S0-BED-098

EQUINOX

First published in May 1993
by GMP Publishers Ltd
P O Box 247, London N17 9QR, England

World Copyright © 1993 Mel Keegan

A CIP catalogue record for this book
is available from the British Library

ISBN 0 85449 200 3

Distributed in North America by InBook
P O Box 120470, East Haven, CT 06512, USA

Distributed in Australia by Bulldog Books
P O Box 155, Broadway, NSW 2007, Australia

Printed and bound in the EC
by Firmin-Didot (France)
Groupe Hérissey

Chapter One

The wink of a red emergency indicator drew Jerry Stone's attention the instant he opened his eyes. He lay on his left side with his arm twisted beneath him, and he had been out long enough for the limb to have cramped. Memory flooded back like a physical blow.

The skyvan had hit hard, tumbled end over end and slammed into tangled root masses which stopped it before it could slither on over the edge, into a stormwater washaway. Stone's head throbbed. In the darkness his fingers felt for the warm wetness of blood on his scalp, but found nothing. The taste in his mouth was metallic.

He lay on the moulded plastic side of the cockpit, hung half in, half out of the flight harness. The straps had probably saved his life. He could have hit the transparent forward canopy like a projectile, launched from his seat by the force of the impact.

Power was still on. The lift motors had shut down automatically but the electricals were alive and he heard a muted rush of air from the ducts. He knuckled his eyes and fought for focus on the instrument panel.

The red enunciator was indicating a fracture in the canopy, and Stone swore. That accounted for his headache while he could find no physical injury. If he was losing pressure he was lucky to return to his senses at all.

But that could not be right. He rubbed his temples and concentrated on the instruments. Pressure in the cockpit was rising, not falling, but at the same time the oxygen content of his gas mix was going down.

He coughed, forced a breath to the bottom of his lungs. Memory was almost random. Where was he? He felt concussed, but the stunned sensation was more likely the effect of whatever he was breathing. He turned on the chemical analysers and blinked at the complex display.

Oxygen was low. Nitrogen was way too high and the air was rich with esters and acids. Memory stirred wilfully. He had come down in the Outfield, a hinterland of dense tropical forest. The plants bled a mild acid and emitted ethanol vapour in their odd photosynthetic cycle. The atmospheric pressure was high but a human could not breathe it. First came drunkenness, then stupor and suffocation.

In the gloom he felt for the crash kit under the control panel. The impact-proof canister popped into his hands as his senses began to spin dangerously. He fumbled with the breath mask, got it over his nose and ran the straps up about his head. The scrubbing filter would clean out the dangerous gasses; the oxygen cartridge gave him fifteen minutes of air he could breathe without falling on his face. He peered at the illuminated face of his chrono and marked the time.

Oxygen filled his lungs and he lay still, waiting for his mind to clear. The last thing he remembered was the rush of half-seen treetops, red lights peppering his instruments as the flight systems shut down. He had taken a hit in the main drive motor and the ground rushed up fast.

How far had he come? As his throbbing head cleared Stone released the harness and took his weight on his hands. He saw lights in the west, not two kilometres away. This far in the Outfield, the only settlement was Station 9. Shooters on the roof must have seen him launch. He was lucky to get out at all.

They would have watched him impact, and they must have been waiting for a fireball. But the skyvan was intact, and Stone gritted his teeth as he tried the canopy release. He must get out, fast. The same shooters who had knocked him down would soon be out here to finish the job. He had minutes.

The gullwing had jammed. He twisted in the seat, braced himself against the opposite side and kicked both boots into the tough plastex. At the third blow it gave, and a stream of warm, moist air gushed into his face. Through the mask he smelt humus, night-blooming fungi and the chemical reek from the aft engine module.

The skyvan was canted on its starboard side, and as he clambered up into the moonlight he saw he had been a whisker away from disaster. The whole side of the van was ripped out, scorched black by the Semtex-3 warhead. Only the firewall between the motors and ride capsule had stopped the blast, or he would have been cut to confetti.

This world's large moon was rising over the forest, gibbous

and white against the stars. The sky was clear, indigo. Stone spared the vault above him one glance before he returned to the crash kit.

A pencil torch; two capsules of oxygen to extend the lifespan of the mask; a radio beacon which would transmit for three hours before its powerpack was dead. He stuffed these items into the pockets of his brown leather jacket, then dove back into the wrecked van.

The HK-440 had been in the footwell when he launched. The magazine was half spent — thirty or so 9mm teflon rounds remained after he had dropped the security men at the hangar. Memory was hazy. Stone could recall only disjointed scraps of image and sound. A figure turning toward him, the shape of a cannon in the hands of a contract shooter, a voice crying out sharply before he was through into the hangar.

The gun had tucked itself under the instrument panel. He pried it out and checked the red LED ammunition counter. He had thirty-two in the magazine. Not much, when half the Station 9 security squad must be in the air.

He heard the approaching bluster of engines as he slung the 9mm machine pistol over his shoulder by its strap and climbed over the side of the wrecked vehicle. A spotlight lanced down, probing the tangle of trees and vines. By day they would have easily seen the scar gouged out of the ground by the headlong, controlled crash, but in the moonlight the dense forest would cover him, buy him a few minutes.

They would be thermoscanning, looking for the still roasting steel and aluminium of the wreck. Stone took the pistol in his right hand, gave the crazily tilted van a single glance, and ran.

Thirty-two rounds and forty minutes of remaining breathable air did not give him many options. He needed transport, preferably the flying variety. He struggled with his disordered memory as he scrambled over the roots of the immense tropical hardwoods. Where was he? What was the name of this planet?

He had made two hundred metres when the thermoscanners behind him located the wreck. Triple spotlights began to circle outward in a search pattern, and Stone picked up his pace. He was headed in the only direction that made any sense — back the way he had come.

Outstation 9 lay two kilometres west. If he could find the maglev track he could follow it directly back to the city dome.

Forty minutes' air would get him there, if he did not have to fight the forest for every step.

Memory swam dangerously. The maglev track was elevated, on an embankment above flood-level. Stone recalled seeing it on numerous landing approaches. He should soon reach it if he kept making his way west. It was the only chance he had.

Bats and night birds fluttered overhead and he ducked. Insects chirped in the tangled vines. He paused for breath and gazed at the stars. The patterns of the constellations were familiar, as good as a route map. On a heading into those star systems from this navigation perspective, he could name five colonised worlds. But only one had a dense, oxygen-poor atmosphere so rich in esters and acids that a human breathing it was out of his skull in minutes.

'Halley,' Stone panted as he recognised the constellations. 'This is Halley... south subcontinent, near the equator. Damn.'

Now he knew where he was, for all the good it did him. Five hundred metres behind the company's contract shooters were tired of scanning. He heard muffled thumps as repeated, random stun discharges slammed over the forest. Anyone standing under the field projectors without a helmet would be comatose in an instant. Even at this distance Stone felt a numb tingling in his nerve fibres.

They would widen the scope of the stun fields to take in more and more of the surrounding jungle. Stone clamped his hands over his ears and dove over a massive snarl of roots and parasitic vines. His foot caught, he went down hard, rolled and was up again with a grunted curse.

As he forced his way through a curtain of narcotic *gammin* flowers, which flurried their white, intoxicating pollen into his face, he saw the elevated maglev track before him. The forest stretched away to north and south, impenetrable, dangerous with life forms he could scarcely imagine. In the west was Station 9, one human outpost in the middle of a million square kilometres; in the east the city of Macao stood on the bank of the Jumna river, by the spaceport.

If Stone could get his hands on a skyhopper he could be in Macao in minutes, lost in the crush of humanity, at liberty to activate the radio tracer, summon a pick-up.

Jarrat was up there somewhere. His eyes roved among the stars as he began to struggle for breath. His senses were like warm honey, so sluggish and dislocated that it took a full minute for him to realise he had begun to suffocate.

He peered at his chrono and swore. The oxygen cartridge was spent, he was getting little more than scrubbed external air every time he heaved a breath, and the oxygen content was not enough to keep a man awake even when he was just standing still.

His fingers were clumsy, his lungs burned as he snapped out the spent cartridge, snapped in a fresh one and forced his spasming lungs to inhale deeply. His head cleared and he marked the time. In thirty minutes he was out of air, and out of luck.

Behind him, the stun fields thumped and thrummed in ever-widening circles. Before him, the lights of Station 9 beckoned like beacons. Stone stumbled out of the grasping roots and vines of the rainforest and pulled himself onto the embankment.

In the open he was an easy target, but he could make faster time. If he tried to cling to cover he had no chance at all. Every breath rasped in his ears as he turned west and ran. The more distance he could put between himself and the wreck, the better his chances became. If he could get back into Station 9 he could steal a aircraft — not a lumbering, underpowered civvy van, but something with the power to throw itself onto the fringes of space.

From there he could get a signal through. Jarrat was never far away. Stone's eyes returned to the stars as he pounded along the side of the embankment. Gravel slithered under his boots. He lost his footing and went down again, rolled back to his feet and did not waste his breath with a curse.

Memory was returning in patches as his throbbing head began to clear. He must have ingested more of this planet's toxic atmosphere than he had realised as he lay unconscious in the wreck. The lights of Station 9 spelled safety, yet Stone's belly churned acidly as he focused on them.

For five weeks he had lived there, and watched his back every second. South side, sub-basement levels, city bottom, deep under the street: they called it Xanadu, but Stone had learned to call it The Pit.

Behind the facade of glitz and glamour was the other face of Xanadu. A 'laboratory' patrolled by security drones and contract shooters, where the best, the purest poison was cut and packaged for supply.

Angel.

For five weeks Stone had worked on the fringes of Xanadu. They knew him as a free pilot, a mercenary down on his luck. There was little he would not do if the price was right.

The face of a man called Morrow swam before his mind's eye as he jogged toward the blaze of neon. How in hell had Morrow known the mercenary was a plant, an agent? Had he known Stone's face from some past encounter? Recognition was always a risk when a NARC entered a deep cover assignment. Everything possible was done to minimise danger, and then a man could only pray, and get on with the job.

The lights were close and Stone's legs had begun to ache when he heard the hissing whine of repulsion and manoeuvring motors up ahead. After five weeks in Station 9 he knew that sound, and dove fast into the rank grasses at the base of the embankment.

The drone had him on infrared and thermoscan. A needle of argon laser light sliced into the ground where Stone had lain half a second before. He was still rolling when it scorched the bullgrass and touched off a tiny spot fire. Flames licked close to his boots but he ignored them, pulled the 9mm pistol up into line and squeezed the trigger.

Five shots ruptured the armoured drone into cartwheeling shards and an expanding envelope of boiling gases. Before the super-hot shrapnel had scythed into the grass Stone was on his feet again.

Station 9 was only a few hundred metres away. He could see the columns of the East Side high-rises, and the brilliant neon spelling out the names of Candydream, Kosmos and Chevrolette. Bats squeaked, winging outward across the forest, but he ignored them and peered at his chrono.

His lungs were burning again and he knelt in the deep shadow of an outcropping to insert the last oxygen cartridge. He drew a breath to the bottom of his chest and forced his feet under him. Just a few hundred metres, and he would be through the gate and on the rink. To the left lay the warren of bordellos and casinos, where Xanadu was the richest and the most terrible; to the right, the hangars where he could get aboard a skyhopper, hot-wire his way around the ignition sequence and launch a second time.

Why had he chosen a waddling civvy van last time? What kind of fool had he been? Memory evaded him. He left the cover of the outcropping and bunched his muscles for effort. From here to the gate he would be in the open. His right hand clenched on the pistol, his eyes scanned the darkness overhead for drones.

When it came, the whining hiss of repulsion and manoeuvring thrusters whispered from behind him and he almost missed the sound in the rasp of his own breathing. A bolt of energy shaved his shoulder, so close he felt the heat, and he flung himself to the ground.

He slammed down on his back and fired one-handed as his body absorbed the jarring impact. The pistol was a bitch to hold on target with one hand as it kicked on its exhaust gases. He held the trigger down, hosed away his remaining ammunition, as close to the drone as he could manage, and then threw both arms over his face as the machine detonated.

He felt the searing heat of the explosion, heard multiple metallic thuds as pieces of the casing smacked into the ground not far from him. When he dared take his arm from his face, the ammo counter read nine rounds, and Stone swore.

The hangar would be guarded more heavily now than when he left. They must have found the body of the contract man he had killed on the way out. The shooter worked for Xanadu though he wore the uniform fatigues of Outstation 9 Tactical. Half the Tac troopers in the outpost worked for the syndicate, which was the reason the Angel was brought in, cut and marketed with such ease.

The sky was clear of drones but Stone was not duped into complacency. Morrow would be monitoring his hunterkillers. He would know exactly where the last had been destroyed, and now that Stone was on his doorstep a squad of contract men would be moving. He clung to cover for vital minutes, watching the dark sky, but saw nothing.

The maglev track ran straight as a ruler into the gateway, under the massive neon Volvo billboard. Shuttles ran between Macao and the Outstations every half hour, and since none had passed him on his run in from the forest, the next must be due.

Stone panted through the last hundred metres and peered at his chrono. He had five minutes of oxygen, then the game was up. The gate was pressure-sealed. A hundred other gates circled the edge of the rink but to gain entry he must have an infrabeam key, and Stone had no such key.

Outstation 9 towered above him, a transparent dome, almost invisible save where the refraction of the neon glare caused rainbows of colour in the night. The sounds of revelry and industry called through the plastex dome, the thundering bass of steelrock from the dance shops and bordellos, the ceaseless beat of the great generators and aircycling machines.

Pressed against the cool, curved surface of the dome, he dropped to one knee, checked his chrono and the ammo counter. Two minutes. Nine rounds. His teeth bared behind the moulded plastic of the mask. He had always sworn a good field agent never relied on luck, but he was down to sheer luck now.

Moonlight turned the maglev track into a blue-white ribbon, and his eyes widened as they raked the distance. 'Come on,' he muttered, 'where the fuck is it? There has to be one!'

Then, there it was — a dazzle of light on the track, rushing closer even as its retro thrusters slowed it for the approach to the gate. Like a big steel animal riding the rail, just above the charged surface, never actually touching, the shuttle slowed, swayed and stopped just metres from the still sealed gate.

Stone sprinted for the rear of the single car, slung the pistol over his shoulder and closed both hands about the couplers. The shuttle was moving again before he had a good grip and he let the sudden tug pull him up onto the back of the car. Feet perched on the couplers, he flattened against the metal and clung tight to the rounded edge of the car.

The gate opened fast, the shuttle slid smoothly into the vast, hangar-sized airlock, and the gate closed again behind. Stone was gasping now, and fought to focus on his chrono.

According to the digital, the third and final oxygen cartridge was dead. And so was he. The air about him was a wind storm as the cycling machines scrubbed out the dangerous gasses and forced in enough oxygen to bring the breathing mix up to levels tolerable to humans.

His lungs burned, his head spun, and Stone tore the mask off his face. If the air was still bad he was done for, but he was finished anyway. The mask clattered onto the stained concrete under the maglev rail and he let himself slither down from his perch on the couplers.

Just enough oxygen hit his brain to keep him conscious and

moving as the shuttle moved off again. It was like running a marathon on the shoulder of a mountain so high the air was almost too thin to breathe. But the inner gate was opening to admit the shuttle, and Stone sprinted to keep pace with the machine. The gate would close directly behind it, and if he was shut in the airlock he was finished.

He tumbled through and fell to his knees as the armoured door slammed. His ears popped as the atmospheric pressure normalised, but inside the air was so oxygen rich he felt almost drunk. He rolled down off the slight elevation of the maglev track and ducked quickly among the trashpacks which clustered beside the gate.

This shuttle was a garbage carrier. As labourers ambled out to load the trashpacks Stone slipped into the shadowed alleys around the periphery of the rink, between Xanadu and the hangars.

Steelrock battered his ears as he scuttled by a dance shop. Angel dreamheads had passed out along the walls. These were the pathetic victims of the drug which had become a disease, and even in his desperate flight Stone spared them a pitying glance. How well he knew their bizarre blend of joy and despair. It was branded into his memory in pain.

They were flying, consumed by the rapture of the drug. In the midst of the phantasm of power, sex and euphoria, the user did not recall that death had moved a little closer with the dose he had just inhaled. Realisation came hours later, with consciousness and despair. The poison of Angel was insidious, inescapable. Yet the glory of fantasies moulded by lust, driven by the lethal golden dust, seduced so many into the trap that Angel had outstripped any plague.

Tactical Response was impotent, fettered by corrupt provincial law, outgunned by the syndicates. NARC, autonomous and accountable only to its own distant hierarchy, had the last fighting chance in the rimworlds and deep sky alike.

With a bitter wave of pity, Stone stepped over the dreamheads. His eyes raked every doorway. The hangars skirted Revolution Square, snug against the side of the dome. As he padded to the end of the alley he saw the inner pressure doors, busy with people waiting for a skyhauler.

Could he make it out with a commercial flight? If he could get a seat, he had the credits in his pocket. Stone slipped the HK pistol under his jacket and stepped into the light and noise.

Faces turned to him. He saw black Tactical uniforms among the crowd and turned his head away. Half the Tac men here worked for Xanadu, and if just one recognised him the company shooters would be on him.

A flak-jacketed trooper lifted his R/T to his lips, and Stone's heart quickened. He hurried his pace, shouldered through the crush to the head of the queue waiting for admittance to the hangar. At the end of the building, past the immense bronze statue of The Revolutionary, was the technicians' gate, used by pilots and engineers. Unless Morrow had already alerted the computer, Stone had the code to open that gate. He had used it many times before.

He had been seen. Tactical men were pointing as he pushed through the crowd, but he could not stop. A keypad was inset in the facia of the gate, with a monitor behind graffitied armourglass. Stone cast a glance over his shoulder, saw the figures in black uniforms striding toward him. If they were genuine Tac officers they were his salvation. And if they were on Morrow's payroll?

Turning his back on them, he punched in codes the computer had accepted only an hour before, and held his breath. His heart hammered, but the machine took them without hesitation and the small gate opened. Stone stepped through and hit the locking control. That would hold them for minutes.

The airlock was dim and red. A perpetual supply of oxygen-charged masks hung in fresh plastic sheaths on the wall at his elbow. He tore one from its plastic, checked the cartridge, ran the straps up about his head and thumbed the control to prime the inner gate. The Tac squad was already trying to hotwire the outer gate — it would not keep them out for long.

But he recalled several skyhoppers and one starship's shuttle in the hangar. He would be out in minutes if he could slip by Morrow's trigger-happy contract goons. If he could steal the shuttle he would hail the carrier for a rendezvous in space. Jarrat would pull the *Athena* out of her high orbit to meet him, he would be home free.

Cold sweat prickled Stone's ribs. He drew the HK-440, adjusted to single-shot operation and flattened against the wall as the inner gate slid open. He glimpsed the ammunition counter as the air stormed about him, equalising pressures.

Nine rounds.

The years of Narcotics And Riot Control training calmed his mind and honed his reflexes. As the gate opened he glimpsed the vast, grey-walled expanse of the hangar: a dozen aircraft, scores of technicians, pilots, passengers boarding an outbound domestic shuttle —

Three black uniforms, bodies made bulky by kevlex-titanium flak jackets, anonymous full-face visors. Stone pulled the pistol into line and squeezed back on the trigger. Two shots, three, spat out of the HK before he saw a shape from the corner of his eye.

Not a Tactical uniform. Jeans, white shirt, white athletic shoes; a squib gun held in both hands, dead on target. Stone spun but he knew it was too late. He felt the needle-prick low in his neck and before he could even feel the burn of drug or toxin his senses dimmed into near unconsciousness.

***

'They just shot him, Captain Jarrat. You can leave it there.' Doctor Yvette McKinnen's voice was shocking in the womb-like interior of the isolation tank. 'Captain?'

'I heard you.' Weightless in blood-temperature air, encapsulated in the lightless bubble, Kevin Jarrat was so dislocated from reality, nothing outside the tank might have existed. He was naked, roughly horizontal, floating in a negative gravity field.

As the biocyber systems engineer turned off the field he righted, and grunted as his muscles took his weight for the first time in over an hour. He felt leaden. The sensor wires which had been tagged into the skin of his scalp and chest began to sting, though he was still too disconnected by the drugs in his bloodstream to notice much.

McKinnen cracked open the hatch, and though she had dimmed the laboratory lights, any light at all dazzled Jarrat after so long in total darkness. He closed his eyes as she relieved him of the sensors, and took a white towelling robe from her as he stepped out. A shot of blocker chemicals fired into his bare thigh and he leaned both flat palms on the metal side of the tank as he waited for his head to clear.

The methaqualone and dexamphetamine neutralised in under a minute and his thoughts steadied almost at once.

McKinnen played a medscanner over his chest to check for toxic shock or withdrawal syndrome, but he felt none of that. His senses sharpened as if he had wound a lens into focus. The drugs were now totally inert.

The lab was quiet at this hour. Several isolation tanks, examination benches, two deactivated robot drones, a sensory simulator and a battery of computers made even the large room seem cluttered. Four monitors displayed endless columns of data. Jarrat gave them a single glance as he belted the robe and lowered himself into a chair. The lab always felt cold after the blood-heat of the tank, and he was grateful for the mug of coffee McKinnen placed into his hand.

'You got your results?' he asked tiredly. These sessions were wearying. After an hour following Stone's every breath, step and feeling, Jarrat felt as if he had run a marathon. Then it would be Stoney's turn in the tank, and Jarrat would make the run for the benefit of the machines.

'Extraordinary results,' Yvette McKinnen said tersely, grudgingly, as she scrolled through a preliminary collation of the data. 'I've never seen the like of it.'

As his eyes began to adjust Jarrat looked into her face. She was forty, a redhead with blue eyes and a thick Paris accent. She had been out from Earth only a month. And she was furious, though she took pains to keep the anger on a tight rein. Jarrat sighed.

'It isn't my project, Doc. If it was up to me, Stoney and I would have been out of here weeks ago. We never wanted to be here in the first place. If you're going to blame anyone, blame the Intelligence engineers who wanted new toys to play with — us!'

She froze the data, picked up her own coffee and perched on the side of the desk to look down at him. Loose white slacks, blue silk shirt and sandals gave her a look of Parisian elegance, but she was a scientist who had been with NARC for almost twelve years. Jarrat never forgot that.

'I don't blame anyone for anything,' Yvette told him, and it was not a lie. Whom could she hold responsible for the hiatus of her own project? She drew a hand through her dark hair and touched his face. 'You look tired. You can leave if you like. It will take hours to process the data.'

'Let me see the preliminary collation.' He swivelled the chair and cradled the hot mug between his hands. 'That was a tough run. Stoney's hurt in three or four places, though he doesn't know it yet.'

The data backed up and McKinnen ran it at normal speed. On the right of the screen was a visual of Stone's run; on the left, a statistical analysis of the data collected from Jarrat's nervous system; across the bottom, a textual transcript of the voice-track Kevin had recorded moment by moment kept pace with the video/data input.

It was surreal. An Intelligence transport took the wrecked skyvan into the testing ground, slung in cargo tractors under the belly of the ship. Stone was already in the craft, drugged, unconscious. The van was deposited on the lip of the stormwater washaway and the aircraft withdrew with minutes to spare before the run began.

Jarrat sipped the coffee and tried to focus on the action on the screens as he listened to his own voice. 'He's waking. Coming to... disorientation. He's cramped. Been lying on that arm too long. Left arm. Shock... he's worried. Headache.' That would be the effect of the drugs, though Stone would not know. Dimethyltriptamine and methylamphetamine in combination with the still classified synthetic, PBH, were never without some side effect. But they made the mind simple to programme.

In the minutes after the cocktail was administered, while Stone was half conscious and before the transport dumped him three hundred kilometres into the NARC weapons testing range, he was given the entire programme scenario. His subconscious mind recorded an entire 'virtual reality' while his own memory was suppressed. The temporary amnesia would last until the drug wore off, or until he received the blocker agent.

On the voice track Jarrat's voice slurred as he responded to the combination of drugs in his own system. They damped the peripheral nervous system, while his brain went into overdrive. His limbs might not have existed, his mind was supercharged. 'He's out,' Jarrat's indistinct voice said from the machine. 'Mask on. Tense. Smell the forest... he's moving. Sweating. He turns quickly...'

Long-range cameras had recorded Stone as he clambered out of the wreck, took his bearings, saw the incoming craft which he believed to be a flier from the Syndicate, and ran. The craft was the same Intelligence transport which had taken him to the site, but the stun fields discharged over the forest were real enough.

Remote cameras flew too high and too far behind for Stone to see or hear them, but they shadowed him as he found the maglev track and began to hurry. 'Can't breathe,' Jarrat's voice gasped from the machine. 'No air, can't —' In the tank, he was so intent on Stone's every sensation, so oblivious to his own body, he might have *been* Stone. Two minds inhabiting one body; two sets of sensations coursing through one nervous system.

The drones hunting Stone were also real, programmed to fire close enough to be convincing, but not to injure. Stone hit them both with dummy rounds which triggered two small explosions, bright gas and scrap metal. Enough for his drug-enhanced mind to warp into major detonations. On the voice track, Jarrat yelped with his partner's pain as Stone dove, rolled, fired. Then he was in the open, making the last run toward the wall of a warehouse.

'Fear,' Jarrat slurred. 'Heart racing. Panting. Waiting. Pressing back against... ah! Running.' On the screen, Stone sprinted down the length of the maglev shuttle and clambered onto the tow-couplers.

Jarrat looked away from the screens. He knew the rest. Stone had never been in any genuine danger. It was all a simulation, augmented reality. The mask was designed to make it difficult to breathe when the oxygen cartridges expired, but the native air was not toxic. Stone could have torn off the mask at any moment.

Instead, he played the scenario through and got further than McKinnen had anticipated. The Intelligence squad was waiting in the warehouse for him. Stone saw it as a hangar. He fired several dummy rounds but the kevlex-titanium armour was impervious. In the tank, Jarrat swore as the dart hit Stone's neck, and he sagged to the ground.

In minutes he was up again as the blocker chemicals neutralised the drugs. This run was complete. On the screen, Jarrat's data curtailed as McKinnen released him from the isolation tank.

She reached over and turned off the monitor, and Jarrat tilted his head at her with a frown. By all accounts the project had almost concluded, which was all the more reason for her to be angry. Her own work was on the shelf, three years' research almost abandoned.

'What do you get out of all that?' Jarrat gestured at the screen. 'The sensory data looks like gibberish to me.'

'Gibberish?' McKinnen smiled thinly. 'Hardly. The machines are analysing the function of the communication between you and Captain Stone. Empathy, artificially engineered by the adept Harry Del during medical treatment following Stone's exposure to Angel. Weapons Research is still eager to make something of it.' She lifted one fine brow at him. 'So far we have learned that no form of scanning we know can detect the transmission of impulses between you, but you are both aware of each other, infallibly, to a range of several light minutes, despite the proximity of radiation sources, positive or negative gravity fields. Neither of you is capable of transmitting or receiving actual thoughts, but you both receive feelings, emotions, intuitions and physical sensations as clearly as radio waves.'

'We could have told you that before you started on us.' Jarrat rubbed his shoulder. He had made a run two days before. Though conditions were strictly controlled, he had fallen from a wall in an attempt to evade a drone which, in his private reality, was trying to kill him. He was still aching, and so was Stone.

Even now Jarrat could feel his partner. Stoney was both physically and mentally tired, frustrated and growing angry. Four weeks as lab rats was not what either of them had enlisted for.

The scientist in control of this project was equally as frustrated, albeit for different reasons. Yvette gathered sheets of printout with short, jerky movements and slammed down the stack. 'I shall inform Colonel Dupre that we have all the data we need.' She looked at Jarrat with smouldering blue eyes.

He got to his bare feet. 'None of this was our idea, lady. Stoney and I didn't beg to be sent here. For my money, your own project is probably more applicable than this one.' His voice rose sharply. 'What the hell do Intelligence think they're going to get out of this? Even if they can figure out what makes us able to do what we do, what good it is? There's no way they can apply it to other field agents.'

'You're wrong, Captain.' McKinnen shoved a chair back under the console and began to turn out the lab lights. The computer would work for several hours, collating data which would be boosted on back to NARC Central on Earth, almost three weeks away by hyperflight. Yvette glared at Jarrat over the hood of the machine. 'I thought Dr Del would have told you.'

'Told me what?' Jarrat demanded. She had lost him.

'Ask him.' The woman marched to the door. She was in the corridor when she turned back. 'Tell him I have nothing against his work. I certainly have nothing against empaths — I've worked with them often before, which is why I was torn out of my laboratory in Paris and sent here. But I think Intelligence is making a mistake. A big mistake.'

With that she was gone, leaving Jarrat confused and annoyed. Ask Harry? Ask him what? What was Colonel Dupre up to? The man may be the NARC Quadrant Director, but he did not own his field agents body and soul. Jarrat stood in the empty lab, listening to the whisper of the computer's cooling system. A single monitor was left on, and as he saw a status report he got moving. The transport had just landed. Stoney was back.

Chapter Two

The medic's fingers probed Stone's back and shoulders as if he did not trust the scanner. Stone leaned over a seat, let the man work as he gazed out at the lights of Venice. From five thousand metres the city looked like a carnival. The spaceport sprawled along the west side, but the NARC transport swung about it, on a heading out of the restricted zone.

The stars were still familiar. Stone gave them a glare. Even in his drugged state he had known these constellations, but this was not Halley, nor was that forest a tropical jungle. And a lucid mind would never confuse the town of Sun Valley with Halley Outstation 9.

The NARC weapons test range was over a quarter million square kilometres of equatorial territory spanning the distance between Sun Valley and Venice. The maglev track bisected the NARC zone but only cargo was carried by rail. Passengers overflew the area at a safe altitude.

Stone sighed. This was Darwin's World, two weeks from Halley on the same nav bearing into the rim star systems. The rainforest was artificially cultivated, just as the sector of desert was manufactured, and the savanna. NARC field simulations were thorough.

And demanding. Stone winced soundlessly as the medic found his bruised bones. 'I took a fall. Just leave it, will you?' he snapped. 'I'll live,'

The young man gave him an indifferent look. 'I have a report to file, Captain.'

Stone knew. Reports, files, records, whole dossiers had been assembled in the four weeks he and Jarrat had been on Darwin's. Meanwhile, the *Athena* was five days away, about to leave its parking orbit over the city of Chell. Captain Gene Cantrell and Lieutenant Mischa Petrov were in command. Telemetry was forwarded to Darwin's daily, as a courtesy, so Jarrat and Stone were never out of touch with the ship.

Their command status had been suspended, not terminated.

Stone wondered to what extent this was candy, intended to seduce them into compliance with the research project. If it was, it had worked, but their patience had begun to wear thin.

A medscanner whirred over Stone's kidneys before the man stepped away. Stone shrugged back into his shirt and glanced at the time. It was just short of midnight. Kevin would be out of the lab, the carrier's telemetry would be in, and he longed to set spine to mattress.

The transport angled over Venice and banked around on approach to the NARC building which towered over the fringe of the city. Stone went forward to the cockpit, stood behind the pilots and watched passively as the prop, the wrecked skyvan, was dumped unceremoniously into a parking bay. The pilot killed the cargo tractors and the transport bobbed up on repulsion toward the landing space on the roof.

City lights dimmed the stars and the equatorial night air was warm, muggy. As the skyhauler pulled out Stone stood at the north parapet, looking out toward the forest. He saw the maglev track which ran to Sun Valley, but the town he had believed was Station 9 lay over the horizon. He breathed deeply, watched the brilliant stern flare of a rimrunner leaving the port on a heading for space, and wished to God he was on it.

The blocker shot had neutralised the drugs, leaving him tired and sore. Stone rubbed his eyes. Jarrat would be just as tired after an hour or more in the iso-tank. Of the two, Stone thought he would prefer to make the run rather than lie in hot blackness, prickled by sensor wires, numb with drugs, mind racing.

As usual, since the run ended he had been 'closed' to Jarrat's empathy. They had made this arrangement privately. The experiments were distressing, the aftermath difficult enough to get through without bearing the double burden of confused emotions and physical sensations. The ability to shut out the conflict of incoming feelings was the only armour he and Jarrat had in this project. Stone often wondered what would have become of them if they were 'open' all the time. He knew they owed Harry Del a debt.

'Captain Stone?'

He turned toward the voice. It was a young NARC officer, just transferred from the Army, judging by the severity of the haircut, the crispness of the salute. He would gradually relax, become a normal human being. He would never be assigned to field service until he did. On the street, a shorn head and military behaviour were like waving a flag, and would get him killed. The ID tag on his lapel read Cheng, D., but his Asian heritage was indeterminate. Most races were so mixed, names and genes often seemed mismatched.

'Captain Jarrat's compliments. He asks if you would join him directly.'

'Trouble?' Stone thrust his hands into the pockets of his jacket and strode stiffly toward the lifts.

'I don't know.' Cheng stood back to let him step into the car. 'But Cap Jarrat looked annoyed.'

Surprising, Stone thought acidly. Kevin had just come out of the tank. Annoyed would be an understatement. The lift took him down five levels and deposited him on an accommodation floor. The apartment they shared was small but comfortable, with a taunting view of the spaceport. Stone set his hand on the palmprint lock and the door opened soundlessly.

The apartment was dim since Jarrat's eyes must still be light-sensitive. Kevin was in a short white robe, barefoot, with a glass in either hand. The quilt on the enormous double bed was turned down, and taps gushed in the tiny adjoining bathroom.

'Drink, bath, bed, in that order,' Jarrat said drily as Stone joined him. 'Then you can take a look at the good news.' His tone was cynical.

'News?' Stone sipped the fiery old brandy and snaked one arm about Jarrat's waist.

'Telemetry.' Jarrat moulded against him. 'The *Athena* is on assignment, shipped out of Kithan eighty hours ago.'

'Is NARC delegating another carrier to Chell?' Stone finished the brandy in one draught and dropped his jacket. He winced as his shoulder pulled, and was grateful for Jarrat's hands on him. His shirt followed the jacket, and Kevin felt for his bruises with more gentleness than the medic... then again, Jarrat knew exactly where they were. Shields eased down and the empathy flared warmly between them, a sensation not unlike a caress beneath the skin.

'Dupre told me we're handing Chell back to Tactical,' Jarrat told him as he rubbed the small injury. 'Seems Gene Cantrell has better things to do to do with our ship.'

'Such as?' Stone leaned over the table, stretched and worked his shoulders as Jarrat's hands moved over him.

'Soak, then watch the transmission.' Jarrat swatted his rump. 'You're just bruised.'

'So are you,' Stone said sourly. 'You've got bruises from the last three runs. You were limping yesterday.' He dropped his pants and stepped into the bathroom without looking back. 'And you're as disgusted with this Intelligence bullshit as I am.'

The hot water eased a dozen small hurts he had only been half aware of. He leaned against the side of the tub as Jarrat shut off the taps. Steam rose in billowing clouds, making the air more humid than the tropical night. Kevin sat on the wide enamel side and trailed his fingers in the water.

'Doc McKinnen said she's got about enough,' he mused. 'She'll tell Dupre the project is complete.' He looked down into Stone's face. 'I think she has a lot less than her bosses wanted, but she's more infuriated with the whole programme than we are.'

Stone snorted scornfully as he dumped a palmful of crystals into the water. 'She's got a damned right to be. Her own work was within a year of practical testing when we happened along. I don't say she'd have shot us dead to be rid of us *and* our empathy, but see it from her perspective. Three years' work down the drain.'

'But who'd have been insane enough to test her gadget?' Jarrat swept back his hair, which was long on his collar, sun-blond, while Stone's was so dark as to be almost black. 'If Central had asked me to test McKinnen's biocyber implant, they wouldn't have liked the answer.'

He was right, and Stone sighed. Yvette McKinnen was a cyber systems analyst. She had developed a brain implant, a transceiver which was being touted as the ultimate monitoring device for agents working in deep cover. But though the device operated on frequencies which were difficult to detect under normal circumstances, its transmission was not totally undetectable. The possibility — some agents said, probability – was that a subspace radio hack would stumble over the signals, decode them, calculate where they were from, and sell the data to the highest bidder on the street. Syndicate moguls would queue to pay handsomely for the information.

If a NARC man was in deep cover, depending on an implant, the day he was even suspected of being an agent, the syndicate in which he was working would only have to scan for the transceiver, and he was dead. McKinnen swore she could find a way

24

to shield the transmission.

NARC was interested enough to fund the project, but even Yvette could see that the strange, natural empathy shared by Jarrat and Stone, the legacy of Harry Del's uncommon ability, was the resolution to a problem of surveillance her own project had only half answered. The bizarre 'cure' to Stone's Angel addiction generated almost as many problems as it solved.

'So she's going to pull the plug on the project,' Stone said as he settled deeper into the water and looked up at Jarrat out of heavy eyes. 'Three bloody cheers. That means we're out of here.'

'Unless Dupre decides the dossier is incomplete. They could keep us here for months.' Jarrat took a breath of the hot, humid air. 'I want out, Stoney. I've had enough. I'm starting to feel like a puppet, and I'm hurting.'

'I know.' Stone laid one wet hand on Jarrat's bare thigh. 'I know everything you feel.'

A flicker of amusement and affection blossomed through both of them as shields lowered again. Jarrat smiled faintly. 'You do, at that.' His hand covered Stone's and their fingers laced. 'I'll call Dupre in the morning, tell him we've had enough.'

It was the primary condition under which they had come to Darwin's World. They had undertaken the test programme on a voluntary basis, with a right of veto if or when it became unacceptable. That point had already been passed, days before, and Dupre knew. Several terse protests had been logged from the terminal in this apartment. None had elicited a response from Dupre's office, but the colonel would know how much latitude he had left. Their veto would come as no surprise.

Stone sat up and leaned forward in search of a kiss. Jarrat's mouth closed over his, possessive and teasing at once. Stone opened to the empathy, let it take him high as a kite.

Better than a drug, he decided. Better than the Angel had ever been. Jarrat's fingers cupped his nape, rubbed him there as tongues twisted together. Relaxation began to replace the tension of the run, but Stone's reluctant body responded slowly. After the chemical overload and the exertion, it was always the same.

They broke apart and Jarrat's grey eyes were dark, rueful. 'This project is wreaking havoc with our sex life. You're too tired, aren't you?'

'Too tired to be energetic,' Stone admitted as he emptied out the tub and stood. 'But you could take me to bed and be gentle,' he added self-mockingly. 'I wouldn't refuse.'

A large towel was draped over his shoulders and Jarrat stepped out of the steam. Stone rubbed sketchily at his limbs as he followed, and stretched out across the bed as the terminal in the corner of the room came on. The monitor flickered to life and Jarrat dropped in a datacube.

Subspace telemetry took three days to cover the distance between Darwin's World and Kithan, where the carrier had orbited high above the city of Chell. It would be several weeks more before the tachyon broadcast was received on Earth.

As the package began, Jarrat sprawled on the quilt beside Stone, one hand on his partner's backside as they watched. An image of the blue-green planet, Kithan, was overlaid by orbital data pertaining to the carrier's flight status, then the screen faded to black and a short version of the day's business appeared in text form.

Replacement officers from Starfleet; requisitions for equipment; an in-draft of descant troops to replenish the Raven units which had been badly hurt in the Death's Head Angelwar. One of the carrier's reactors was off line for maintenance; the shuttle in which Stone had been shot down was back in the air. Several NARC operatives were on leave, others were at the end of their enlistment. Surgeon Captain Kip Reardon had attended a hangar accident, when an armoury tractor collided with an engineer's cargo sled, and a man was crushed. No irreparable injuries.

The routine business was second nature. Jarrat thumbed the remote to skip through the data. He had seen it often before, and it was not the normal business of the ship which was on his mind.

The hand on Stone's left buttock patted. 'Here it is. Assignment orders, transmitted from Dupre's office, Venice Central, Darwin's, received four hours before this telemetry was dispatched.'

Stone lay propped on an elbow, one arm about Jarrat's waist as he read. 'Effective immediate, terminate Chell assignment, transfer *Athena* to Zeus system, best speed. Assume Elysium assignment earliest possible. Refer to code-access brief.' He looked up at Jarrat's tense profile. 'Did they send the brief?'

'They did.' Jarrat touched the remote. The screen blanked and the text was replaced by a video. 'We ought to be there, Stoney.' He leaned back against Stone's sturdy legs. 'McKinnen must be getting the same data from us, over and over — we're no use to anybody here. Just a couple of dumb lab rats.'

He was furious, tense, and feelings of frustration cut into Stone like a knife. He shut them out with the ease of many weeks of practice before Kevin could exhaust them both. One arm caught Jarrat about the shoulders, pulled him down, and Stone held him tightly as they concentrated on the screen. Every muscle in Jarrat's body was tense.

The background video was a documentary, probably culled from an educational pack. It opened with a diagram of the Zeus system: a G3 yellow star, several barren outer planets, one massive gas giant and sixteen moons, of which two were hospitable to humans. Terraforming had tamed them. Most of the population of just under one billion lived in the colony of Avalon. The capital of the autonomous territory was Elysium, founded ninety-four years before by a corporate empire acclaimed as far away as Earth.

Equinox Industries. The name was intimately familiar to anyone in NARC or Starfleet. Equinox was a major supplier of electronics and software. Even equipment manufactured by rival companies often used the cheaper, compatible components packed under the Equinox label.

A video compilation replaced the data file, and Jarrat thumbed on the sound. An unseen female narrator spoke against a kaleidoscope of images: crowds thronged beneath the towering buildings of Elysium; massive machines stripped the minerals from barren worlds; heavy lifters shunted mammoth cargoes of ore from a pulverised asteroid to the nearby smelter.

The screen depicted an excavator the size of a town and the mass driver which fired its rubble into orbit. 'This,' read the narrator, 'is the heart of Equinox Industries. For almost a century the company has supported the economy of Avalon, providing employment for much of the population.

'This industrial Titan manufactures everything conceivable from virtual reality games to the flight systems controlling the most sophisticated ships flown by Starfleet and NARC. But now this system is exhausted. Little remains to be quarried and for

Equinox to survive here it must win a new development contract.

'With the outer planets and satellites spent, Equinox turns its attention to Zeus itself. The atmosphere of the giant is fluorine-rich, and could provide continued revenue for the next century. Fluorine remains one of the most powerful fuel sources for the starclippers linking the rim systems with the deep sky.

'The people of Elysium are uneasy. Equinox has not held the reins of government since Avalon became a sovereign territory sixty years ago. Many businessmen are supportive of Equinox, but rival factions among the people would be happy to see the company leave, which Equinox has threatened to do if rights to the atmosphere of Zeus are not finalised soon.'

Pictures of the city replaced those of the systematic destruction of the planets. Stone studied the edited images of a big multiracial community. Crowds congested the broadwalks; in the sky loomed the dusky green face of Zeus.

'These people,' the narrator continued, 'say their system is reduced to toxic rubble, its population exploited. Their space is filled with meteor-sized debris. Ships operate flak screens every second, or risk fatal collision. Since civil pilots cannot access such military hardware, Avalon's nonmilitary "free-pilots" are effectively captive. Spaceflight in the Zeus system is almost totally controlled... by Equinox.

'Worse, the process of extracting and refining fluorine is tipped to lay a veil of debris into the orbit of Zeus which, over a century, could hinder sunlight, radially altering the climate of Avalon and her populated sister moon, Eos.

'Elysium is angry. A rival political faction is headed by Senator Tigh Grenshem, whose object is to rid this system of Equinox. But without this company the colony of Avalon will be impoverished as well as polluted.'

Cityscapes were replaced by multiple stills of Grenshem. His personal file rolled through the left of the screen: fifty-two, widowed eight years before, once worked for Equinox and then left to enter politics. Not a handsome face, but an intelligent one, Stone decided.

The narration continued without pause: 'With Equinox gone, the clean-up could begin. Grenshem claims his system has other resources. The export of software and flight systems would replace the support lost with Equinox. Tigh Grenshem has fought a running battle with Equinox Director, Randolph Dorne, for over a year. Three weeks ago he solicited Tactical protection after receiving numerous threats of violence.'

Another image and file replaced Grenshem. Stone rubbed his jaw as he looked into the pale blue eyes of Randolph Dorne. Born on Earth, of multiple nationality, indeterminate race, he was forty-six, unmarried, no children; his residence was listed as Skycity.

The background video ended and the NARC file began. Colonel William Dupre's face appeared against the department emblem, a steel gauntlet, palm-upward, cradling a white dove. Dupre's brown face was bleak, his soft Barbadian voice brusque.

'Good evening, Gene,' he began, speaking directly to Captain Gene Cantrell, for whom the file was earmarked. 'You'll leave the Chell assignment a month early. Pull out as soon as you can pass all offices into the hands of Tactical, make your best speed for Zeus. You may have been keeping abreast of developments there... things seem to be coming to the boil faster than expected.

'I've a brief from Central for you, and a Tolstoy-size dossier for your computers... take a look at this short version.' His brows arched. 'Make what you can of it. It's a tough one. You'll want to forward this to Jarrat and Stone — feel free. It may turn out to be their business anyway.'

Dupre smiled into the camera, reached out and turned it off. The screen blanked and the transmission from Central began. The quality was poor though it had been cleaned up and enhanced. Subspace dropout was unavoidable. With a familiar sense of bitterness, Stone absorbed the text and voice-over.

'To Col. W. A. Dupre, Quadrant Controller, from C-in-C, NARC Central. Incidence of Angel abuse in Avalon during the past two years is through ten percent, invoking automatic NARC involvement. Surveillance began six months ago. The system's habitable worlds, Avalon and Eos, are Angel saturated, but Intelligence has been able to locate neither a source of manufacture, nor an import route. Carrier assignment is effective immediate upon receipt of this signal. Documentation follows.'

There the brief ended, and Jarrat turned off the monitor. He rolled over, flat on his back, and arched his head into the mattress. 'They shipped out three nights ago,' he said quietly.

'And it's about three days' hyperflight.'

'Cantrell and Petrov are going to be in over their heads.' Stone's fingertips traced the curve of Jarrat's throat. 'Gene hasn't done much field work in years, and Petrov hasn't had the experience.'

Jarrat closed his eyes as Stone's fingers dipped into the neck of his robe. 'Like I said, we ought to be there.'

'So we talk to Dupre in the morning.' Stone's lips brushed Jarrat's forehead as he loosened the garment. His hand moulded about Jarrat's chest and he luxuriated in the hot velvet skin, muscle and bone. His thumb brushed the sensitive peak of the nipple and Jarrat stretched responsively as the empathy blossomed.

'Dupre might not release us,' he warned. 'McKinnen has a hunch her bosses are up to something with Harry Del.'

'With Harry?' Stone lifted his head in surprise. 'He wouldn't be in anything questionable. You know the man better than that.'

'I know him. But McKinnen was adamant. I was saying there's no way Intelligence can apply anything they get out of us to other field agents. She said I was wrong, she thought Harry would have told us. Unquote.'

A frown creased Stone's brow. His hand played over Jarrat's flat belly but his mind was preoccupied elsewhere. 'They're working on something, some project we haven't been told about,' he guessed.

'That's what I thought.' Jarrat's right hand rested lightly on Stone's and urged it downward.

The prickle of musk, the heat of the velvet-over-steel shaft returned Stone to the present. His fingers curled about Jarrat's cock, worked lazily while his mouth hunted Kevin's tongue. Empathic shields dropped completely, pleasure doubled as sensations echoed and re-echoed through them.

With an eloquent groan Stone went down flat and held out one arm. 'Come on, Kev. I'm bushed, honey. Make it easy for me.'

'Be gentle?' Jarrat teased as he lifted himself onto the bigger, broader body. His long legs splayed about Stone's sturdy thighs and he leaned forward. Cocks crossed like sabres and began to duel. 'This project,' he panted as he began to move, 'is wrecking my love life!'

Stone caught his head, smiled against his lips. 'You wanted to fuck?'

'Of course I wanted to fuck!' Jarrat paused, kissed him and began to move again. 'Just once I'd like to hit the mattress with enough energy to get it right.'

Get it right? Stone's eyes closed, his hips humped in Jarrat's easy rhythm. Pleasure surged about him and bounced back from Kevin's nerves like breakers on a beach. But Kevin wanted more, and frustration was a whisker away. Stone's hands swept down across his supple back, palmed his buttocks and pulled him in tight.

'Stoney?' Jarrat took a breath.

'Roll me over,' Stone suggested, a bass growl.

'You're tired,' Kevin said doubtfully.

'Not that tired.' Stone leaned up to have his mouth, then tipped him off and turned belly down. With a pillow under his cheek he relaxed, spread his long legs and smiled as he felt Jarrat's fingers trickle from his nape, down his spine, into his cleft and zero in on the heart of him. He closed his eyes, and heard the cap twist off a tube.

He was 'open' now, not just physically but empathically. As slick fingers entered him he let the feedback overwhelm him and heard Kevin's soft groan of reaction. What one felt, the other felt. It hardly mattered who played the active role. Stone held his breath as Jarrat spread him and replaced his fingers with his cock, and then took a deep gasp as pleasure surged through him.

Hot and heavy, Kevin rested on his back. Teeth worried gently at his nape, and Stone shivered... was it Jarrat's nerves which scintillated with delight, or his own? Full of him, over-loaded with throbbing pleasure, Stone panted into the pillow. Musk and fresh sweat prickled the nostrils; Kevin's breath scudded moistly over his ear as Jarrat began to work deeply into him.

It never lasted long enough. Limp in the aftermath, he watched with groggy eyes as Jarrat produced a warm washcloth for him. The quilt swathed them, and as Jarrat snapped off the dim lights Stone turned over into his embrace.

'We're leaving. Tomorrow.' His teeth worried Kevin's lobe, branded the base of his neck. 'No more simulations.'

Jarrat's voice was slurred with sleep. 'Dupre won't like it.'

'Dupre,' Stone groaned, 'can do the other thing.' He punched the pillow to comfort and let his eyes close at last.

***

'You asked for my professional opinion, I gave it to you.' Yvette McKinnen stood rigidly, hands clasped behind her, before Colonel William Dupre's desk. Her dust-green jump-suit looked almost paramilitary. 'I believe you are making a grave mistake. I have considerable experience with cases of natural and artificial empathy.'

'And that experience,' Dupre said levelly, 'is that such people carry an emotional burden which ultimately destroys them. I understand what you're saying, Doctor —'

'You just don't agree with me,' she finished. Dupre clasped his hands on the desk. It was a genuine antique, brought from Earth at great cost, a personal whim. In the corner of the office Harry Del leaned on the water cooler, eyes closed, massaging his temples as if his head was throbbing. Baggy slacks and an even baggier shirt gave him the look of a Bohemian artist. Jarrat and Stone sat in the mock-leather armchairs beside the desk.

Their faces gave little away. Dupre could read more from their body language. They were in denim and jackets, clothes suited to travelling, as if they would walk out and keep walking, if they found they had come here only to be ignored.

Both of them were past the point of no return. In fact, they had endured more than Dupre had anticipated, though less than the Intelligence specialists wanted. Jarrat, always the more fiery of the two, was beginning to look ragged about the edges. Not sleeping, Dupre guessed, living on his nerves. He needed a week's R&R, or a return to active duty. Stone looked grim, sullen. His temper was not as quick or sharp as Jarrat's but he was on the edge. His last psyche profile indicated that the eruption was imminent, and when it came it would be a spectacle, since Stone kept his temper on a tighter rein than Jarrat, perhaps for too long.

Without doubt, Intelligence had pushed them hard. Perhaps too hard. Stone was half a hand's span taller than Jarrat and much more muscular. His hair was very dark, and worn short, where Jarrat's was a tousled mane of sun-blond and brown, long on his collar. But Narcotics And Riot Control had not hired them for their undeniable good looks, and the very spirit and skill which had brought them into the department could now urge them out of it.

On the desk before Dupre was a memo from Intelligence. They wanted more. They wanted to increase the work load, double the number and difficulty of the simulations. See how long it took Jarrat and Stone to break? Dupre wondered. Testing to destruction was the way a new weapons system was analysed in terms of strength and weakness. But men were not machines — something Intelligence was inclined to forget.

The memo was specific, demanding, but Dupre regarded it sceptically. Authority here, as in any matter, rested in his own hands. He looked up at McKinnen, then at Del who was drinking from a glass beaker. Jarrat and Stone were simmering. Two resignation statements lay beside the memo, and Dupre was abruptly out of options.

He could close the data-gathering part of McKinnen's project, tell Intelligence to analyse what they had and ease up on two men who had just drawn the line; or he could try to coerce, perhaps to bribe Jarrat and Stone back to work. McKinnen would erupt first. She was nearer the edge than either of the 'lab rats', probably because they were fatigued by hard physical work and constant narcotic stimuli. And Yvette had just as good a reason to blow up.

Dupre drummed his fingers on the memo. 'Harry, I know you don't agree with Dr McKinnen's statement.'

'How could I agree?' Del thrust his hands into the pockets of his baggy blue slacks and turned to face Dupre. 'I've been an empath all my life, I've spent more years dealing with my own kind than Yvette ever will. With all due respect, Bill, she's dead wrong. Many empaths are the most stable people, so long as they're in touch with their emotions. Ask Kevin or Stoney. They're in control. They're won't destroy themselves physically or mentally, not next week, not next year.'

The woman's fists clenched. 'Time and again, Colonel, I have seen artificially induced empathy or telepathy result in mental instability, even madness and suicide.'

'But their empathy is natural,' Del argued. 'To them, it's as normal as breathing and eating, or making love!'

'But ten weeks ago they'd never been empathic in their lives,' McKinnen insisted. 'Natural empathy is born in the individual.

Anything else is totally artificial.'

Harry rubbed his temples once more. 'Yvette, you're a biosystems analyst, and a good one. But you work with machines, biocyber implants. The instances of instability, insanity and suicide you've seen are due to the human brain's inability to adjust to implants. The machine/brain fusion has never been successfully achieved. There's always danger. Even a simple mechanical fault. An implant 'flutters' for any one of a thousand reasons... the mind maddens. All you can do is sedate the subject, because by the time the fault shows it's too late. Jarrat and Stone are different. Their empathy is as natural as if they were born with it.'

Dupre held up both hands to stop them. 'Please! You've said all this at least twice. Repetition is getting us nowhere. From what I see, you're at stalemate. Dr McKinnen, you view the work from the biocyber perspective. Dr Del, you see it from the standpoint of natural empathy. If Dr McKinnen is correct, Captains Jarrat and Stone will break. If she is wrong, they're stronger than they ever were. Correct?'

'In principle.' Harry Del smiled wearily. 'Strong or not, Bill, you can break them. Shove them back into that lab, let your Intelligence division test them to destruction, and they'll break. Being empathic doesn't make them superhuman.'

'Yes.' Dupre's eyes flickered over the memo, and he cleared his throat. 'According to your report, Dr McKinnen, you have all the data you need.'

'More than was needed,' she said tartly. 'Repetition, as you said, is unproductive. Intelligence is greedy.'

'And thoughtlessly cruel,' Del added. 'These simulations may be more or less harmless, but for the subject caught in the middle of them, it's a fight for life. Mind and body respond to every crisis with peak effort and the result is physical and emotional exhaustion.' He stabbed a finger at the younger men. 'They've run three simulations per week each since they arrived. It's rest they need. As a doctor of medicine —' he glared at McKinnen, who was an engineer '— I would prescribe sixteen hours' sleep, two days of total rest, and then a return to duty. Something to occupy mind and body productively.'

Dupre sat back, head cocked as he regarded doctor, engineer and field agents one by one. Jarrat and Stone had not said a word in fifteen minutes, but were missing nothing. Stone's hot

34

blue eyes were fixed on the back of McKinnen's head. Jarrat was studying the painting of a China clipper which hung by the water cooler. Both were tense as athletes under the gun. A word, and they would walk, leave NARC, with two identical resignations.

At last Dupre sighed and deliberately put his signature to a document which had been prepared days beyond. He turned it toward McKinnen. 'Project... suspended, Doctor.'

'And Jarrat and Stone?' McKinnen asked curtly.

'Ah.' Dupre stood, hands on hips, elegant in grey slacks and white uniform shirt with the NARC insignia. The field agents watched him warily. 'Dr Del recommends that you are perfectly capable of returning to duty. You agree?'

'Colonel!' McKinnen's fist thumped the desk. 'You have not been listening to a word I say!' The French accent thickened with anger.

'On the contrary,' Dupre said ruefully, his own Barbadian accent languid, 'I've heard every word.'

'And you choose to ignore me in favour or — of an outworld *healer!* You brought me here to humiliate me?'

The outburst was not unexpected. Dupre passed a hand before his eyes. 'I wanted your professional opinion to balance that of Dr Del, and you gave it to me. What conclusions must be drawn from two conflicting opinions are my concern.'

He spoke softly but the woman was already angry. The door whisked open and she was gone, leaving Harry Del to breathe a sigh of relief. He sagged onto the couch and took his aching head in his hands.

'With respect, Bill,' he groaned, 'she is wrong. You can take my word for it. Jarrat and Stone are stronger than they have ever been. If they break, it'll be because you let the Weapons Research division destroy them... and I hope to Christ they would have better sense than to sit on their asses and let it happen!'

'Indeed.' Dupre picked up the resignations, folded them and placed them in Stone's hand. 'I don't think we'll be needing these.'

For the first time since he and Jarrat had made their statement, Stone spoke. 'Then if we're not going back to the lab, are we returning to the carrier? We've been reviewing our telemetry every night, Colonel.'

'Then you know the *Athena* is en route to Zeus.' Dupre perched on the edge of the desk and frowned at Del. 'Sixteen hours' sleep and two days' rest, you said?'

Del leaned back and massaged his neck. 'And a return to productive activity. Put them back where they belong, Bill, before they go stale and it costs you another million credits in retraining.'

The Quadrant Controller tugged at the lobe of his ear. 'You may be right.' He looked into Jarrat's wary eyes. 'You saw yesterday's telemetry?'

'The situation on Avalon is still under Tactical's control.' Jarrat looked sidelong at Stone. 'The carrier won't make orbit for a few hours yet. The problem seems to be, we can't work out how the Angel gets in... the rest of it is purely political, way out of our jurisdiction.'

'Yes.' Dupre folded his arms. 'If I were to reassign you, don't imagine that I'd completely ignore McKinnen's warnings. I've no experience with empaths, and the outside chance remains that Harry may be wrong.' He smiled at the surgeon. 'Not that he's been wrong to date! But if I put you back aboard the *Athena* you'll be under surveillance yourselves. Gene Cantrell will remain aboard.'

Stone's eyes narrowed. He felt the kick of Jarrat's annoyance and carefully tuned him out. 'In what capacity?' he asked carefully.

The Colonel's brows arched. 'Observer. Gene will watch, listen and report to me.' Dupre shrugged expressively. 'I'm still not used to all this.' He waved vaguely at the two younger men and Del. 'This empathy. Maybe Harry's right.' He looked away. 'Or maybe I'll be burying you two. I don't know that I want it on my conscience. If I thought you were as unstable as McKinnen thinks, I'd bust you to civilian. At least you'd stay alive.'

'But you know better,' Del added. 'Yvette is a talented engineer, but she's stronger on the cyber aspect than the psyche. Let Cantrell monitor them. Call it a field test. Send his reports to Intelligence. They'd just love to have them.'

'They would.' Dupre sighed heavily and gave Jarrat a shrewd look. 'You know what the boffins want? Harry told you?'

A thread of Jarrat's tension licked through Stone's belly almost like an echo of lust. He shut it out and concentrated on what Kevin was saying.

'McKinnen mentioned something, but Harry hasn't said a word. I guess that means it's classified.'

'Restricted information, at least,' Dupre amended. 'We asked Harry to keep it quiet until we find out if there's any ground to be gained out of it.'

'Like what?' Stone leaned forward, elbows on his knees.

The empath stood and paced between the window and the water cooler as he spoke. 'Your bosses want me to see if I can do it again,' he said caustically. 'Take another two field agents, link them empathically as I linked you, as a form of undetectable surveillance for deep cover assignments. On one hand it's a relief to work with people who are not like the bloody-minded bigots I suffer at home! Here, empathy isn't censured as a certifiable perversion, and that's refreshing.'

Stone was stunned. 'Can you do it?'

'Oh, yes.' Del turned toward him, hands in pockets, brow furrowed. 'The question is, should I? Do I want to risk taking two perfectly sound lives and wrecking them.'

'You didn't wreck us,' Jarrat said quietly, and was answered with a smile.

'Special case. Emergency.' Harry sighed. 'You two were already in love, though not yet lovers.' He frowned at Dupre. 'I'm dead against the rest of it, Bill. The risks are terrible. I told Jarrat before I did it to them, if he didn't put an exceptionally high price on Stone's life, he'd end by killing him to be free of him. Friendship can turn to hate like that.' He snapped his fingers. 'Living with another person under your skin could become a nightmare.'

'Unless you loved the other person,' Stone added.

'Right.' Harry arched a brow at Dupre. 'I'll make Intelligence a deal. Bring me partners who are committed, handfasted or at least long-time lovers, and I'll try. Otherwise, forget it. You think I want to be responsible for driving people to violence, murder or suicide?'

'You told McKinnen empaths are the most stable people,' Dupre said slowly.

'I said,' Del corrected, '*many* empaths, who are in touch with their emotions, are stable! Jarrat and Stone are in touch, in control and in love. That is their stability. And even in their case I was damned reluctant to do it.'

Dupre toyed with a pen though his eyes were on the field

agents. 'All right. You'll place yourselves under Dr Del's care. A few days' rest, first.'

'Then we're on assignment?' Jarrat was on his feet.

'Don't be so puppy-dog eager,' Dupre chuckled. 'A month ago, before you arrived, I told you there's a job coming up that's a ball breaker. This is it, and I don't envy you. I'll fix you a ride with Starfleet that'll get you to Zeus a few days after the carrier. You'll have the chance to study the background documentation en route. The short version you saw last night is superficial.' He waved them away. 'Go. Doctor's orders. Sleep! I'll buzz you when your flight is due.'

Eager to breathe free air, Stone was out of the office before Jarrat and Del, and did not stop till he was on the fifth floor balcony. The view over Venice to the spaceport was impressive. Ships left hourly; soon he and Jarrat would be aboard one of them.

The tropical air was sultry, the sky overcast. A storm was coming in from the south. As Jarrat's arm circled his waist Stone began to relax, and looked back to find Harry regarding them with a curious expression.

'You'll make it work,' Del said in answer to Stone's unspoken question. 'I've no doubt of that. Bill wants Cantrell to keep an eye on you — fine. Don't resent the concern. It's genuine. But you won't make a balls-up of your job.'

'Thanks.' Jarrat looked out over the city. 'When will you be going home?'

'I've a few weeks' work left here,' Harry mused. 'They might find me some lovers like yourselves to work with, but I'll try to axe the experiment before it starts... it stinks.' He shrugged off the introspective mood. 'I'm more interested in working with the Narcotics division. The devil's claw concoction of mine, which we used to buy you time, Stoney, is being researched. It won't wean an addict off Angel, but it may prolong life, and improve the quality of life.' He sighed heavily. 'I'm hoping to do better. They also asked if I'd try to adjust the brain chemistry of a test subject to render him impervious to Angel, the same work I did for you. The object is to see if we can make it impossible for what happened to you to ever happen again.'

'That,' Jarrat said thoughtfully, 'sounds reasonable.'

'Perhaps.' Del sounded less than sure. 'The trouble is, I can make mistakes if I mess about with the chemistry of a healthy brain. Leave a man allergic to nitrogen, or perhaps he'll get drunk on water! Without the neural damage of Angel addiction to key on, I'm almost lost. Which means,' he added bleakly, 'if NARC wants to experiment, the subject will have to volunteer for addiction and then pray I can do my stuff.' He shuddered. 'I see the value of the research, but it frightens me. I don't know that I want the responsibility. I prefer to work with simple plant narcotics. I'm sure there's a substance somewhere that will counteract Angel.'

Stone slipped his arm firmly around Jarrat. 'If there's an answer, you'll find it,' he said tiredly. With relief came exhaustion, and many aches he had been only dimly aware of. Neither he nor Jarrat had slept more than a few hours at a stretch in weeks. Emotional stress, exertion and chemical loading took a heavy toll.

'I believe,' Harry said wryly, 'the colonel placed you under my supervision! Rest, he said. That was an order.'

An order which was easy to obey. Jarrat was already asleep when Stone stumbled into bed. He laid his cheek on the warm, hard plane of Kevin's shoulder and closed his eyes. The last he knew was the slight vibration through the frame of the vast building as a Starfleet lighter touched down on the roof far above.

The dreams came later.

He ran, but knew he would be caught. Shadowy shapes pinned him down with crushing weight. A capsule broke with a sharp plastic pop, and acrid golden dust filled his head and stole his thoughts.

Angel.

Horror rampaged through his mind. The drug was like sweet poison. Angeldeath awaited him — no one survived the one-way track into the nightmare. But first came the Angeldreams. Fantasies torn from the deepest realm of the subconscious were clothed in sensual flesh that seemed so real. Stone threshed as the bitter dust stung his nose, choked him, but even then the fantasies had stirred to life.

He saw Jarrat again, the focus of his dreams, now as before. The chimerical creature with Kevin's face rose from his memory: emerald skinned, winged, his body adorned in paint, gold, rings and chains, he deliberately seduced a man he loved. His beauty inveigled, beguiled, and Stone was lost once more.

Engrossed in the golden dust he writhed, frenzied with the drug-induced, fantasy-driven lust which would rage as long as his body held out...

Angel.

The word crept into the midst of the phantasm and Stone recoiled from the incubus he had created. It wore Jarrat's face and body but it was not Kevin. Lips curled back over razor-like fangs, talons ripped his skin as the carnal dream became horror at the mention of a word.

Now he fought, but knew he could not win. Angel was a disease. Some reasoning part of his mind knew it for what it was. A synthetic, a narcotic designed in the lab, so powerful and seductive that it had built empires, and torn them down.

Angeldreams were the kind a man would die for: he might swim in diamond, hear the song of the stars, master the sky with the power of living flight. Rampant with sexual energy, lord of every scene, he commanded any lover his imagination could conjure. No act was impossible, sensuality was infinite.

Until he was so rotten with the drug and the physical punishment wreaked upon his helpless, overworked body, his existence could not be called living. The only escape was death. Stone fought like a madman as the agonies of withdrawal assaulted him. He could inhale another draught of poison, flee into the dreams, one step closer his end. Or he could die here, tonight, in torment.

He was disgusting. Flying, out of his mind, his enslaved body fucked the floor or the bed in its senseless euphoria. He was a user. A rutting Angelhead. In months the addiction must deepen, the dreams would fly his mind ever higher while the rest of him decayed. Horror at his own corruption nauseated him and he screamed, hoarse and helpless.

It was not the first time Jarrat had shaken him awake in the night and held him tightly enough to bruise. He gasped air to the bottom of his lungs, buried his face in Jarrat's chest and inhaled the clean, male scent. This Jarrat was living, real and alive, not the beguiling Angel illusion.

'I've got you. You're all right, love.' Kevin was still only half awake, his voice slurred with sleep, trembling with reaction to Stone's terror, which had invaded his own sleeping mind. Strong arms held on tight. 'Same dream?'

'Yeah.' Stone fought off the last clinging tendrils of the

nightmare. 'Christ, I'm sorry.' He sat up, chest heaving, skin slick with an icy sweat.

Jarrat stroked his back as they both got their breath back. 'You ought to tell Harry. He'd be able to do something.'

'He's on a NARC research contract now,' Stone said shakily. 'He'd have to report this crap I keep dreaming to Dupre. You want me in a psyche clinic?'

'No.' Jarrat caught him by the shoulders and pulled him down. 'Come here. Tell me about it.'

'Told you last time. It never changes.' Stone lay against him and struggled to control the leftover shivering. Jarrat's mouth covered his and he felt a little warmth seep back into his bones.

'Tell me how to help,' Jarrat whispered. 'Is it like what you did for that kid you picked up, Rikki Mitchell? Is it booze, a meal, sex, you need?'

'I'm not craving. I'm not an addict anymore,' Stone said gently. 'Harry saw to that.'

'Then tell me what to do.' Jarrat's fingers tightened.

'You're doing it.' Stone pulled the sheet over their heads. 'Just don't let go. It's rich, isn't it? Let go of me in the night, and the bogeyman grabs me and stuffs my nose with that shit. And I try not to breathe it, but —'

'Stoney.' Jarrat's mouth silenced him. 'You're the only man who ever came back from Angel addiction. That makes you one of a kind. No one else ever lived out what you're going through to know what it's like. The alternative was a slab in the morgue!' He gave Stone a shake. 'Tough it out, try counting your bloody blessings. You have to be alive to feel like hell.'

For the first time Stone glimpsed the absurd privilege of the nightmare. It should have been ridiculous to be grateful for the terror and disgust which assaulted him one night in three, but Jarrat was right. He was alive, and if the price of his life was a cold sweat, broken sleep, it was cheap.

He settled gratefully into Jarrat's embrace and closed his eyes. 'I'm okay now. You can let go.'

'I could,' Jarrat muffled against his neck. 'But I'm not going to. Shut up and get some rest.'

'Romantic,' Stone accused groggily, but Jarrat was already past hearing. Stone banished the dream with an effort of will. He set his head back on Kevin's shoulder and closed his eyes.

This time his sleep was peaceful.

Chapter Three

Lift engines roared and cast an acrid draught across the security section of Venice Spaceport as the Starfleet courier *Ariel* was prepped for flight. She still shimmered with heat after landing, and would be airborne again within in an hour. Jarrat turned his eyes from the brilliant stern flare as the main motors were testfired, and looked back at the car. Stone sat on the hood of the Rand Falcon, idly smoking as they waited for the Starfleet crew to call them.

The night wind was hot and blustery, the stars obscured by an overcast and light smog, which reminded Jarrat keenly of Chell. That city was once more the responsibility of Tactical. The Angel syndicate, Death's Head, was destroyed, but Jarrat would never forget the dockside labyrinth, the people, the conflict.

His old injuries were well healed but he still felt them after exertion, when mended bones and joints ached. After the physical demands of McKinnen's repeated simulations, perhaps only Stoney knew how worn down he had been. And Harry, Jarrat thought. The empath could rarely be fooled.

Unbroken sleep and two days of indolence and lovemaking were Harry's prescription. Jarrat felt reborn. Hands in the hip pockets of his jeans, he turned back toward the Rand, where Stoney lounged on the starlight blue hood. The humid wind scudded across Kevin's bare chest as he stepped into the halogen wash of the driving lights. Stone's eyes roved over him, making his skin prickle.

The cigarette fell into the gravel, and Stone held out his hand without a word. Jarrat went to him, was scissored between Stone's knees, and laced his fingers behind his lover's neck. The shields were down; shared emotions raced through them, phantom echoes of every kind of sensuality they had indulged. Jarrat's eyes closed to savour the exquisite sensations as Stone's flat hands caressed his bare back. Stone was elegant in white slacks, black silk shirt, platinum chains about his neck and left wrist — Jarrat's gifts, bought days before in a Venice thieves' market.

A crackle from the R/T dispelled the moment of closeness. Stone took it from his pocket, and the voice of the courier's pilot said sharply, 'We're prepped, Cap Stone. We launch in ten.'

Their bags were already aboard. Jarrat shrugged on his pale green shirt, thrust it into tight grey marble denim as Stone slid off the long hood of the Rand. The jets whined up and Kevin took the car through a wide arc toward the Starfleet craft. It was sleek, aerodynamic, designed for speed in atmosphere; its hyperflight engine module remained in orbit.

As Jarrat swung the car in beside the roasting stern a young sergeant in NARC fatigues stepped down the boarding ramp. He took the wheel from Jarrat with a sketchy salute.

'The whole Zeus dossier is loaded. Colonel Dupre's instructions. A duplicate of all data processed by your carrier in the last three days, Cap.'

'Thanks.' Jarrat arched one brow at Stone. 'That means about half a million words of reading and ten hours of videos. Where do you want to start?'

'With the summary,' Stone said drily. The pilot was at the top of the ramp, waiting to lock up. As they boarded Stone took the man's hand in greeting. The ID bar on his breast read Voskov, C., and he wore the lieutenant's insignia. 'How soon can you get us to Zeus?' Stone asked quietly as the ramp growled up.

Voskov gave him a cheeky, freckle-faced grin. He was a redhead with skin like milk and pale blue eyes. 'You'll find we're a little faster than the ships you're used to, Captain.'

'Four days from Darwin's to Zeus by carrier,' Jarrat said indifferently.

'We'll have you there in two, sir,' Voskov promised. 'These couriers are the fastest things Starfleet fly. If you'd take your seats, we're on prelaunch procedures.'

The interior was cramped, cool, discreetly lit, dove grey and black. It boasted no cabins, no amenities, no comforts save the reclined acceleration couches which could be angled up or down to serve as chair, bed, bench, for up to six passengers. Before each was a terminal, and two had been prepared for use.

'Oh, nice,' Stone muttered. 'Two days in this bucket? You sure you can't do it in one, Voskov?'

The pilot was not offended. 'Not even in this, Cap. You want to outrun this mother, you hire a speed jockey with a chopped race bird. Those, Starfleet does not operate.' He sounded disappointed.

Jarrat tried the couch for fit, felt it mould about his body, assuming his shape almost sensually. The flight harness buckled about him and he marked the time. His chrono was set for several time zones. In Venice, midnight was two hours away. In Chell it was morning. In the city of Elysium, in the sovereign colony of Avalon it was evening, and aboard the *Athena*, shiptime, a little after noon. The longer a man spent suspended between worlds, the less time meant.

The engines rammed to peak thrust and held while systems were tested a final time. On the monitors before them the display counted down to zero and Jarrat held his breath for the blow in the back of acceleration. These ships were not designed for passenger comfort, but for speed.

The whole airframe shook with the tremendous vibration as repulsion offset gravity and the heavy lifters kicked the courier into the air. Three gravities crammed crew and passengers into the couches, and Jarrat gritted his teeth as his apparent weight soared. Breathing was difficult, blood pressure rose steeply. In minutes the courier levelled off, the display read eighty kilometres' altitude, and gravity seemed to normalise as the acceleration diminished.

With a grunt, Stone released his straps and touched a key on the board before him. Jarrat unbuckled and strode forward in search of coffee as Stone began to read. Voskov would be tracking his hyperflight engine module. They would dock in minutes and be out of the system soon after. A styrene beaker in either hand, Jarrat stood behind Voskov and his copilot, a tall, olive-skinned woman. The forward ports were flak shielded, the sunlight harsh and glaring as the *Ariel* nosed up toward its massive engine section.

The drive module's smoothly contoured hull housed fusion reactors and three Kestrel engines, and dwarfed the slender, aerodynamic lighter. The *Ariel* rotated delicately; manoeuvring thrusters nudged her into line. A metallic impact hammered through the airframe as twenty electromagnetic clamps mated the two craft together.

The control surfaces came alive as Jarrat watched, and Voskov commenced the full preflight checklist on his powerplant and hyperflight engines. Jarrat left the Starfleet crew to its work and returned to the cabin.

The Avalon data had just begun to display on the monitor before Stone. With a grim look, he backed up the file and started it again as he took a beaker of coffee.

'You're going to love this,' he warned as Jarrat brought the couch up to mould him like a seat.

'Surprise me.' Jarrat ran a hand through his hair and focused on the screen. 'Oh. When did that happen?'

'The show was already on when the *Athena* arrived. Not an Angel packriot, but Tactical squealed for NARC just as soon as the carrier was there.'

Jarrat absorbed the scenes of mass rampage and destruction with a frown. A building was ablaze; cars lay wrecked; a skyhopper gouted flame and smoke on the median strip in the middle of a ten-lane clearway. The crowd had gone mad. 'Not a packwar? You sure?' The scene had all the hallmarks of one.

'Civil disobedience,' Stone said cynically. 'That's the pro-Equinox faction at war with Senator Tigh Grenshem's disciples.'

'It's not our concern,' Jarrat mused. 'Supposing they rip Elysium to shreds, it doesn't involve NARC. We're not political, we never have been.' He angled a frown at Stone. 'Tac wanted us in?'

'Soon as the carrier made orbit.' Stone ran a text file accompanying the video. 'The man in command of Elysium Tactical is Colonel Vic Duggan. Central put him in the picture as soon as Elysium drew NARC attention. He's worked with our surveillance team for six months, so he knew the carrier was en route.'

'And Cantrell deployed the Ravens?' Jarrat reached over and skimmed through the data. 'Ah. Gene told Duggan he was on his own. NARC is not the Army.'

'I'll accept that as an aphorism,' Stone said acidly. 'Duggan is fairly pissed, as you'd expect. Tac took a thrashing that night. Statistics... fourteen men dead, nineteen lifted out by medevac.'

'Civvy casualties?' Jarrat was intent on the streetwar on the screen. Reduced to two-dimensional images, it was no less appalling. 'Jesus Christ, Stoney, they're armed! Phosphor grenades. Flak curtain.'

'And an energy weapon. They shot down a Tac flyer.' Stone searched for specific data. 'Eighty-four civilians killed, three times that number taken out by medevac to clinics around Elysium.'

Jarrat stabbed a finger at the screen, where a man was being torn apart in a welter of scarlet as he ran into a wall of flak. 'Military weapons. Have Tac got any idea where the crowd came by them?'

'Not according to this transmission,' Stone sipped his coffee and reviewed the textual data in silence for a time. Jarrat was intent on the images of devastation. 'I've got Gene's personal report to Dupre on Darwin's right here.'

The screen froze, and Jarrat turned to the text. Cantrell had dispatched his report within two hours of assuming orbit over Elysium, and in so short a space of time he sounded terse with anxiety and was asking for official counsel.

'The situation on Avalon is desperate. In the city of Elysium it's at flashpoint, these people are on the edge of civil war. Tac has lost control – if it ever had control. They're too busy burying their dead and licking their wounds to worry about what's happening on the street! Colonel Duggan was on the comm before we assumed orbit, begging for a full complement of gunships, but I refused. We're apolitical. I made the usual excuses. If we're drawn into politico-military service, we're a squad of bloody mercenaries, we could be used by every questionable government to crush civvies. The old speech. But Duggan's men were getting mauled, he wasn't impressed and I don't blame him. I gave him a challenge: prove some connection, any connection that links the war between Grenshem's group and Equinox to the Angel trade, and I'll deploy. Trouble is, both Elysium Tac and the NARC surveillance team have been trying to make that connection for six months, while this circus brewed up. So far, zilch. I'll watch Duggan like a hawk, he could invent the evidence to get us where he needs us. Right now, he's mad enough to spit. The shit is about to hit the fan, and when it does, Bill, I wouldn't like to be down there among it.'

More followed, but Jarrat stopped the flow of text. He sat back, eyes closed, and digested Cantrell's misgivings. 'What have we got on this Duggan?'

'They sent his whole file.' Stone punched it up. 'Most of it's pretty accurate.'

'What do you mean, most of it?' Jarrat cracked his eyes open, but before Stone could answer they caught their breath.

The whole frame and hull of the Starfleet courier seemed to buck, there was an instant of freefall, like riding the top of a parabolic arc in a plane, a second's sensation of hollowness or falling, and then velvet smoothness.

'We're in hyper,' Stone grunted, and pressed a hand to his belly. 'Jesus, I hate that.'

Jarrat rubbed the back of his neck. 'Try it on a troop transport with a squad of chicken rookies peeing themselves in fright. Seventeen years old, first time out, on their way to a hotzone... that's the point of no return, and they know it. All they want is to run home to daddy.'

Stone regarded Jarrat soberly. 'You went through that.'

'But I had nobody to run home to.' Jarrat felt the old pangs of regret as his memory filled with scenes of childhood. A hospice, three weeks from Earth. A friend, adolescent lover, dead in his arms. Angeldeath was ugly. Other images overset the older ones: it was Stone, then, head lolling stupidly as the Angel commanded his brain. Fingers of ice gripped Jarrat's insides and squeezed.

'Hey.' Stone's voice was choked as Jarrat's feelings hurt him too. 'Kevin. Kev!' He caught Jarrat's right hand tightly. 'You all right?'

'I'm fine.' Jarrat shook himself hard. He passed a hand over his eyes and leaned over to kiss Stone's mouth briefly. 'And what did you mean, most of Duggan's file is accurate?'

'Just that.' Stone began to relax again as the storm of Jarrat's emotions ebbed away. 'It's as accurate as a dossier compiled from routine file research can be.' He smiled faintly. 'But I knew Duggan almost ten years ago. I was a rookie.' The smile widened.

'You served on Avalon?' Jarrat was surprised. 'You never told me. I thought you transferred out of London Tactical straight into NARC.

'I did. Duggan was on Earth when I knew him. He was an instructor in crowd control. I shouldn't think he'd remember me. It's been a lot of years and I was just one face among hundreds. Thousands. Tac recruits come and go frequently, you know. Most people sign on for a two-year hitch and take the training. They try the job, find they can't take the heat and get out again.'

Keys pattered, and Jarrat ran the file. Duggan's picture appeared at right of the screen. 'Victor Healey Duggan, forty-eight years old, educated on Earth and at Moswell-Chow

Technical College on Dalago. Never married —'

'Wrong,' Stone interrupted. 'Intelligence didn't dig deep enough. Vic Duggan was married when he was studying for an engineering degree.'

'Divorced?' Jarrat wondered.

'The guy died.' Stone looked away.

Jarrat felt his heart squeeze. Or was it Stone's reaction?

'Angel?' He set a hand on Stone's arm. 'Duggan married a guy who was a user?'

'The way I heard it,' Stone said quietly, obviously forcing his thoughts into focus, 'the addiction was listed as accidental. A campus prank. They were all skulled out, it was silly season. Some dickhead cut the party treats with that crap.'

'My God.' Jarrat looked back at the screen, where Duggan's face was displayed. He was handsome, seeming younger than his years; very tanned, dark haired, brown eyed.

'Yeah.' Stone released the display to continue. 'Duggan was doing a course at Moswell-Chow. He left after the funeral, brought Dominic's body home to Earth for cremation, and he enlisted with Tactical a few days later.'

For a moment they were silent, then Jarrat cleared his throat. 'Was Duggan on a vengeance crusade when you knew him?'

Stone's brows arched. 'I don't think so. It would have been fourteen years after he lost Dominic, when I knew him. If he'd started out on a crusade, that kind of idealism gets kicked out of you fast in Tac, believe me.'

'About as fast as the Army kicks it out of you,' Jarrat said ruefully as he scanned Duggan's service report. 'He's earned commendations and medals. Good record. Doesn't look like the kind of man who'd write his own evidence to drag NARC in where we're not supposed to be. He asked for the assignment to Avalon seven years ago. No reason given here for why he'd come out this far and then elect to spend years working in an industrial rat-trap.'

'Check something,' Stone suggested. 'Seven years ago... would that be about the time the percentage of Angel dependence started to reach noticeable levels?'

Data hustled through the screen. 'Uh... right.' Jarrat leaned back and propped his booted feet on the work surface between the couches. 'Duggan's style, would you say? He's on a crusade, but he's not stupid. If you can plug the gaps before the leak becomes a deluge you might, I say *might*, keep the Angel out of a population as relatively isolated as Avalon.'

'That'd be Vic Duggan,' Stone agreed. 'Then, what went wrong? He managed to keep the Angel situation under control until just two years ago. See these statistics.'

They had been put into chart form, instantly visible. When Duggan arrived, Avalon and Eos were by no means free of Angel, but the import route was swiftly traced. Duggan stopped a smuggling racket operated by baggage handlers on the Orion starclipper line. With supply cut off, the system was clean for three years. Existing addicts drew their licenced supply, and since the life expectancy of the user was often measured in months, three years after Duggan's arrival, Angel use was almost completely unknown on Avalon.

'And then, overnight, it exploded,' Stone finished as he and Jarrat read off the statistics. 'It went from nothing to huge levels of addiction, in ten months, and the stats were bad enough to draw NARC surveillance two years ago.'

The latest Tac Intelligence report was in, transmitted along with Cantrell's data. Jarrat skimmed through it fast. Where the Angel was coming from, no one yet knew. Duggan's last prayer was that the presence of a NARC carrier could conjure a trick of magic.

The files awaiting them detailed every aspect of the sovereign colony, from its economy to its topography, by way of politics and industry. Jarrat looked at the flight elapse time chrono, which counted down to the estimated entry to orbit over Avalon. Twenty-three hours, forty minutes.

He dropped a hand onto Stone's shoulder and levered to his feet. 'I'll get us a meal and a drink. We've got a lot of ground to cover.'

It was the part of an assignment he liked least, and yet his life and Stone's might depend on the local knowledge they squirreled away at this point. Study was as much a part of the job as the violent action and fireworks which drew more public attention.

Given the time-lag in tachyon band communications, Gene Cantrell would receive Dupre's notification to expect the *Athena*'s captains with hours to spare before the courier entered the Zeus system. Jarrat's teeth worried at his lip as he consulted the menu on the side of the robochef. For himself, chicken and noodles. For Stone, white fish and rice.

49

As he waited for the food he watched the Starfleet crew idling through their duty in the open cockpit just ahead. The normal blackness of space had warped into a maelstrom of lurid blue, like peering into the eye of a cyclone. Jarrat looked away as the machine delivered a tray and two meals.

They had work to do.

Chapter Four

Before he entered the outer limits of the Zeus system, Voskov dropped into normal space, raised his flak screens and signalled Elysium Control. Leaning on the back of the copilot's seat, Stone studied the CRT displays. To the naked eye the system seemed clear enough, but tracking told the truth.

Space was full of rubble, the last remnants of planets which no longer existed. Piecemeal, they had been smashed, hurled into the smelters which were parked with station-keeping thrusters wherever they had been employed. Six asteroid belts followed the orbits of the outer planets. Debris was a fine haze, like a veil of gravel, slowly spiralling inward to the distant G3 primary.

'Starfleet Courier 119 to Elysium Control,' Voskov called for the fifth time. 'Starfleet courier to Elysium ATC.' He adjusted his equipment. 'Jeez, Cap,' he commented over his shoulder in Stone's direction, 'there's so much interference I'm going to have to use a subspace squirt, or we'll never get through at all.'

'Do it,' Jarrat's terse voice said, a pace behind Stone. 'And signal the carrier. Tell Cantrell we're here.'

'Will do.' Voskov looked back at them. 'I can get in on flak screens, we don't need a tug, but they'll give me the safest approach route. Saves me sitting here for two hours scanning the whole shitty system for a decent way in. Christ, look at the mess they made. It used to be nice here once.'

'You local?' Stone asked as he watched the confusion of planetary rubble on the tracking displays.

'I'm from yonder.' Voskov gestured toward galactic south. 'Belgaris. But I got relatives here, we'd visit by clipper when I was a kid. D'you know, Cap, the clippers have to stand off and wait for a couple of tugs — takes two, one to move the ship in by a safe approach, the other to generate a flak screen big enough for a ship that size. Soon as you get up some velocity, this crap would punch straight through your hull like missiles if you didn't have deflectors.' He shook his head ruefully. 'I had an uncle on Avalon. He used to be a pilot, thirty, forty years ago — back in the days when you could still dare to stick your nose into orbit.'

Stone lifted a brow at Jarrat but they made no comment as the lieutenant tuned his equipment and hailed Elysium Control on the tachyon band. The belts of rubble, asteroid debris and meteor-sized fragments were constantly shifting. Between one flight and the next, an approach angle one assumed was safe could become a suicide run.

The whole assignment dossier was compacted into five data cubes, which Jarrat had retrieved from the terminal an hour before. They drank coffee with Voskov while the computer piloted the *Ariel* through the labyrinth of wreckage. Fifteen light minutes from Avalon, Stone's ears picked up a warning from the proximity indicator, and he leaned into the cockpit.

The sun was rapidly expanding, the forward viewports would soon begin to darken. 'What's that?' Stone gestured at the winking red enunciator.

'Just coming up on a smelter, Cap.' Voskov panned his cameras to starboard and zoomed on the object. 'Equinox had over nine thousand of those. They tore this whole system to wreckage.'

The nuclear smelter was the size of a city — derelict now, abandoned, radio-marked for safety. The reactor was shut down and the gaping maw of the immense machine seemed like the pit of hell. Riding astride the tail, like a terrier humping a wolfhound, was the mass driver which had fired semi-refined material to the fleet of freighters in one direction, fused slag and slurry in another.

The proximity alarm silenced as the ship cruised by, and Stone returned to the cabin. Jarrat was reading through the notes he had made, pad in one hand, buzzbox razor in the other. Stone raked his nails through his own stubble and reminded himself, on Darwin's World it would be evening. On the carrier, where they would soon dock, it would be early afternoon.

As Jarrat finished he held out his hand for the razor. One grey eye winked at him as Kevin returned to his notes. Their baggage lay by the docking port.

'Cap Stone?' Voskov called. 'I raised Captain Cantrell. He sends his regards. They've got a shindig on, he's busy. We'll dock in five. Coming up on Zeus now. God... look at that son of a bitch.'

The face of the giant world was dusky green. Neither Jarrat nor Stone had ever served in this system, and it was not a holiday destination. They had seen Zeus only in video images. The reality was stunning. The gas giant seemed to fill the heavens, gibbous, brooding. Overwhelming.

Orbiting well out of the radiation belts, Avalon, Eos and several uninhabitable satellites appeared like blue-white crescents against the immense, sullen visage of their parent. Jarrat whistled softly as Voskov cut speed to approach Avalon on a pre-calculated, logged flightpath.

'They want to rip the insides out of that monster,' Voskov said offhandly. 'It's been in the news lately. The rest of the system's finished, totally fritzed. Now Equinox wants to start in on that.'

'We heard,' Stone said evasively. The less Voskov knew about their business here, the better.

Jarrat stirred and pointed into the velvet darkness beyond the swelling half-disk of Avalon. 'There's the carrier.'

The sterntubes of the *Athena* glowed a dull cherry red. She was like a leviathan in space, and Stone was never unimpressed by the sight of her. Most of the crew never saw her from the outside.

'Picked up their acquisition signal,' Voskov reported unnecessarily. The displays were a mass of guidance data. Range, speed, deceleration parameters, attitude and rate of roll, pitch and yaw. The computer was in command. Voskov merely monitored his systems while the co-pilot yawned. To them, it was another 'red eye special', shuttling documents and passengers to an obscure, inaccessible location.

Like a remora on a whaleshark, the courier nudged in alongside the big ship and caught on with a metallic clatter. Red lights peppered the hatch release panel and swiftly turned green as Jarrat slung his bags over his shoulders. The hatch hissed open. Fractional differences in pressure equalised with a stirring breeze.

Lt Mikhail Petrov thrust out his hand in welcome, and Stone took it. Big, burly, yellow haired and ruddy faced, Petrov was gaining weight. It would be his undoing at the next physical, and Stone knew he would be in the gym, hours every day, struggling with his stubborn physique. He always ate more when he was irritable. As Stone released the man's hand he dealt the growing midriff a prod.

'Getting stuck into the stroganoff? What's your trouble, Mischa? Five weeks with Gene, and you look like hell.'

'Feel like hell,' Petrov added as he gave his hand to Jarrat. 'Thank bloody Christ you're here.'

'That bad?' Jarrat flicked a glance at Stone as the hatch behind them locked. Winking instrument lights announced that the shuttle was about to undock.

The Russian's eyes rolled to the ceiling in search of divine guidance. 'It's not Cantrell's fault. There's sweet bugger all he could do.'

'About what?' Stone shouldered his bags and led the way to the lift bay. 'Trouble on Avalon? Cantrell signalled there's a shindig on.'

'Understatement,' Petrov said sourly. 'What's the last telemetry transmission you had?'

Jarrat's eyes narrowed. 'Just before we left Darwin's. Couldn't get anything in-flight.' He shot a glance at Stone. 'The situation's changed?'

'Developed,' Petrov said sourly. 'The ops room is busy. Gene hasn't slept in two days. If you want to get your feet wet, I know he'd love to crash out for a few hours. I'd better get back there. The Blue Ravens deployed two hours ago. There's been some heavy fire.' He shook his head, tight lipped. 'It's bad. Very bad.'

A familiar ball of tension knotted in Stone's middle. He felt the kick of Jarrat's feelings, mirrors for his own. At the lift Petrov left them and hurried forward toward the operations room. Stone stepped into the car and thumbed for their deck.

'The Blue Ravens deployed?' Jarrat said quietly. 'Gene would never get involved in political manoeuvring.'

'Which means Vic Duggan made his Angel connection.' Stone's brows twitched. 'It would have to be good to convince Gene. He's a born sceptic.'

The digital on the lift's control panel gave shiptime as 14:45. Jarrat switched the chrono on his wrist over to *Athena* time. It would take a few days for them to readjust, but for the moment any feeling of late evening fatigue had been swept aside.

Their cabins were sealed, untouched. Stone merely touched the palmprint lock on the nearest accessible door, shoved his bags inside and stood back to wait for Jarrat to dump his own.

They were in the ops room minutes later, and Jarrat swore beneath his breath as he read the status board.

Gene Cantrell was almost sixty, and he looked every year of that age as he leaned on the back of the radio man's chair, a cigarette in one hand, the other massaging the bridge of his nose. He was in white slacks, black shirt, sport shoes — plain clothes, the privilege of an officer. He looked as if he had been subsisting on speed and nicotine for days. Petrov was watching real-time video telemetry and barely looked up as the carrier's commanders appeared.

But Cantrell managed a smile as he stubbed out the smoke and gave his hand first to Jarrat, then to Stone. 'Got a buzz from Bill Dupre. I'm glad to see you.'

'I'll bet you are.' Stone gestured at the status board. 'What's all this? Petrov said you deployed Blue Raven two hours ago. You've got Red Raven in the air now.'

'Take a look.' Cantrell swung out a chair and parked his backside on it. 'Streetwar, Stoney. Casualties that'd do a battle zone proud.'

'Duggan called?' Stone asked quietly.

'Several times.' Cantrell rummaged for another cigarette, found the packet empty and lobbed it into the waste bin by the tracking console. He rubbed his eyes tiredly. 'Vic's got a pretty strong case this time... one I can't disprove. Till we refute it and the shouting starts, we have no excuse to refuse the man his gunships.'

Jarrat was watching aerial transmission from the shuttle. 'Who's flying observation?'

'Curt Gable.' Cantrell turned up the audio. 'I was out there myself till an hour ago. It's a mess.'

'Christ.' Jarrat's breath hissed through his teeth.

'Look at the stats,' Cantrell told him. 'That's a pretty good reason to send Duggan a couple of gunships.'

'That's a pretty good reason to hang it up and send for the Army!' Jarrat stabbed a finger at the screen and glared at Cantrell. 'You've got two hundred civilians dead and five hundred injured!'

The older man winced visibly. 'I can read, Kevin. And before you pop your cork, the nearest warship is the *Ambush*, and she's two weeks' flight from here on active service. I doubt they could pull her out of the trouble on Braegan in time to do us one iota of good.'

A knot of tension ravelled in Stone's insides. It was hard to tell if it was his own fury or Jarrat's. Kevin was looking at the NARC casualty list now. Blue Raven 3 was dead, two more slightly injured.

'Military weapons,' Stone said bitterly. 'I don't suppose Duggan managed to find out where they're coming from?'

'Nope.' Cantrell leaned back and looked up at the two younger men. 'Duggan is up to his nuts in a war. I shouldn't think he has time to worry about where the phosphor grenades and Avenger missiles came from. You put a lid on the situation and then you kick ass later for answers... that's Tactical procedure, isn't it, Stoney?'

Stone ignored the jibe, reached over Cantrell and touched the transmit key. 'Athena to NARC Airborne. Curt?'

A brittle burst of static, and Gable was on the air at once. 'Is that Stoney? When did you get in? They said you were on your way over from Darwin's!'

'A few minutes ago.' Stone glanced over Cantrell's head at Jarrat. 'Hand over forward observation to Red Raven gunship and get back here, Curt. I think we'd better take a first-hand look at the hotzone.'

'With the greatest of pleasure, Cap,' Gable breathed. 'You're welcome to it.'

Straightening, Stone dropped a hand on Jarrat's arm, and Jarrat nodded. Without a word they left the ops room and hurried aft and down, to the hangar level in the carrier's belly. The shuttle bay was already depressurising as they stepped into the Ravens' suiting rooms. The Blue Raven audio thundered over the open speakers, a confusion of invective, narrative, warning and response. They heard Gil Cronin, Blue Raven 6, barking over the audio clutter; then an answering shout from his second, Joe Ramos, Blue Raven 7. They were groundside in Elysium and under fire. Jarrat gave Stone a level, sober look but said nothing.

In twin lockers just off the Blue Raven suiting room were their own hardsuits. Stone felt a familiar flutter as he saw the mirror-polished black surfaces and locust-like helmets. Jarrat was a pace ahead of him, already breaking out the pieces of his lower body armour.

'Taking no chances,' Stone said quietly.

Locking on the first sections, Jarrat neutralised their punishing weight. 'Not after what happened last time, over Chell. First, they knocked you down with a heat seeker up the tailpipe. And then there was you, me and Mavvik under Drummond Park.' He glanced up, brows knitted in a bleak frown. 'Taking chances is the last thing I've got in mind, Stoney.'

He was, Stone thought, magnificent when the light of battle lit in his eyes. Many centuries before he might have marched with Alexander or fought with the Celts against the awesome might of Rome. In fact, Kevin Jarrat had never set foot on Earth before he was twenty-four years old.

Stone touched his smooth cheek, making Jarrat turn toward him. Stone said nothing. They had no need of words. The empathy rang like a bell, reverberating with love, lust and everything between. Jarrat's eyes darkened as his pupils dilated, and he smiled.

'You're so beautiful,' Stone told him with a wry, selfmocking grin. 'Times like this, you make me think of a puma. I could eat you alive... in fact I will, later, and that's a promise.'

The grey eyes closed and Jarrat concentrated. Stone gasped aloud, physically winded by the body blow of Kevin's feelings. The pulse pounded in his ears and he stepped back a pace as if he had been struck. Then Jarrat's eyes opened, smoke-dark, and Stone took a breath.

'Oh, yeah,' Kevin said, husky with transitory, cherished affection stolen in the midst of turmoil. 'Later, Stoney.'

Later. The word was redolent with promise and Stone's heart beat harder as he began to clamber into his own armour.

The kevlex-titanium was bulky, heavy, punishing his muscles in the moments before he turned up the repulsion, kilo by kilo. He divided his attention between the riot armour, the Blue Raven radio traffic and the adjoining shuttle bay status display. Spinners and sirens sent flight crews scurrying into safe compartments, and Stone felt vibration through his booted feet. The hangar door rumbled open in the belly of the ship, admitted Gable's aircraft, and growled shut.

Furnace temperature air blasted from the cycling units, returning the hangar to normal pressure and temperature after it had been exposed to the freezing vacuum. The status board lit green just as Stone settled his headset. He locked down his helmet and screwed the twin air and power umbilici into the chin sockets. The helmet instrumentation came on automatically.

The loop chattered in his ears: Cronin, Ramos and Reynolds,

the Blue Raven gunship pilot were crosstalking with Cantrell and Petrov; Engineer Budweisser was arguing with mechanics on the Red Raven gunship. And Stone heard another voice, almost familiar, which he had not heard in more years than he cared to recall. Vic Duggan sounded furious as he yelled for the Red Ravens to drag a Tactical squad out of a blazing vehicle.

Before he could speak Gable's voice cut in. 'The shuttle's all yours.'

Jarrat's gauntleted hand hit the bay door release. 'Thanks, Curt. Grab a break while you can.'

'Kevin!' Standing by the beautiful, gull-grey shuttle, Curt Gable unlocked his helmet and lifted it off. 'I wondered if you came back with Stoney... there was some talk about them splitting you up. I never got the full story, just some half-assed bull about it being classified.'

Footsteps rang on the steel decking. 'Tell it to you later,' Jarrat promised as he passed Gable and slapped steelmeshed palms with him. 'You got a full ordnance load aboard?'

'Yep. I kept high and about a klick downrange, shooting long-range videos. It's hot as hell down there, Cap. Stay out of it if you can—these buggers are armed the way Death's Head was armed, and there's a lot more of them.'

One hand on the scorching hull, about to climb after Jarrat into the forward cockpit, Stone paused and swivelled his helmet to see Gable clearly. The younger man's dark hair was tousled. 'Where's Tac 101 set up?'

'East side of Mount Clavel, overlooking Sciaparelli, about ten klicks from the hotzone. Cap Cantrell warned them to get the fuck out of there... remember the way Death's Head rocketed Colonel Stacy's field base above Chell?'

Stone was unlikely to forget. In that assault a boy called Rikki Mitchell was killed. Icewater pumped through his veins for a second before he banished the memory. Jarrat's empathy was almost closed, or he would have been aware of the sudden rush of grief and bitter resentment.

'Thanks, Curt. Get out of here. Have a coffee while you've got the chance.' Stone adjusted his weight to fifty kilos and climbed the side of the shuttle by the hardpoints. He settled into the forward cockpit, buckled the flight harness, and with the ease of long practice his eyes skimmed the instruments. 'Observer to Cap Cantrell. With your permission, Raven Leader is airborne.'

A note of genuine gratitude came through in Cantrell's voice: 'Acknowledged. Blue Ravens units, Red Raven units, Raven Leader is on launch procedures.'

A flurry of responses came in fast. Loudest among them was Gil Cronin. 'Lieutenant Petrov!' he barked, as if he might have bitten a chunk out of the Russian's haunch.

'Negative.' Stone chuckled mirthlessly as the cycling machines depressurised the hangar and the outer hatch rumbled open once more. The brilliant, cloud-swept face of Avalon glared up, and his helmet visor dimmed automatically. 'It's Raven 7.1 and Raven 9.4. We just got in.'

'Jesus!' Cronin gave a whoop over the radio clutter. 'Blue Ravens! Cap Jarrat and Cap Stone are back.'

Ramos: 'Outstanding! Gilly, get down here and knock this fucker off my back. He's somewhere in that building with a missile tube, and my thermo-imaging's screwed!'

Cronin: 'I'm with you, Joe... I see him. There's two of them. They're going to... incoming! Get down!'

With a familiar lurch in the belly, Stone felt his mind and nerves slide smoothly back into gear. How often had he and Jarrat done this? The shuttle's twin engines rammed up, he kicked in the repulsion, edged out of the hangar and put the nose down.

She bucked through re-entry, wings glowing poker-red, and he homed on the radio traffic. In the rear cockpit Jarrat was already running recorders and every long-range scanning device he had. Stone heard him muttering beneath his breath as he watched the CRTs.

'What is it, Kevin?'

'Take a look.' Jarrat piped an edit of the data forward. 'They're cutting that side of the city up for scrap. They've been going at it four, five hours, according to what I'm reading here. Tac wouldn't have stood a chance.'

'What the hell is NARC doing?' Stone demanded. 'It's two hours since Blue Raven deployed! The whole action should have taken less than half that time.'

'They're trying to prevent property damage, at a guess,' Jarrat mused. 'I see nine building fires, four aircraft down. One of them's a medevac skimmer. Christ, they're trying to pull the wounded out of the wreck.'

'Trying to prevent property damage?' Stone echoed, disbelieving. 'Gene!'

'Here, Stoney,' Cantrell's voice responded at once. He was listening in, as if he was at Stone's elbow. 'And before you blow your stack, we're holding off at the express request of Vic Duggan. Or we'd have locked down the Sciaparelli sector two hours ago.'

'I see.' Stone gazed up at the brooding malachite face of the gas giant which seemed to fill the sky. 'Okay, Gene. NARC Raven Leader to Tac 101. Get me Colonel Duggan.' He waited five seconds, ten. 'NARC Raven Leader for Tac 101!'

Static, white noise, then a flustered woman's voice. 'Tac 101. I'm sorry, sir, there's nobody here.'

'What do you mean, nobody there?' Stone barked. 'Where's Duggan, goddamn it? Who is this?

'I'm Officer Sherry Weintraub. A medevac lifter just limped in on one engine, sir,' she protested. 'Everybody's down there trying to douse the fire till they get the casualties out!'

She was furious enough to spit the words at him, and behind his visor Stone grinned. That was the kind of spirit that sustained Tactical against the odds. The old Tac camaraderie returned. 'Okay, Weintraub. Give me an acquisition signal and I'll join you. Buzz your colonel, tell him NARC Raven Leader is on approach.'

The acquisition beam was broadcast at once. Stone jinked the nose about as Weintraub made a swift acknowledgment and fled. Ten kilometres downrange, twenty thousand metres high, Jarrat picked up the battle zone and whistled. 'I've got them. Better fly by high and wide, Stoney. They're shooting some heavy duty crap, and till we find out why Duggan's had a muzzle on Gene we'd better not shoot too much back.'

'Roger that.' Stone swung south and maintained altitude. Unless the shooters on the street had sophisticated tracking equipment they would never know the shuttle had passed by. Gable was smart to stay well out. Memories of the battle over Chell haunted Stone. He had learned the hard way.

'There's Tac 101,' Jarrat said a moment later. 'On the shoulder of that hill... looks like they're set up in a park. Or what was a park. Christ, look at the mess. The poor sods.'

The CRT at Stone's elbow displayed the pictures Jarrat was watching. The medevac lifter had been abandoned. Gushes of chemical smoke poured from its engine cowls. One side was ripped away, carbonised by the blast. A ragged line of casualties stretched away across the grass at a safe distance. Two medics, themselves smoke-blackened and coughing, scurried between the victims.

Stone cast about for a safe landing site. He saw the rank of Tactical vehicles, radio truck, command truck, several squads. To their west side was an open area between the mess truck and a quaint ornamental fountain. The shuttle rotated to fit the space before he cut the engines and feathered down on the hot, blustering repulsion.

'Are we safe?' he asked as he popped the canopy. 'We're far enough out of the zone?'

'Nobody's going to drop an artillery round on us,' Jarrat assured him. 'From what I can see, they're shooting line-of-sight, fire and forget, unguided stuff. Shut your eyes, pull the trigger and hope.'

'But there's a lot of them,' Stone added.

'A mob only needs weapons to turn into an army.' Jarrat had his flight harness off and vaulted lightly over the side. He hit the grass without a sound or a jolt, at an apparent mass of fifty kilos, lifted off his helmet and stood back to watch Stone. 'This doesn't smack of a dopehead riot, Stoney. You'd better find out what this old mate of yours is up to. If he's falsified his documentation, I wouldn't be him when Central gets to hear of it.'

'Vic Duggan was never a mate of mine,' Stone said drily as he unlocked his helmet and lifted it off. 'I was a rookie kid and he was an instructor. He won't even remember who the hell I was.'

He was wrong. At forty-eight, Duggan was lean, hard and fit, his face unlined, his hair still rich red-brown, worn long and tied at his nape. He wore the black Tactical fatigues and flak jacket, and carried a service machine rifle slung over his left shoulder.

The mobile command base was a chaos of Tac and civilian wounded. Duggan was shouting into an R/T, trying to arrange a transport, and having no luck. Stone lifted off his helmet, tucked it under his arm and strode across the ploughed grass.

On his heels, Jarrat ran a hand through his hair and resettled his headset. 'Blue Raven gunship.'

'Over the hotzone, Cap,' pilot Tanya Reynolds reported.

'We've got sixteen assorted civvy casualties.' Jarrat's nose wrinkled on the acrid draught from the burning medevac skimmer. 'Tac are out of resources. Launch me whatever you've got, get these people out of here.'

'All I got aboard is the engineer's tractor,' Reynolds warned.

'It'll do.' Jarrat adjusted the earpiece as Stone, who had been listening, turned toward him. 'Tell Duggan to clear some landing space. He'll have to move his trucks.'

White noise sheeted out the R/T, and Vic Duggan returned it to his belt with a curse. Fists on hips, he surveyed the smoking wreck and the pall hanging over the Sciaparelli sector. A shake of his head was his only comment. He had never been a man of big words, Stone remembered.

'Colonel.' Booted feet soundless on the grass, he came to rest behind the officer who had once been his instructor. 'We just rejoined our unit. NARC Raven Leaders.'

Duggan turned slowly. Brown eyes narrowed against the smoke, focused on Stone's face, and then the auburn head nodded. 'I've been expecting you, Stoney.'

Genuine surprise stalled Stone's demands to know why Duggan had bridled Cantrell. 'It's been a long time.'

'Ten years.' Duggan looked him up and down before he flicked a glance at the silent, wary Jarrat. 'I heard when you transferred to NARC. I heard when you made Captain.' He took a breath, coughed on the laden air. 'I knew you'd go far.'

The surprise redoubled. 'When I was a rookie,' Stone said acerbically, 'you told me I had to work harder, much harder, or I'd never amount to shit. Unquote.'

A humourless smile quirked one corner of Duggan's wide mouth. 'You had the potential, Stone. If you'd been useless I'd have let you dope and screw like the rest of the kids. You had the aptitude to be more... you obviously took my advice.'

'Yeah.' Stone blinked on the smoke. 'You were a good instructor. But now it's our show, Colonel. We've got one dead man and two injured, and you've had us pratting about on low power in Sciaparelli for over two hours.'

'It's starting to get dangerous,' Jarrat added. 'That crowd is armed with gear that could do a gunship a lot of damage. A reactor spill in the city —'

'I'm aware of the danger, Captain Jarrat.' Duggan had read the name stencilled on Jarrat's breastplate.

A wave of anger rolled through Stone, his own and Jarrat's combined. 'Then maybe you'll tell us what this is about?' He waved a hand at the wreckage. 'Ten more minutes, Colonel, then we pull all NARC units out and you're on your own. When we fight, we do it to clean up a mess, not make a bigger one.'

Duggan bit his lip, rubbed his eyes and gestured at the heavy command truck. 'Let's get out of this smoke.'

'And move your vehicles,' Jarrat added with a glance at the sky. 'The best we can do is an engineer's tractor, but it'll get the casualties out if you give it landing space.'

'Thanks.' Duggan lifted the R/T to his lips. 'Bob, Rachel, Mack, shift the trucks. A NARC tractor's coming in for the wounded.'

The command vehicle was ponderous and squat, riding a powerful repulsion field. Under the combined weight of two suits of riot armour it almost grounded out before the automatic system shunted up to compensate. Duggan slammed the door, closing out the bad air. Inside was a cluttered office, a mass of equipment, monitoring officers, machines processing a barrage of realtime telemetry.

Sweeping a stack of printout off the corner of the desk, Duggan sat. A muscular woman in the familiar fatigues put a beaker into his hand and he drank gratefully. The ID code on her shoulder read 79866/Weintraub. Stone accorded her a nod as he waited for Duggan to speak.

'Cantrell told us you made your Angel connection,' Jarrat prompted as Duggan crushed the foam cup and threw it into the disposal. 'So what's your trouble?'

'I... almost made it,' Duggan growled, as if the admission had been tortured from him. 'I'm still waiting for data.'

Stone was speechless. Jarrat slammed his helmet down on the corner of the desk. 'Narcotics And Riot Control is not a mercenary army, used to crush civilians when some half-assed local government drives its captive population over the edge into anarchy!' His voice rose sharply. One steel-gloved finger stabbed in the direction of Sciaparelli. 'If that isn't an Angel packriot, you and your balls are going to be heading in three different directions!'

The older man did not recoil or wince. Stone watched Duggan closely. He had not changed. He was still tough, immovable. So sure of himself that he did not feel the need to stand, he was content to perch on the desk and look up at Jarrat.

'It's not an Angel riot, Captain, but it's Angel connected.

When I can prove it, when I can cover my ass, I don't give a fuck if you thunder and lightning merchants don't leave two bricks standing on top of each other in that sector. But I'm still waiting for the data.' He gestured with the R/T. 'It's coming. It's overdue. And if I sat on my duff waiting for it before I pushed the panic button there'd have been a thousand dead and ten times that number injured.'

Jarrat took a calming breath. His temper was on a tight rein; it crackled through Stone's nerves. Stone set down his helmet and leaned on the side of the vehicle.. His eyes followed Weintraub as she sorted datacubes and printout. 'What's this Intelligence, where's it coming from?'

'I have a squad in Belreve, north of Elysium, trying to make contact with Senator Tigh Grenshem. You were briefed?'

'Thoroughly.' Jarrat paused to listen to the headset as the command vehicle's jets whined up and the truck shuddered into movement. 'Your transport's on approach, Colonel.'

'Thanks.' Duggan rubbed his smoke-sore eyes. 'I can't raise my squad... I can't raise Grenshem. I sent a man after them two hours ago. He hasn't called home either.'

The NARC men looked sidelong at each other. 'Grenshem has your Angel connection?' Stone asked, and at Duggan's nod he swore. 'Grenshem squealed for Tactical protection weeks ago. Numerous threats on his life, wasn't it?'

'We sent him two bodyguards, an armoured groundcar and a skyhopper to fly topcover for him.' Duggan's brows arched. 'There's not a hell of a lot more we could do, Stoney, short of putting the man in a cell and locking the door.'

'You're well acquainted with Grenshem?' Jarrat asked shrewdly. 'You trust him?'

'I do.' Duggan stood. 'He told me last night, this streetwar was coming. He was meeting with some informant. I never got the name. A whistleblower from Equinox.'

He paused as they heard the thunder of heavy lifters and the whole vehicle shook. Not twenty metres away the tractor was setting down in the ruins of the park.

'Your connection is between Equinox and Grenshem?' Stone echoed. 'That's political! This is not our scene, Duggan. NARC isn't your private Army.'

The Colonel hooked his thumbs into his back pockets and studied his old student with genuine appreciation. 'You're a good company man, Stoney. Keep the firm's image clean, is it? But you're going to have to trust me — and Grenshem.' He indicated the hotzone with a nod of his head. 'That's military hardware. Grenshem knows where it comes from. He told me he has a feed to where the Angel is coming from... and the two sources are either close or identical. Like, maybe Angel money is paying for weapons. Or maybe master smugglers run both into this system right under our noses, Christ knows how.'

And that put an entirely different complexion on the situation. Jarrat exhaled, a hiss through his teeth. 'Call your squad in Belreve.'

'Tried, just before you got here,' Duggan admitted.

'Try again,' Stone said brusquely.

The R/T crackled with static. 'Tac 101 to Wildcard.' He called repeatedly over two minutes and then quit in disgust. 'Nothing. I...' He gave Stone a glance which betrayed the anxiety he was nursing. 'I got the proverbial bad feeling.'

'Yeah,' Jarrat agreed. 'So have I.' He tapped his chin with one steel fingertip. 'How far out is Belreve?'

'Thirty minutes by road, ten by skyvan.' Duggan took a breath. 'You could be there faster.'

Stone picked up his helmet. 'We'll be in touch, Colonel. Get us some background on this circus. What it's about, what sparked it, why now and not next week, who's running it.'

'You got it.' Duggan opened up the rear of the truck and moved aside to let the massive, riot armoured figures step down and out. 'And Stoney...'

At the foot of the boarding ramp, in the act of lifting on his helmet, Stone turned back.

'...it's good to see you again,' Duggan said quietly before he slammed the door on the smoky, toxic air.

Jarrat screwed in his umbilici and cut back into the comm loop as the engineer's tractor rammed up for takeoff. It blanketed the whole hillside in heat and noise. The squat, stubby, grey-hulled transport rose away on blistering repulsion and arced southward, away from the hotzone.

'Well, well,' Jarrat mused softly, under the radio chatter. 'So Vic Duggan doesn't remember who the hell you ever were.'

Stone gave the command vehicle a deep frown as he locked down his helmet. 'I guess I'm unforgettable,' he said drily, and led the way back to the shuttle.

Chapter Five

The onboard deck was preprogrammed with comprehensive data covering the city of Elysium and most of Avalon's northern continent. Stone recalled what he needed as the shuttle bobbed up over Tac 101, and at an altitude of two thousand metres he turned the nose into the cloud-scattered northeast.

Belreve was a country town, similar to Shiloh, Orleans and Albany, settlements strung out along the great, sweeping arc of Northbound 5. The ten-lane clearway cut through the glacial hills, busy with ground traffic while skyvans and suborbital skimmers bustled overhead.

'Big population,' Jarrat commented as Stone took the shuttle up in a backbreaker, over the hills above Elysium. Zeus filled the canopy, drawing his eyes away from the CRT. Bands of green, blue and gold circled the gas giant with strange, sensual beauty.

Stone made no comment as he watched his instruments. Tigh Grenshem lived in a mansion on Haarlem Boulevard — the heart of a rich people's ghetto? Stone cut speed. The wings and canards outswept as the spaceplane fell in over Belreve. Some sixth sense raked his nerves a moment before Jarrat spoke.

'Switch down to Channel 44.' Kevin's voice was taut. 'I'm reading local radio... Belreve Tac and the bucket boys. I think there's been trouble.'

'You could put money on it,' Stone said bitterly as he switched to the domestic frequencies. But he had already seen the finger of smoke which pointed into the southwest, driven before the light breeze. 'There it is. Damn. House on Haarlem Boulevard. Want to place a bet?'

The long, curving road was cordoned at either end by two Tactical squads. Three vehicles were wrecked; one was still hot, a mass of greasy chemical foam as it was hosed down by masked figures. A coroner's skyhopper had parked on the lawn of a white-walled mansion, but the four bodies had not yet been loaded. They lay under groundsheets while the medics completed the customary reports.

Clipped trees, wide lawns and statuary, slate roofs, antique marble and old world elegance were the privileges of the nauseatingly rich. Stone viewed the scene below with cynicism as Jarrat spoke to the Tac lieutenant. The NARC aircraft hardly needed identification but Jarrat gave it anyway, and Stone feathered the aircraft down between the west cordon and the third wreck.

A fresh-faced young trooper jogged out to meet them as the canopy whined up. She was blonde, skinny, not long out of college. Stone left his helmet in the cockpit, cut his weight to forty kilos and landed lightly beside Jarrat as the kid sketched them a salute. Her ID bar read 92117/Lucas.

'Sorry for the mess, chief, we weren't expecting NARC,' she apologised.

'Who's in charge?' Jarrat demanded without preamble. 'You wouldn't know what the hell is going on here?'

Lucas gestured toward the house. 'That's the Senator's place. He's, uh, dead.' Her mouth twisted. 'Happened three, four hours ago. They put a bomb under his groundie.'

'They? Who?' Stone asked sharply.

But Lucas could only shrug. 'Search me, I only work here. Lieutenant Curry knows more than I do — and that's damn all. He's in the house, trying to get the Senator's secretary calmed down.' She shook her head sadly. 'Poor kid's in bits. He was Grenshem's lover too. They'd lived together for years. It's a miracle they weren't both in the Chev when it went up.'

The Chevrolette limousine had probably been an Eland or a Springbok. It was difficult to tell. The front half was ripped open; only the impact-proof engine capsule had survived the blast, as it must. It contained a hotcore generator which could have poisoned the whole town with radiotoxicity if it had ruptured.

As they strode up Grenshem's crazy-paved driveway, Stone cast a grim look over the peeled-back, stripped aluminium. 'You thinking what I'm thinking?'

The breeze stirred Jarrat's hair. 'Maybe Duggan's right. Grenshem was onto something, and he died for it... the question is, had he sniffed out a trade in military arms, or Angel smuggling?' As the light overcast scattered and the sun brightened he shaded his eyes and surveyed the other smashed vehicles. 'That one will be Duggan's Wildcard squad, coming out for Grenshem's data. Too confidential for transmission. The last wreck will be the man he sent out to find them.'

'They were thorough,' Stone mused. 'And that smacks of an Angel syndicate.' He paused on the drive to watch the medics load the four covered bodies. One was inside sealed plastic tube. Stone gave the shattered limousine a frown. 'There wouldn't have been much left of Grenshem.'

Movement at the house's open polished wood door had caught Jarrat's attention. A man in Tac uniform stood there, hands in pockets, watching the medics. 'Lt Curry?' Jarrat went ahead.

The riot armour was better than an ID badge. Curry was fifty, bald, lined by worry and long hours. Pale blue eyes read the name on Jarrat's breastplate and he stood aside with an expression of relief. 'You're here to take charge? Thank God for small mercies.'

'Sorry to disappoint you,' Jarrat said aridly. 'We were looking for Senator Grenshem.'

'You missed him.' Curry nodded at the van as the medics sealed the rear hatch and the pilot fired the jets to idling. 'They made a good job of it. He never knew what hit him. The device was wired to the main engine ignition.'

'So we see,' Stone agreed. 'Colonel Duggan of Elysium Tac was waiting for some data of Grenshem's. Was the house broken into, anything stolen?'

'I'm afraid so.' Curry thrust his hands into the pockets of the black uniform trousers. 'You'd better talk to Stuart. Go easy on the kid, Captain. He's shocky, doped to the gills. He and Tigh were very close.'

'Lovers,' Jarrat said quietly.

Stone felt the twist of Kevin's raw emotion and swallowed hard. They lived on the edge, worked with risk almost every day. This was a scene that could be waiting for them. By the odds, it was already long overdue. Stone looked over his shoulder, found Jarrat's grey-green eyes brooding on him, and then Kevin slammed up the shields and the distressing empathic feedback was gone.

The house was quiet and cool. Polished parquet floors; the whisper of discreet fans; plaster-cream walls, glass-lined shelves housing books which were centuries old; genuine antiques, crystalware and spirits. A original Hennessy bottle stood on the rosewood table before the window in a room which doubled as office and lounge. The blind was closed, the light muted.

On the shelves, amid an audiovisual library, were framed images of Grenshem and his young lover. They looked, Stone thought, so happy, so fulfilled, he would have suffered pangs of aching envy only weeks ago, before he found himself in Jarrat's embrace.

On the leather couch the young man sat with his head in his hands, and Stone felt an unbidden flutter of emotion. He was dark, curly haired, pale skinned, clad in white denim, barefoot and bare chested. Curry knelt beside him, touched his shoulder gently.

'Stuart, love, you've got to answer some questions. There's a couple of NARCs... that is, some officers from Narcotics And Riot Control.' He looked up at Jarrat. 'Sorry. We don't see a lot of you guys out here.'

'No offence.' Jarrat moved carefully in the confines of the room. The armour seemed more massive between walls. 'What's he taken, Curry?'

'Dreamsmoke, I guess. Anything he had. He was screaming when I got here. I told him to dope up and then sleep. I didn't expect you.' Curry shook the young man's shoulder once more. 'Stuart? Come on, sugar. Christ, how much did you take?'

The old animal sixth sense prickled Stone's skin. He leaned down, took the boy's chin in one steel-meshed but very gentle palm and lifted it.

Doe-soft brown eyes blinked at him, but the young man was just drifting, almost concussed by shock. He had not begun to cry yet; tears would come later, when the shock wore off and reality hit him hard. He was lovely, with snub-nosed charm and the soft, smooth curves of youth. Stone relaxed and lowered himself lightly to one knee.

'Relax, Curry, he's not overdosing. You know him well?'

'Since he was born.' Curry scrubbed his face. 'Stuart Wymark. He's twenty-three, born over in Orleans, educated in Elysium, came to work for Tigh when he was nineteen, never left. Belreve is a fairly small community, Captain. I won't say everybody knows everybody, but, shit, everybody knew Tigh. He was a kind of local icon.'

The brown eyes cleared a little and Stuart leaned back into the couch. Leather squeaked beneath him as he ran both hands through his black, curly hair. His chest was smooth, his nipples rose-brown. His legs were long and slender, his muscles well worked for the pleasure of looking and feeling good. Stone glanced up at Jarrat and shared Kevin's expression of regret. The kid deserved better than this — and he was alive by a miracle.

'NARC?' Stuart's voice was slurred.

'I'm Jerry Stone. This is Kevin Jarrat.' Stone broke the wrist seal and lifted off his right gauntlet so as to take Stuart's hand. 'Can you answer some questions?'

'Questions?' Stuart took a deep breath and blinked at his fingers, which lay in Stone's palm. 'They killed Tigh.'

'We saw.' Jarrat came closer. 'You know who?'

The dark head shook. 'Never saw them.'

'But you know what Tigh was working on,' Stone prompted. 'They broke in, looking for his data?'

'Yes.' Stuart blinked up at Curry. 'I told Pete.'

Curry sat on the couch beside him. 'Tell it again.'

'Two men,' Stuart said vaguely as his thoughts began to drift once more. 'Last night. Didn't trip the alarms. Tigh was asleep but I heard. I woke him... he saw them leaving.' He gestured toward the back of the house. 'They searched the safe and the computer.'

He closed his eyes, as if to drowse, and Stone grasped his hand more firmly. 'Did you find anything missing?'

'This morning.' Stuart took a breath. 'They took everything.'

With a groan, Jarrat stepped back. 'Then they read the data, and Grenshem didn't live the morning out. Christ, it must have been the real thing, Stoney.'

But was it Duggan's Angel connection or a steer to an arms smuggling crew? Stone bit his lip. Stuart's hand was soft, as one would expect of a secretary. Stone thumbed his palm to stir him again. 'Did you and Tigh work together? Stuart!'

'Wha—?' Stuart snapped back to the present. 'Oh. All the time. Tigh never did anything without me.'

'Then you know what he was working on,' Stone prompted. 'Come on, honey, it's important. Stuart!'

But he was drifting as the drug took hold, and Curry swore. 'I'm sorry, Captain. If I'd known you were coming I'd have told him to wait.'

'Sure.' Stone stood and let the boy relax. 'He'll have his

comedown pops around here somewhere. Find them, get him sobered up long enough to talk.'

'Uh, yeah. Bathroom,' Curry guessed. 'Tigh never touched the stuff but Stuart likes the buzz now and then.'

As the man hurried away Stone joined Jarrat at the window. Kevin had lifted the blind. The coroner's crew were slamming hatches and the lift engines which had been idling rammed up to takeoff thrust, shaking the windows. The trees bordering the wide lawns thrashed in the downwash as it took off, and they watched its white hull dwindle with distance against the dusky face of Zeus.

With one fingertip Jarrat adjusted his headset, and his brow creased. Stone watched his partner's expression darken.

'You listening to Elysium?'

'Some trigger-happy bastard's taken a shot at the Blue Raven gunship.'

'Damage?' Stone felt the kick of Jarrat's anger, and a creeping coldness.

'Damage report coming in now... the hull is sound but they've lost their high-gain antennae. Can't talk to the carrier directly. They'll shunt their comm and telemetry through the other gunship.' Jarrat touched the headset again. 'Raven Leader to Blue Raven gunship.'

As he waited for a response Stone retuned his own headset and listened in. Pilot Tanya Reynolds was livid. 'The fuckers hit us, Cap. I've got them on scanners. My gunners can waste them in two seconds!'

'Hold your fire and move out to a safe distance,' Jarrat said shortly. 'You are not cleared to fire, Reynolds!'

The pilot swore passionately. 'Then what the Christ are we doing here, Cap — giving a pack of civvy shooters some target practice?'

'Pull out and observe,' Jarrat repeated. 'Where are the Blue Ravens?'

'Same place they've been for hours,' Reynolds snapped. 'Playing hide and seek on the street. Duggan's got us hamstrung. Can't shoot back, we'll damage property and people will get hurt.'

'So you're making manual pickups?' Stone guessed.

'Picked up two, three hundred civvies.' Reynolds paused. 'I've pulled out, two k's downrange... the Ravens are screaming blue murder. Are they abandoned, or what?'

Jarrat rubbed his eyes and regarded Stone levelly. 'They've been in there a long time. Get them out, give Gold Raven a run?'

'Do it,' Stone agreed.

'I heard that,' Reynolds said eagerly. 'Blue Ravens, withdraw to the extraction point for pickup. Red Raven gunship, you got us on carrier relay?'

A crackle, a man's voice: 'Affirmative that.'

Stone lifted off the headset and left Jarrat to monitor the situation as Curry reappeared. In his right hand was a rose enamelled case containing a hypo gun and several capsules. He clicked one into the gun and pressed the muzzle against Stuart's shoulder. The shot of blocker chemicals popped through the boy's skin, leaving a ruddy brand.

Almost at once the brown eyes cleared. Stuart lifted his head, rubbed his face and blinked blindly at Curry. Stone moved into his field of vision and dropped lightly to one knee beside him. Stuart seemed fully aware of his company for the first time as he saw the massive, mirror-black armour.

'It's okay, sugar,' Curry told him. 'This is Captain Stone. Can you answer some questions?'

He drew a shuddering breath, clenched both hands into the curly hair and met Stone's eyes uncertainly. 'You're a NARC, aren't you? I kind of thought you'd come sooner or later.'

A pulse beat in Stone's temple; he heard Jarrat's soft intake of breath as Kevin felt the quickening of Stone's heart. He forced a smile to his lips, hoping it would reassure the boy. 'Colonel Duggan told us to talk to Grenshem, but we're too late. His data was stolen last night. You're the last link we have, Stuart, and it's important. There's a war in Elysium, and we still don't know if we should be part of it. What do you know, son?'

The boy's lightly muscled arms hugged about his chest. 'Tigh met a man here yesterday ago. He was scared shitless, kept saying they were right behind him.'

'They?' Stone glanced up at Jarrat, who had tripped the recorder on the shoulder panel of his armour and was getting every word.

'Shooters. Contract men.' Stuart rocked to and fro. 'His name is Jack Spiteri. He worked for Equinox till six, seven months ago. He had information.'

'A whistleblower?' Jarrat asked quietly as he checked his

sound level and moved a little closer.

The dark curly head nodded. 'He'd seen things, heard things, while he was at Equinox, and after. Meetings.' Stuart looked woundedly at Stone. 'He was a project designer. Didn't work with the top brass, but he knew their faces. And he saw them — on the street in Elysium, city bottom. I mean, big men slumming with low life like Wozniak and Buchanan, in dens like Rawhide.'

The names meant nothing to Stone, but Jarrat was recording. Elysium was Duggan's territory. Details would be easily come by. Stone stood. 'So Spiteri saw big wheels from Equinox slumming. So what? They might have been on the town.'

But Stuart's face twisted cynically. 'Not men like Buchanan. He's ex-Starfleet. Flies industrial cargo charter between here and the Cygnus colonies. Equinox business.'

'They have their own fleet,' Jarrat observed. 'Why would they charter a private pilot?'

'Why indeed?' Stone studied Stuart Wymark's pinched face. The kid was going down fast. 'And Spiteri overheard their business — Equinox men and this low life?'

'So he told Tigh.' Stuart's eyes flooded with tears. 'I don't remember it all. Tigh recorded it for Duggan.'

'Weapons?' Jarrat asked in a low tone. 'Or Angel? Come on, son. It's important.'

Stuart struggled with the tide of his grief. 'Spiteri was sure. He saw an Equinox director and a security task force in plain clothes in Rawhide, meeting Buchanan. Got close to them, overheard some stuff. I don't know much more, but I heard Tigh talking about Angel. And I know the Cygnus colonies had the biggest Angel lab in this quadrant before NARC busted it a few months ago. It was on the vidcasts.'

On that assignment, the carrier *Valkyrie* had been parked in orbit over the colonial homeworld while the *Athena* was above the city of Chell. Jarrat and Stone had read the details when the powerful Black Unicorn syndicate was broken.

'Buchanan,' Stone said slowly, 'shows every indication of being a smuggler. Suppose the *Valkyrie* destroyed the Cygnus lab but missed an enormous stockpile of Angel.' He stood back and regarded Jarrat bitterly. 'Duggan said he guessed the connection to the weapons and the Angel was either close –'

'Or the same,' Jarrat finished. He arched his brows at Stone. 'It's not bad. Not conclusive, but not bad.' He looked down into

Stuart's flushed face. 'Think, now. You heard Tigh talking to Spiteri about Angel. They could have been making smalltalk.'

'No way,' Stuart protested. 'Spiteri was mad as hell, Tigh was trying to smooth him over. And I heard Dorne's name.'

'As in, Randolph Dorne?' Stone echoed. 'The Equinox director?'

'Spiteri was saying something about Zeus,' Stuart went on, stumbling over his words as he scrubbed his eyes. 'Something about Buchanan, and Angel, and Dorne, and this fight, today. Oh, I don't know. I wasn't really listening.' His face crumpled.

'Doesn't matter, kid.' Stone touched his shoulder. 'Get yourself another buzz. You need it. Look after him, Curry.'

'I will.' The Tactical man rummaged in the enamelled case and produced a packet of cigarettes.

A lighter flicked several times, and before the NARC men stepped out of the house they smelt the distinctive, sweet odour of the dreamsmoke. Stone pulled on his glove and locked the wrist seal. 'Dorne and Buchanan, Angel... a smuggler out of the Cygnus colonies; weapons, Angel. A war on the street, Grenshem's faction getting trashed by Equinox supporters, armed by Christ knows who.'

'I'm buying,' Jarrat said shrewdly as they returned to the shuttle. 'It's thin, but I went into Hal Mavvik's palace on less than that, and gut instinct turned out to be dead right.' He touched the headset. 'Raven Leader to Red Raven gunship, give me a status report.'

The comm loop was alive with crosstalk. The pilot's voice cut over the chatter like a knife. 'Blue Ravens extracted, their gunship shoved off for minor repairs. I'm two thousand metres over Elysium, out of heat-seeker range. Red Ravens are getting restless. Someone is going to start shooting back soon, Cap, no way to stop it unless you pull everybody out fast. Gold Ravens are on re-entry, they'll insert in ten.'

'You getting this, Stoney?' Jarrat asked quietly, and when Stone nodded he addressed the gunship pilot once more. 'Hold up where you are, wait for Gold Raven. Deploy everything you've got. Put a lid on the situation, any way you like, fast as you can. Raven Leader will be with you before you go in. Relay that to all units. You are cleared to fire. Repeat —'

'Roger that!' The pilot gave a bitter cheer and then switched to the open loop to pass on instructions.

Stone eased the mass of his armour into the forward seat and buckled the harness. 'It's pointless sounding a two-minute warning. There can't be anybody in Sciaparelli who doesn't know there's a streetwar on.'

The canopy whined down and the engines fired with a banshee scream. In the rear, Jarrat punched up the NARC telemetry transmission and reviewed the last half hour's data at high speed. Repulsion hammered, and Stone threw the spaceplane upward, back over the glacial hills to Elysium.

The evening sky was overcast, growing dimmer by the minute, and a strange twilight was about to fall. Across Elysium the city lights came to life, a blaze of neon and halogen which replaced the failing direct sunlight. Avalon and Eos were only moons. Sunrise and sunset were geared to their orbital cycles about the giant. With the sun eclipsed, Zeus was a great, velvet blackness in heavens, and night would last for days. But when Avalon was on the sunward side of Zeus even midnight in Elysium was not dark, for the face of the giant world reflected a flood of blue-green twilight.

The city was mapped out by its shimmering neon, a criss-crossed latticework of straight lines and curves marking high-ways, bridges, landing fields, the spaceport. Monolithic build-ings reared into the sky, capped by glaring commercial boards: Orion Spaceways, Silver City... Equinox.

'There's Gold Raven,' Jarrat said as the shuttle arced in on the flank of the Red Raven gunship. 'Okay, let's see what we've got down there. Switching to thermoscan.'

The CRT at Stone's elbow displayed an edit of his data, and Stone's teeth closed on his lip. He counted more than sixty armed individuals still holed up in buildings which were little damaged as yet, since NARC had not been permitted the right of returning fire. Tactical did not have the firepower to retaliate and most of the damage done to this point had been inflicted by the rampaging street army. In other cities, at other times, it would be the Angelpack waging war upon vigilantes crusading to destroy them, or rival syndicates intent on victory at any cost. Here, now, the Angel connection might be more tenuous but Stone had that gut instinct Jarrat had spoken of. The connection was very real.

The gunships formated high above the city and then dropped in low. Repulsion and floodlights turned the street into a storm, and Jarrat's lenses closed on the action, recording everything. The shooters were pinpointed before the gunners in the belly-mounted weapons pods opened up, and when the order to jump was given the Gold Ravens were in little danger between ship and ground.

Stone dropped lower, and on the CRT watched the jump bay open in the belly of the gunship. Inside the darkened bay, the descant troops had been on standby since they launched from the carrier.

Twenty-five mirror-black locusts dropped from the bay and fell fast toward the street. Tracer spat at them from a roof here, a doorway there, but suppressing fire from the ship doused it quickly in eruptions of masonry and smoke. Stone watched the armoured figures go down, then transferred his attention to the CRT.

The kevlex-titanium riot armour was identical to the hardsuits he and Jarrat wore, but the descant troops were armed. On the right forearm, a 9mm rotary cannon, cycling fifty rounds per second, actuated by an eye-blind trigger mechanism. On the left forearm, a stun cannon projecting a field which would overload the brains of anyone in range who was not helmeted. On the left thigh, the snapper, a coiled lash connected to the back-mounted powerpack, just three metres of uninsulated cable carrying enough voltage to drop a man as if he had run into a wall.

The street was a litter of dead and wounded. With the continual crossfire, medevac had been unable to reach the casualties. Stone wondered how many people had died where they lay while the hotheads kept up a barrage of grenades, flak, phosphor and missiles.

Even if they had expected a fight, Grenshem's supporters could not have anticipated this. They had walked into a war, and since Angel was still a relative newcomer to Avalon, perhaps it was the first real streetwar this city had seen.

Sensors, cameras and recorders running, Stone passed low over the rooftops, circled the Silver City building and closed on the area where the Red Ravens were mopping up.

A Tactical skyvan stood in a storm of floodlights in the middle of the deserted six-lane clearway which bisected the city centre. The back ramp was down, and Tac officers were shackling prisoners as the Red Ravens delivered them.

Some were less fortunate. A medevac skimmer stood by,

loading casualties, but Stone had little compassion for them. These were the shooters who had knocked down another medevac craft, and taken suicidal shots at the Blue Raven gunship. Did they know that if they damaged the gunship badly enough they could poison half the city, and themselves with it? Stone regarded the scene bitterly, and looped back over the rooftops to rejoin the Gold Ravens.

A dozen fresh fires raged in the night, but as soon as the Ravens pulled out they would be doused from the air. The loop was a muddle of invective, callsigns and reports, but Jarrat's cameras told the truth.

It was almost finished. Stone consulted the chrono and smiled humourlessly. Seventeen minutes. He felt Jarrat's acid satisfaction overlaying the needle-like slivers of regret and anger. Any kind of war was a waste, and the price was paid by innocent bystanders. How many had been trapped in the crossfire?

'That's about the last,' Jarrat judged as he made a thermo-scan pass over Sciaparelli from two hundred metres. 'There's nothing twitching down there now. I see a lot of bodies, fires, not much else. Those that were dumb enough to stand up and fight didn't make it. Say, seventy, eighty arrests, and their mates disappeared into the woodwork. Correlate data with Tac to-night. I'd say, all-clear, Stoney.'

'Raven Leader to Tac 101,' Stone called sharply.

Duggan must have followed every word of the NARC radio traffic. 'Can I get fire control in, Captain? I'm looking at about a billion credits' worth of wreckage from here!'

'I think so.' Stone would have reckoned the fire damage at worse than that. 'Red Ravens, Gold Ravens, extract. That's it, boys, out you get. It's Tactical's show now.'

But the shuttle's nose rotated back toward Mount Clavel rather than lifting toward the sky, and space. Stone cut speed, approached the ruined park in a glare of floods and spinners, and called Duggan as he settled the plane in an empty area which had been an athletics field.

The mobile command vehicles were closing up and would soon move out. Duggan stood in the midst of a confusion of debris, transports and walking wounded, hands in pockets, his flak jacket at his feet, his shirt unbuttoned and flapping in the scorching engine draft as Stone touched down.

The man looked, Stone thought, sick. Bareheaded, he and

77

Jarrat landed lightly in the charred grass by the hull of their aircraft, and Duggan joined them without a word. The sky was silver-green. Stars glittered in the east, the far west was still faintly flushed by sunset, and overhead Zeus loomed like a thunderhead.

'You found Grenshem,' Duggan guessed as Jarrat ran his fingers through his sweat-damp hair. 'I haven't been able to get an answer from my squads. I'm wondering if some asshole in Sciaparelli has been jamming my frequencies.'

'Your men are dead,' Jarrat told him quietly. 'They don't answer because they can't. Tigh Grenshem is dead too. We talked to his secretary, his lover, Stuart Wymark. You know the kid?'

In the glare of the quadruple halogen driving lights as the command vehicle started up, Duggan's face was white. 'I know him. He and Tigh were like fingers in the same mitten. How did they get him?'

'A bomb under the Chev you assigned him,' Stone told him. 'Grenshem was being watched. Maybe they saw his informant at the house yesterday. They broke in last night, stole the data. Grenshem detonated the device when he tried to ignite his main motor. It must have been very quick.'

Duggan closed his eyes for a moment, as close to an expression of shock as Stone had ever seen him allow. 'I'll send a forensics squad.'

'Tac Lt Curry has been there since it happened,' Jarrat told him. 'He's looking after the kid.'

'You spoke to the boy?' Duggan's eyes were clear now, he was back in control. 'Vic and Stuart shared everything, every word of every campaign. Stuart would know the business.'

'He did.' Stone stirred, stood aside as the command vehicle backed up with whining jets and roaring repulsion fields. 'Get us everything you can on a man called Jack Spiteri, ex-employee of Equinox, worked as a project designer until maybe six months ago.'

'And while you're doing it,' Jarrat added, 'get us Spiteri himself. The man is the key to this, Duggan.'

'Then Tigh was right.' Duggan's eyes widened in the harsh glare of the floodlights. 'He made the Angel connection?'

'It could be a charter pilot, name of Buchanan,' Stone affirmed. 'Runs between here and the Cygnus colonies. We'll find him via his civil registration and flight logs. Chances are that's your smuggler. NARC busted one of the biggest Angel operations we ever saw in the Cygnus colonies, about the same time as Kevin and I were running our own show on Kithan.'

'I heard about it. The Black Unicorn syndicate.' Duggan cocked his head at the younger man. 'I heard about the Death's Head bust as well, Stoney.'

Stone's brows arched. 'You been keeping tabs on me?'

The Colonel shrugged expressively. 'Let's say, I was always interested to see how far you'd go.'

'Then you weren't disappointed,' Jarrat said drily. 'We want Jack Spiteri, fast.'

'I'll do what I can.' Duggan slid pad and pencil from his pocket. 'I might be able to find this pilot for you. If he's on Avalon, I'll pick him up.'

'Try a place called Rawhide,' Stone suggested. 'What is that, a dance shop?'

'Fronts as a dance shop.' Duggan slid the note pad away. 'Two basements down it's a fuck shop... very rough. We keep an eye on it, make sure they don't work the kids over too bad, keep juveniles out of there. You get a lot of dopers fucking for fix money. They don't care what they do, and half the time they're too wrecked to know what's being done to them, but you got to draw the line somewhere or you'll sweep the dead meat out with the beer cans in the morning. Buchanan drinks there? It's a place to start.'

'We'll be waiting.' Jarrat set one steel-gloved hand on Stone's massive, armoured shoulder. 'There's nothing we can do here, and we've got two squads to debrief and a pile of data to process.'

'He's right, Vic.' Stone was watching Officer Weintraub. R/T in one hand, machine pistol in the other, she was shouting at the roadies to get the command trucks moving. Memories he thought he had forgotten were close to the surface, and he knew Jarrat was aware of his feelings of deep reminiscence. Tactical was a way of life. He forced his mind back to the present and gave Duggan a nod. 'Like he said, we'll be waiting.'

The shuttle kicked off with a whining howl of jets. Ten thousand metres over Elysium the wings and canards swept in and back, giving the spaceplane the flight dynamics of a missile. Stone stood it on its tail, opened the throttles and threw it fast toward space, and the ominous face of Zeus.

Chapter Six

The debriefing was routine, thorough but quick. The Blue, Red and Gold Ravens watched the videos, reviewed their audio and made the relevant personal reports before Petrov dispatched the telemetry package. It would be routed through Dupre's office, then boosted on to Central, on Earth, via the tachyon band. Gene Cantrell survived the debriefing and then headed for his quarters to sleep.

The ops room closed down, the carrier was entrusted to her Starfleet crew, and Jarrat and Stone took the opportunity to unpack, shower and eat. Until Duggan's data came in they could do little more.

Shiptime, it was 23:00 as Jarrat threw the debris of their meal into the disposal. Stone was still towelling his short, dark hair and Kevin was damp, his skin flushed after the scalding water. On Darwin's World it would be almost dawn, but crisis energy had dispelled fatigue. Even now they were too restless to settle. The aftermath of an action was always the same. It could take a full day to wind down, then fatigue set in with a vengeance.

The monitor displayed a constant stream of data. Jarrat watched idly as Stone towelled down, but nothing had arrived from Duggan yet.

'Give the man a chance,' Stone counselled. 'He'll have to sort out his own casualties first. Tactical got shit kicked out of them. They'll be short handed, which won't improve Duggan's track record. He was good, ten years ago. From what I saw, he still is.'

Kevin caught the towel as Stone tossed it to him, and dumped it into the chute. They were in Jarrat's cabin. The common door connecting it to Stone's stood open, but both were identical and where they slept was unimportant. Stone sat against the moulded bedhead and patted his lap.

'Come to daddy,' he invited, sultry, enticing.

Smouldering grey eyes looked him over, and Jarrat's body stirred to life as Stone watched. Lithe and tawny, lean and still very boyish, Kevin went to him, knelt astride Stone's muscular thighs and leaned in to kiss. Stone caught the wide, bony shoulders, held him to the plunder of his mouth until Jarrat chuckled and broke away. Shields dwindled a fraction at a time until empathy was so clear, so intense, that if the sensations were not shared they would have been distressing.

'You're eager.' Jarrat's hands moulded about Stone's breast. Thumbs flicked nipples, palms skimmed the dusting of dark chest hair. He felt the caresses in his own nerves and wriggled pleasurably.

'Objecting? Don't con me.' Stone's own hands delved between Jarrat's widespread legs and grasped the elegant genitals he loved. A waft of musk prickled his sinuses as Kevin began to turn on powerfully, and they both groaned. Stone arched into the bed and looked up at his partner. What need to say, 'I want you?' Jarrat knew. He could feel every throb of the desire Stone was nursing.

A smile, a kiss, and Jarrat settled on him, rocking and rubbing. Stone's arms closed about the slighter body, lifted him and settled them on their sides. For a long time they moved smoothly together, from one position to the next. Jarrat slid down to suck, fetched Stone to the brink and stalled him with a firm tug on his balls which made both men cry out. Stone turned him, repaid him in kind with a hot, generous mouth, before he found himself on his back again while Jarrat humped, belly to belly. It could have been an hour or a century before breath began to pant, and Stone was unaware if it was his own heart racing or Kevin's.

His fingers clenched into Jarrat's muscular buttocks and Kevin threw back his head. His eyes were dark, almost doped as he looked down at Stone. Without a word he leaned over, rummaged through the bag he had dropped by the bed hours before and produced a small ceramic tub.

The lube was chill, unscented. It slid on like velvet. Stone held his breath, moaned deep in his chest as Jarrat's long fingers swept about his cock. Kevin blew on him, made him gasp as his shaft danced with a life of its own, but it was Jarrat whose skin prickled and who shivered.

Stone pulled himself up against the bedhead and caught him by the hips. 'Don't torment me,' he whispered.

'Torment?' Jarrat straddled him, reached back to find him and held him at just the right angle.

The shocking thrill of pleasure drew a cry from them both. Stone was dizzy, eyes squeezed shut as Kevin settled on him a fraction at a time. His fingers worked under Jarrat's buttocks, found the place they joined, the blade of himself sheathed in a living scabbard. Jarrat's head tossed as he moved, and Stone was swamped with sensation, so overloaded that his senses spun.

A sharp flicker of pain, a wellspring of pleasure. It was always the same. Jolts of excitement rippled into Stone's thighs and belly like expanding rings on the surface of a pool. His fingers clenched into Jarrat's arms but he felt them bruising his own; Jarrat slammed down hard, but he felt Kevin's thrill ignite his own prostate, and gasped.

The end was volcanic, and Jarrat collapsed on him, hot and heavy. Still immersed in him, too lax to move, Stone stroked his back while the world righted and reality began to encroach. The rich odour of sex was heavy in the room, but aircycling fans were already humming. Jarrat enlived at last. He propped himself on leaden arms and lifted his hips to uncouple them, and Stone shared his sensations.

Feeling very empty, throbbing a little, Jarrat ducked into the shower stall. He hit the taps, turned his back to the stream and bent forward, hands on his knees. A balled-up washcloth landed unceremoniously on Stone's belly.

'That was worth waiting for,' Kevin said ruefully as he towelled down.

'Promised you, when we were suiting.' Stone lobbed the washcloth back. 'Told you I'd eat you alive.'

'You did.' Jarrat stretched both arms over his head. 'I feel better than I've felt in weeks.'

'I know.' Stone tapped his nose. 'I also know you're worried. About Grenshem's data?'

'Yeah.' Dry, glowing, Jarrat slid into the bed and turned onto his belly. 'If Stuart Wymark turns out to be wrong, we'll be reprimanded, Stoney. We just deployed NARC descant troops in something that might not have been an Angel packwar.'

Stone dimmed the lights and pulled up the single sheet. The cabin air was evenly warm. 'We're playing percentages. The odds are, the kid remembered right and Grenshem told Duggan the truth. If the Ravens hadn't deployed that battle would still be raging.'

'And if Stuart heard wrong?' Jarrat's voice was muffled.

It was a decades-old question. Within two years of the formation of Narcotics And Riot Control, an unscrupulous governor attempted to use the carrier *Lysander* to crush a civil war unconnected with the Angel trade on the rimworlds of Vereal and Macedon. The incident became textbook required-reading. NARC was not a private army and would not be involved in politics without specific orders from Central. Military action undertaken by the department must be at the behest of the government of Earth — a situation that had never occurred.

NARC could, Stone admitted as he drifted on the fringe of sleep, be a terrible weapon if its mobility and striking power was placed in the hands of a corrupt regime. The thought was chilling.

A chime from the comm stirred him and he peered at the chrono. 06:32. Watch crews would be changing according to the Starfleet roster, but the NARC officers obeyed their own schedule, quite apart from the carrier's running crew. Jarrat was barely awake, and Stone reached over his back to select voice-only on the panel by the bed.

'Stone.'

'Incoming data, Cap.' It was Kiveris, a radio technician monitoring the NARC band. 'It's coming in on priority... you waiting for something from Tactical?'

Stone sat and rubbed his face. 'We'll take it here.'

'On its way, Cap.'

'Kev.' Stone swatted the shapely backside beneath the sheet. 'Kevin!'

'I heard.' Jarrat rolled over and yawned eloquently. 'Get me a coffee, will you? I'll see what Duggan's got for us.' He was out of bed as he spoke, and shrugged into a robe, scarlet Macedon silk embroidered with sea dragons.

The transmission was brief, concise and not what they had hoped for. Tactical was trying to trace the informant, Jack Spiteri, without success. The pilot, Buchanan, had logged a flight to Eos and had not yet returned, but the security squad at Elysium Field were alerted to seize him as soon as he touched down.

In the meantime, a brief file on Spiteri had been rushed together, and Duggan had transmitted a quick summary of data he had gathered from the civilian shooters arrested in the hotzone. Clad in slacks, barefoot and barechested, Stone fetched two coffees from the robochef. He put Jarrat's into his hand and pulled a chair up before the terminal.

Half a paragraph into the report, Jarrat made cynical sounds. 'There's your cause for the streetwar. It would have started as a protest meeting, escalated into a riot, then somebody started shooting.'

A referendum had been taken two days before they arrived; votes had been counted, the result broadcast hours before violence erupted. It seemed the vast bulk of the population had voted to grant Equinox mining rites to the atmosphere of Zeus. A man did not have to be particularly perceptive to smell the rat.

'"Grenshem made a broadcast the night before he died,"' Stone read, '"alleging that the referendum was fixed." Predictable. The man had guts.'

'To take on Equinox publicly, when he already had information from this Spiteri, that Equinox moguls are socialising with the likes of Buchanan?' Jarrat shook his head. 'Grenshem was stretching his luck. And it broke.'

'Yeah.' Stone leaned back in the chair, one arm about Jarrat's slim hips. 'Nine out of ten people arrested in Sciaparelli last night say they were fighting because of the fixed vote. The tenth is saying nothing.'

'And the weapons,' Jarrat mused as he paged down through the file. 'Damn. Duggan got nothing out of them.'

'He wouldn't have used sophisticated interrogation techniques,' Stone reminded him. 'For a start, he'll still be burying his own dead. Then, these guys have to be convicted before Duggan can touch them with serums or cyber devices, or you'd have a flock of legal eagles shredding Tactical.' He looked up into Jarrat's watchful face. 'The more sophisticated the technique, the nastier it is.'

'I know.' Jarrat drained his mug. 'I saw it all in the Army, remember. They did some experimental crap in Intelligence that'd curl your hair.' He set the cup aside. 'Anyway, the ordinary street hoon wouldn't know where the weapons came from. Duggan's not going to find the source that way.' He returned to the screen. 'If Buchanan is on Eos he won't be hard to find. You notice he was well out of the way when the streetwar started.'

Stone broached the third file, labelled Spiteri, Jack, D. An image filled the right ride of the screen, probably pulled from a licence application. He was twenty-seven, darker than Bill Dupre's Barbadian complexion, with cropped, crinkly black hair and narrow features. He was handsome but looked weary, as if he carried a merciless burden. Stone skimmed the educational and employment details without a comment, and then they saw it.

'Ah.' Jarrat tapped the screen with one forefinger. 'Here it is. Recently bereaved. Jack married an engineer, Michael Rogan, died six months ago. He was with Equinox... looked like a brilliant career. He worked in the construction of launch facilities. Have we got the cause of death here?'

At the touch of a key the text scrolled on, and Stone grunted as he saw the coroner's postscript. 'Angel. Christ, we should have known.'

'So Spiteri lost his mate to Angel six months ago,' Jarrat mused. 'Both of them worked for Equinox.'

'Hardly surprising,' Stone added. 'Seven out of ten people work for the company.'

'And now Spiteri is whistleblowing.' Jarrat folded his arms on the scarlet robe. 'Grenshem may have been on track.'

'We'd better hope.' Stone frowned at the screen. 'What would make a man in Michael Rogan's position use Angel? He had a brilliant career, prospects. According to this they lived in an upmarket sector of Albany, ran a suborbital aircraft, and were rolling in money.' He arched a brow at Jarrat. 'That's not the profile of your typical Angelhead.'

The typical user was mid-late teens, violently emotional, depressive, often poorly adjusted, or simply miserable. The misery could be the product of poverty, a failed relationship, hopeless prospects. Psychologists from the rim to the deep sky had written millions of words on the subject. None of it meant a damn. If a man was sufficiently depressive his last choice might seem to be Angel or the nearest roof. There was no way back from either.

A shiver prickled Stone's spine. Jarrat felt it at once and his arms slipped about Stone's bare torso. 'You okay?'

'Yes. No.' Stone buried his face in the silk. It smelt of Kevin's body and he inhaled deeply. 'I'm just thinking.'

'Of the Angel ride you took?' Jarrat stroked his hair.

'Thinking of Rikki Mitchell, actually.' Stone hugged Jarrat

about the hips and released him. 'He was your typical user. Young, isolated, emotionally bruised. All bravado on the surface, bleeding underneath.'

'We've all lost someone we cared for to Angel,' Jarrat said quietly. 'Don't punish yourself.'

'I'm not —' Stone began, and then stopped. He was. He was telling himself, if he had left Rikki at home on the island of Outbound, he would still be alive. Harry Del might have worked the strange empathic healer's magic for him, changed his brain the way Stone's own brain was changed.

Jarrat was waiting, and at last Stone lifted his head, showed him flushed cheeks and solemn eyes. Kevin stooped to kiss. 'Things happen the way they happen. First law of the universe.'

'That doesn't mean I have to like it.' Stone stood and turned his back on the screen. 'Call Duggan, see if he's picked up Spiteri yet, and if not, why not.'

The razor buzzed against his jaw as Jarrat made the call. Stone stood out of range of the lens and listened to the voice of his old instructor. Duggan was tired, sore, angry. Jarrat did not push, and at last Duggan relented.

'I'm doing the best I can, Jarrat,' he said tersely. 'Thirty million people in Elysium. You want me to find *one* who doesn't want to be found. Jesus, you're asking for a bloody miracle!'

'All right,' Jarrat allowed. 'What have you got on the Equinox directors?'

A pause, then Duggan said cautiously, 'The directors? You asking me to run surveillance on the luminaries who make this system tick?'

'I'm asking for what you've got on them,' Jarrat said with spurious blandness. 'Don't tell me you don't keep files, Duggan, because I don't believe you.'

The Tactical man hissed through his teeth. 'You're going to get me into shit up to my armpits, Jarrat. Okay, I got files. But I'm not transmitting them.'

Jarrat shot a glance at Stone over the hood of the terminal. 'Is this frequency being monitored?'

'Maybe. Maybe not. If I take dumb-ass risks I can follow Tigh Grenshem!'

Switching off the razor, Stone stepped into view of the camera and looked into Duggan's face on the vidscreen. 'If you've got information we'll meet you.'

'Do that.' Duggan looked as weary as he sounded, and as angry. 'I traced Neil Buchanan to Eos for you. At least, that's his last logged destination, and he didn't leave the system.'

'Keep tabs on him,' Jarrat said tersely. 'We'll be with you in a couple of hours, Colonel. You still at Tac HQ?'

'Yeah.' Duggan dragged both hands through his hair. 'I thought I'd crash here. Hardly worth going home. Nothing to go home to.' His eyes flicked from Stone to Jarrat and back again. 'I'll pull those files.'

'Thanks.' Stone reached over and blanked the screen. 'What do you make of that?'

'I reckon Duggan's got more sense than Grenshem had,' Jarrat said drily as he dropped the robe and swiped up the razor. 'And it all points to Equinox Industries. You rub the wrong man — or men — up the wrong way, and you die.' He thumbed the razor and applied it to his jaw.

***

Tactical HQ towered over the Rheims sector on the west side of Elysium. Skimmers and skyvans swarmed about its roof, and Jarrat stood off at a safe distance, waiting for landing permission. The shuttle touched down between a troop transport and an air ambulance carrying the decals of The Argyll Mercy Clinic.

The NARC men were in plain clothes, and as the canopy rose they clambered out into the blustery mid-morning wind. The armour was in storage, in compartments beneath the deck plates, and the shuttle was fully armed. Elysium had a nasty reputation. Angel involvement or no, the city could metamorph into a hotzone in minutes, and NARC officers and property presented prime targets.

In tight green slacks, beige shirt, sport shoes and amber glasses, Jarrat looked good. Stone admired him without verbal comment, though Kevin picked up on his feelings and gave him a smile. Stone examined his own reflection in the smoked glass doors which led into the reception bay. The white slacks and grey shirt hugged his body. Jarrat liked what he saw, and Stone was satisfied.

Their ID had been transmitted along with a request for landing instructions. The young receptionist barely looked up as they appeared. She had been crying. Her mascara bled, carbon black, over one cheek as she blew her nose. On the desk at her elbow was a framed holosnap of a smiling boy in Tac uniform. A casualty of the night's bitter streetwar, Stone thought, and felt a rush of compassion.

Fans rustled the papers strewn across Duggan's desk. The man sat with his chair tipped back against the wall, a cheroot in one hand, a bourbon in the other. He was off duty, Stone knew at a glance as he and Jarrat stepped into the cool, cluttered office.

The windows overlooked Rheims. Sciaparelli was five kilometres away, easy to pinpoint by the column of greasy smoke which still rose from several building fires. Zeus loomed in the sky, brooding and magnificent, and Jarrat paced to the wide window, hands in hip pockets, to absorb the view.

The chair thumped back onto all four feet and Duggan stubbed out his smoke. A datacube rattled across the desk. 'That's the lot. And if you let the bastards know you got it from me, Stoney, you're signing my death warrant.'

Stone parked his rump on a clear corner of desk and slipped the cube into his breast pocket. 'All right, Vic. You can trust me.' He studied the older man's face closely. Jarrat was not missing a word, but did not turn back from the view. The building trembled as something heavy lifted off the roof. The Argyll Mercy ambulance dropped smoothly by, down toward the street. 'What do you know, Vic?'

'It's in the file.' Duggan massaged the bridge of his nose. 'Or is it personal opinion you want from me?'

'You taught me to trust instinct, first and last,' Stone said levelly. 'That's how I've always worked.'

'Trust your instinct, use routine leg work to back it up.' Duggan quoted an old unwritten law and smiled faintly before he leaned both elbows on the desk and gestured with the bourbon. 'Help yourselves.'

'Not right now.' Stone twisted his neck to read the cover legend on the top file of a stack. Death certificates.

'All right.' Duggan tossed down the spirit. It roughened his voice and he cleared his throat hoarsely. 'Tigh swore to me he had a link to corruption that goes right to the top.'

'Of Equinox, or government?' Jarrat turned back from the window.

'What's the diff?' Duggan laced his fingers, studied his palms.

'Okay, the official version states that Equinox hasn't controlled government here in six decades, since Avalon was granted autonomy. That's horse shit. Grasp that fact, and you'll start to make sense of things here.'

'They buy their politicians?' Stone guessed.

Duggan yawned deeply. 'Put it this way. Nothing happens in the Zeus system without their say-so. And what they want, they get. Top of the ladder is Randolph Dorne, and let me tell you, on Avalon, God comes three rungs lower.' He smiled cynically. 'Dorne worked his way up through the ranks, invested heavily, came to own controlling shares about the same time I arrived here.'

Jarrat and Stone shared a glance. 'Then Dorne controls the power, government, funding, the lot,' Jarrat mused. 'Neat. So he sent his shooters to get Grenshem's data and make sure the senator was silenced permanently... which reminds me, Duggan. You ought to pull Stuart Wymark out. He can't be safe. As soon as Grenshem's killers know they missed him, they'll be back.'

'Done and done, Jarrat,' Duggan snorted. 'What do you take me for? Pete Curry's got Stuart somewhere so safe, even I don't know where the kid is. He's been sweet on Stuart since the kid got out of college.'

'Okay.' Jarrat permitted himself a smile. 'Drop that cube in the machine, Stoney. Let's see what we've got.'

The monitor dimmed, red type on black. A menu of files appeared, a dozen names which meant nothing to Stone; two which he recognised. Dorne himself, and Wozniak. 'Tell me about this one. Wozniak.'

'Contract man, and good.' Duggan forced his feet under him, rounded the desk and poured another bourbon. 'In fact, Kjell Wozniak is so good we can't touch him legally. Not even worth trying. I know that asshole has killed at least four people who got in Dorne's way. It's probable he did the job on Tigh. But a half-matched voice print, a long-range shot from a video remote, a very dodgy DNA ident... a good lawyer would string me up by the balls. I'd be on the next clipper back to Earth, with a whole career up in smoke.'

Stone looked up from the screen with a grin. 'You never were the kind to write your own evidence.'

'Honesty's my one weakness.' Duggan swallowed the whisky

and recapped the bottle. 'If you want Wozniak, I can pick him up but I can't hold him. He's on Dorne's payroll. Works on Skycity. I got no solid evidence to indict him, and he has all of Equinox behind him. Like somebody once said, you can't convict a billion credits.'

'Let's take a look at Dorne,' Jarrat said thoughtfully. 'Skip the minions, go straight to the top.'

Keys pattered, and Randolph Dorne's face appeared. 'Born on Earth in the international sector of Florence,' Stone read off. 'Nationality reads Euro-American, nothing specific. Never married, no children. Educated in Japan, qualified in corporate law, arrived on Avalon at twenty-six, on an Equinox contract. Got the reins between his hands by the time he was forty.' He looked up at Jarrat. 'Damn. Now, how did he do that? I never got the hang of making money.'

A sound of genuine humour escaped Jarrat. 'That doesn't mean he did it illegally. And even if he did, a corporate lawyer would chop Tac up for dog meat if they tried to prove it.' He straightened and frowned at Duggan. 'Grenshem swore he was tapped into corruption that went right up to Dorne?'

'He was certain.' Duggan sighed.

'Angel?' Stone pressed. 'Or illegal arms trafficking? Come on, Vic! One is your business, the other is ours. You give us something that links Equinox to Angel, and we'll blow them sky high for you. Otherwise we can't get involved.'

The colonel leaned both shoulders on the wall by the window and laced his fingers at his nape. 'I've got nothing concrete. Just a bunch of allegation and supposition. Understand that, Stoney.' He looked piercingly at Stone. 'Sixty-seven Equinox employees have died of Angel in the last two years.'

Jarrat's brows arched. 'So? When you consider the way your population's soaked in that crap, that's hardly surprising. You've got ten percent addiction, double that on your campuses, and seventy percent of your labour force is on the Equinox payroll.'

'But very few of Equinox's Angeldeaths fit the profile,' Duggan said stubbornly. 'Qualified people, thirty or forty years old, married, happy, successful. Then one day they cram Angel up their noses and suicide just as surely as if they dove off a roof.' He glared at Jarrat. 'That sound typical to you?'

'No,' Jarrat admitted.

'Michael Rogan,' Stone said quietly.

'Jack Spiteri's better half,' Duggan agreed. 'He's just one, Stoney. There's dozens, scores like him. It's on the cube. Makes depressing reading.' He reached over and popped the datacube out of the machine. 'I'm manacled hand and foot, can't make a move in any direction. Tigh tried, and he's dead. You get the picture?'

'Oh, yeah.' Stone took the cube, fingered its white metal casing and met Jarrat's eyes in conference. 'I want to talk to Randolph Dorne.'

The bald statement made Duggan choke on a cynical chuckle. 'Good luck, kid. I've been trying to get two words with the bastard for the last six months!'

'He can give Tac the evasion treatment,' Jarrat said with deliberate smugness, 'but he can't screw around with NARC, and if he's a lawyer he knows it. There's a line in our fine print somewhere. Something about refusal to cooperate being a confession of culpability. The kind of legal double talk that can mean anything we want it to.' He accorded Duggan a wink. 'He'll talk to us. What about Buchanan?'

With a yawn, Duggan turned off the monitor, stretched out on the couch beside his desk and closed his eyes. 'Like I said, he's on Eos. He hasn't logged a flight out of the system and when he sticks his nose back into Elysium airspace you got him.' He pried open his eyes. 'Unless he hears you're after Dorne, in which case he could cut and run, straight out from Eos, and you won't see his nasty ass in this system again.'

'Do you monitor radio from Skycity?' Stone asked shrewdly.

'We do.' Duggan shoved a cushion under his head. 'We'll pick up a call if one's made, but important data goes coded. We get zilch. And if Buchanan's quick he'll be gone before you can spit. Now, bugger off and let me sleep. I popped a handful of speed last night and it's wearing off with a vengeance.'

Hands in pockets, Stone glared at the face of Zeus, framed in the wide windows. Aircabs darted to and fro between the towering buildings; the sky was cloudy and the wind blew a flurry of rain into the glass.

On the couch, Duggan's breathing settled into a light snore and Jarrat touched Stone's arm. 'We're wasting our time here. Duggan's given us all he's got.'

The shower had stopped when they stepped through the

glass doors into the windy expanse of the landing bay, high over Elysium. The sky was still deeply overcast; the light reflected from Zeus made the air seem green, and it was cool, almost chill. Jarrat lifted the shuttle's canopy, climbed up and perched on the side of the cockpit. With the canopy like a vast armourglass parasol above him, he pulled on a headset.

'Raven 9.4 to carrier.'

To his surprise Gene Cantrell's voice answered. 'Carrier.'

'You got the ops room busy, Gene?' Jarrat's tone was sharp as he looked down at Stone, who stood in the lee of the hull.

'Just processing a load of data,' Cantrell told him. 'Finishing off last night's work. I crashed before I got through it. What can I do for you, Kevin?'

'Launch the standby gunship,' Jarrat said slowly. 'Full descant unit.'

'Roger that.' Cantrell paused, and his next remarks were directed to the carrier's NARC complement. 'Blue Ravens, go to launch alert. Launch in ten.' Then, 'Destination, Kevin?'

'Switch to Channel 77,' Jarrat instructed, and waited until Cantrell had complied, shifting into the security band specific to NARC. Even military specialists could not easily break in. Then, 'Destination is Eos.' Jarrat extended a hand over the side as Stone began to climb. 'Check civvy registration. Pilot by the name of Neil Buchanan, flies some sort of cargo charter, and it's something major, because he's running flak deflectors, which is more than most civil pilots can afford. In this system, that means a probable direct link to Equinox. Don't impound the ship, don't let the man know he's under surveillance, but if he tries to do a runner, grab him. Tell Gil Cronin, if he lets Buchanan slip through his fingers I'll personally break his kneecaps.'

A snort of ribald laughter cut across the comm loop, and Cronin's voice intruded. 'I heard that, Cap. You want the man, you got him. Alive, I presume?'

'Dead won't do us much good,' Jarrat said drily as he settled in the acceleration couch and strapped down. 'Get moving Gil... and watch your open transmission. I think you may have some eavesdropping.'

'Source?' Cronin's humour was gone the instant the lives of the twenty-four men under his command were in possible jeopardy.

'Skycity,' Jarrat told him as the canopy whined down and

locked.

'Dorne's mansion?' Cronin was obviously unsurprised. 'Okay, Cap, copy that. Blue Raven 6 out.'

Then Cantrell again: 'Gunship reports launch procedures initiated. Are you coming home, 9.4?'

For a moment Jarrat hesitated. Stone had pulled on his own headset and cut into the security channel. 'We'll let you know, Gene. We might pay a social call first.'

'Standing by. *Athena* out.' Cantrell shut down.

Rain spattered the canopy and Stone watched the rivulets streak the armourglass. 'You want to buzz the man's home?'

'His mansion in the sky.' Jarrat was punching keys. 'Ah, here it is. An Elysium phonecode, restricted access.'

Again keys tapped, selecting the number and voice-only. Stone adjusted his headset to the civilian band as a young man's cultured voice said,

'Skycity. The Dorne residence.'

'My name is Jarrat. Captain Jarrat, Narcotics And Riot Control. When can I speak personally with Mr Dorne?' The blunt statement and request were made without inflection, and would hit the target like .60 calibre.

The pause was stunned. 'I'll inform Mr Dorne that you called, Captain.'

'I said,' Jarrat repeated in a barbed tone, 'when can I speak with him?'

'I'm not sure, sir.' The young man was probably only a minor secretary, and flustered. 'If you'd like to wait, Captain, I'll find out. I assume this is NARC business.'

'It is, and I'll wait.' Jarrat's fingertips drummed on the console beside the navigation deck as the line silenced. 'Put the cat amongst the pigeons, Stoney?'

Stone laughed shortly. 'Stir, and see what comes to the surface. If Buchanan tries to run I'd be happy to read that as a connection between either Equinox, or Dorne, or both, and the Angel smuggling here.'

'So would I.' Jarrat trailed his fingers over the inside of the canopy, following the rain.

The earplug crackled and Stone swallowed his comments as the secretary returned. 'I'm sorry, Captain, Mr Dorne won't be available till this evening. If you'd care to come to Skycity then, you would do so as house quests. To the entertainments, that is.'

'19:00, Elysium time?' Jarrat asked.

'Perhaps an hour later, Captain. Do you require transport?'

'No. Inform Mr Dorne that Captain Stone and I are on official business. This is not a social call. Goodbye.' Jarrat cut the connection, tightened his flight harness and fired the lift engines with a series of sharp gestures betraying annoyance. 'Raven 9.4 to Tac Flight Control, give me takeoff instructions.'

'Tac Flight. Incoming traffic from the southwest. Wait for my signal before launch.' A woman's voice, harassed and short tempered. Jarrat turned his head to watch as a troop transport lumbered in out of the overcast. The storm of engine noise and repulsion, floods and spinners, blanketed the roof before the squat, ugly vehicle set down. Hydraulic shockers flattened beneath it, the floodlights and spinners doused, and Jarrat ran up his own main lifters.

'Tac Flight to NARC Airborne, launch anytime.'

'On our way.' Jarrat pulled gently back on the cyclic stick, lifted the shuttle a hundred metres above the Tactical building and performed a sensor sweep of surrounding airspace before he turned the spaceplane's nose up, swept the wings and headed fast for the carrier.

Before the sky had darkened through mauve to black Cantrell was on the air, and the comm panel flashed a Channel 77 warning. 'Blue Ravens are away.'

In the rear, Stone keyed in a schematic of the near Zeus system. 'Eos is about two hours out by gunship. Check my figures, Kevin.'

A glance at the CRT at his elbow, and Jarrat agreed at once. He felt a lick of excitement from Stone. 'You want to rendezvous with the Blue Ravens?'

'That's what I'm thinking,' Stone mused. 'They'll be running about in panic at Dorne's place for some time, but if they're going to signal Buchanan, they'll do it soon. We could be on Eos before Buchanan even knows he has trouble coming.'

'I heard that,' Cantrell called. 'Kevin?'

'Tell Blue Raven to hold up, take us in tractors and pull us aboard,' Jarrat affirmed. 'Are you monitoring signals out of Dorne's establishment?'

'Every second,' Cantrell assured him. 'Three calls have gone out in the last six minutes. I think they're trying to locate the boss. Looking for instructions, at a guess.'

'Stay with them, and tell Blue Raven we're coming up,' Jarrat said brusquely as he watched his screens.

Stone was tracking the carrier. The gunship was a smaller mark, even then three thousand kilometres downrange. Its acceleration curve levelled out as Cantrell relayed instructions, and Stone piped the ranging data from the rear cockpit observer's CRT to Jarrat's. The nose came about a few degrees and Jarrat kicked the twin throttles wide open.

The gunship's acquisition beams and spinners were on, but Jarrat released the controls five hundred metres out when instruments informed him the tractors had connected. From that moment, the pilot sat back for the ride.

In the belly of the gunship, aft of the bay from which the descant troops jumped, a hangar door slid open. A sheet of white halogen light spilled into space, and Stone's eyes narrowed, his irises protesting the brilliance as the tractors took them aboard.

'Return to manual,' Jarrat called as the plane crossed the threshold into the hangar, and instruments reported that the tractor had released him.

The shuttle touched down lightly on the broad, black steel deck and the bay rumbled shut. Air pressure and temperature soared, but it was still cold when the canopy rose and Stone lifted himself out.

Like the carrier, the gunship's flight crew was Starfleet, but the descant troops were NARC, under the command of a man with whom Jarrat and Stone had served for years. Sergeant Gil Cronin was a giant, in height and breadth. His head was shaven, his features square, his skin brown with an even spacer's tan, accumulated under UV lamps during off-duty hours. He was waiting for them as they left the hangar to the maintenance crew.

'You eaten yet? You got time before we make Eos.' Cronin gestured over his shoulder at his squad. In the characteristic white tee-shirt, dark blue uniform pants and soft soled, deck-friendly boots, most of the Blue Ravens were lounging in the ready room between the hangar and the jump bay.

'Thanks. And get me a headset.' Stone lifted a hand in greeting at Cronin's second, Joe Ramos, Blue Raven 7. Enormous, swarthy, Ramos wore his hair uncut, roped over his shoulder in a thick braid. As usual when he was not in the hardsuit, he was fondling a deck of cards.

The ready room was quiet, designed to quell nerves, kill time and review data in the minutes or hour before deployment. Screens flickered in a bank along one wall, the briefing table was a litter of printout, but most of the men were eating, gambling or reading. Lurid photos adhered to the bulkheads. Stone spent a moment trying to work out what the two pneumatic young women were doing in a hammock. More to his taste were the bronzed Adonises working out in the poster tacked up alongside.

'Headset.' Cronin proffered it, dangled from one thick finger. 'Cap Cantrell ought to be listening to Skycity.'

As he selected a meal from the robochef menu, Jarrat glanced over his shoulder at Cronin. 'You seen the palace?'

'On videos.' Cronin's weight sank the padding of a seat and he swept up his cards. 'Haunts of the stinking rich. You don't see many of them assholes on the street. Most fly from Skycity to the landing bay on top of Equinox Towers, and don't get no lower.'

'You've been watching them?' Stone took a plate of chicken and salad from Jarrat, settled his headset and swivelled a chair in at the end of the table. He heard the muted comm loop from the flight deck, crosstalk between gunship and carrier. Jarrat pulled up a chair and chewed mechanically as his eyes skimmed the lewd pinups.

'Petrov was born suspicious,' Cronin said indifferently. 'He runs surveillance on everybody, everywhere.'

'This time he might be right.' Jarrat leaned over and took the datacube from Stone's breast pocket with one finger, a fleeting, private tease which made Stone smile. 'Let's take a look at this.'

The nearest terminal swivelled to face them, and Cronin threw down his cards to watch as they examined Duggan's files. Randolph Dorne seemed immaculate on the surface, but Duggan's excavations had turned up small incongruities.

Such as the presence on his staff of men like Kjell Wozniak. As he saw Wozniak's name and face, Cronin swore. Stone frowned up at him. 'You know the man?'

'He's the Equinox security chief.' Cronin folded his big arms on the breast of the tight white tee-shirt. The fabric stretched about biceps Stone might have envied. 'That's now. Elysium scuttlebutt is, he was a king shooter not long ago.'

'Syndicate?' Jarrat paused, fork halfway to his lips.

'Maybe.' Cronin passed a hand over his smooth dome. 'Check the file. He's from the Cygnus colonies.'

'Not that he was there when Black Unicorn was broken,' Stone added. 'Which only means he pushes his luck as far as it's safe, then bugs out before NARC shows up. How long's he been on Avalon?'

Jarrat searched the file. 'His travel permits say he shipped in fourteen months ago.' Both brows arched. 'Which was about the time NARC took an interest in Cygnus. Damn.'

'Neat.' Stone returned to his meal, marked the time and listened to the crosstalk on the loop. Avalon's sister moon of Eos lay seventy minutes away.

'Any signals from Skycity?' Jarrat asked softly as he saw Stone's eyes on the time.

'Plenty. According to what Gene's getting, they've called five offices, a bordello in Belreve and a health club in Orleans.' He smiled grimly. 'Dorne ought to leave a note of where he's going.'

'Him?' Cronin snorted as he returned to the game. 'The man owns this whole shitty system, Cap. He'll be in hell two days before anybody knows he's dead.'

The assertion made Jarrat smile, and he returned to the files, this time running the brief notes Duggan had included on the sixty-seven Equinox employees who had suffered Angeldeath in the last two years. A footnote to the file added a further dimension. Jarrat drew Stone's attention to it with one finger on the screen.

'Before this run of Angeldeaths inside the company — and it amounts to something like two or three a month, every month — you had just five in the previous four years.'

'Curiouser,' Stone said drily, 'and curiouser. And I don't believe in coincidence.'

'Two years ago...' Jarrat pushed his plate away and sat back. 'Dorne got the reins of Equinox in his fists four years before that.' He stopped with a quiet gasp as he felt the prickle of disturbance from Stone, which he recognised as the physical thrill of an intuition. 'What?'

'It wasn't much over two years ago,' Stone said tersely, 'that the company formally requisitioned the mining rites to the

97

atmosphere of Zeus, which they thought they'd be handed without question, since they owned a bunch of key senators —'

'And the local population threw a fit.' Jarrat swirled his coffee in the bottom of the styrene cup. 'That's pretty slick, Stoney. I'm buying.'

Stone's eyes flicked back to the time. The gunship would make Eos in forty minutes. And the voice of the pilot, Tanya Reynolds, whispered sharply in his ear:

'Signal from Skycity. Dorne's calling home... damn. They cut in scramblers.'

'Decode,' Stone said quickly.

'They're trying,' Reynolds' voice assured him. 'Give 'em time. This is some pretty tough shit.'

'Patch me to the carrier.' Stone looked into Jarrat's watchful face. 'They've found Dorne, but they've scrambled the call. Now, why would they do that if it was an innocent message that he's getting a little visit from NARC tonight?'

'How long till we make Eos?' Kevin looked at the chrono.

'We're making best speed,' Stone mused.

Then Mischa Petrov's voice cut over the crosstalk: 'Can't decode, Stoney. It's not military, not Starfleet, not one of ours. Christ knows what the system is. Probably something they designed themselves, they've got the resources to do it. Could take half an hour to break it. You want it that bad?'

'Yes.' Stone bit his lip. 'And keep your ears on, because if we're right there'll be a signal out of Skycity for Eos in about the next five minutes.'

'You want we should jam it?' Petrov asked.

'Let it go through,' Stone said quickly. 'If we can get a reaction out of the pilot, Buchanan, we're halfway home.'

'Roger that, and standby,' Petrov responded. 'I'll buzz you if we get an intercept.'

If? Stone's fingertips drummed a rhythm on the table as they waited and watched the time. Then, there it was, eight minutes after Dorne's scrambled call. Jarrat took a quick breath as he felt the kick through Stone's nerves, and the Russian's thickly accented voice said sharply in Stone's ear,

'Coded signal outbound from Skycity. Same scrambler system, Cap. We'll break it if we can but it'll take time. UHF transmission is high power, narrow beam. You're going to get lucky.'

'Thanks.' Stone gave Jarrat a thumbs-up. 'Reynolds.'

'Yo,' the pilot called over the background chatter.

'Put your foot on the loud pedal,' Stone told her. 'Buchanan's warned, as of now.'

'I can get a bit more our of her,' Reynolds said doubtfully. 'Coming up on Eos.'

Jarrat stood, both hands running through his hair, a small betrayal of the electric tensions of which Stone was acutely aware. 'Call Eos Flight Control, tell them to stall him, hold him on launch procedures. Claim equipment failure, anything.'

'I heard that,' Reynolds told Stone.

'Priority, channel 88,' Stone said quickly. 'Use a recent military code. At least it'll slow Buchanan down.'

'We'll make Eos high orbit in ten,' she informed him as she set up the transmission. 'He won't outrun us, Cap.'

'Stoney.' Jarrat set a hand on his partner's shoulder. 'You want to jump, or shall I?'

'I'll go.' Stone stood. 'Help me suit up. You can monitor this show from the flight deck.'

A klaxon called a squad of eight men to duty, including Cronin and Ramos. Most had been watching the time and were on their way into the suiting room without prompting. The jump bay was already darkened, the range counters and CRTs alive with orbital data and enhanced views of Eos.

The shuttle's deck plates lifted out and Jarrat held the kevlex-titanium sections while Stone worked his body into them. Piece by piece they sealed, and by the time Kevin handed him the helmet, repulsion had cut his apparent mass to fifty kilos.

'Be careful,' Jarrat said quietly as he stepped back. Stone settled the helmet, with its featureless visor, and screwed both umbilici into the chin sockets. 'This is the first time we've seen a live action since...'

'Since Hal Mavvik,' Stone's metallicised voice said via the transducers, which he had set at minimum.

At maximum, he could magnify his voice to a hundred decibels, and the floodlights across the brow of the helmet generated a quarter million candlepower. Such light and sound alone constituted weapons, but Jarrat was arming the suit for him as they heard the Blue Ravens' final call.

The 9mm rotary cannon clamped to his right forearm and he

shifted his head inside the helmet to test the eye-blink trigger. The stun projector clamped to his left forearm, and as Jarrat jacked it into the powerpack mounted between his shoulders Stone read his power levels.

The final test was beyond machines, beyond technology. Stone dropped the empathic shields which had become like second nature and invited Jarrat's emotions to touch him deeply. His vision dimmed as Kevin's feelings rolled into him, powerful, as pervasive and overwhelming as the most intense sexual sensation, though Jarrat had not set a finger on him. Some regarded empathy as a kind of 'mind fuck'. Stone was not sure, but from Jarrat he read the concern of one lover for another; affection, anxiety, tension. Kevin was strung up like a thoroughbred.

Sweat prickled Stone's ribs as mirror, echoing sensations threatened to overwhelm him. One big steel gauntlet cupped Jarrat's cheek with seemingly absurd gentleness. 'You monitor me. You can do it better than any bloody machine.'

'I'll be here.' Jarrat turned his face to the chill metal for a second. 'Check your telemetry channels, start your voice recorder. Bill Dupre only let us out on our own on condition we ran this whole circus as a project for the buggers in Intelligence.' Then stepped back. 'Go.'

Stone walked lightly out of the hangar and into the jump bay, but he was more aware of Jarrat than of the massive figures around him. Cronin and Ramos were at the head of the descant squad. He took his place with them, eyes on the CRT displaying the rust-brown face of Eos as the ranging data came up.

'Time to drop?' he asked, strangely dislocated as he followed Jarrat's progress. He was on his way to the flight deck. Muscles in his legs, pulse in his throat, tightness in his chest and belly. He was jogging toward the blunt bow section, where the flight crew perched above the nose gunports... anxious, tense, eager to get it right.

'Three minutes,' Cronin told him. The faceless black helmet swivelled toward him. 'You always did want to be in on this. What is it, a macho trip of yours?'

'Keep polishing your ego,' Stone told him aridly, 'and you'll slither right off it. Flight deck!'

'Here,' Jarrat's voice responded, slightly breathless. 'Coming up on target. Standby.'

The rusty face of Eos filled the CRT. The rangecounters read 04/06 and the deck trembled with vibration as the hatch slid open. Stone's eyes skimmed the instruments. It was night over this part of Eos. City lights glared out of the velvet dark; the ambient temperature was 43°C, with a hard wind driving off the iron oxide desert.

Eos was not a pleasant place. File material stated that dangerous industries were quarantined here, where a radiation spill or a chemical explosion could be contained without the population of Avalon being at risk. The pay was triple-time, and still nobody wanted to work on Eos.

Stone was not surprised. 'Where is he, Kevin?'

'Docked on the east side,' Jarrat told him. 'Tried to launch five minutes ago but Control are stalling him. You're coming up on the bay. We'll drop you in the nearest alley, but you're not going to have much surprise. Spinners and sirens are on, you've got civvies making tracks in all directions. He's in Bay 16. We're on approach now.'

The range counter read 01/00, and Stone looked down through the hatch to see the vast, floodlit concrete basin in which sat Neil Buchanan's ship. It was an industrial cargo hauler, heavy, not fast, but it would batter its way through the asteroid rubble filling this system where a faster, more sophisticated ship would be smashed. The hull was steel blue, unmarked; obese engine modules thickened the stern and the cockpit was in an impact-shielded capsule on the nose.

The concrete walls were stained black by the exhaust of countless ships. Buchanan's engines shimmered with heat. He was idling, awaiting clearance. And by now he must know he had company. Would he run? The gunship loomed over the bay, making launch impossible.

'Jump!' Cronin's voice cracked like a whip in Stone's ears.

Around him the eight Blue Ravens stepped out into the air, and Stone jumped with them. The repulsion buoyed him up, he went down like a feather in the wind and landed lightly. His heart quickened as he swivelled his helmet. Below was the alley between Bays 16 and 17, where the rimrunners set down. The dim sky was filled by Zeus. A few stars shone through what seemed to be an overcast but which Stone knew was a pall of red dust. Rain never fell on Eos.

The Ravens turned up their floods and the alley blazed with

harsh white light. Stone cast a glance at the gunship, which hovered low over the launch bay, effectively blocking Buchanan from that route of escape. 'What you got, Kevin?'

'He's still aboard, sending coded signals,' Jarrat reported. 'He knows he's in trouble.'

The blast-armoured doors which closed off the bay in the event of fire or explosion were twenty metres ahead. Cronin and Ramos were already flanking them. The doors were sealed, which was routine when a ship was about to launch. As Stone joined them Cronin accessed the control panel and delicately punched keys with one steel finger.

Nine rotary cannons swung up to cover the bay as the shield doors slid open to left and right. The concrete bowl was murky with airborne sand, kicked up by the stinking, roaring exhaust, which lifted the air temperature to 200°C. A red light winked in Stone's helmet, recording the temperature on the skin of the armour, but the cooling system compensated automatically.

Cronin had taken a step into the bay when Jarrat's voice sliced over the comm loop like a knife. 'Watch it! He's moving! Cargo hatch opening in the starboard flank!'

Even from this distance, Stone felt the jolt of Jarrat's tension. A knot ravelled in his belly and he fell back against the wall. From their vantage point the observers on the gunship had glimpsed the hatch seconds before the ground troops, but Stone saw the dark shape plunging down the loading ramp in the same instant Jarrat saw it.

'It's a demolition tractor,' Cronin barked. 'Jesus! Get out of here!'

The industrial machine was designed to tear mountainsides apart with a geocannon. The gaping muzzle came about as the gunner rotated the barrel, keyed on the helmet lights. In the instant before it fired Stone dove into the sand which had drifted against the wall.

The demolition shell was impact detonated, heavy ordnance. The whole entrance to the launch bay erupted with a chemical fireball of muzzle flash and explosives. If Stone had not already been down the concussion would have flung him off his feet, riot armour and all. Helmet audio struggled to blanket the hundred-decibel blast and his instrument lights blinked. Masonry pelted the armour and he found himself on his side. He was blanketed by rubble, heart pounding, breath caught in his throat.

'Stoney! Raven Leader to Raven 7.1!' Jarrat's voice rose over the confusion of signals. 'Stoney!'

'I'm okay. It's a tractor —'

'With a geocannon, I saw,' Kevin snarled. 'Gil, get them out of there. You're not going to dent that. Give me some manoeuvring space and I'll immobilise it. *Move!*'

'Moving,' Cronin bawled. 'Cap Stone! Stoney! Where the fuck are you?'

At that moment Stone was digging. He had keyed his apparent mass up high to gain leverage, and had thrown the shattered slabs of ferroconcrete off his legs. Steel spars thrust out of the ripped sections like lances. He grasped them in both fists, wrenched, and all at once he was out.

'Go!' he barked at Cronin. 'Get them out of here!'

Out of the corner of his eye he saw the squat barrel tracking again, coming around for another shot. A pulse hammered in his head as he keyed the repulsion high. He shed apparent mass fast, bounced to feet and dove furiously after Cronin and Ramos.

The muzzle flash enveloped him in incandescent gases, the concussion picked him up and tossed him into the alley like a broken toy. Stone landed hard in a tangle of armoured limbs with Ramos and Blue Raven 17. The shell tore twenty metres out of the wall of the launch bay, flung masonry and steel bars high into the air.

Stone rolled, scrambled to his feet and shook his head clear. 'Kevin! Kevin!'

'I'm doing it!' Jarrat shouted. 'Get your ass out of the way, damn it!'

Bolts of argon laser light stitched down from the weapons pods in the belly of the gunship. They were paired, port and starboard, in five sections between bow and stern. The forward guns were biased to defend the flight deck, those amidships protected the jump bay and the tail guns defended the reactors, the power plant which was the most vulnerable part of the gunship.

And Buchanan must have known that. Stone's mouth dried as he watched the squat barrel begin to elevate. 'Jesus Christ. Kevin! Kevin!'

This time Jarrat did not answer — there was not a tenth of a second to even think of speaking. Stone dove, lay on his back, eyes wide, consumed by icy, numbing horror as he watched the barrel track up and around. How much elevation could Buchanan get? The hull hovering over the bay was so long, 75° would be more than enough.

If he put a shell into the engine deck, even if he did not rupture the reactor housing he might hit the coolant tanks or the waste sump. At the very least, the danger of a radiotoxic spill was very real, and imminent. The gunship would pull out fast, its crew would evacuate by pod and the computer pilot would throw the ship into space on a ballistic trajectory, in a desperate bid to safeguard the city beneath. At worst, the blast that was coming would light up the sky for a hundred miles. He could be loading with a geodetic nuclear shell. The gunship could be vaporised, and everything around it, in a nanosecond. Vengeance and suicide in one.

These thoughts rushed through Stone's mind like a hot wind as the barrel tracked upward. Along the belly of the gunship ten laser cannons pulsed great gouts of blinding energy into the tractor. Every part of Stone's mind and body keyed on Jarrat. Kevin was sweating, spine stiff, muscles aching: those belly cannons were on remote, controlled from the flight deck. The guncrews had not been stood to — this should have been an arrest, not a battle.

The argon laser eruptions continued without pause as the barrel swung up toward maximum elevation. Was Kevin targeting on the traverse, the motors, hoping to stop it manoeuvring? Stone was not breathing as the barrel rose through 70°.

Then the world seemed to explode around him, and for an elastic, elongated second he was sure Buchanan had ruptured the reactor housing and the gunship was going up.

But that could not be right. If the reactors had blown the concussion would have been over in a single, blinding flash. Yet the eruption went on, blast after blast, like being caught in the heart of a thunderstorm. Stone's suit electronics overloaded, instruments went out and his helmet darkened. He was blind, deaf, gasping on the little air between nose and visor as he rolled over and over in the rubble, and the skin temperature soared above 400°.

Repulsion was out, he was pinned under the full weight of the armour, it was like being chained to the ground. With the power out he was not transmitting telemetry. The receiving computers would report that Raven 7.1 was destroyed. Jarrat knew better. Stone could feel him even now: a flashfire of dread, then an icy wave of relief as the natural empathy continued while technology failed.

He had tumbled to rest in the angle of a wall, wedged there. He felt the onset of asphyxia, and only the automatic reflexes of exhaustive training made him unscrew the left umbilicus. The outside air burned his sinuses with heat and chemicals but at least he could breathe. He wiped a glove over his visor and peered up.

The gunship was still there, a ghostly shape glimpsed through a pall of dust and smoke. Stone coughed, reached around with one leaden arm and tried the cable junctions just beneath the powerpack. One was loose, ripped half out of the socket. He rocked it back in tight and wheezed in relief as instruments, air, cooling and repulsion went back on line.

The comm system came alive in the same instant, and he heard Kevin's voice. 'Gil! Gil, for Christ's sake!' A pause, and then in a calmer tone he called, 'Come on, Stoney, I know you're alive. I can feel you. You're bruised but you're breathing. You've got power back on. You're not burned. Stoney!'

'Here.' Stone screwed in the air umbilicus and dragged a cool, clean breath to the bottom of his lungs. His repulsion was high and he clambered shakily to his feet. 'I'm all right, Kevin.'

'I know you are,' Kevin said shortly. 'But I'm not getting an answer from Gil. Do you see him? He's not transmitting anything.'

'Blue Raven 6?' Stone turned around on the spot and for the first time, as the smoke began to clear, got a glimpse of the tractor. 'Jesus, what happened to that?'

The machine had been peeled open like a can. The barrel was gone, it was canted on its side with the treads ripped and scattered. Stone tore his eyes away from it.

'Blue Raven 7. Ramos! Joe! Where are you?'

'Here, Cap,' Ramos called from fifty metres down the alley. 'We've got two dead. Gil's knocked out cold, but I think he's okay. I'm getting biosigns. His transmitters are busted, so he's not sending.'

Stone huffed a sigh and relax. 'You got that, Raven Leader?' he asked breathlessly as he followed Ramos' voice along the rubble-strewn alley.

Ramos was on one knee beside Cronin's tumbled figure, peering at the biosystems panel, located on the right shoulder of the armour. A medic must sometimes read most vital signs without being able to open the armour to a toxic battlefield environment. As Stone approached Ramos looked up and waved.

'I heard.' Jarrat paused. 'You've got fire control and Tactical coming your way. Reading your breathing mix now... I think you ought to be able to crack the helmet.'

'If you stretch a point.' Stone screwed out his umbilici, lifted off the helmet and groaned in the hot, smoky, dusty night air. His hair was plastered down with sweat. He drew one filthy gauntlet over his face and settled the headset more firmly as he saw the approaching spinners of two fliers. 'Okay, Kevin. What the hell did you do? I thought the gunship had gone up!'

'We were close,' Jarrat admitted quietly. 'Too damned close. Couldn't pull this bucket out fast enough to stop him taking a shot. As the barrel tracked up, the first target he was going to pick up was the engine deck. I acquired on his muzzle, put about a dozen shots down the barrel, best I could do at short notice.' He hesitated, and Stone felt the squeeze of his heart as if they were one body. 'You weren't far enough away. I... took a risk.'

'And it worked, Kevin,' Stone said in the same quiet tone. 'That's the way this game is played.'

'Yeah.' Jarrat heaved a breath, audible over the loop. 'Buchanan made his shot but the barrel was distorted. It split, blew back through the breach and detonated the magazine. The whole lot cooked off. We estimate eight or ten shells. Nothing nuclear, thank God. The cabin section is sound — these tractors are built to take it. We'll have to cut it open. I'll send you a couple of engineers.'

Two skimmers had bellied up out of the night as they spoke. One rumbled on to douse the gutted launch bay in fire retardant, the other set down in the gloom at the end of the alley. Stone tucked his helmet under his arm and walked out to meet it. He read the Tactical decals on the side as the pilot stepped down.

Beyond it, city lights were hazed by dust and smoke. A few faces appeared through the pall but no one dared come closer than the warehouses on the other side of the street.

The Tactical pilot was a bemused man, twenty years Stone's elder. He had pulled on a crew cap and watched the battered NARC troops assemble at the mouth of the launch bay's access alley. The flak jacket he wore seemed ludicrously inadequate. His ID code read 79296/Grumman.

He had an accent Stone almost recognised, something close to home, certainly from Earth. 'You wouldn't like to tell me what's going on here?' Grumman peered at Stone's breastplate, where his name and rank were stencilled. 'I can't read that for slime. Who the hell are you?'

'Stone. Captain.' Stone looked up at the gunship. 'You've got a mess in Bay 16. In fact, you haven't got much of a bay left. It was a NARC operation, Lieutenant. Unavoidable damage.'

Grumman's mouth flopped open. 'That's all you're going to tell me?'

'We're still trying to make an arrest,' Stone elaborated unhelpfully. 'An industrial pilot, Neil Buchanan. Check with Flight Control.'

'I did,' Grumman growled. 'They've been dancing to your tune for the last half hour. You got your man?'

'I don't know yet.' Stone turned and peered back into the smoke-gouting alley. 'Raven Leader, are those engineers down?'

In his right ear, Jarrat sounded fatigued by relief. 'They've got the fire doused. Going to cut him out of the cabin with a couple of laser torches. Come back up any time you like, Stoney. It's over.'

'Copy that,' Stone responded with genuine gratitude. He gave Grumman a nod and lifted his helmet. 'I'm being recalled to the gunship,' he lied smoothly. 'Any queries, Lieutenant, call the carrier. The details are classified.'

'But —' Grumman began.

Stone was already stalking into the pall of smoke, eyes on the ship, searching out the red spinners which marked the jump bay. Ramos and two Ravens had slung Gil Cronin's armour between them. He was still out cold. Repulsion neutralised all but a fraction of his mass as they manoeuvred him directly under the hatch.

They keyed the repulsion higher yet, and Stone watched as they feathered up toward the ship. He hung back to peer into the launch bay. Fire-retardant foam and spilled fuel formed a stinking, greasy lake between Buchanan's ship and the few surviving concrete walls.

A squad of engineers in environment suits stood on the side of the half-overturned tractor, and two cutting torches ignited. They would take minutes, perhaps a quarter of an hour, to slice into the impact-shielded cabin. Buchanan could still be alive.

If Stone told the truth, he did not care if the man was alive or dead. The mass destruction Buchanan had attempted to create made the senses reel. If he was alive, in this system he would not remain alive for long. Under Avalon law, what he had done would earn him capital punishment, and not all the influence of Equinox Industries' legal department would save him.

With a last glance at the engineers as the torches began to cut, Stone hit the repulsion and rose like a feather toward the gunship's open jump bay.

Chapter Seven

A scanner whirred over Stone's back, but the exam was cursory and the medic sergeant released him from the gunship's infirmary at once. Stone had not inhaled enough of the chemical fallout from the blast to be dangerous. In worse shape was Gil Cronin, who was still groggy, nursing severe concussion, when the engineers signalled that they were through into the cabin of the demolition tractor.

Jarrat sat on the edge of a diagnostic bed in the corner of the infirmary, watching Stone without a comment as he listened to the talkback from the flight deck. Stone stretched, straightened his shirt and pulled his hands through his hair. He turned toward his partner with a rueful expression.

'Got a report to file,' Jarrat said quietly. 'Intelligence will want a personal report from us, extra to the standard telemetry.' He touched the earpiece as the information he had been waiting for came up. 'Hold on, Stoney... go ahead, Lieutenant, I'm listening.'

It was Ed Suzuki, an ex-Army engineer with seven years' service in NARC carriers. 'We're into the cabin, Cap. The medic says he's alive, but he's rough.'

'Can you move him?' Jarrat frowned at Stone.

'Doubtful. We can try. But I don't think he's going to make it through two hours' flight back to Avalon.'

'Get him up here, we'll put him in cryogen.' Jarrat stepped aside and motioned Stone out of the infirmary.

'He's busted up?' Stone guessed. 'He almost took us, Kevin. We walked right into that.'

They ambled aft, to the Blue Ravens' ready room and the jump bay. Jarrat stepped into the darkened bay and knelt by the hatch to watch as engineers and medics strapped Neil Buchanan into a frame to immobilise his whole spinal column. They attached a repulsion unit and lifted him out of the tractor.

They came up fast, and Jarrat swore beneath his breath as Buchanan was carried by. Blood streamed from both his ears.

His brain must be badly damaged. Without comment, Jarrat and Stone followed the medics to the infirmary and watched as Buchanan was placed into a cryogen tank.

His life processes would be indefinitely suspended, he would at least live until Surgeon Captain Kip Reardon could work on him. Beyond that, there were no guarantees. Jarrat could find no compassion. Blue Raven 4 and Blue Raven 22 were under sheets in the corner of the infirmary, and if Buchanan had made his shot half of Eos could have been irradiated.

The gunship was already pulling out as Stone eased into the padding of a chair in the ready room. Jarrat punched for coffee and paced between the briefing table and the bank of live screens. Anger was like a fist under his heart.

It was always easier to be part of the action. Exertion purged a man of adrenalin. Playing the part of observer was equally as important to the assignment, but at the end of it Jarrat always found himself overstressed.

'Kevin.' Stone's voice was quiet, chiding. 'Why don't you hit something? Then sit down and write that report.'

Jarrat halted, took a draught of scalding coffee and turned to face Stone. 'The whole squad came this close. The risk I took —'

'Was necessary.' Stone leaned forward, elbows on his knees. 'If you hadn't done that, we'd have lost the gunship.' He forced the ghost of a smile to his lips. 'Next time we'll move faster.'

'Next time?' Jarrat drained the cup and turned his back on Stone. Several of the Blue Ravens were watching. Joe Ramos took a battered deck of cards from his pocket and shuffled them from hand to hand. Jarrat drew both palms over his face and, with a sigh, pulled a chair up to the nearest keyboard. 'We can have this logged by the time we reach the carrier.'

The report was brusque. The psyche evaluators would not miss the curt wording. They would read his tension and anger in every line — and they would expect to see those reactions. The situation had escalated from standard pickup to full-scale battle without a second's warning. And they had been lucky. Depending on luck to bail you out was, Jarrat thought as he signed and closed the file, a recipe for suicide.

Ten kilometres from the carrier, the gunship hove to and the spaceplane dropped out of the aft hangar. The main infirmary was already standing by, waiting for Buchanan. The telemetry package was even then on its way to Dupre's office on Darwin's World. Jarrat shunted forward his throttles and nosed out into space. He looped around, under the gunship, and tucked back into the carrier's own shuttle bay.

In Elysium it was early evening. On Randolph Dorne's Skycity the 'entertainments' would just be gearing up for the night. According to Petrov, the house party had started four years ago and had yet to slow down. Jarrat drummed his fingers on the control panel as he watched the hangar pressure and temperature gauges. A familiar feeling kindled in the pit of his stomach and intensified as he lifted the canopy and climbed down.

Stone was introverted, pensive. His face was still streaked with grime, his hair mussed and sweated. Jarrat caught the sharp tang of his sweat as they fell into step, toward the service lifts. Fear made a man sweat, and Stone had felt plenty of that. Perhaps only Jarrat knew how much.

'You're playing a hunch,' Stone observed as they rode the lift up.

'Randolph Dorne,' Jarrat said caustically. 'In two years of trying, Vic Duggan hasn't found a shred of hard evidence to indict the man.'

'But you're going to nail him,' Stone said in the same acid tone.

'To a wall,' Jarrat finished as the car stopped. They stepped out. 'Shower and gladrags, mate, in that order.' He twitched his brows at Stone. 'We seem to be invited to the party.'

A pace ahead of him, Stone pulled his shirt over his head as he stepped into the cabin. His nose wrinkled on his own sweat and he leaned into the shower stall to hit the taps. 'Like to wash my back, soldier?'

The offer was too good to refuse. Jarrat groaned pleasurably as the jets of scalding water pummelled his skin, but deep relaxation was elusive. He soaped his hands and his fingers dug into Stone's tense back muscles as Stone turned his face to the stream.

'Dorne'll have a hard time talking his way out,' Stone mused. 'We've probably broken their radio code by now.' He turned, set his shoulders against the tiles and rested both hands on Jarrat's slim hips. 'Will you cool down!' Kevin's tension was snapping like a whip, goading Stone's own body to stress.

'Can't.' Jarrat turned his face away. 'I almost bloody killed you back there. You think I'm going to forget that in a hurry?' Wet and slippery, he slithered out of Stone's hands.

'I shouldn't think you'll forget it as long as you live.' Stone let him go, soaped his hair briefly and let the torrent sluice away the suds.

Standing in the middle of the cabin, skin and hair streaming, hands on hips, eyes downcast, Jarrat fought with his feelings. Duty and necessity were in head-on collision with his personal loyalties... the very predicament the NARC psyche evaluators warned against, time and again.

Don't get involved, never get involved. Fuck till you're incapable but never, never blunder into the trap of emotional involvement, it'll kill you every time!

How often had he heard those words from his instructing officers in the early months of his enlistment? They were right. On the one hand was a billion-credit operation, on the other, two men whose feelings were so entwined that passion and personal loyalty overrode reason.

Except that Jarrat had not let it happen. Even in the heat of battle he had done what he must. It was only now, reliving the event in memory, that he realised how close to the edge they had been.

Pain flicked through him, savage as a physical beating. It hurt Stone too and rebounded to assault Jarrat a second time. He struggled with the empathic shields, could not quite manage to raise them, and seemed to be a lightyear away as Stone turned off the water and reached for a towel.

'Kevin.' Wet skin glided on warm, wet skin as arms slid about Jarrat from behind. Stone nuzzled his neck. 'Honey, stop it. There was nothing else you could do. We all had one chance to live and two to die. We got lucky. Next time we'll be more careful.'

'Next time?' Jarrat's voice was hoarse as he leaned back heavily into Stone's bigger, broader and stronger body. Stone's hands splayed over his breast and belly but he felt no spark of desire.

'It's going to happen again,' Stone said softly against his ear. 'Like I said, this is the way the game is played. We told Dupre we could handle it. If you want out, say so and we'll resign.'

'I don't know what I want,' Jarrat admitted as he turned into

Stone's arms and plastered himself against the muscular body he loved.

'Yes you do.' Stone nipped his shoulder with sharp teeth, branding him there as his palms cupped Kevin's buttocks and kneaded. 'You want to nail Randolph Dorne to the wall. After that, we'll take another look at this whole mess.'

'Mess?' Jarrat drew back, both palms spread over Stone's chest. 'We're doing the work we do best, the job we trained for years to do. We begged for the right to get back here.'

Stone's hands dealt his lover's buttocks two simultaneous, stinging slaps. 'Then jettison this gloom and get dressed. We're going to a party.' He kissed Jarrat's mouth briefly but deeply, swept the towel off his own shoulders and draped it about Kevin's neck. 'Petrov told me, a million credits wouldn't buy a ticket to Dorne's 'entertainments', yet here we are with an invitation, and you're blue.'

'Not blue.' Jarrat began to rub his hair. 'Let's say I'm having second thoughts.' He gave Stone an unconvincing glare. 'That's the first time your neck has been on the chopping block since... I didn't like it, Stoney.'

'I'd be worried if you did.' Stone stooped and kissed the curve of his back with a warm, wet tongue.

At last Jarrat responded with a deep sigh, a cat-like purr. He lifted his foot onto a chair, patted his calf, but his eyes followed Stone into the next cabin, where Stone opened a closet and rummaged for clothes.

He chose the black slacks and white shirt, body-hugging, seductive. Boots. Platinum chains for his neck and both wrists. Stone dressed swiftly, combed his hair while it was still damp and surveyed himself in the long mirror.

For himself, Jarrat chose tight white denim, a loose, filmy shirt the colour of spice and the bracelet and emerald ring Stone had bought for him weeks before in Chell, before they shipped out of Kithan. They had joked about the ring, and about formally handfasting, which in some cultures was symbolised by an exchange of rings. Jarrat had been the first to laugh. Tonight, he studied the emerald with a frown as he slipped it onto his left hand.

His misgivings were still strong but he had his thoughts under control now and the empathic shields were up. Stone got only vague fragments of his feelings.

Strong hands fell on Jarrat's back as he regarded the ring, and stroked him through the thin saffron fabric. Almost reluctantly he relaxed.

'I'm all right,' he said, and meant it as he turned into Stone's embrace. 'You just wait till it's me, groundside, and you up here with your finger on the button.'

Stone winced. 'I'll worry when the time comes.' He held Jarrat at arm's length to genuinely admire him. 'You look good enough to eat.'

With a glance at his chrono, Jarrat snorted. 'Let me shave, and that might be halfway accurate.'

'Don't shave on my account,' Stone chuckled. 'Two day's worth of beard seems to be the height of fashion in Elysium right now. I can't say I mind it myself.'

But Jarrat was unimpressed. 'Where I come from, you wouldn't even get into a city bottom dance shop with a face like a broom.'

'Sheckley.' Stone leaned on the back of a chair to watch as Kevin smoothed his jaw. 'That's where you're from?'

'Till I was seventeen.' Jarrat paused as memories he had half forgotten assailed him. 'It's only a staging base between the rim and the deep sky. Makes its revenue out of servicing and fuelling the rimrunners. It was rotten with Angel by the time I was twelve or thirteen. I might have been lucky to escape.' Satisfied with his face, he tossed the still buzzing razor to Stone.

'Lucky?' Stone echoed as he tackled his own dark, stubborn beard. 'You had no home, no family. I wouldn't call that lucky.'

'I did okay,' Jarrat said guardedly. 'The hospice was safe, I forced down what education I needed and bounced straight into the Army. What else was I going to do, Stoney? Bum around the docks, looking for a sugar daddy, run with the dope pack and end up with a nose full of Angel by the time I was nineteen?' He closed his eyes. 'The day I was nineteen, I was on a troop transport, headed for Kelso Prime.'

They were silent for some moments before Stone threw down the razor and cocked his head curiously at Jarrat. 'Pain, Kevin?'

'Not really. It was rough but I did all right.' His eyes glittered with self-mocking humour. 'I found a sugar daddy after all. An Airlift colonel with very nice bedside manners and a taste for lightly battered chicken in service greens.'

'Lightly battered chicken? Sounds,' Stone said generously, with a salacious lick of his lips, 'delicious.' He looked Jarrat over from head to foot and back. 'You must have been a knockout at that age.'

Jarrat returned the lecherous scrutiny. 'I like to think I matured well.'

'Like fine wine.' Stone's arms opened invitingly.

Jarrat went to him but his mind was on the time. His teeth closed none too gently on Stone's lobe. He snatched a swift kiss and fended him off. His thumb hit the comm, voice-only, as Stoney drew a gold-banded chrono onto his wrist. 'Ops Room. Petrov?' The Russian responded at once. 'Any joy with the decodes?'

'We're getting nowhere,' Petrov said disgustedly. 'Their scrambler code is like nothing Intelligence has ever seen. The computers are running, trying to find the root, but it's more like an arbitrary substitution code than any kind of exchange cipher.'

'Which is to say,' Jarrat mused, 'you unscramble the transmissions into words, and the words read as gibberish.'

'Right first time.' Petrov sounded exasperated. 'If we had maybe ten times as much material to work with we'd get it, but the maximum duration of both transmissions combined was about fifty seconds. Imagine trying to convert Russian to Japanese, using a dictionary with ninety percent text erasure.'

Jarrat met Stone's eyes, brows arched. 'Stay with it, Mischa. Even a partial decode would help. And maybe we can manoeuvre Dorne into another transmission.'

'Sure,' Petrov agreed. 'The more we have, the easier it gets. I'll let you know if we come up with anything.'

'Thanks.' Jarrat thumbed the comm again. 'Infirmary.'

He waited almost a minute for a response, and Surgeon Captain Kip Reardon sounded irritable. 'If it's Gilly Cronin you're asking after, I gave him a pill and sent him back to his own bunk. If it's Buchanan — what in Christ's name did you do to the man?'

'He did it to himself, Kip,' Jarrat said flatly. 'Tried to blow a gunship out of the air over Eos. What are his chances?'

'Pure shit,' Reardon told him without hesitation. 'His brain turned to jelly in the shockwave. He's comatose. I'll do what I can for him in the morning. I've drained the edema and got the blood out of his brain, but I don't think even that magician of yours, Harry Del could fix this one. Was Buchanan important?'

'We're fairly sure he was an Angel smuggler.' Jarrat watched his lover patting on a palmful of aftershave. 'Do what you can, Kip. We're not asking for miracles... we already had one tonight.'

Reardon snorted. 'You mean, the gunship that came home in one piece? I had a medic's report on Stoney. He got half a lungful of something toxic, but it seems he'll live.'

'He's... fine,' Jarrat agreed as his eyes roved lazily over Stone's body. Stone poised, hips canted provocatively, and Jarrat bit back a chuckle. 'I'll talk to you later, Kip.'

They were on the shuttle deck minutes later. Engineer Budweisser was methodically examining the keel plates of the Blue Raven gunship, taking hull integrity readings after its proximity to the immense detonation. Jarrat returned the veteran's wave as he passed by toward the waiting shuttle. He clicked his chrono over to Elysium time and saw 19:40.

A military axiom swore that punctuality was a virtue. It was a cardinal sin to be late for a firing squad. Jarrat gave the maxim a thought as he settled into the forward cockpit, fired the lifters and plugged into the loop.

'Hangar Control, clear the bay. We are ready to launch.'

Sirens whooped, technicians scurried to safepoints and the crescent face of Avalon glared up through the open hatch. Jarrat eased his throttles forward a fraction and put the nose down.

Elysium Air Traffic picked them up as they bucked into the upper atmosphere. Sensors informed Jarrat that he was being scanned, and he hailed Control with a terse message. 'NARC Airborne to Elysium ATC. We are en route to Skycity and do not requite landing or navigation services.'

In the rear cockpit, Stone was already tracking what Cronin referred to as Dorne's 'mansion in the air', and he whistled softly. 'There it is. Come right, 118°. It's floating on repulsion at ten thousand.'

The size of a football stadium, shaped like a discus, Skycity was a domed platform riding on immense repulsion motors. At four points about the thick wedge of the disk were the manoeuvring thrusters, station-keeping engines which held the platform more or less over the same patch of ground. Below,

Elysium was lost in a haze of industrial smog, dim with evening shadows, but at this altitude Skycity was still in sunlight as the shuttle approached.

An acquisition beam activated, and Jarrat cut back to a hover. 'Skycity Control, this is NARC Airborne. Captain Jarrat and Captain Stone to see Mr Dorne.'

They were expected. A woman's voice answered, smooth as velvet. 'Please follow your guidance beam to the landing area, Captain. Space has been reserved for you. Please enjoy your stay on Skycity.'

'Courteous,' Stone observed.

'Prudent,' Jarrat amended as he jinked the nose about to follow the beam. 'There it is... looks like a hangar.'

A small landing bay opened to the sky and running lights marked out the interior taxiway. Jarrat nudged inside at minimal speed, landed lightly and shut down his systems. The hangar was floodlit, grey decked, lined with equipment, test benches, fuelling ports. Behind them, the armoured doors sealed; before them a transparent pressure lock led into the domed platform itself. Beyond the transparency they saw trees, lanterns, a fountain. Jarrat's finger was on the canopy release when he hesitated, and Stone was all too aware of the crawling sensation in his gut.

'What is it, Kev?'

'Call it intuition.' Jarrat reached down between his feet, lifted out a deck hatch, and from the compartment beneath selected a palm gun. The tiny Cooper .30 calibre was not powerful, but it was easy to conceal, mostly plastic and so difficult to detect, and effective enough over very short range. 'I feel a tiny bit exposed,' Jarrat said ruefully as he checked the ten-round clip and slipped the weapon into his right pocket. 'Arm yourself. I don't believe in taking chances.'

The R/T was equally discreet. Jarrat handled it almost nostalgically. A gold cigarette lighter which, at the touch of knowing fingers, converted into a powerful transceiver. The short aerial extended, he selected a restricted NARC band and brought it to his lips.

'9.4 to carrier.'

Even if Dorne's radio crew were monitoring, they should not be able to eavesdrop on the NARC frequency. Petrov's voice whispered from the device. 'Carrier. Trouble, Cap?'

'Testing voice contact,' Jarrat corrected. 'I'm going to leave this channel open, Mischa. Stay with us.'

The Russian skipped a beat and then came back stridently. 'I'll put Red Raven on standby. If you think you're walking into some kind of trap, Dorne'll find himself rubbing shoulders with riot troops faster than he knows how to shit.'

'Do that.' Jarrat slipped the tiny R/T into his shirt pocket and cracked the canopy.

Service technicians in blue uniform coveralls hovered, but they stood back from the aircraft. Stone took a few paces, secured the canopy with the infrabeam and pocketed the key. He gave the technicians a dispassionate nod and led the way to the pressure lock.

A rush of equalising air, a slight pop of the ears, and it closed behind them. Vast cycling machines produced a gentle breeze, oriental lanterns nodded among the frangipani and jacaranda. The air smelt sweet as dreamsmoke. Beyond the dome, the sky was crimson and gold; in the east the first stars had appeared. Arching overhead, the dome itself was invisible.

Lawns stretched away toward the mansion, bisected by a white broadwalk. To left and right as they headed for the house were fountains, statues, forms plucked from centuries long past. A martial woman driving a team of chariot horses; a massive, ponderous Hercules in marble; a slender, virile Poseidon in bronze.

Guests cavorted across the lawns and Jarrat turned as he heard the splash of water. Beyond the frangipanis was a pool, floodlit from the bottom and filled with bubbles from hundreds of oxygen hoses which made the water seem to effervesce. Lovers cavorted there also, in twos, threes and groups. Some looked stoned. Only the blond boys, fucking enthusiastically in the near corner, seemed to know what they were doing.

The whine of electric motors announced company, and Stone's hand on Jarrat's arm held him back. A girl drove toward them in a buggy, cutting across the lawn on a light repulsion field. She wore Dorne's uniform blue, a sheer fabric bodyskin stretched about narrow hips, long legs and weighty breasts. Black hair, streaked with scarlet, tossed in the artificial breeze as she smiled.

'Captain Jarrat, Captain Stone. I'll take you to Mr Dorne directly. He is expecting you. Will you dine with him?'

'This is not a social visit.' Jarrat mounted the buggy, slid onto the rear bench and looked sidelong at Stone. The moment Stone was aboard, the girl swung back toward the house.

The mock-Roman architecture was impressive in any century. If Jarrat had thought of Hal Mavvik's mansion above Chell as a palace, he knew he had overestimated it. In none of his travels had he seen anything to rival Dorne's citadel in the clouds, and he clearly felt Stone's amazement.

'My God,' Stone murmured. 'Dorne put all this together?'

Their driver glanced back. 'Magnificent, isn't it? Do you know, the artworks are genuine. Mr Dorne is a collector. Every piece on Skycity is unique and original.'

'Magnificent' might not have been the right word, Jarrat thought ironically, on a planet that was smashed by industry and rancid with Angel. He regarded the frolicking guests with cynicism. How many were users? How many were high tonight, and would not live out the year?

Most of the revellers were visitors, but some were professionals, and it was easy to pick them — the young men, almost too physically perfect to be real, who pretended to be amused and attracted by corpulent men three times their age. Jarrat lifted a brow at Stone as the buggy came to a halt before a portico fluted with marble columns.

Their driver left them with a smile as a tall, ebony-skinned woman stepped out of the house. Her hair could never have been cut in her life. It hung to her knees, veiled her body. It was all she wore, save a great deal of yellow-gold jewellery and cosmetics. Her fingernails were scarlet talons.

'I am Natasha.' The voice was rich and deep, the accent not unlike Dupre's. Green-lidded eyes flicked from Stone to Jarrat and back. 'I will take you to Mr Dorne.'

'You're his butler?' Stone asked flippantly.

Jarrat choked back any expression of humour and gave Stone a warning glance.

The woman was as tall as Jarrat, with long bones and small, high breasts. He wondered if she had been born female or had been modified. Either way, the effect was striking. Small, rouged nipples drew the eyes, then she was leading them into the house and he caught a glimpse of buttocks through the cloak of her hair.

The light was muted, the air rich with some kind of joss Jarrat had never smelt before. He waited for the buzz, but it did not seem to be narcotic.

Their guide took them along a gallery lined with art treasures, some of which even Jarrat recognised. Stone had spent his youth on Earth and knew many more. The Dying Gaul; Ramses II; David. No wall was bare of similar treasures which spanned centuries. Leonardo, Caravaggio, Fragonard.

At the end of the gallery was a flight of stairs. Without a word, Natasha climbed, turned right onto a long balcony and brought them to a walnut-panelled door. Her knuckles rapped, she inclined her head before the NARC men and was gone.

Servomotors swung open the door. Amber lamplight spilled from within, and Jarrat's nostrils flared as he smelt scents he did not recognise. The last lick of sunset bathed the room in scarlet, through windows overlooking the city. They were on the very edge of the platform. Clouds wisped by the pressurised glass. He gave the vista a long glance and turned his attention to Randolph Dorne.

The man sat in a red leather recliner beside a live fire which flickered in a hearth surrounded by Greek bas-reliefs. A balloon of brandy was cradled in one hand; one long leg was crossed over the other, and Dorne did not offer to rise. His file quoted his age as forty-six, Jarrat would have guessed thirty-five. His hair was dark blond and thick, his face unlined, angular, his features broad and lushly handsome. But the brown eyes were Dorne's most striking attribute. Jarrat felt their gaze almost arrest him in his tracks. Almost.

Dorne was dressed in burgundy slacks and tunic which hugged a slender body. He toyed with the brandy, swirled the priceless fluid in the bottom of the balloon. 'I presume you have an excellent reason for this intrusion, so I shall ask you to state it, come to the point swiftly and leave.' His voice was deep, the accent as inspecific as the offworld speech of habitual travellers like Jarrat. The words were brittle and sharp as broken glass.

'Very well.' Stone's eyes covered Dorne from head to foot, a deliberately rude scrutiny. 'Why don't you tell us about Neil Buchanan.'

The hesitation was a tenth of a second too long to be effectively concealed, though Dorne tried. He lifted the brandy to his nose and inhaled the Hennessy vapours. 'What do you want to know?'

At least he was not disavowing all acquaintance, but alarms clamoured in Jarrat's head. He had seen the momentary dilation of Dorne's eyes, an involuntary response to stress which not even a genius could control. 'You use him as a contract pilot?'

'Sometimes.' Dorne took a sip.

'Why?' Stone asked bluntly. 'Equinox runs a whole fleet.'

'Because it makes ridiculous sense to dispatch a ship twice the size of your carrier to deliver a small cargo.' Dorne studied Stone imperturbably. 'And although we run several small couriers, they are frequently engaged. Sometimes it is wise economy to subcontract.'

'What kind of cargoes does Buchanan carry for you?' Jarrat held Dorne's eyes, trying to read some expression. The man was good. His face was a mask.

'Anything from perishable medicines to heavy industrial machinery.' Dorne sniffed brandy vapours. 'None of this has the slightest to do with Narcotics And Riot Control.'

'No?' Stone smiled cynically. 'Buchanan got out of the Cygnus colonies just before NARC became involved there.'

'How interesting.' Dorne set the glass on the antique table at his elbow and folded his hands.

Annoyance stitched through Jarrat's insides. 'We intercepted your transmissions, Mr Dorne.'

'Which transmissions?' Dorne's fair brows rose. 'Many thousands are processed by my communications facilities here and in Equinox Towers every day.'

Jarrat took a step closer but it was Stone who said, 'The signals you sent to Eos. To Buchanan.' No flicker of expression crossed Dorne's face.

'They were decoded,' Jarrat lied fluently.

The statement produced a faint smile. 'That is a lie.'

'Is it?' Jarrat turned away, strode to the windows and leaned both palms on the cold glass. Below, Elysium was a blaze of lights, lines, loops and curves following clearways, road bridges, the river and the spaceport. 'Buchanan is critically injured. We have him in a cryogen tank aboard the carrier. He probably won't live.'

'Very sad. I heard your goon squad blew him up.' Dorne's tone was indifferent. 'We monitor the Tactical band, of course, in case we can provide assistance.'

'Of course.' Stone gritted his teeth as he felt the tension of Jarrat's spine, the acid ripple of his anger. 'You signalled Buchanan that NARC had taken overt interest in you at last. Your satellites tracked our gunship out of orbit and you gave Buchanan an early warning to get out.' It was a calculated risk, an educated guess.

Jarrat pivoted from the window. 'And like a good little boy, Buchanan tried to cut and run. Tell us why.'

Again, the hesitation before Dorne covered smoothly. 'An adroit ploy, gentlemen. Most imaginative, but in this case hardly warranted and quite ineffective. You are lying when you say you decoded my transmissions, which renders all else you say supposition, defamation and intimidation.' He reached for the brandy. 'Equinox codes are cyber governed, changed every seven seconds, randomly. Even my computers cannot decode my own signals without access to the Determinant, which establishes how and when the codes change.'

He smiled. 'The Determinant is not transmitted, but installed with the receiving hardware. To use one of our terminals, an operator places his left palm on a scanner and verbalises a nine-digit access code. The device is programmed to detect the voice patterns of drugging or stress. A gun in the operator's back, dope in his nose, or an electronic voice simulation backing up the use of his captive hand by force, and everything in a two-metre radius is reduced to cinders.' Dorne finished the brandy. 'It is impossible for our codes to be broken or stolen. Now, tell me why you are trying to dupe me with lies.'

The ruse was almost up, but a few moves remained. Stone played one of them. He lifted his chin and met Dorne's eyes levelly. 'We know exactly how your code system operates. The information cost us two million credits.'

Fair brows arched, creasing Dorne's forehead. 'Now, that is interesting. Enrique!'

A door clicked open along from the fireplace, and a slender young man appeared. He was brunet, smooth faced, with wide blue eyes and handsome features. Clad in a black kaftan which flowed about his limbs, he was a little flushed and tousled, as if he had just hurried out of bed. The effect would have been charming if Enrique had not answered Dorne's summons with such eagerness.

'Access the Neapolitan file.' Dorne tapped his fingertips

together and shifted his long legs. 'Quickly, Enrique. If these officers are telling the truth, Equinox security has been severely compromised.'

'At once, Mr Dorne.' Enrique gathered the kaftan about himself and stepped out again.

'The Neapolitan file,' Dorne said conversationally, 'is a summary of the profound psyche surveillance that is performed daily upon every operative who has access to the Determinant you claim to have purchased. If one of our people has gone rogue, I'll know who it is momentarily, and you can have him, on a silver platter, with my blessings.'

Stone felt Jarrat's flurry of annoyance, echoing his own anger. Dorne was too clever to be caught this way. The game would be up as soon as the secretary returned.

He was back in minutes, a little more combed and poised. 'Nothing, Mr Dorne. Our operatives are sound.'

'Then, there you have it.' Dorne looked up with a smile. 'Thank you, Enrique, I'll call if I need you again.' He paused as the young man stepped out, sat back in the chair and steepled his fingers on his middle. 'Now, why don't you tell me why you're lying to me?'

Eyes on the lights of Elysium, Jarrat considered their options. Dorne had the winning hand tonight; he was a company lawyer by profession, his mind a steel trap. Stone was mute, concealing a smouldering anger, as if he barely trusted himself to speak. He was still filled with raw, recent memories of the battle on Eos, while the man who had surely triggered the fracas was untouchable.

'All right, Mr Dorne.' Jarrat turned back from the window and thrust his hands into his pockets. 'We haven't broken your codes yet, it's true. But it doesn't take a genius to guess the content of the transmissions. Buchanan is fresh from Cygnus. We believe he was an Angel smuggler, proof is only a matter of time. We already have plenty of data connecting your company with the Angel trade —'

'Hard evidence?' Dorne's voice developed a razor edge.

Stone's mouth quirked, hardly a smile. 'Not yet. Like he said, proof is only a matter of time.'

'We'll get it,' Jarrat added evenly. 'Fair warning, Dorne. Equinox was short-listed when the Elysium file opened. If you're as innocent as you claim, and someone else within your company is responsible for smuggling Angel and military weapons, you'd be well advised to assist us. We'll finish the Angel trade, with or without you. And if it's without you — '

'You'll try to hang culpability on me.' Dorne stood and smoothed the burgundy tunic. He was not a tall man, slender and fine boned. 'Spare me the intimidatory rhetoric, Captain. I own majority shares of Equinox but I do not control every employee under our banner, nor am I responsible for whatever criminal activities they undertake when they leave the premises.' For the first time emotion was evident, and he glared at the younger men. 'Equinox Industries maintains a well-manned and faultlessly equipped private army, barracked within our Elysium facilities. After what you have informed me, I shall initiate my own investigations, and I can assure you of their thoroughness. If I have Angel or weapons smugglers on my staff, gentlemen, they will be rooted out like the disease they are.'

'And you'll be in touch as soon as you have something to tell us,' Stone finished.

'Naturally.' Dorne's eyes lit with anger.

'Then if you'd care to divulge the content of this morning's coded signals,' Jarrat said smoothly, 'we'd be pleased to leave.'

'Personal business,' Dorne said offhandly. 'Nothing important. My secretary had considerable difficulty finding me. A minor personnel crisis here on Skycity.'

'And for that, you used the company scrambler?' Stone sounded disbelieving.

Dorne lifted his chin. 'The encoder is installed as part of the hardware in my skyhopper, Captain Stone. It is an automatic and unavoidable part of any transmission I make from my aircraft.'

'And the message was not recorded, of course,' Jarrat said cynically.

'Why would I record trivia about spoiled fruit and an entertainer with a fractured arm?' Dorne demanded.

'And the signals between here and Eos?' Stone added, by now merely fascinated to hear what Dorne had contrived.

'Business,' the man said sharply. 'Buchanan was carrying a small but somewhat dangerous cargo. I wanted to know if it had been safely delivered.'

'The cargo?' Jarrat's brows rose. He could have guessed.

'A demolition tractor with a magazine preloaded with ten rounds.' Dorne clasped his hands behind his back. 'From what I hear, Buchanan seems to have used the machine to attack your gunship. A regrettable incident, but as I have already pointed out, I am not responsible for the lunatic actions of a chartered pilot. A dead pilot,' he added darkly. 'If Buchanan is dying, he will pay the ultimate price for his actions. The tractor was a legal shipment. I can show you the freight manifest.'

'I'm sure you can.' Jarrat stirred, pinned on a smile and withdrew to the door. 'You'll hear from us again.'

'Unless,' Dorne added with razor-edged blandness, 'you hear from me first. If you're right, and Equinox is being used as a front for the Angel trade, I shall cut the corruption out by the roots and hand the culprits to Narcotics And Riot Control to deal with as you see fit.' He gestured expressively with one long-fingered hand. 'I have always enjoyed the best relationship with Tactical and your department. I am a lawyer, as well you know.' He touched a key on the panel by his chair. The walnut door swung open on discreet servos. 'Now, why don't you enjoy my hospitality? A banquet, the finest entertainment, my art collection, music, or perhaps you would prefer a boudoir, a Companion and the drugs of your choice.' He smiled. 'Nothing illegal, naturally. Natasha will be your guide.'

The woman materialised as he spoke her name. Stone's gaze swept over her. 'I like your taste in butlers.'

A chuckle, and Dorne returned to his chair. 'Natasha is the mistress of this household. Anything you want, ask her.'

It was a dismissal. Jarrat stepped out, Stone a pace behind him. Before Dorne could key the door closed he turned back. 'You have a man on your staff. Kjell Wozniak. Head of Equinox Security. If you're as virtuous as you claim you'll appreciate a word of friendly advice. Get rid of him. The man is a contract shooter. Tactical would like to roast him on a spit for a whole list of top-level assassinations, every one of them linked with your company. When Tac busts Wozniak they'll use him to bust you. Goodnight.'

As the door closed, leaving Dorne once more mask-faced, Stone gave Jarrat a sidelong glance. 'Was that wise?'

'Why not?' Jarrat looked coolly at Natasha but spoke to Stone. 'It seems we misjudged Mr Dorne. It'd be too bad if Wozniak took him down. I expect the shooter will be off the payroll in the morning.' Only Stone knew the words were a feint. Kevin smiled thinly at the woman. 'You know Wozniak?'

Natasha's dark head tilted at them. 'I don't see him often. Elysium city bottom is his playground. Dance shops, sex shops. You want to know where to find him out of hours?'

'Rawhide?' Stone guessed.

'Maybe.' Natasha stood aside. 'And try Flex. What's your pleasure? Dinner, whisky and a string ensemble? The Companions have arrived. One or two are delicious.' As she spoke she led them back to the gallery, and paused by an open window, overlooking a courtyard. One scarlet taloned hand held aside the satin drapes. 'Take your pick. On the house.'

The courtyard was lit by antique carriage lamps; the balmy air was heady with dreamsmoke and roses. Four young men were lounging against a fountain in the shape of leaping dolphins, waiting for company. They were naked, save for fine gold chains about necks, waists, hips, bracelets, cockrings and nipple-rings. Jarrat heard Stone's quick intake of breath, felt the rush of his pulse and knew what he was thinking.

Once, he had confessed to this fantasy. In his Angel dream it was Kevin decked out for a night on the town in jewellery and sultry smiles. Jarrat hid just such a smile and admired the young Companions.

'They're beautiful,' he said courteously.

'Take the blond with the ruby tit-rings, he's the best,' Natasha advised. 'Or, you prefer women?' she studied them from beneath lowered lids. 'I wouldn't have thought so, but if you follow me I'll show you what we have.'

The offer was almost indifferent, as if the Companions were joints of meat. Stone cleared his throat. 'Not tonight. I think we've seen all we need to.'

'Then, I'll send for a buggy,' she began.

'We'll walk,' Stone decided. 'This place is incredible. I'd like to enjoy the sights.'

Natasha inclined her head. 'As you wish. May I suggest you walk by the olive groves? We have marbles and bronzes of Priapus which you may interest you.'

With that she stalked away. When she was out of earshot Jarrat slipped the R/T from his pocket. On the base was an indicator which would warn if they were under video or audio surveillance. It was quiet, and Jarrat addressed the mic. '9.4.

You got that, Petrov?'

'Right down to the bronzes of Priapus,' Petrov reported dutifully. 'Pissy little Roman kid with a dick like a moose on heat. Got the lot, Cap. He's smooth. You buy all that crap?'

'Not a word.' Jarrat leaned both elbows on the window ledge and inspected the Companions. The perfect, well-worked bodies, flawless skin, silken-cape hair and rich jewellery tugged hard at him. Lust flickered like live flame through his groin, and beside him Stone swore softly. Jarrat turned his back on the courtyard, gave Stone a look of reproach and lifted the R/T. 'Log the voice track for analysis and close down. You can stand down the Red Ravens, too. We're not in jeopardy here. Dorne wouldn't dare lay a finger on us.'

'You staying for the party, Cap?' Petrov asked acidly.

'No. 9.4 out.' Jarrat deactivated the R/T and slipped it away. 'What's the matter Stoney?' he asked when they were unmonitored, free to speak personally.

In answer, Stone nodded at the Companions. 'I'm looking at them and thinking of Lee, the kid you had in Mavvik's palace. You chose me. I'm... not much by comparison.'

'Idiot.' Jarrat laced his fingers at Stone's nape. 'I told you once before, I got what I wanted.' He searched for Stone's mouth, kissed him soundly. 'You want it in three short words?'

'Such as, "I love you?" I might.' Stone murmured, and opened his mouth for Kevin's tongue.

Jarrat took all he offered, repaid him with interest. Stone held him tightly, possessively, and then released him. Jarrat looked at him out of sultry eyes. 'You want to look at the Roman kid with the moose cock?'

'Sooner go home and...' Stone cast a glance at Jarrat's groin and licked his lips suggestively.

The flicker of desire was back, magnified, nurtured. Jarrat eased down the empathic shields to let lust reverberate between them. 'That,' he said drily, 'is the best offer I've had all night.'

Chapter Eight

'We're going to need a man on the inside.' In the darkened operations room the tip of Petrov's cigarette glowed brightly as he inhaled.

The same thought had been on Stone's mind for an hour. The ops room was shut down. The computers were still running, but after Dorne's claims for the impregnability of Equinox code structures, the effort seemed futile. The only way to break those codes was to be entrusted with the Determinant. The only way to know what was going on in the heart of Equinox was to be there.

The point of stalemate was reached early, in almost every assignment. This was where deep cover work began, where the training and experience of NARC field agents paid off. Stone was watching Jarrat's face in the light of the blue CRTs. Kevin was not happy about what they both knew was imminent. About as happy as Stone had been when Jarrat boarded an Orion clipper at Gateways for the last leg of the journey to Chell, with forged papers, bogus ID and the reputation of a king shooter which existed only in clever computer hack work.

It was past midnight and they had technically been off duty for hours. Spent coffee cups and the debris of a meal scattered the work surfaces. Petrov was crypto qualified, but he had drawn a complete blank with Dorne's transmissions. He could see the deep-cover assignment impending as surely as Jarrat and Stone.

'It may not be necessary,' Jarrat argued as Petrov swept the litter into the waste disposal. 'Duggan must locate Grenshem's informant soon. He's as keen to see Dorne nailed as we are, so he'll have half of Elysium Tac out looking for Spiteri as soon as they've buried their dead.'

'That was late this afternoon.' Petrov rubbed the back of his neck. 'It was vidcast. Long rank of caskets, Tac and civvies, one-way ticket into a furnace in Sciaparelli. Grenshem was cremated in Belreve, full honours, flag and anthem. You didn't see it?'

'We'll catch it later.' Stone leaned back in the swivel chair by a telemetry monitor. 'With Senator Grenshem dead, who takes his place?'

'There has to be an election.' Petrov rummaged for a datacube, dropped it into the machine and searched for the file material. Some was a video grab, made directly off the news vidcast, some was Tactical telemetry.

Stone knuckled his eyes and forced his attention to the screen when all he really wanted was a soft mattress, cool sheets, warm Jarrat. He saw several overviews of the funeral in Belreve, the grieving family, a knot of politicians and local Tactical officers. Notable by his absence was Stuart Wymark. So Curry was keeping him out of sight. The eulogy was read by a friend. In the background were clergy in the green robes of the Temple of Gaia.

'Two candidates are contesting for Grenshem's job,' Jarrat read off the text file. 'One was Grenshem's protégé, she'll follow in his footsteps like a shadow. Lenore Maddigan.'

On the screen was a woman in her forties, elegant, sophisticated. She looked intelligent, but brains had of a sudden assumed less importance than guts and cunning. 'See what you can find out about her,' Stone told Petrov. 'If Maddigan is going to continue Grenshem's work she'll be the next target.'

'While you're doing that,' Jarrat added, 'see if Kjell Wozniak is junked off the Equinox payroll in the morning. Three hours ago, I told Dorne he's a contract shooter, get rid of him, we're running surveillance on him.'

Petrov took a last deep dag and stubbed out the smoke. 'Was it smart to tip off Dorne?'

'A gamble.' Jarrat stirred restlessly. 'According to Dorne, his end of Equinox is totally legit, he knows nothing.'

'You don't believe that shit?' The Russian demanded.

'Oh, sure. I believe in leprechauns too.' Stone slid an arm about Jarrat's waist. 'You don't amass a fortune that big, that fast, and do it legally. I'm not saying you can't get rich quick, but not that rich, that quick.'

'Find out if Dorne was ever audited. Access his tax declarations,' Jarrat mused. 'Go back ten, fifteen years. See if you can dig deep enough to find where he jump-started his money machine, and how. What about the voice track analysis?'

Every word of the meeting between Dorne, Jarrat and Stone

had been recorded, and the computers had taken it all apart. The evaluation was exhaustive, but Petrov made a face as he handed over the summary printout.

'Inconclusive. The bastard's good. Syllable stress and spacing says he's probably lying, but he could just as easily be mildly drunk, slightly stoned or in a post-coital sweat. Try to indict on this, and we're chopped liver.'

'The secretary, Enrique, looked like he'd just rolled out of bed,' Stone said drily. 'Scratch that. Who's the other contender for Grenshem's job?'

'This one.' Petrov advanced the file as he made notes.

It stopped at the image of a man who seemed a disturbingly sensual cross between professional Companion and intellectual. The hair was black and cropped short to his skull, the eyes were blue and piercing. Stone could not have said what generated the instantaneous dislike, but he felt the reaction from Jarrat too.

'Bryce Ansell, an engineer,' Petrov told them. 'Sunny side of thirty, good looking, brilliant. Dorne discovered him in college and groomed him. He's a company man right down to the balls. Predictable. Now he's dabbling in Avalon politics but he keeps an office in Equinox Towers.' The Russian paused. 'And we're going to need a man on the inside.'

'Maybe.' Jarrat folded his arms, a deliberately defensive posture. 'Maybe we'll get lucky elsewhere.'

'I'll buzz Duggan in the morning.' Stone yawned expressively. 'If Grenshem's whistleblower was determined enough to put his neck on the line once, he'll do it again.'

'Unless he values his ass,' Petrov snorted. 'He got lucky last time — Grenshem bought the ranch, not him. Next time?' He drew one finger over his gullet.

Hands thrust into his hip pockets, Jarrat paced to the door. 'Might depend on how much this Jack Spiteri even wants to stay alive. He buried his spouse six months ago, remember. Michael Rogan died of Angel.' The grey eyes closed, and when they opened were dark as a storm sky. He almost glared at Stone, pivoted and was gone without another word.

The assault of Kevin's emotions left Stone winded. He was aware of Petrov frowning at him but he covered, shuffling printout. Petrov was not so easily decoyed.

'Tell me the truth, Cap. No bullshit. Can you two cut it?'

'You mean, can we handle a deep-cover assignment?' Stone tipped back his head and blindly studied the darkened ceiling. 'That's what we're here to find out, isn't it?'

'You know Cantrell is watching you?' The Russian spoke discreetly. 'You got regular telemetry going back to Dupre and Intelligence.'

'We know.' Stone focused easily on Jarrat. Kevin was resigned to the impending action, but he was fretting. Muscles and lungs worked as he strode aft to the cabins. 'Cantrell's job is observe and report.'

'Surveillance.' Petrov sounded disgusted. 'They're using you. I heard some of the stuff you were doing in the lab. Simulations. You let the bastards take liberties.'

Stone discovered a moment's genuine humour. 'I never knew you cared. Stop worrying, Mischa. We're big boys. And I think we can handle it. We'll never know till we try. Kevin isn't wild about the idea. We can delay a few days, see what Duggan comes up with. Spiteri is the key to it. Find him, and a deep-cover job may not be necessary. But if it is, we'll do it. That's why they pay us the big bucks.'

He paused as he felt the vibrations of Jarrat's sensations in his own nerves. Kevin was undressing, stretching his spine through the brief routine of exercises that kept him supple. Stone shivered, and shivered again when he felt the cool caress of sheets as Jarrat slid into bed. Yet Kevin was brooding, and not bothering to shield the anxiety.

With a quiet sigh Stone got to his feet. 'I'm going to crash. They don't hire me by the hour and this shift's been a bugger.'

'Sleep well,' Petrov called after him.

Sleep was the last thing on Stone's mind. The cabin was in semi-darkness but Kevin was wide awake. He turned over as Stone dropped his clothes, and shuffled over in the bed. Stone found himself on a patch of linen warmed by Jarrat's body heat. He pulled Kevin hard against him and buried his face in the soft, unruly hair. Jarrat's intense misgivings jabbed like needles even as they kissed.

'We can do it,' Stone said, muffled against his tongue. 'If we couldn't we'd have screwed up in simulation.'

'I know.' Jarrat's fingers left bruises on Stone's back. 'But I don't have to like it.'

'I'm not thrilled about it myself.' Stone rolled him over,

pinned him to the bed with his weight and shifted till Jarrat's growing erection slipped between his legs. Kevin's hands caressed down his back to his cheeks. 'We've a few moves to make before we have to look at a deep-cover job.'

'Spiteri, Maddigan, Dorne's financial records.' And then Jarrat gasped as Stone began to hump.

Coherent thought fled from his mind. Stone felt it go, banished by a tumult of lust. Kevin took him to the brink and backed off, making him howl. Lost in the shared sensations, Stone ground his teeth until he had a rein on his glands. When Kevin wriggled around he found his head pillowed on a long, lean thigh, his mouth filled with the heat and taste he could never forget, never get enough of.

Bittersweet was Jarrat, like no other flavour Stone knew. Like the unique signature of his musk. He sucked avidly as his own cock slid smoothly into the welcome of Kevin's lips. The darkness was a cocoon, a haven. Passion was a liberation from anxiety, and they clung to it while they could.

Every glorious pang of pleasure Jarrat felt shafted into Stone's nerves. When Kevin's fingers worked between his buttocks and entered him he might have cried out if he had been able. Jarrat cried out instead.

His head lifted, his spine stiffened as he felt the invasion of Stone's body as if it were his own. Stone wriggled on the fingers, probed Kevin's swollen balls, shared the ripples of delight. He took the beautiful cock down deep and struggled to breathe as Kevin held his testicles between encouraging fingers. A moment later Jarrat's mouth enveloped him once more, and they were coming.

For a long time they lay still, panting woundedly. Jarrat's spent shaft was heavy, musky against Stone's neck. Stone kissed it, moved up and set his head on the pillow with a gratified sigh.

For the moment, misgivings were soothed and sleep was easy... dreams were not. Stone slept soundly for several hours before he wrenched awake as the recurring nightmare of Angel addiction began. This time he jolted to consciousness in time to stop it before it could control him, but he knew his fitful tossing would disturb Jarrat.

He slid out of the wide bunk, padded into the adjoining cabin and settled on his own. Rest was as important as sleep, and with a glance at the time he schooled his body to stillness.

He was showered, shaved and dressed when the comm buzzed for attention. Kevin had not yet stirred. The sleep of the just, Stone thought fondly as he helped himself to tea from the robochef and touched the comm. The chrono read 08:14.

Gene Cantrell appeared on the screen. 'You slept well?'

'Not particularly.' Stone sipped the scalding liquid. 'What you got for me, Gene?'

'Messages.' Cantrell consulted his notes. 'Kip needs you in the Infirmary. Buchanan died two hours ago.'

'Counter-signature on the certificate of death, find the next of kin, if any, authorise disposal of the deceased.' Stone cradled his cup between his hands. 'And?'

'Engineers report trouble with number three reactor. They shut it down. It's been giving trouble since we left Kithan. They're requisitioning replacement components. We'll need a Starfleet tender. The nearest is servicing the *Valkyrie*, about two weeks from here. Or we can petition the Army, get a tender in maybe eight days. That's your decision. They're waiting for the word.'

The question was routine, though only the carrier's NARC captains could answer it. 'Signal the Starfleet tender,' Stone said at once. 'We're not going anywhere in the next week, we won't need main engine ignition. Two on-line reactors are plenty. Anything else?'

'Tactical called. Equinox put their internal security on alert at midnight. Coded transmissions are up twenty percent, in and out of Skycity and Equinox Towers. Colonel Duggan left a message. He's got some priority data for you, but refused to transmit, even on military scramblers. He'll be back at Tac HQ at 14:00, Elysium time.' Cantrell paused. 'I think you and Kevin will want to be there.'

Stone's heart quickened. 'Thanks, Gene. Is that the lot?'

'Just about.' Cantrell set aside his notes. 'Petrov reports no joy with the crypto work. You want him to keep trying?'

'Where's the point?' Stone stirred as he heard a rustle of linen in the next cabin. 'Without the Determinant we're beating our heads against a wall.'

Bare feet pattered, the shower started as Cantrell said, 'We can require Dorne to provide us with the Determinant. We have the authority.'

'And it comes supplied with a concealed command which

automatically alters the text it's being used to decode, into anything Dorne wants us to hear,' Stone said sourly. 'We'd be going through the motions, Gene. The second they gave it to us, they'd change every code to stop us eavesdropping on subsequent transmissions, and we'd be left with a fistful of air. Worse, we could play right into Dorne's hand. He trusts the Determinant to us, lets us eavesdrop on totally legit signals for forty-eight hours while he organises a case of industrial espionage based on compromised security. Equinox loses half a trillion credits... guess whose rump gets kicked?'

'Dorne would do that,' Cantrell agreed. 'You've considered the options, Stoney?' His brows quirked.

'Deep-cover assignment?' Stone smiled humourlessly. 'Tell me about it. Let's see what Duggan has for us this afternoon.'

'You've got your fingers crossed,' Cantrell observed.

'If you mean, I'm not overjoyed at the prospect of either Kevin or me going groundside for weeks and getting crap beaten out of us again, you're dead right.' Stone looked up as Jarrat stepped into the cabin. He was towelling down, listening without comment.

Cantrell smiled ruefully. 'There's a lot to be said for being sixty. They don't give me that work anymore.'

'Lucky you.' Stone winked into the lens and cut the connection. He perched on the edge of the desk and watched Jarrat appreciatively. 'We may be about to get lucky. Duggan called. He has data he wouldn't even transmit scrambled.'

'Spiteri?' Jarrat dropped the towel into the chute and padded away in search of a pair of black denims.

Restless, Stone followed him. 'Buchanan turned up his toes. You want to counter-sign the forms before or after breakfast? Then I'm going to hit the gym, hard. I've got a week's worth of fury under my lid.'

The denims zipped and Jarrat pulled a shirt over his head. 'That's not a bad idea. Kip'll be waiting for us.'

In fact, Surgeon Captain Kip Reardon was breakfasting on coffee and croissants in a corner of the office, just inside the Infirmary, while he watched a video. Stone caught a glimpse of the screen, saw an open viscera, a denuded heart beating as some new surgical technique was demonstrated, and looked away. Reardon popped the last bite into his mouth, put the video on hold and stood. 'Squeamish, that's your trouble,' he accused. 'If you had my job you'd be less trigger-happy.' He searched for a folder, took out a standard form and turned it toward Jarrat and Stone for twin signatures.

Cause of death: cerebral haemorrhage. Jarrat scanned down the certificate, signed without question and passed the pen to Stone. 'Damage done in the concussion of the explosion?'

'Yup. From what Cronin tells me, Buchanan was bloody lucky to survive the blast. The engineers have been digging pieces of shrapnel the size of warheads out of the keel of the gunship. You know you almost got a hull breach?'

'We'll get Budweisser's report in due course,' Jarrat said quietly. 'It was close, Kip. No one's denying it.'

Reardon folded his arms on his white surgical smock, leaned back in the squeaking swivel chair and stretched out his legs. He was neither young nor handsome, but he was the best combat surgeon NARC had, and a good man to call a friend. His eyes were honest, his manner forthright. Stone had liked him from the moment he came aboard, and he, even more than Jarrat, owed Reardon a debt. Kip had covered for them when he could have thrown the book at them.

Just once, in Chell, Jarrat bought Angel on the street and Stone used it. Reardon had known where Kevin was going, what he must do, when they bundled the semi-conscious Stone into the shuttle. But he had mentioned the episode to no one.

Even now he was studying Stone from beneath knitted brows as if he could scarcely believe what he saw. Stone was alive, free of the Angel — the only victim who ever made it back. Stone signed the certificate, handed it to him and waited.

'You're well, Stoney?' Reardon asked quietly.

'I'm uptight,' Stone admitted. 'This assignment could be easier. But I guess you mean *that*.'

Reardon's face creased in a smile. 'Cravings?'

'Angel cravings?' Stone shook his head. 'I get cravings for good sex, food, the occasional shot of booze or a smoke, but not Angel.' He glanced at Jarrat, felt the warmth of Kevin's affection. 'All I need, I'm getting.'

'Amen.' Jarrat dropped the empathic shields and bounced Stone's pleasant feelings right back at him like a ball.

Both men drew a sharp breath, and Reardon whistled. He took a scanner from his breast pocket and played it over Stone, chest and groin. 'Heart rate and blood pressure up, testosterone and androgen levels increasing, sperm count —'

'Kip!' Stone swiped the scanner out of his hand. 'That's none of your business.'

'Want to bet?' Reardon's fingers drummed on the computer hood. 'You think Intelligence wants me to report on the weather? You know you're on monthly physicals till further notice?'

Jarrat groaned. 'Christ. Give me one good reason!'

'Dr Yvette McKinnen's recommendation to Bill Dupre's direct superiors.' Reardon's teeth worried at his lip. 'Seems she logged a report outlining the instability of empaths.'

'Bloody woman,' Stone breathed. 'That's crap, and you know it, Kip.'

'Do I?' Reardon recovered his scanner and toyed with it. 'You're stressed out, Stoney. So's Kevin. You want a pill?'

'What we need,' Jarrat said acidly, 'is a hard session in the gym. I'm going to pump iron till I drop, then take a sauna. If that doesn't thrash the gremlins out of me, nothing will.'

'Good for you,' Reardon approved.

'When's the first physical due?' Stone asked dutifully as they withdrew from the office with a glance along the dimmed observation ward. It held six empty beds and a battery of equipment. Exam rooms, two ORs, cryotanks and the morgue flanked the ward to left and right.

'A couple of weeks.' Reardon waved them away. 'I had Harry Del's last report sent over. Unless you two jumped your track on the way here, that'll hold for a while.'

With an expression of relief, Stone stepped out.

The gym was down two decks, forward of the machine shops. Both Starfleet and NARC crews had free access, but instructors had to be booked. Weights and aerobic machines, taikwando and kendo equipment, judo mats, rings and bars filled the single long hall.

They had the facility almost to themselves. A dozen crewgirls were bouncing each other off the mats; two Gold Ravens were punishing their already massive bodies with repetition sets under the kind of grav-loading Stone doubted he could have lifted more than two or three times. They grinned wickedly at him as he paused to watch. He lifted two fingers at them and followed Jarrat into the locker room.

Clad in brief white shorts, with the loading set twenty percent under his limits, Jarrat worked without a break until Stone was distressingly aware of his pain. Sweat gleamed on him, his face was a grimace of effort. His muscles were distended, veins roped beneath the skin. Stone was working hard, but Jarrat seemed to be deliberately driving himself.

On his back on the bench, Stone pressed his own body weight, working doggedly through the fifth of nine sets, but his eyes were on Jarrat. If the contraption in which Kevin reclined had stood in a dungeon, it would have been called a torture device. Padded bars drove his thighs and arms apart with the identical pressure he could exert on them. Sensors adjusted the force every second, so that even as he began to tire his output remained at a safe peak, till the moment he actually quit.

He was hurting. Stone's body reverberated with punishing strain which was not his own. 'Kev? Kevin!'

Grey eyes blinked on a veil of sweat. 'I'm fine,' Jarrat said hoarsely.

'You're not.' Stone locked the bar in its cradle and turned off the grav-loading adjustor.

He swung his legs over the bench and rested both elbows on his knees. Jarrat's body was protesting, near exhaustion. A moment later he quit, and as he ceased to exert pressure on the machine it stopped with him. The bars retracted with a whine of servos and he flopped forward, palms on his thighs.

'You're hurting,' Stone said quietly.

'I said, I'm fine.' Jarrat straightened with an effort.

'You can't lie to me,' Stone reminded him. 'You want to tell me what's eating you?'

Jarrat shoved himself out of the machine and stalked into the sauna without looking back. Stone followed, grabbed a towel and stepped into the steam. After a workout it was the best way to sweat out the toxins. Jarrat dropped the shorts, tucked a towel about his hips and settled on the bench with his back against the amber tiles.

Slitted eyes watched as Stone stripped and followed. They were alone, but Jarrat had slammed the shields up on his empathy. Stone struggled to read anything through the armour. Once, the empathy had been distressing. Now, the total absence of Kevin's feelings was strange and disturbing.

He twisted on the bench and studied Jarrat soberly. 'That woman's right, isn't she?'

The question reached Kevin at last. 'What woman?'

'McKinnen.' Stone passed a forearm over his face. 'She told Dupre this would happen. What did she say? Mental instability, madness in the end. Empaths! Christ.'

'Oh, Stoney.' Jarrat exhaled noisily and tousled Stone's dark hair with rough tenderness. 'That's not it. I'm all right, I'm just bloody worried, and I've got reason to be.'

'Worried?' Stone was wide open and still getting nothing. He made a small wounded sound. 'Kevin, let me in. Don't do this to me.'

'I'm sorry.' Jarrat leaned back and closed his eyes. His armour fractured little by little. 'This what you want?'

Pain blazed from his hard-worked body, exhaustion, and behind the purely physical sensations was an acid knot of foreboding. Stone took a breath. 'Yes. Don't shut me out when something's wrong. Tell me.'

'It's you,' Jarrat admitted. 'Your turn groundside.'

'Deep-cover work?' Stone put his head back on the wall and closed his eyes. 'Is that all? I thought it was something major.'

It was the wrong thing to say. Jarrat was on his feet, fists balled. 'Damn you, Stoney! You think you're immortal? They can do to you what they did to me — smash every bone you've got, punch your ass and dump you for dead! You think it can't happen? Jesus, where's your mind? Not something major?'

'Kevin, it's my job.' Stone recoiled under the emotional lashing. It was the first time Jarrat's anger had slipped the leash and been directed at him. Techniques Harry Del had taught them were all the protection he had as Jarrat's fury and fear scorched through him and left him gasping.

'Your job.' Kevin took a breath, wiped both hands over his sweating face. 'I wish to God —'

He said no more, and Stone winced as a lance of agony embedded in his chest. Jarrat began to pace. Stone stood, reached for Kevin's shoulder to stop him, but Jarrat brushed him aside and strode into the adjoining cubicle. Cold water pummelled him, made his heart jump, and Stone felt that too. He was silent now. Nothing they could say would be right.

They did not speak for minutes. It was not till Stone felt his own anger begin to kindle, and buttressed his defences against the painful empathy, that Kevin relented. Stone's temper was always slower to ignite, burned with less heat and spent itself faster. NARC psyche tests rated him more stable because of his higher flashpoint, but Stone was not so sure.

'I'm sorry.' The apology was surly but genuine. Jarrat would not look at him, but concentrated on his denims and boots. 'If I didn't love you I wouldn't give a toss what happened to you. But I care, damn you.'

'And you think what happened to you last time will happen to me.' Stone ran a comb through his short, damp hair and settled his collar. Jarrat stamped his boots to comfort and still would not look up. Stone took a breath and chose his words carefully. 'To start with, lightning doesn't strike twice so fast. In the second place, I'm a big boy, I can look after myself. All I need is the best backup in the business — and honey, that's you. Lastly, I'm not in the game to take stupid risks. If the water gets hot, you pull me out of Equinox the way I wanted to pull you out of Death's Head the night that toad, Vazell, put a dart in you.' Jarrat flinched with memory and turned to him at last. Stone nodded. 'I wanted to get you out that night. It was your decision to go back.'

'I wanted the mule,' Jarrat whispered.

'We might have got him some other way,' Stone said with brutal truth. 'You put yourself into that scene, Kevin, when you ran risks nobody would have asked of you.'

Jarrat took a long, deep breath. 'You may be right.'

'I am right.' Stone took him by the arms, felt the steel of overworked muscles, the cording of his sinews. 'And if you think I'm going to run any kind of risk, forget it. I expect you to monitor me every minute. At a hint of trouble, I'm out. Fast. You lose contact with me, I'll remind you. Like this.' He closed his eyes, concentrated well below the belt and had the satisfaction of hearing Jarrat groan.

'Christ.' Jarrat leaned against the wall between the lockers. 'I can't get it out of my head, Stoney. Every time I see you in deep cover, I see you on the ground in an alley.'

'That was last time.' Stone touched his face. 'You have to let it go. You know what this is, don't you?'

'Yes.' Jarrat pushed away from the wall. 'Delayed stress syndrome. It's been in my subconscious, waiting for a trigger, and this is it. I buried it so deep, even McKinnen couldn't find it. I'm doing the best I can. I wish to God I could talk to Harry Del. He'd know how to straighten out my head.'

Stone felt the squeeze of his heart and longed to hold him, but the gym was not the place. He settled for a brief hug. 'When we're finished here we'll be due some leave. Harry'll be pleased to see us.'

'Yeah.' Jarrat cleared his throat and pulled his shoulders back. 'I'll manage, Stoney. I'm not trying to say you can't handle yourself, groundside... and I'll hold my half of it together. You can trust me.' He gave Stone a tired smile. 'How many times did your instructors tell you, when you transferred to NARC, never get involved. Never fall in love.'

'I lost count,' Stone admitted. 'They were right. It makes the job a hundred times harder. Still,' he added with forced cheer, 'I wouldn't trade what we have. Not for any damned thing you can think of.'

A thread of pleasure wound through Jarrat's belly, dispelling a little of the painful apprehension. 'Thanks. I needed that.'

'And look on the bright side,' Stone reminded him. 'Duggan might have something positive.' He glanced over Jarrat's head at the chrono. 'Speaking of whom, we'd better get airborne.'

He stood aside to usher Jarrat from the locker room, and paused to frown at the weights and machines. How much had McKinnen detected in the course of the endless psyche tests? She had been so adamant in her assessment of empaths as unstable, prone to irrationality, even madness. Stone turned after Jarrat with a flicker of concern, which he was careful to shield.

***

Vic Duggan looked five years older, but Stone expected it. He would have spent the morning talking to the families of the Tactical officers killed in the streetwar. Saying, over and over, 'Your son died doing a lousy job and doing it well, and we're all poorer without him.' How often had Stone heard that speech? How often had Duggan made it?

He was late. The NARC men had been sitting in his office ten minutes before he appeared. He swallowed a large bourbon and glared into the street for some time before he could speak. On the couch, Stone motioned Jarrat to silence, and at last Duggan rubbed his face and said,

'I found your man. I know a few of his friends, and I talked to Mike Rogan's family. I put the word out, NARC wants to pick up the pieces, if only Jack's a good lad and calls home. He called in the early hours this morning. I wasn't here, and even if I had been, I wouldn't have transmitted what he gave me.' Duggan cast a glance in the direction of Chandler sector, to the north, where the immense Equinox Towers dwarfed the next tallest buildings. 'You know they monitor the NARC bands?'

'We know.' Jarrat leaned forward, elbows on his knees. 'You've got Spiteri?'

'No. I don't know where he is, but I know where he'll be at 19:00 tonight.' Duggan leaned over the desk, twisted the monitor about and produced a map. 'You know your Avalon geography?'

'Not in any detail.' Stone moved closer to study the screen. 'Two continents, small oceans. Elysium is about fifteen hundred k's north of the equator. So?'

'So Spiteri's gone to ground.' Duggan touched the screen. 'Here, half the planet away. He's at the old Caitlin-B field.'

'Which is?' Jarrat's eyes flicked to Duggan's face.

'A gas field. They worked it out to provide power for the terraforming engineers in the first decade. Things were pretty rough here then. The quickest ship from Earth took three months and the terraformers had to make this rock what you see today. All the comforts came later.' He produced a larger scale chart. 'There's a rough navigation reference. Spiteri has a skyvan. He'll give you a twenty-second pulse on open UHF from those approximate co-ordinates, and you'd better be there inside five minutes, or he'll split. The man is shit scared, and I don't blame him.'

Stone straightened from the screen. 'He didn't make it out cleanly after Grenshem was killed?'

'He says they're behind him. They've missed him three times already.' Duggan slopped another bourbon into his glass. 'I believe him.'

'Equinox shooters?' Stone shot a glance at Jarrat. 'He's got them so stirred up, they're chasing him halfway across this planet. Kevin?'

'They only ever tackle the one with the ball,' Jarrat said wryly, and Stone felt the kick of his pulse.

'He wouldn't give me his data.' The raw spirit roughened Duggan's voice. 'But I managed to piece some of it together from a few crumbs Grenshem threw me. Spiteri's your man.' He stabbed a finger at the chart and co-ordinates. 'Be there, Stoney, for godsakes, don't blow it.'

'You know me better than that.' Stone felt the quick, heavy beat of Jarrat's heart. 'You heard anything about Dorne's man, Wozniak?'

'Not a squeak.' Duggan lowered his backside onto the chair behind his desk. 'I've had surveillance on him for months. It's business as usual. He threw a bimbo out of his penthouse on the Oberon building just after dawn, took an aircab to Equinox Towers, same as he does four days a week. Why?'

'Dorne should have dumped last night,' Jarrat said with deep satisfaction. 'You know what I'm thinking, Stoney? We might pick up Wozniak.'

'Interrogation?' Duggan asked doubtfully. 'You're getting into deep shit. Under Avalon law, interrogation other than routine questioning is prohibited until after conviction. Some kind of legal double-talk to protect harmless, innocent civvies from brutes likes you.'

'And you,' Stone added. He smiled thinly. 'Stop worrying. Avalon legal-eagles will know exactly what we choose to tell them. Pick him up.'

Duggan rolled his eyes to the ceiling. 'On what charge?'

'Invent one.' Jarrat made a note of Jack Spiteri's nominated co-ordinates and time.

'How about a nice, ripe rape?' Duggan suggested. 'Not the kind of thing a man denies on the doorstep or talks his way out of in a minute. The way Wozniak uses scrubbers, he won't be surprised to be picked up. It's been on the cards.'

'Rough?' Jarrat arched one brow.

'Very.' Duggan made a whipcrack motion with his right hand. 'I'll put a squad in Rawhide. He's sure to show up there one night soon. When he does, he's yours. You want him on the carrier?'

But Stone made negative noises. 'It'd be more anonymous if you held him right here.'

'And it'll be my ass in a sling when he screams for his lawyer,' Duggan added.

'He has to remember what happened before he can yell,' Jarrat argued. 'There's a couple of drugs we use that'll damp his memory for a few days, and by that time it's too late to protest.

We deny ever being here, Wozniak gets the rep of a dopehead who's forgotten how to tell a trip from reality.'

'Dope-testimony isn't worth the cube it's recorded on,' Duggan reminded him. 'Don't try to bust Dorne on that.'

'Which is why you release him after he's said what we need to hear, even if he gives us the whole story.' Jarrat flexed his fingers. 'No matter what he says, it's only verbal testimony. Legally worthless. But Wozniak could plug us into Dorne's private business, and we'll dig for what we can use to bury them. It was the same in Chell, the Death's Head job.' Jarrat glanced at Stone. 'Unless Spiteri knows enough to close this assignment, we're down to the option of placing a man in Equinox.' He looked at Stone as he spoke.

For a moment Duggan said nothing, and then he swore. 'Rather you than me. If one of you goes in, you'll want all you can get to work with — hence, Wozniak, and a nose full of some narco shit.' He held up his hands as if at gunpoint. 'All right, I'll send a squad into Rawhide and tell you when I've got him on ice.' He looked from Stone to Jarrat and back again. 'Which of you does the deep cover?'

'If it comes down to it, me.' Stone's shoulders twitched in an offhand shrug. 'It's my turn.'

'Like I said, rather you than me.' Duggan swallowed the dregs of his bourbon. 'That's all I got for you, Stoney. Can't find the source of the military weapons trade. It's like a door's been slammed.'

'And Equinox, or Dorne, slammed it.' Jarrat folded the notes he had made and slipped them into his pocket. 'We'll see you, Colonel. If Spiteri has something choice, we'll let you know. You can pick Wozniak up along with Dorne and the rest of them, and lock the cage.'

'Don't I wish.' Duggan gave his hand to Stone in passing. 'Good luck, kid. You'll need it.'

On the roof, standing by the shuttle in the shifting wind and sporadic sunlight of afternoon, Stone glared at the brooding face of Zeus. The lore in the NARC ranks was that the instant a man began to rely on luck he should get out, because that luck had just expired.

With a passionate curse, Stone scaled the side of the spaceplane and dropped into the rear cockpit as Jarrat fired the main lifters.

Chapter Nine

The complete charts for Avalon's south continent were displayed on the plotboard in the ops room. At two kilometres per centimetre resolution, surface features were individually labelled.

'Locate on the beacons,' Stone advised. 'They have some sort of equipment there, so tall it's radio marked for the safety of civvy aircraft. You'll ride straight down the signal, pick up Spiteri and get out fast.'

Jarrat's face was wreathed in surreal shadows, lit from below by the illuminated plotboard. His eyes returned to the chrono for the third time in ten minutes and he chided himself. The thoroughbred was on his toes, less than an hour before the race. A certain amount of stage fright was healthy, but past that point it was a killer. Jarrat wished he knew where the dividing line lay.

Delayed stress syndrome was a post-trauma condition he had studied but never personally experienced. It was a dance of phantom images, sounds, sensations, like shadows on the periphery of his mind. He would see faces — Mavvik, Roon, Viotto — hear gunshots, engines, voices. He would feel the blaze of pain from his broken body, then it was gone again, and he would snap back to the present to discover twenty seconds missing.

He swallowed hard, felt the prickle of sweat down his spine and met Stone's eyes levelly. Only Stoney was aware of his difficulty. Cantrell and Petrov had noticed nothing, nor would they. Jarrat was in command of face, voice and limbs. When in doubt, he fell back on basic NARC doctrine. Training, experience, logic and intuition built an efficient officer, no matter the wreckage of his private life.

Petrov had on a headset and was listening to the loop. 'Flight crews have serviced and armed the shuttle, Cap. You're carrying a full ordnance load. Carrier pilots are standing by for manoeuvring.'

'Any time they're ready.' Jarrat straightened his back and felt a knot release in his middle. Anticipation was worse than doing. With the show under way his ghosts receded.

'Flight deck,' Petrov called. 'Conform orbit and commence groundscan.'

Several CRTs lit as the carrier drove out of her orbit over Elysium. She had been parked on station-keeping, holding position relative to the city's co-ordinates on engine power. Elysium slid down over the horizon as the *Athena* crossed the terminator into the night side.

'19:00, Elysium time, the man said,' Stone murmured as they watched the orbital data. 'Forty minutes, Kevin. They're waiting for you.'

'On my way.' Jarrat pulled on a headset. 'Load the onboard deck with everything you've got.'

'Get into the hardsuit,' Stone said tersely as Jarrat strode away from him.

Jarrat hesitated. 'You think that's necessary, for a simple pickup?'

'The Buchanan pickup should have been easy too,' Stone reminded him. He touched Cantrell's shoulder as he left the plotboards. 'I'll help you. You don't have much time.'

They were in the lift, and Jarrat was adjusting his chrono to the timezone of his destination when Stone said quietly, 'Are you okay, Kevin?'

'Yes.' Jarrat lifted his chin. 'It's the waiting that kills me. I won't have time to see ghosts when I get moving. If I tell you the truth, I'd sooner do the deep-cover job than sit up here and watch you do it.'

'This one's not yours to run,' Stone said darkly. He gripped Jarrat's shoulder. 'If you can't handle it up here —'

'I can.' Jarrat covered Stone's hand with his own. 'The ghosts of Death's Head won't master me, Stoney. Not after we beat the real, live bastards. I won't let it happen — end of statement.' He smiled faintly. 'You know what they say about falling off a horse. It's time we both got back in the saddle for real. Simulations don't count.'

The lift opened and he stepped out into the cold, breezy air of the shuttle bay. The spaceplane's sterntubes shimmered after testfiring. A munitions sled was still parked under the nose, and a flightcrew was checking the missile load. The plane was armed with the Hawk, Maverick and Phoenix III weapons

NARC had acquired even before the military had them. At the time there was a public outcry, but the packwar on Earth itself silenced the critics when a syndicate called Ronin held most of Yokohama to ransom.

As he suited up, Jarrat listened to loop. The carrier had dropped into an adjusted orbit, low over the co-ordinates of the Caitlin-B gas field. Stone lifted on the breastplate; Jarrat closed the neck seal and neutralised the weight. Looking down, he watched Stone brush his thumb over the name and rank stencilled on the gloss black kevlex-titanium.

Stone's blue eyes were hot as he looked up, and his voice was harsh. 'You be bloody careful,' he said roughly, as if he must bluff around his concern.

'Don't con me.' Jarrat touched his face with one steel finger-tip. 'I'll be home in ninety minutes. Less.'

'Here.' Stone slapped the helmet into his hands and stepped back. 'I'll be with you... in more ways than one.'

The empathy flared brightly, ringing between them for a breathless moment. Jarrat nodded soberly and lifted on the helmet. Instrument lights flickered and stabilised. He checked the digital a hand's span from his nose and screwed in the twin umbilici. 'Raven 9.4, about to launch. Clear the bay and give me a groundscan update.'

His right hand fell on Stone's shoulder for a moment, and he stepped by into the hangar as sirens whooped and yellow spinners sent the technicians scurrying. Stone was still at the armourglass observation window as he climbed into the air-craft. The bay was sealed and already depressurising. The computers were loaded, the navigation deck was on line, and his gauges were all in the green.

'9.4, launch, any time,' Petrov's thick Russian voice told him. 'Groundscan over the gas field reports zip. We don't even see the skyvan your man is supposed to be flying, so he's already at the site. Monitoring for his UHF marker signal.'

The bay opened to space as Jarrat shunted up the repulsion. He dropped out over the velvet night side of Avalon and turned the nose down. 'Fifteen minutes to contact. When you get that signal, yell. Stoney?'

'Right here.' Stone's voice was low and soft in his ears, like crushed satin. Jarrat felt the rush of Stone's emotion too, affection, concern, pride.

'Just checking,' Jarrat admitted. 'Voice recorders are on. We're supposed to report to Intelligence, remember.'

'I'm not likely to forget,' Stone said drily. 'Okay. For the benefit of Intelligence, I am open and keyed on you. I can even feel you itch.'

Behind the visor, Jarrat grinned. The itch was beneath his left shoulder. He rubbed it against the backplate as he inspected his instruments. 'Three thousand klicks downrange. You got that signal yet?'

'Nope. Still monitoring,' Stone said smoothly. 'Nothing on groundscan in your area. There's a domestic airbus out of Elysium, south-bound, five thousand k's to your north-east, but according to Elysium Air Traffic it's a regular milk run.'

The south continent of Avalon was only lightly populated. Towns and cities were smaller and more sparse. Lights shone like jewels in the semi-darkness. Jarrat took a visual bearing on the city of Domingo and brought the nose about a few points.

The night was not really dark. Zeus blocked the stars over half the sky, but Eos was up, waxing, almost full, a brilliant disk in the east. The bloated face of the gas giant reflected a flood of sunlight. The sky was a blue-green twilight as Jarrat thundered in toward the extinct gas field.

He picked up the beacons marking the disused industrial complex, cut speed, swept out the wings and canards and cruised across the snow-capped peaks of a spinal mountain range. 'I'm two hundred k's downrange at ten thousand. I'll hold here till we get the UHF bearing. I can be all over Spiteri like a rash before he hears my jets. I'm not tracking anything, Stoney. I got a feeling we're home free.'

'You watch yourself, Kevin,' Stone said sharply. The unspoken message rang clear as a bell: *Don't be cocky! Get complacent and you're in trouble!*

'I will.' Jarrat boosted his UHF gain. 'Where the hell is this — got it!' He felt the leap of Stone's pulse in the same instant, a companionable feeling, as if Stoney was close enough to reach out and touch.

'Move,' Stone called. 'He won't wait for you.'

Before he had spoken Jarrat had already shoved the throttles to the stops and the aircraft bucked like a startled horse. He looped over the hills above Caitlin-B, left a sonic concussion like a thunderclap and howled down off the high country, over the wilderness which remained after industry laid waste what had been virgin prairie.

In the eerie, blue-green twilight he saw an endless plane of asphalt, punctuated by the corroding skeletons of refineries abandoned many decades before. Instruments reported the mass of metal below, and buried dumps of toxic waste. Caitlin-B was the garbage tip of the planet.

The twenty-second transmission had been silent for two minutes when Jarrat cut speed and hovered over a tangle of immense pipes, gantries and girderwork. He kicked in the floodlights and watched the CRT as he rotated the aircraft for a visual survey. If Spiteri's skyvan was here, it was expertly hidden.

'Can you see him?' Stone asked shortly.

'Not on groundscan or visual,' Jarrat reported. He touched the comm panel with one fingertip. 'Where are you, Jack? NARC Airborne to Spiteri. You've had a good look at me. If you want a ticket out, show yourself.'

A crackle of interference as transmission was distorted by the mass of metal and the powerful beacons, and the voice he had waited for said, 'Nose about, ninety degrees.'

Jarrat rotated the spaceplane and saw a light in the deep green twilight. Two flashes — off; two flashes — off, a hand torch no more than a hundred metres away. The shuttle covered the distance just above the cracked asphalt, then he dropped the landing gear and sent up the canopy.

The man did not step out of the ravel of tumbled girders, and Jarrat switched his helmet display to thermographic to pick him out of the metal. Spiteri crouched in the cover of a mountain of pipes, and he was armed. Frightened, Jarrat guessed, distrusting everything and everyone.

'Jack Spiteri,' he called, 'Duggan sent me.'

'You — you're NARC?' Over the R/T, Spiteri panted with fear. 'How do I know you're not from Equinox? They've nearly had me three times. I'm warning you, I'm armed.'

'Use your eyes.' Jarrat released the flight harness and lifted himself onto the side of the cockpit. The locust-like riot armour glared the lights. 'Don't you know NARC when you see it?'

'Jesus. Yes.' Spiteri's voice broke. 'You scanning the area? I saw them. They overflew me hours ago.'

'There's nothing,' Jarrat told him levelly. 'Are you going to come out and talk? You want a ride?'

'No. That is, I'll talk, I don't want a ride.' Spiteri had edged out of cover.

As he stepped into the open Jarrat returned to normal visual. One hand up to shield his eyes from the glare of the floods, Spiteri shuffled toward the plane.

'You're not safe,' Jarrat warned him. 'Let me take get you off Avalon.'

In his right hand Spiteri carried a machine pistol, and he wore the paramilitary fatigues which were chic on the streets of Elysium. He was tall and well built, with cropped, crinkly black hair and skin a few shades darker than Dupre. And he was agitated with terror.

'I can't leave,' he shouted across the asphalt as he shoved the R/T into his pocket. 'I got family, man. They're dead meat if I walk out on them.'

Jarrat bit his lip. 'You getting this, Stoney?'

'Every word,' Stone assured him. 'Tell him I'll send a transport for his family if he'll give me the location.'

'Okay, Spiteri.' Jarrat dropped lightly from the side of the cockpit with his apparent mass set at fifty kilos. 'Calm down. Tell me where your family is, I'll get you a transport.'

'Transmit their location?' Spiteri's dark eyes widened. He spun, flung his arm at the sky. 'They're listening, man! You think they don't hear you *breathe*?'

Stone: 'He may be right, Kev. Groundscan shows nothing moving, but that doesn't mean they're not there. Watch yourself.'

'Come here, Jack.' Jarrat held out one gauntleted hand. 'I'll take you out now, send a transport for your folks later.'

'Forget it.' Spiteri shook his head violently. 'I can't trust you. They get every word you say on the air. Jesus, you got to be on relay to your ship right now! For all I know they might have tapped your intership comm loop!'

'*Kevin!*' Stone barked. '*Don't!*'

Monitors in the ops room had displayed a glitch as Jarrat broke the helmet seal. 'Bugger the telemetry,' he said bluntly. 'Spiteri might be right. Dorne's one jump ahead of us, no matter where we go. You monitor me, dammit! He can't tap that. This is what we're here to test! Close down.'

The helmet lifted off and he took a breath of the warm night

149

air. He smelt dust and some iron tang as he lifted off the headset and ran steel fingers through his hair. 'Okay, Jack,' he said levelly as he placed the helmet on the wing. 'You wanted to talk. No telemetry, no recorders.' Only the empathy which burned fiercely along every nerve in his body as Stone seemed to take possession of him from two hundred kilometres' altitude.

'I told it all to Tigh Grenshem,' Spiteri muttered as he approached the aircraft. 'Oh God, did I get him killed?'

'Maybe.' Jarrat cast a glance about the wind-swept wilderness. 'They missed his lover. The kid gave us your name and you were damned hard to find. What do you know, Jack? Make it quick. Let me give you a ride somewhere safe.'

'Safe?' Spiteri dragged both hands over his face. 'I've got somewhere safe. I left my brother and his kids there this morning. Nobody on Avalon knows where, and I'm sure as shit not telling you.'

'Then tell me about Equinox.' Surreptitiously, Jarrat touched the audio recorder. He was not transmitting, but every sound Spiteri made would be captured.

The man hugged his arms about himself. 'You know I worked for them? So did Michael. Mike Rogan, my man. That's how I met Mike, fell in love with him. We worked together. He was everything I ever wanted. We married.'

Pain seemed to flay the flesh from Spiteri's bones as Jarrat watched. 'I know he's dead. He died of Angel, six months ago.'

'Yes.' Spiteri swallowed the grief. 'I kept him going. I kept him alive three months longer than the medics gave him. He lived two years. Two whole goddamned years on that shit.'

'Why?' Jarrat asked hoarsely as his memory haunted him with images of Stone's terrible addiction. 'Why would Michael take the drug?' Some sixth sense told him, the answer to that was the key to everything.

'He would never have used it,' Spiteri said bitterly. Tears were iridescent in the blue-green half light. 'He went out one night. I was working, he wanted to go dancing. He had this favourite dance shop in Elysium. Valhalla. He... didn't come home. I found him the next day, skulled, rancid with it. Oh, Christ.' He sagged to his knees. 'They gave it to him.'

'Equinox?' Jarrat's blood cooled by degrees. 'Who? He saw faces, got names?'

'You can't be serious.' Spiteri dragged his sleeve over his face.

'Michael had a couple of beers, went to the pisser. Hand on his mouth, gun in his neck. It's so easy. They dumped him among the trackpacks behind Valhalla and left him. He might have been dead. I got a call from a kid who'd been at the dance shop.'

Ice shivered the length of Jarrat's spine. 'What makes you say it was goons from Equinox?'

Spiteri had a grip on his grief now. Fury supplanted it and he fought to his feet. Jarrat gave him one big gauntlet to pull him up. 'Michael was a clever man, but he had a big mouth. He fought with the bosses. He was with Grenshem's party, you know? Liberation from industrial tyranny. Get Equinox out of this system so we can start to clean up the mess. Mike was always hassling the company directors, giving Grenshem live ammunition to fire at them in the courts. He pushed them. He pushed too far, too hard, and —'

'And he paid the price.' Jarrat fought down his anger. 'I'm sorry. If it's any consolation, you're not alone. This is not uncommon. Angel is a more sophisticated kind of murder than a gun or a knife, but it's murder just the same.' His heart squeezed at the sound of his own words. 'Is this what you told Grenshem? Corruption that goes right to the top? Murder, Angel handling?'

'Part of it.' Spiteri cleared his throat. 'You see, when Mike died I was half dead myself. The funeral was... bad. But I saw the kid there, the one who called me when he found Mike among the trashpacks. He was a Companion.'

'A hustler?' Jarrat was not surprised.

'Yeah. A real beauty. The kind who works on Skycity, for big money. He wasn't hustling in Valhalla, just went there to dance. Even hustlers need a night off. Besides, the guys who drink at Valhalla couldn't afford Jesse Lawrence. We're talking about a Skycity showpony. Anyway, it turned out, Jesse and Mike were friends. I used to work a lot of late hours and Michael would go to the dance shop, meet the Companion there for a drink, just sociable.' Spiteri tipped back his head. 'Christ. All the fights Mike had with the bosses... the fights that got his nose crammed with that pigshit! And all for what?' He sniffed noisily. 'That kid knew it all. Jesse Lawrence already knows enough to rip Equinox inside out and bury Randolph Dorne so deep Avalon would forget who he was.'

Jarrat's heart beat hard at his ribs. This was what they needed.

151

'The Companion attended Michael's funeral?'

'To pay his respects.' Spiteri rubbed his face. He told me how Michael was slow-murdered. He knows them all! Buchanan and Wozniak, and the company moguls, looking for cheap thrills in city bottom dens like Rawhide.' His eyes gleamed ferally. 'I went there. I sat in a corner in Rawhide and watched. I saw everything Jesse already knew. They never knew I was eavesdropping, but I heard them.' He glared at Jarrat. 'It's on the street in Elysium that you killed Buchanan.'

'It didn't happen quite like that, but the man's dead, yes. You have the data, Jack?' Spiteri nodded distractedly. 'The hustler gave you what he learned on Skycity? Angel, military weapons for the crowd?' Jarrat felt for Stone, wondered how much of his elation Stone was getting. The empathy was clearer than open radio, all he had to do was concentrate.

But when Jarrat diverted his attention from Spiteri and focused on Stone all he felt was a mute scream of warning which tore the breath out of his lungs and made him spin to gaze out over the asphalt.

He saw the winking red running lights of an aircraft, and a tenth of a second later heard a growing howl of repulsion. Swearing lividly, he dragged the headset on. 'Stoney! Stoney, what is it?'

'You've got company,' Stone shouted. 'Coming your way fast — I tried to warn you. Something just lifted out of the blind spot under some mess of machinery about half a klick from you. Could be anything. Move!'

'I'm moving,' Jarrat panted. He had grabbed Spiteri by the arms as Stone spoke. Jack was staring at the lights like a mesmerised rabbit. His wits were already tattered, it would take little to break him. Jarrat lifted him in both gauntlets and heaved his weight upward. 'Get in there! Spiteri! Get in the plane!'

Hands scrabbled, he got one boot onto the wing as Jarrat crammed on his helmet. With one hand he screwed in the power umbilicus, with the other he propelled Spiteri upward while his eyes followed the winking lights and tried to judge distance. In the instant the helmet instruments lit he had the data at his fingertips.

Thermographic showed him a skyhopper, something big, armed and armoured, like an executive aircraft. It was stationary in the twilight, four hundred metres out, just hanging there, as if —

'Get in there!' Jarrat bawled, and thrust Spiteri up with the full force of his arm.

A dozen shots pelted the side of the shuttle and left a series of shallow depressions. Several whanged off Jarrat's armour; he felt the impacts, the slight shove as they pushed him aside. He keyed his weight to ten kilos and jumped.

He bounced like a ball, caught the side of the cockpit and pulled himself in. Spiteri was draped, half in, half out, and his blood looked black in Zeus' eerie half-light. Jarrat lifted him into the rear cockpit and used his own armoured body to block the incoming fire for the precious seconds it took to run up the flight harness. Rounds slammed into his back and shoulder but the armour was impervious.

'Kevin!' Stone shouted. 'I felt shots!'

'It's a long-range hit,' Jarrat panted. 'I'm on thermo, I can see the bugger. It's a skyhopper, looks like a Yamazake. I've got Spiteri aboard but he's in bad shape.' He lifted the man's head, looked into the blood-spattered face. 'He's alive.'

'Try and keep him that way,' Stone said tersely.

'The thought occurred to me.' Jarrat twisted, dumped his own weight into the forward acceleration couch and dropped the canopy fast. The repulsion came up with a blistering roar. He folded the gear and bobbed up to fifty metres for a full groundscan of the area. 'Damn. The shooter's running.'

'Tracking him,' Stone called. 'Heading north fast enough to burn his tail feathers. Making altitude fast.'

'I'm right behind him.' Jarrat sent the shuttle up as fast as he dared. He thought of the man in the seat behind and groaned. 'I'm going to kill Spiteri with high-G's if I throw this thing around too hard. Jesus, Stoney, he may already be dead.'

Stone's breath hissed over the air. 'Did you get what we need? Do not transmit data!'

'I wasn't considering it. And yes, we got enough to work on.' Jarrat punched keys and the CRT at his elbow showed him the rear cockpit. Spiteri was lax, lolling with the roll of the aircraft. 'He's out cold.'

'Then catch that skyhopper,' Stone said acidly. 'The way that mother's making altitude, I'd swear he's heading for orbit. I'll launch you a gunship.'

'I can take him!' Jarrat snapped as he shoved the throttles wide and pulled the cyclic stick back sharply. The skyhopper was on his screens, a single track on a backbreaking trajectory. 'I don't think it's armed, or they'd have taken a shot at me before I got off. Civvy joy toy, maybe.'

'It's fast,' Stone observed. 'You're closing on him.'

And the shooter's pilot knew it. Jarrat watched his instruments, saw the range to target decreasing until he was almost clear to try a shot. The skyhopper rolled and dove, trading altitude for speed. Jarrat stood the spaceplane on one wingtip to stay with him. Wings and canards swept in and out automatically, changing the geometry of the aircraft from moment to moment.

Ten thousand metres above the lights of Domingo, the skyhopper pulled up and cut a scorching arc into the north. The range was extreme, but Jarrat flicked the guards off the trigger on the side of the cyclic and armed a Hawk. The missile leapt away into the twilight before him, leaving a brilliant flaretail which chased the skyhopper, on the very edge of his visual contact.

The pilot was good. Jarrat gave him his due as he watched the CRT. Stone whistled as his own instruments told the story. The skyhopper rolled into a suicide dive, pulled up in the shadow of a mountainside and stood on its tail. The Hawk was not as quick to act or react as a human pilot. The explosion as it ploughed into the mountain sent a yellow fireball high into the air.

'Don't lose him,' Stone warned. 'He's on the deck, hard to follow on groundscan. You've got a better chance of keeping a track on him than we have.'

'I know.' Jarrat still had the Yamazake, a blip on the forward CRT, growing indistinct as it began to dodge about low-level concealment and obstruction. A radio mast, power pylons that marched across the southern hills, immense groundstation antennae. His speed was down now, but the low level acrobatics were desperate, foolhardy. 'He knows he can't outrun or outgun me,' Jarrat muttered. 'The bugger's going to try to outfly me.'

'Looks...' Stone hesitated, '...like he's playing tag with the squirrels.'

'He is.' At two hundred metres Jarrat pulled up, took a forward scan and crammed on all the speed he dared. 'Now you see him, now you don't. Oh, Jesus. I've got a town ahead.'

'That'll be Orlando,' Stone supplied. 'Careful with your missiles.'

'Stoney!' Jarrat protested as he pulled up to five hundred and scanned for air traffic. 'You tracking anything civvy in the air ahead of me?'

'Only your runner. And he's turning west.'

Jarrat followed, thundering over the rooftops of the outdistrict town. Complaints would inundate local Tac, irate objections to joy-riding jet-jockeys. Jarrat smiled mirthlessly as he opened the throttles a notch and Orlando was suddenly far behind.

Before him, the skyhopper lived up to its name, agile as a gymnast as it bounded over a pine plantation, a ridge, and shot low into a broad river valley. The kick of unease through Jarrat's belly broadcast to Stone, clearer than radio.

'What's wrong, Kevin?'

'Nothing,' Jarrat said tersely. 'It's just too damned long since I did this kind of work, and this guy's trying to fly me into the ground.'

'We've lost him,' Stone called a moment later. 'He's off our screens.'

Jarrat handled the spaceplane with intuitive delicacy. The instinct of a human pilot outpaced the computer. The wings were outswept, the ground was never more than fifty metres below. Trees, ridges and hills loomed up out of the twilight, but he kept the speed up.

The radiant, superhot engines of the Yamazake skyhopper were in acquisition range of his heat seekers, if he could only get a clear shot. The river valley wound unpredictably, filled with random obstruction. Groundscan radar supplied a constant stream of data but the human pilot's instinct was several leaps ahead every time.

'I've still got him.' Jarrat bobbed over a granite outcropping and pulled hard to starboard as a pine plantation rushed out of nowhere. 'Damn. Our man's local. He knows this rabbit warren like his own backyard.'

'We still don't see him,' Stone said evenly. 'Is he down?'

'Airborne at twenty metres, on the deck. River valley. Christ, he's good. Best I've seen outside Starfleet. Whoa!' He snatched the stick up hard and opened the throttles as the valley came to an abrupt end. The skyhopper had pulled up a tenth of a second sooner, since the pilot know the area. Suddenly they were in free air, and the NARC spaceplane was no more than a hundred metres behind.

A Phoenix III leapt away from the port wing, and Jarrat was intent on his instruments. 'Missile has acquired... I've got him. Clear air. He won't outrun this one.'

A fireball of blazing gases and cartwheeling shrapnel blossomed in the twilight. Jarrat roared through, came about in a wide arc and scanned the site of the impact. Spot fires burned brightly where wreckage had ploughed in, but the Yamazake was gone.

'Bandit destroyed,' Jarrat reported. 'Inform Orlando fire control they have a couple of small grassfires at these co-ordinates. Can you raise Duggan?'

Stone: 'He's been listening in since showtime.'

'Patch me through.' Jarrat paused a moment. 'I've got your man, Colonel, but he's in bad shape. They were waiting for me, been here for hours. They used me to make Spiteri show himself in this wilderness, but they'd have targeted him anyway, as soon as he moved. He couldn't hide forever. Your security band is shot, Duggan. Your comm lines are hacked. He was dead in the water as soon as he called you.'

A painful silence answered before Duggan said bitterly, 'I worked that out for myself, Captain. You want to tell me what you think I can do about it?

'I could make a few suggestions,' Jarrat said acidly. 'None of them legally or anatomically possible.'

'Will Spiteri make it?' Duggan asked in subdued tones, as if he had accepted Tactical's responsibility for a man's death.

'I don't know.' Jarrat lifted the nose, inswept the wings and opened the throttles. High above him, the *Athena* was a green mark on the CRT. 'I'm taking him to the carrier, it's closer than Elysium. Stoney, tell Reardon I'm coming home.'

Chapter Ten

A gurney team waited in the service lift as the hangar repressurised. Kip Reardon was already gowned and the main OR was decontaminating as Jarrat touched down. Stone felt the rush of his anger as the cycling machines blasted furnace-hot air into the bay, but Jarrat's face was unreadable as he lifted off the helmet.

The canopy was up, the gurney team hurrying across the deck as he sat on the side of the cockpit and peered down at Spiteri. 'He's alive, Kip,' he called, addressing Reardon via the loop. 'He's bleeding badly. I'm afraid I threw him around a lot, trying to catch the shooter.'

It might have been better, Stone reflected silently, to let the skyhopper go and get Spiteri aboard in one piece, if he could have been guaranteed to make it to the carrier alive. The 'if factor' made any decision precarious. Jarrat looked piercingly at him. They never shared actual thoughts, but sometimes they were thinking so close, they had no need to.

'Out of the way, Captain, please!' Faith Macefield was Reardon's assisting surgeon, an ex-Army woman, twice Jarrat's age and size. The command was barked in drill-sergeant tones.

He dropped to the deck and watched as the medics clambered up the ringing steel steps of a boarding platform. Stone hung back, watchful, his attention divided between Jarrat and Spiteri. Kevin was so angry he could barely speak, and when he found his voice his words were barbed.

'Bloody Tactical!' He slammed his helmet from one hand to the other. 'They've got holes in their security you could drive an airbus through!'

'Hardly their fault, is it?' Stone demanded quietly. 'They're not exactly up against a pack of amateurs. Equinox have got us against a wall too.'

'And every time we get screwed, we get blown on the ground,' Jarrat snarled. The fury spent itself like a summer storm. 'Equinox is into Tactical so deep, Duggan must know his department is in Dorne's back pocket!'

'Wouldn't be the first time it's happened.' Stone sighed. 'Let me help you out of the hardsuit.'

'Not yet.' Jarrat set his helmet aside. 'Maybe Kip can give me a word with Spiteri before they put him under. He might not make it.'

Stone felt a flare of emotion from him. 'You trying to tell him you're sorry? You didn't get him shot, Kevin. That skyhopper was four million credits' worth of raceplane, and it was concealed in a scanner blind spot before we began tracking. No way was Spiteri going to get out of there alive unless you were clairvoyant. You're an empath, not a magician! Don't launch into a guilt trip.'

The undertone lecture made Jarrat pause. His brows arched and Stone felt the anger begin to defuse. 'You sure?'

'Review the data for yourself.' Stone stood back as the gurney team hurried Spiteri toward the emergency lift which would deliver them directly to the OR. 'We got a good look at the aircraft. We read it as a Yamazake Corona, manufactured in the Cygnus plant, so expensive the likes of us can only dream about it. So fast, it's debatable if it should be in civvy hands at all. And this unlikely joy toy came out of nowhere in the middle of an industrial wasteland, dead on cue. If you hadn't made Spiteri show they'd have waited till he tried to get off in a crappy little skyvan, and knocked him out of the air.'

They stepped into the lift, flanking the gurney, and Stone looked into Spiteri's brown face. He was as good looking in the flesh as in the file picture. His lashes fluttered, his lips worked as he saw Jarrat. Bare whispers left his lungs, and Jarrat bent closer.

'Tell me, Jack, I'm listening.'

The words were so soft, Stone did not even hear them. The lift rose fast, and when the doors slid open they stepped out into the white light of the Infirmary. Through the wide observation window they saw a prepped table, a battery of machines, two nurses, and Reardon in surgical greens. The decontamination light was on, and Jarrat and Stone pulled up short as Spiteri was whisked inside.

They stood at the window, watching silently as Reardon began. A cryogen tank stood open. Spiteri might be relegated to hibernation as a last resort. Not long before, Stone had stood before this same glass, watching Reardon. That night it had been a Chell money man on the table.

At last Jarrat turned away, cracked the wrist seals and took off his gloves. 'Ah, the hell with it. I need a drink.'

'Cantrell wants to look at your videos and debrief,' Stone reminded him.

'He can wait,' Jarrat said sourly. 'He's aboard as an observer, remember? Things get done in our time.' He strode toward the lift and spoke over his shoulder. 'I think Spiteri gave me enough.'

With a glance into the OR, Stone followed. As he helped Jarrat to de-suit they played back the covertly captured voice track. His brows knitted as the playback ended, and he popped the datacube out of the recorder mounted on the left shoulder of Jarrat's armour.

It turned over and over in his palm. 'Jesse Lawrence.'

'A Companion,' Jarrat added. 'According to Spiteri, a prince among his kind, so beautiful and so skilled, he's one of a select stable who get work on Skycity. You remember them? They were so far out of our price bracket it was funny. He's seen and heard it all, and he keeps his mouth shut... the kid's got a brain.'

'The last thing Spiteri said to you,' Stone murmured as his hand closed on the cube, 'before they took him into the OR. I didn't make it out.'

Jarrat slammed the locker on the last piece of his armour. 'A name. Schaefer. I don't know what it means, he hadn't mentioned it before. He said, "Schaefer, ask Jesse." And then he went out.' Jarrat's face shuttered and he looked away, but Stone felt the burn of impotent grief.

'Kevin.' His fingers closed on Jarrat's arms. 'You want that drink? You look like you could use it.'

'Yeah.' Jarrat shook himself hard. 'And then we'd better find Jesse Lawrence, fast. Without,' he added caustically, 'any help from Elysium Tac!'

He stalked away like a hunting cat, and not for the first time Stone thought how magnificent Jarrat was when he was angry. Despite the situation, he smiled faintly as he watched the swing of his hips, the toss of his head and the flex of long legs. Spiteri had called the Companion a showpony, but before Stone was a colt not yet broken to saddle or spur. God forbid that Jarrat should ever be tamed, he thought fervently as he followed his partner in the direction of their cabins.

With a double brandy under his belt, Jarrat began to settle. He drank a second slowly and rinsed the tumbler in the basin in the shower stall. Stone sat on the bunk, waiting for the comm to buzz. Cantrell would not be patient for long.

Sure enough, as Jarrat set down the tumbler Petrov called from the ops room. Stone touched a key. 'All right, Mischa, we'll be there.'

'Got a call from Orlando Tactical,' Petrov told him. 'They're scraping up bits of wreckage. You want 'em?'

'Send them to Elysium,' Jarrat said indifferently. 'If Forensic makes anything of it, great. We already know what we're up against.'

The anger had quelled to brief flashes of annoyance. Stone slipped an arm about his waist. 'That was some of the best low-level flying I've ever seen. Circus stuff. I was proud. Gene was impressed.'

'I was just plain scared,' Jarrat confessed with a rueful look. 'It's a long time since I did anything like that. You stayed with me, dead on target, same as the simulations.'

'The empathy?' Stone hugged and released him. 'The more agitated we get, the clearer it is. At first I tried to match what I felt against your telemetry. In the end, I stopped even looking at the machines. They're too slow and inspecific. But you gave me a fright.'

'When I curtailed telemetry?' At the door, Jarrat hesitated. 'Stoney, it's not just Tactical that might be hacked. Have you thought, Equinox might be into us?'

The thought had occurred to Stone, and it chilled him. 'I'm trying not to think about it,' he admitted. The white metal cube from Jarrat's voice recorder caught the light as he held it between thumb and forefinger. 'This might be the key.'

The grey eyes were like gimlets as Jarrat looked at it. 'It had better be. Blood's been spilled for that. Spiteri won't make it. The best Kip can do is shove him into cryogen and see if his family want to cover the repair bill or terminate.' His face hardened. 'If his family survives. Equinox might find them.' He looked levelly at Stone before he stepped out and turned toward the lifts.

The ops room was dim. Petrov and Cantrell had organised the shuttle's video, and Stone played back the voice recording without comment. Jarrat helped himself to coffee and sat in the chair at the end of the table, chin in his palm, eyes on the monitor, where the pictures from his nose camera recounted the fight, flight and wreck in graphic detail.

The older officer whistled. 'That's some fancy flying, Kevin. You were fighter qualified after coming into NARC?'

'I trained with a Starfleet squadron.' Jarrat sipped his coffee. 'A week of theory, four of simulation, two in the air with an instructor made of equal parts ice and sulphuric acid, then six weeks flying every mission set-up the computer could devise. Stoney did the same.'

'Three months of hell,' Stone said drily, 'but I never regretted it.' He leaned both elbows on the briefing table among a litter of printout. 'Jesse Lawrence is the last chance we have. And we're worried, Gene. Every time we make a move, Equinox is in before us. We don't know if we're being blown through Tactical... or if Equinox is into us.'

Cantrell's eyes widened. 'You think we've been hacked? The carrier?'

'It's not impossible.' Jarrat frowned into his cup as if it were a crystal ball. 'Equinox has technology the Army is still dreaming about. A lot of the electronic guts of this ship were assembled either with Equinox hardware or components made by their licensed subsidiaries '

'This is true,' Petrov mused. 'Equinox designs the software Starfleet will be using next year.' He stopped there, and the colour drained from his face.

'Right.' Jarrat took a breath. 'And NARC uses mainly Starfleet flight systems. Get on the stick, Gene. Find out which of our components are based on Equinox materials. Shut everything down till we find out if we're carrying a leech.'

The thought was terrifying. Cantrell flicked a lighter but did not hold it to the small cigar between his lips. 'You know what you're saying?'

'I know.' Jarrat massaged the back of his neck. 'We don't dare trust our computers or communications.' He looked sidelong at Stone, brows arched.

Eyes closed, Stone grasped the problem by the horns. 'Leech' was an apt colloquialism. An inbuilt device, or an obscure corner of a programme so sophisticated its operators had no real understanding of how it functioned. The parasite listened, recorded, and waited until it was activated. Then it used the very equipment it was designed to control to fulfil its basic purpose. Espionage.

The carrier's own computers could be informing Randolph Dorne of every move NARC made, instants after a decision was taken. And the leech could have lain dormant in the electronics since the equipment was installed. It had occurred in Starfleet, on rare occasions.

With a sick expression, Cantrell stood. 'I'll have Budweisser start a major diagnostic. It'll take time.'

'And time is one thing we don't have,' Jarrat said softly. 'Equinox is moving, Stoney. They're covering their tracks as fast as they can. If we drag our heels, and if they even suspect Jesse Lawrence, the kid is dead meat... and we lose the last link in the data chain.'

Stone rubbed his face hard and looked at the chrono over Petrov's bowed head. 'It'll be about 22:00 in Elysium. That'd be a Companion's busiest time.'

'I'd say.' Jarrat drained his cup. 'He'll have an agent.'

'Makes sense,' Stone agreed. 'But we don't dare call from here.' He swivelled his chair out and stood. 'Get Bud busy, Gene. Shut everything down. Final signal to Central — inform Dupre we're going dark till further notice. Say it's routine servicing on the tachyon transmitters. There's no sense in telling Equinox we've woken up to them. Kevin?'

'Right behind you.' Jarrat fell into step beside him as they left the ops room. 'Can you trust Duggan? I mean, are you sure?'

For a moment Stone bridled, then hesitated. 'You mean, Duggan might have been bought?'

'He wouldn't be the first.' Jarrat thrust his hands into the pockets of his jeans as they walked. 'If they offered you ten million credits, a penthouse in Geneva, a Volvo Ajax in the garage, a bedwarmer like Jesse Lawrence... you may not have the tenacity to turn them down.'

Stone winced. 'That stinks, Kevin.'

'So, can you trust Duggan?' Jarrat pressed.

The question was loaded, and Stone did not answer too fast. 'If you'd asked me ten years ago I'd have said yes, no reserva- tion. Now... it's been a long time. When I was in rookie school Duggan was an idealist. He had this light in his eyes. Fanatic. Zealot. He was on a crusade, and if it cost him his life, he'd die smiling. He was married, like Spiteri.'

'I haven't forgotten.' Jarrat puffed out his cheeks. 'For what it's worth, I think we can trust Duggan. Gut feeling. He's still on the crusade, just older and wiser. He knows he may not win, but that doesn't stop him tilting at windmills.'

They stepped into the lift and were silent until the car deposited them on the hangar deck. Flight crews were working on the Blue Raven gunship. Powertools whined and Stone waited for a moment's quiet before he summoned a big, thickset man in uniform fatigues.

'The comm loop is out,' he cautioned. 'We're going dark, the whole ship. Inform your unit verbally. But first, tell hangar control we want to launch.'

The man had sergeant's stripes up, which meant he had several years' NARC experience, but he was stunned. Stone watched him hurry away and bit his lip, but it was Jarrat who put it into words.

'You were on three other carriers before you were assigned aboard this one. You ever done this before, Stoney?'

'Shut down telemetry, run silent?' Stone shook his head slowly, deliberately. 'You?'

'No. In fact, I've only heard of it being done in lunatic battlefield simulations.' Jarrat beckoned a passing crewgirl. 'You on duty, sweetheart?'

She was a cute little thing, with red hair cut short about her ears and a freckled snub nose. One shoulder insignia was NARC; the other was Starfleet. 'Just going off shift, Cap.' She looked up at him curiously. 'Something's wrong, isn't it? I just spoke to a tech sergeant. He said we're on radio shut down. I thought he was trying to have a joke on me.'

'No joke, kid,' Jarrat told her. 'Get me a couple of Ravens. We want the armour stored under decks in the shuttle. And have a crew replace the missiles I used.'

Her eyes widened, and she fled to do as she was told. Stone watched the flight crews, saw the expressions of sheer disbelief ripple through NARC and Starfleet personnel alike. 'How long will it take Budweisser to run a diagnostic?'

'Hard to say,' Jarrat mused. 'We could be dry-docked right here. It may be paranoia, but if we're carrying a leech it's also possible we're bugged in the nav or drive ignition. We're using a lot of Equinox components. Unwittingly, we install a parasite.

It sits dormant for years, till this ship shows up in this system. How'd you like to attempt main drive ignition and get an engine implosion? There wouldn't be much left of us.'

Stone recoiled. 'That would mean — years ago Equinox, or someone in the company, took defensive measures against the day when NARC would arrive here.'

'It's possible.' Jarrat watched a sled trundle out to replace the missiles as two Gold Ravens appeared with the armour on a trolley. 'When Angel use on some world crosses the ten percent line, NARC won't be far away.'

'Good Christ.' Stone was cold to the bone. 'No, I don't buy it, Kevin.'

'You mean it scares the daylights out of you, so you're going to deny the possibility,' Jarrat retorted.

The concept rocked Stone. 'Budweisser will find it,' he said quietly. 'If it's there.'

'I hope you're right.' Jarrat looked levelly at him. 'Because if we installed a load of booby traps along with our electronics, they could be rigged to activate at the touch of a button... and Dorne may have his finger on it. So until Bud either finds the parasites, or until he gives us a clean bill of health, we don't do anything to excite Dorne. Yes?'

Before Stone could answer his name was called, and he turned to see a flustered messenger. 'Cap Cantrell is in his cabin, he wants you there, immediately.'

The comm loop was dead. If Randolph Dorne's specialists were eavesdropping they would soon guess they had been suspected, if not detected. First they would assume a fault in their own equipment. Any time NARC could get was valuable.

At a knock on Cantrell's door, he opened. Lieutenant Karl Budweisser was already inside. Short, muscular, Canadian, he was past his best years but one of the best combat engineers in the business. He wore NARC fatigues by preference; as an officer he could have worn plain clothes.

On Cantrell's desk, the terminal slaved to the carrier's computers was turned off. Beside it, a portable sat in an open carrycase. Its screen displayed a schematic of the ship. Budweisser was making notes and barely glanced up as Jarrat and Stone appeared.

'We could be in trouble,' Cantrell said without preamble. 'You'd better tell them what you told me, Bud.'

The Canadian set down the notes, thrust his hands into the pockets of his black uniform pants and gave the younger men a grave look. 'What makes you think we've got a leech?'

'It's either us or Tac, or both. We can't afford chances,' Stone said evenly. 'Booby traps installed along with listening devices are a logical progression, and the real rub is, if we do have them, we installed them ourselves, years ago. Standard replacement components... complete with parasite devices.'

'Shit.' Budweisser ran his palms over sparse hair which was swiftly greying. 'It's feasible. This carrier was commissioned twelve years ago, built by Mitsubishi at Kure, same as a lot of our big stuff. Now, most of the original electronics are Yamazake, but eight years ago some smart-ass in some office decided to use cheaper compatible parts from a competitor, as a cost-cutting exercise. Starfleet got the same order, it came down from the top. As you can guess —'

'Equinox undercut Yamazake,' Jarrat murmured. 'For eight years, every time we blew a fuse we installed an Equinox replacement.'

'Fuses, we don't worry about,' Budweisser said acidly. 'It's guidance, reactor governors, engine ignition sequence, weapons control, tachyon transmission gear. These, you should sweat over.' He swivelled the portable terminal. 'Now, we're safe to use this machine, because it's mine. I bought it a couple of furloughs ago, last time we were on Earth. It's never been connected to the ship's computers, so you can forget about contamination.'

'Contamination?' Stone echoed. He looked sharply at Jarrat and pulled up a chair. 'You'd better explain.'

Cantrell had poured four glasses of malt whisky. He placed one into Stone's hand, passed one to Jarrat. 'Drink that. You'll need it.'

The engineer savoured the malt with a pensive expression. 'I accessed the tech library, nothing an eavesdropper would notice. We've installed Equinox components all over this ship, on every refit, for years. There's maybe sixty million Equinox chips scattered through our electronics. The good news is, I can find them. The bad news? It'll take months, and even when I find them I don't dare rip the buggers out. To start with, we don't have enough replacements to get us back up and running. Even if we did, they'd be Equinox junk, replacing shit with shit.

And they're not the problem. They're inert, like a grenade without a fuse.'

'And the fuse?' Stone had glimpsed where Bud was going, and his skin was ice cold.

'Commands hidden in the flight system software,' Jarrat whispered.

'Right.' Budweisser tapped keys and produced another diagram. 'The brains of this bucket are a clone of Starfleet's Skylark computers. They run the most sophisticated progs yet designed, upgraded on every major overhaul. On the last three refits, we installed updates of the QuantumData system. It runs guidance, drive, communications, defence, every critical function.' He paused. 'It was designed in an Equinox lab.'

Jarrat groaned expressively. 'What did you mean, a minute ago, contamination?'

'Suppose we did install parasites along with our hardware,' Budweisser said darkly. 'They're like limbs without brains. Their brains will amount to minor routines hidden deep in the QuantumData which makes this ship tick... and any ship like it. The software parasite could spread like a virus, computer to computer, ship to ship, hitch-hiking with transmissions of common data. Then it sits like a bomb, waiting for one of two triggers.'

'One,' Stone said slowly, 'a signal from daddy. Sooner or later Angel gets to be a problem on Avalon, a carrier enters this system and Randolph Dorne has a spy aboard, it's been aboard in stasis for years.'

'The other trigger?' Jarrat asked, though it was all too easy to guess.

'We know that our leech, if we got one, is someplace in the QuantumData. If it's smart enough,' Bud said acerbically, 'it'll know the nanosecond when I start cutting off its legs — the actual hardware devices. There may be a logic bomb. A command that only triggers if realises it's being attacked.' He shrugged expressively. 'Main drive ignition, out of sequence... we'd be a billion bits of scrap metal in orbit.'

A sliver of ice wormed through Jarrat's belly and Stone shivered. 'Then we don't dare take the system apart,' Kevin said quietly.

'Worse,' Budweisser added. 'I don't dare even look into the software. If I poke around in the brains of this ship, I may let it know what I'm doing, and it could defend itself.'

'Jesus.' Stone's fingers tightened on the empty glass. 'Okay, Bud, I'm open to suggestions. This is way out of my field. What options have we got?'

Budweisser studied the screen of his personal terminal. 'There's two things we can do. I'm down to one option, personally. I can't trust the blueprints of this ship, as stored in the tech library. When we installed Equinox components, we got Equinox schematics with them, and they'll show anything they want us to see.' He exhaled through his teeth. 'I'll scrutinise every centimetre of our electronics, use synthetic aperture scanning and build a holo blueprint. In virtual reality mode, inside a terminal that's never been connected to the main computers, I'll test each individual component. I'll find the bugs, the arms and legs.'

'How long?' Stone asked tersely.

'Say, eight or ten days to re-blueprint the whole ship,' Bud guessed. 'And two, three years to run —'

'Years?' Jarrat was on his feet.

'Sixty million chips,' Budweisser growled. 'Get me a hundred extra terminals like this baby, I'll do it for you in a couple of weeks. Just don't supply anything made by Equinox or its subsidiary, or any company that uses their components.' He reached for the bottle and helped himself to another malt. 'And don't yell for help on any comm system, tachyon or otherwise. Write a letter — but not on a terminal slaved to the ship.'

'We get the picture,' Stone said softly. 'Okay, the other option?'

'Get a cyber specialist out here.' Budweisser rolled the glass between his hands. 'What we need is a tapeworm prog that'll slither through every circuit we have, looking for redundant, extraneous, irrelevant subroutines, read 'em, tell us where they are.'

'And turn them off,' Jarrat added.

'Ah.' Bud took a sip. 'That's the sticky part. Like I said, it could defend itself. Machines don't think infinitely fast, only at the speed of light.' He smiled bitterly. 'I'm a combat engineer, and a bloody damned good one, Cap. I'm not a cyber specialist.'

'Get one.' Stone stood and gave Cantrell a hard look. 'Send Curt Gable groundside with civvy ID and travel passes. Put him on the next clipper to Darwin's World, get this whole story to

167

Dupre, on paper, if necessary! Get a cyber systems analyst here by Starfleet courier, as fast as they know how to move. Say, six days turnaround.'

Jarrat made cynical sounds. 'If she's still on Darwin's, they'll send Yvette McKinnen, God help us.'

'Bill Dupre told me a little about her,' Cantrell said thoughtfully. 'She's not a keen supporter of yours. She told Bill to have me watch you both for delayed stress syndrome after the Death's Head job.' He arched his brows at the younger men. 'Any sign of that?'

'Not a flicker, Gene,' Jarrat lied. 'She just doesn't care for us. It's nothing personal, but we screwed the biocyber implant project she had years invested in. She's still the best I ever worked with, Bud.'

'I know her by rep.' Budweisser closed up his portable. 'I'll get busy.'

He was gone with that, and Stone regarded Cantrell with a frown. 'Get Gable on his way. Keep the comm system dark until you can rig something.'

'Like what?' Cantrell gathered glasses and bottle. 'Get the audio boys to use portables, put together a loop of forty, fifty hours of immaterial chatter? Put that on continuous playback while we run about with bits of paper and verbal messages? It'd fool Equinox. For a while.'

'You could do worse.' Jarrat stepped to the door. 'It might mean survival, Gene.'

'Where will you be?' Cantrell asked. 'We won't be able to contact you while we're dark. It'll take time to organise a code system for voice contact.'

'We still have to find Jesse Lawrence,' Stone reminded him. 'We'll be in Elysium.'

'Civvy ID, cash and cards,' Jarrat added. 'Give us twenty-four hours. With luck we'll be back by then, with a very beautiful kid in tow, alive.'

'Be careful,' Cantrell called after them. 'I'll get the loop on line as soon as I can. A few hours. Equinox might assume we had a fault.'

A fault? Stone thought as he led the way toward his cabin. They had a fault which could run like a disease through every thinking machine in NARC, Starfleet and the Army alike. He watched Jarrat search out the civilian ID they had not used in over a year. The travel passes were open-dated, the credit cards drew on an unlimited account on Earth.

With a sense of urgency Jarrat changed into white denim, a black silk shirt, black boots, and laid a brown leather jacket on the bed. Before he put on the jacket, he shrugged into the shoulder harness of an old friend.

The Colt AP-60 had not seen use since he had left the streets of Chell, but it was in superb condition. The magazine held eighty rounds; the capsule of pressurised gas which propelled the teflon-coated, hollow-nosed .60 calibre rounds was fresh. Jarrat checked the weapon instinctively, down to the short, perforated barrel shroud. It cycled ten a second and those projectiles would carve through two centimetres of steel plate from a range of one hundred metres. Its weight was welcome against his ribs as he slid it into the holster.

In the adjoining cabin, Stone dressed in the familiar Tactical-issue pants he liked, a beige shirt, sport shoes, and laid out an elegant beige leather jacket. His own weapon was a 9mm Ingram-Kalashnikov, shorter than Jarrat's by a scant centimetre, lighter by two hundred grams. It cycled only seven a second and though the magazines held only forty rounds they were so quick to change, he could carry one weapon and assorted clips preloaded with explosive, incendiary, teflon, and regular anti-personnel ammunition.

'Cash and cards.' Jarrat was preoccupied as he sorted a wedge of local bills, travel papers, ID and credit cards. 'We used them on Sheal last year, but they'll serve again. Crenna, John J.' He held the photocard up beside Stone's face, and slipped it into his breast pocket. 'Landham, Raymond T.' He frowned at his own card and slid it into his wallet.

'We'll be in trouble if the Elysium authorities try to verify those,' Stone said quietly. 'We're not entering via commercial channels. The spaceport won't have a record of us.'

'Don't give them a reason and they won't check.' Jarrat pulled on his jacket and looked at his chrono. 'It's midnight in Elysium, and that's perfect.'

'Kevin.' Stone laced his fingers at Jarrat's nape to hold him. 'You want me to stay here and monitor you? We've got no telemetry, no way to yell for backup if it goes bad.'

'The best backup I know is standing right here.' Jarrat leaned over and searched Stone's mouth with a restless kiss. 'This is the first time we've been one jump ahead of Equinox, Stoney. We can't afford to waste the advantage.'

He was right. Stone nipped his ear with sharp teeth, tousled his hair affectionately and gave him a push.

They were on the hangar deck minutes later. The flight crews had been cautioned to radio silence, and Gil Cronin tripped the spinners and sirens to clear his unit out of the bay. He slapped palms with Jarrat as Stone climbed up the hard-points, and then jogged away to relay verbal instructions to the hangar controllers.

Without a word spoken over the dead loop, the bay depressurised and Stone took the spaceplane out and down toward the city of Elysium.

Chapter Eleven

The Taipan Hotel towered over the rambling Alexandria sector on the low side of Elysium. The blaze of neon filled the night in the north, but to the south the rising hills were marked out by the lights of a more sparse urban jumble.

The shuttle cruised in at two hundred kilometres per hour, five hundred metres over the rooftops, holding a speed, course and altitude which made it look, on any tracking screen, like a civilian airbus. In the night sky only its acquisition lights were visible.

A fast orbit had taken the plane about the planet, away from the carrier. Stone entered the atmosphere half the world away and dropped low, under the tracking network. In the rear cockpit, Jarrat watched the groundscan CRT, navigating by geography and the radio beacons which marked the derelict industrial fields.

They approached Elysium at the speed and height of the civilian craft they often derided, and Jarrat searched the data files for a likely landing point. They needed a hotel with a roof stressed to take something the weight of the shuttle; it must be well out of town, with an enclosed hangar. The choices were few, and in minutes he picked out the Taipan.

The roof landing area was brilliantly illuminated. Stone stood off to watch a skycab pull out, tuned into the local radio traffic and called the building. Invitations to land were cordially extended, and as a guidance beam was broadcast he eased closer.

A little way off, wreathed in darkness, he backed off the throttles and Jarrat consulted the observer's instruments. 'We lucked out — and it's about time,' Kevin reported. 'They don't seem to employ a night shift hangar crew, so the only person who'll see us approach is the controller, and he'd never identify this bird for certain in the dark. Too unusual on civvy street. Their surveillance videos are off.'

'That's illegal, isn't it?' Stone asked drily.

'Also cheap,' Jarrat added. 'Most of these places are run by accountants. They turn off almost everything between midnight and dawn. Everyone's asleep, who's going to know?'

Half the roof was enclosed, protecting million-credit vehicles from the elements. Limousines and sport planes were parked in orderly niches, and as the shuttle slid into the hangar Stone gave them a glance that could have been envious.

In the back, Jarrat almost chuckled. 'None of those toys flies as high, as fast or as far as us, and there's not a missile among them. Be satisfied.'

'But I don't own this crate,' Stone added as he rotated the shuttle and parked it in the corner between a Chev and a scarlet Rand stratoskimmer. 'Let's get her covered, fast.'

The hangar was deserted as they climbed down. Out of the cargo compartment in the belly Stone drew the case containing a thin, tough kevlex sheet. In a hotzone it was enough to protect the aircraft's delicate systems from electromagnetic pulse; in civil surroundings, from interfering hands and prying eyes. Despite its thinness its area was enormous, and its weight, but repulsion units made it easy to handle.

It tugged quickly over the back of the shuttle and Stone sealed it about the landing gear with a code from the infrabeam. He stood back, considered the amorphous, anonymous shape under the cover and lifted a brow at Jarrat.

'Good enough,' Jarrat decided, and pointed him at the frosted glass doors which led into the building.

Emerald carpets, mint green walls and a drowsy receptionist greeted them as they stepped inside. Jarrat produced his ID with a smile and signed for a room. Nothing exceptionally expensive, nor too cheap. Nothing to draw attention.

The room was five levels below, with a view of Elysium stretching from the Alexandria sector, right below their windows, to Sciaparelli, on the horizon. Complimentary cognac stood by a king-sized bed with an oyster-grey quilt; vidphones flanked the French lace pillows and a terminal was dormant in the corner. An amber tiled bathroom opened to the right, with a hot tub, salts, oil, soap and a choice of towels or hot air turbodryer. Not quite all the comforts of home, but not bad.

Stone frowned at the city as Jarrat turned on the terminal. Every city looked the same an night. The neon glared, the steelrock beat out a brazen, pagan rhythm which clouded the senses, masked the terrible reality of day.

Down in those streets, one kid in ten between fifteen and twenty-five was dead on his feet. Angel scythed through the population like a plague, left tides of grief and despair, and yet in the night the waves of joy were almost tangible, shouting out of city bottom and the rich men's ghettoes alike.

Sex, power, ego, fantasy. All were magnified by Angel. The drug lifted the darkest dreams out of the roots of the mind and cloaked them in flesh that seemed so real. The addict returned, over and over, craving the golden dust as if he would suffocate or starve without it. Death was a year or two away, but decay came first, and the insensible fucking, the animal response of a body driven without mercy by a mind in delirium.

Dreamheads passed out among the trashpacks, and for all they knew they could be on Skycity among the elite. The truth was told in rancid flesh, ruined health, atrophied physique and a mind so removed from reality that it soon desired only the dreams. Stone shivered as he remembered all too well.

Jarrat felt the shudder and left the terminal as the screen brightened. His arms circled Stone's torso from behind, drew him close, turned him. 'What is it? That felt bad.'

'Just remembering.' Stone buried his face in the curve of Jarrat's neck. 'City streets have that effect on me. They're full of Angelheads. And I was one of them.'

'Not by choice.' Jarrat gripped him hard. 'And the men who did that to you are dead. You're tired. Go to bed.'

'And Jesse Lawrence?' Stone gestured at the screen.

'Is a professional.' Jarrat's fingers ran through Stone's dark hair. 'He'll be with a client till morning. We're not talking about a ten-credit blow. He's supposed to be the best money can buy, the kind that gets the diamonds and furs and cars, the offer of a penthouse if he'll only live in and pretend he loves the fat old exec with the bald head.' He rasped his fingernails gently through Stone's late-night stubble. 'Go to bed. I might have to call a dozen agencies before I find him, and he won't be free till dawn. We can grab a few hours' sleep. You need it.'

'So do you,' Stone whispered. 'But I wish you'd fuck me.' He felt a backwash of warmth from Kevin as he spoke.

'Do you?' Jarrat nuzzled his mouth. 'I might be able to manage that.' He sucked Stone's tongue for a moment and then gave him a push. 'Lie down. Let me find this hustler, and then I'll sort you out.'

So Stone stripped off clothes and sidearm, sprawled on the grey satin quilt and propped his head on his hand as he observed the hunt. Jarrat skimmed the commercial pages of the Elysium phonecode list, zeroed in on the Companions' Agencies and started at the top.

Velvet Kiss produced the offer of two boys who did a double act for the lucky client; Summer Wine produced a harassed proposal of a possible booking for Steve or Marco or Joe in three days' time. Jarrat hung up and tried again. He drew a blank at Young Bucks, Leather And Lace, and Black Pearls, but Stone saw him begin to take notice as he called Wild Stallions.

'It's a particular young man I'm looking for,' he told the yawning receptionist. 'I'm calling all over town for him! You don't agent for Jesse Lawrence, do you?'

The receptionist smiled and twisted the gold ring in his right ear. 'We do, but he's busy. Did you want to book him, or do you need to speak to him urgently?' He looked at his wrist for the time. 'I can probably reach him for you. The customers want to catch forty by this time.'

'Where is he?' Jarrat asked pleasantly.

'On Skycity.' The young receptionist consulted a schedule. 'May I ask who referred you? That is, I don't recognise you, so I know you haven't booked with us before.'

'My name is Raymond Landham,' Jarrat lied. 'Jesse spent a few nights with my business associate about two months ago, and when my friend got home to Orleans, I heard about nothing but Jesse for weeks. I'm here on business myself, and I just have to find this boy.'

'Ah.' The receptionist wore a smug look. 'He's a treasure. I'll do the booking first, make sure you have him as soon as we can manage, then I'll see if I can reach him. When would you like to meet?'

'As soon as he's available,' Jarrat said quickly. 'In the morning, if possible.'

'Not morning.' Brown eyes looked doubtfully out of the screen. 'He'll sleep past noon! As it happens, he doesn't have a booking tomorrow, you're in luck. Now, it's a thousand credits, payable by card before you hang up. You know Jesse doesn't do rough work? The usual fuck, suck and safe games, no dope, fists or pain.' A radiant smile. 'Any problem?'

'None,' Jarrat purred. 'Tell him I'm at the Taipan, room 716, unless you can reach him for me now. I'd love to talk to him. Ready for my card?' He pressed the credit card to the bottom left of the screen and waited a few seconds.

'That's fine, Mr Landham. Let me call Skycity for you.' The receptionist beamed at him. 'One moment.'

The screen blanked and Jarrat sat on the side of the bed. Stone shuffled closer, snaked one arm about him and pressed his face against the curve of Kevin's back, through the body-heated black silk. His hand delved into the warm nest between Jarrat's lean thighs and moulded about the growing hardness.

Then the vidphone flickered and Stone paused as Jarrat returned his attention to the call. On the screen appeared a face which was familiar, and Jarrat took a breath in surprise. Stone was out of the scan-angle of the camera, and watched the screen with astonishment. It took a moment, but then he had the young man. They had seen him through a window, in a courtyard in the light of several antique carriage lamps. Skycity.

'Damn,' Stone murmured. 'He was there that night!'

He was honey brown, with long, dark blond hair and fine, chiselled features. The rings in ears and nipples were gold, as were the clasps about his upper arms, the chains about his neck and those suspended between the nipple-rings. Wide, violet eyes looked out of the screen, unsuspecting. Behind him was a boudoir; he seemed to be sitting on the side of a vast bed. A shape lay asleep behind him.

'I'm Jesse,' he said in the slightly broadened vowels of the Elysium accent. 'You're Raymond Landham? You booked me?'

'That's right.' Jarrat took a breath. 'I've a friend who told me I had to see you. Jack sends his best.'

'Jack?' Jesse drew his hand across his chest, disturbing the filamentary chains.

'You remember Jack and Mike,' Jarrat purred. 'Jack told me I must find you.'

For another moment the violet eyes were puzzled, then they widened and the young man's throat bobbed as he swallowed. 'Uh, yes, I — that is, I remember. I can't talk about it here.' He glanced over his shoulder at the shape in the bed and dropped his voice. 'I'll meet you.'

'Come to the hotel,' Jarrat invited. 'I gave your agent the address.'

'No,' Jesse said at once. 'I'll tell you where.'

175

So he did not trust, Stone thought, and approved. He had more sense than to walk into someone else's set-up. This kid lived on his wits and had stayed alive when Grenshem and Spiteri, and God knew how many others, were dead.

'All right,' Jarrat said evenly. 'Tell me where, and when. I'll meet you on your own ground.'

Jesse's mind was clearly racing. 'There's a dance shop. You know Valhalla?'

'I'll find it,' Jarrat promised. 'When?'

The violet eyes strayed aside, probably to look at the time. 'Say, 09:00. I can get there by then, Mr Landham.'

'It's a date, kiddo,' Jarrat told him. 'I'll let you get back to work. Sleep well.'

'Fat chance,' Jesse said drily, and the screen blanked.

Jarrat turned off the vidphone and leaned back into Stone's waiting arms. 'Well, well. Valhalla, at nine.' He turned his hand and peered at his wrist. 'We have seven hours, Stoney. Get some sleep, take a bath, have a meal.'

'Fuck me,' Stone said softly. Slowly, deliberately, he eased down the empathic shields which protected him from the worst, and best, of Jarrat's stormy emotions. Lust, love, tenderness and wanting thrummed between them until Stone could barely breathe.

'Oh, yeah.' Jarrat pressed him down, pinned him to the quilt, covered his mouth, and Stone's hands splayed across the black silk.

It lifted out of Jarrat's belt. Stone's hands slid into the tight white denim, cupped Kevin's supple buttocks and kneaded. Jarrat groaned, rolled to his feet and stood in the lamplight to strip. Stone thought of Jesse Lawrence for just a moment as Jarrat set aside the Colt and folded his clothes. Then the image of the Companion was gone.

In his arms was a hard body, lean and muscular, artless and sublimely masculine. Stone was enthralled, as always. Kevin went over him with hands and lips, teased, bit and sucked until Stone was whimpering. Jarrat's skin prickled with the mirror sensations. He rolled over, inviting Stone to play him with mouth and hands as if he were an instrument.

Rose-brown nipples seduced Stone's tongue while his hand curved about the sturdy, beautiful cock which would soon be inside him. Jarrat arched into the bed, spread his legs and dug his heels into the mattress. His musk was sharp, so familiar now. Intense pleasure ripped through Stone's own body as he took a grip on the blood-hot shaft and gently bit into the nub of Kevin's left nipple.

They surged up, close to climax, and Stone took his hands and mouth away before it was too late. Jarrat's eyes were dark, rueful, self-mocking. He dragged a breath to the bottom of his lungs and sat up.

'There was a time I could make foreplay last all night,' he said in wry tones. 'I wish I knew what happened to my technique.'

'I'm irresistible,' Stone said glibly, and kissed the middle of Jarrat's smooth back. 'We're still new, honey, so's the empathy. In six months or a year we'll get it right. Not that I'm complaining, mind you.'

'I should think you're not!' Jarrat pushed to his feet and investigated the bathroom, which lay to the right of the bed.

'I saw a bottle of body oil,' Stone said lazily as he turned over on his back and crooked his knees.

His eyes followed Jarrat as he returned with a ceramic bottle, dwelt on the bob and sway of his cock. Usually smooth and golden, it was ruddy with desire now. He held out his palm to receive it. Kevin stepped closer and slipped into the waiting hand.

'This is gorgeous,' Stone said honestly. 'Then again, it's part of you.'

'Flattery will get you — ' Jarrat began.

'Everywhere?' Stone lick-kissed the throbbing head of him.

'I was going to say, fucked.' Kevin sank the mattress beside him. 'Go on, lie back and enjoy it. I want you just the way you are, loverboy.'

'On my back?' Stone wriggled down and spread his legs. Jarrat knelt between them and both long-fingered hands grasped Stone's eager genitals. He closed his eyes to savour the deep, racking pleasure. 'Oh, Kevin.'

'I love you,' Jarrat said, not quite unexpectedly. 'Maybe I don't say it often enough.'

'You don't have to.' Stone was breathless. He gasped as his legs were lifted over Jarrat's broad, bony shoulders, and with slitted eyes he saw the body oil glistening on Kevin's fingers. Then thought was torn from his mind as his body was plundered for pleasure.

177

The empathy might have been distressing a month before, but they had learned to control it, to relish it. Stone's face creased in concentration as he heard Kevin's soft grunt of pain, a response to Stone's fleeting discomfort as first two and then three fingers opened him. In moments pleasure began, and the fingers were replaced by Jarrat's cock. Stone held his breath, intent on the empathic bonding.

There! As Jarrat slid in he felt the tumult of sensation in his own nerves. Pleasure raced through every fibre and Stone cried out. Kevin echoed his shout a moment later, and the grey eyes looked down at him. Mouth open to pant, cheeks flushed, Jarrat was beautiful. Stone would have told him so, but could not find breath to speak.

Instead, he slipped his legs down, hugged tight about Kevin's torso, and as Jarrat began to rock, moved with him.

***

Five levels above a holotheatre, Valhalla opened off a busy arcade in downtown Capri, on the west side of Elysium. An aircab delivered them to a parking bay on an adjoining building, and from there they shouldered through the crowds. Gyrobikes wove along the kerb and the thoroughfare was congested with traffic, some on wheels, some riding blustering repulsion.

Theatre, arcades, dance shops and sex shops never stopped, but they had their quiet times. The haul from dawn till noon was as quiet as Valhalla would ever be. The sound system was low, steelrock was replaced by bluesy music. Inside was a dim, humid cavern, a vast dance floor that would be packed at midnight. To the left, the bar was softly lit; in the back were tables and booths where the weary could rest.

A few Angelheads had collapsed along the wall opposite the bar. They were spent, rank, exhausted. Stone gave them a glance of genuine pity. How easy it would have been for him to be one of them. Kevin and Harry Del had brought him back. Without the love of one and the incredible gifts of the other, Stone wondered where he would have been.

Perhaps he would have been like these hopeless victims, crumpled, discarded and forgotten in the shadows when the revellers went home. Waiting to die, and in the end wanting to. He shook off the thoughts with an effort. Kevin was frowning at him, painfully aware of his bitterness. He gave Jarrat a mute nod and moved on.

At midnight dreamsmoke would thicken the air and strobes would flicker hypnotically. At nine the air was merely candy sweet and the strobes were off. Jarrat and Stone stood in the doorway, searching for a face.

He was in the back, sitting at a table, hands about a glass, and he looked almost asleep. A sky-blue silk robe was tossed over the back of the chair. The cavern was so humid, Stone found himself sweating the moment he stepped in, and was not surprised Jesse Lawrence had thrown off the robe. He was naked, aside from his jewellery and swathes of body paint about his hips and left leg. He was as beguiling in the flesh as Stone remembered.

As they approached, Jesse stirred awake, put down his glass and stood. He was just under Jarrat's height, and much lighter, with supple muscles, a long, smooth cock and lovely, taut balls. Was he twenty-two? Stone wondered. The boy held out his hand in a nervous greeting, and Kevin took it. The dim lights shone on the rings in his ears and nipples. Several bracelets and a fine gold cockring lay on the table with his wallet and sunglasses.

'I know you,' he said quietly as he clasped Jarrat's hand. 'I'm good with faces. I've seen you before.'

'You saw us on Skycity.' Jarrat glanced at Stone.

'Oh, Christ.' Jesse snatched for his wallet and tried to dive past Jarrat, but the breadth of Stone's body stopped him. He struggled, threshed and kicked.

'Easy,' Jarrat hissed. 'You're safe.'

'You're Equinox security — Wozniak's goons,' Jesse sobbed. 'Jesus, how did you find me?'

'We're NARCs,' Stone told him. 'Jack Spiteri sent us.'

The boy froze. Blond hair veiled his face and he twisted his head, almost the only movement he could make as he lay trapped against Stone's body. 'NARCs?'

'You have a carrier over Elysium, did you know?' Jarrat glanced at the ceiling.

'I heard.' Jesse took a quick breath. 'I thought... you know what I thought.'

'That you were about to go follow Grenshem and Spiteri?' Jarrat touched his cheek. 'Stop worrying. You're probably safer now than you've been for months.'

Footsteps clattered from the direction of the bar and Stone

heard the characteristic rasp of a weapon charging. He remained still as a man's voice snarled, 'Put the kid down and get your hands up. You okay, Jesse? I said *put him down!*'

Stone released him and held his hands out from his sides. Jesse raked his hair back and smiled ruefully at the barman. 'It's okay, Tino. It's not what I thought it was.'

Slowly Stone turned. Tino was a burly man with Asiatic features, a large belly and a Steyr .44 pistol levelled on the whole group. 'Be sure, sugar,' he told Jesse. 'One yell, and I'll chop these good old boys to bits.'

'I'll be all right. Thanks, Tino. I... misunderstood,' Jesse said as he stepped back from Jarrat and Stone.

The barman put up his weapon and returned to his trade, and Stone looked the Companion up and down. His chest was heaving. His honey-coloured skin was slick with the sudden sweat of fear and the filamentary gold between the nipple-rings shuddered with every breath. He was terrified. The blue and silver body paints had smudged, leaving a faint mist of colour across the flat belly and beautiful genitals.

Jesse reached for his drink and swallowed it without taking a breath. He slid in behind the table and drew the robe about his shoulders. 'I'm sorry. I thought you were Wozniak's. I saw you with Natasha.'

'We were meeting Dorne,' Jarrat told him as he also sat. 'Natasha offered us your company.'

'Yeah? Company's my job.' Jesse hugged his arms about his chest in an effort to still his shivering. 'He's spectacular, isn't he? But not my kind.'

'He?' Stone appropriated a chair from the next table and sat.

'Natasha. He was a man six months ago. Decided to get modified. They say they put his balls in cryogen, in case he decides to change back. He's spectacular, but not my type. Treats me like I'm just a... a hole.'

Jarrat and Stone shared a glance. 'We got that impression that night,' Jarrat agreed. 'It's a pity we turned down the offer of you. It would have saved us a lot of trouble, and maybe saved Spiteri's life.' He slipped his fingers into his shirt pocket and turned on a tiny voice recorder. The boy did not even notice.

'Jack's dead?' Jesse's voice shook.

'I don't know,' Stone admitted. 'He called us with some information, Equinox was there. He was badly injured, he might be in a tank by now. The repairs could cost a fortune, and that's down to his family.'

'What family?' Jesse's eyes flooded as he looked up at the NARC men. 'His family was Michael, and Mike's dead!'

'Michael Rogan?' Jarrat leaned back, shoulder to shoulder with Stone. 'Tell us about them.'

'Get me a drink.' Jesse's hands clenched tightly. 'I need it. You scared shit out of me.'

A wave of Stone's hand brought the barman. Jesse was drinking a mild local spirit; Jarrat opted for a beer, Stone declined the offer of a drink altogether. The boy fought the shakes under control with an effort, sipped something he called a 'grancuzzi' and marshalled his thoughts.

'What can I tell you? Jack and Michael were — well, like you two look. Close. They were so happy, I was jealous. I knew Michael years ago, while I was still in school. We used to come here to dance.' He cast a glance about the dim cavern of Valhalla. 'Just to dance. We never fucked. Never got around to it, then Mike married Jack.' He pulled his wallet closer and produced a creased holosnap. 'Mike gave me this. I wasn't there when they handfasted.'

In the image the two men stood, loosely embraced, on the steps before a Temple of Gaia. Stone studied it and felt a deep pang of regret for their trouble.

'Mike was beautiful in those days,' Jesse said quietly. 'Before the Angel cut his heart out.'

Jarrat sampled the beer. 'Spiteri said he and Michael were sure it was a forced addiction.'

'Bet you ass it was forced,' Jesse hissed. 'Christ, why would Mike want that horseshit? He had a home, a project of his own at Equinox, a Rand Falcon in the yard. And Jack. They had it all, and you're asking me to believe he'd trade it for a nose full of Angel? No way.'

'I'll accept that.' Stone sat back, one hand on Jarrat's lean thigh. 'Spiteri said Mike had a lot of run-ins with his bosses. He supported Grenshem.'

'Yeah.' Jesse toyed with the cockring, spun it on his forefinger as he thought. 'He'd give Grenshem inside info he could use in the campaign against Equinox. Jack was working late. I'd meet Mike for a drink or to dance. I told him he was getting into hot water. Mike was an idealist. He thought he could get Equinox

181

right out of this system.'

For some time they were silent, before Stone leaned closer and dropped his voice. 'Jack said you know the lot. The info he gave Grenshem, that got the Senator killed, came from you. True?'

'Sure.' Jesse tipped back his head and closed his eyes. The lids were faintly blue-shadowed. 'A Companion hears things. You don't have to deliberately listen. You're in bed, or in the bathroom, cleaning up after a session. A call comes in. People must think we spontaneously turn deaf! I've worked on Skycity scores of times, and been in a lot of penthouse pads. Some imbeciles hire a Companion to entertain when they get their business buddies in. So I strip on a table, get fucked a few times, and then I'll use the bath and they talk like I'm not even there.' He hugged himself. 'Some of them have big mouths. After they've done me they lie back and smoke, and brag.'

A nerve flickered in Stone's belly, he felt an echo from Jarrat. 'Spiteri told us to ask you about someone called Schaefer. That's all he said, just the name. Mean anything?'

'Good old Jack.' Jesse sighed. 'Straight to the heart.' He shook off his drear mood and frowned at his fingers, which tugged the expensive cockring, as he spoke. 'Gary Schaefer joined Equinox a couple of years ago. About the time Randy Dorne started getting so rich, even he doesn't know how much money he has. Gary shipped in from the Cygnus colonies, somewhere out that way. He books me a lot. He's enthusiastic in bed — no bloody good, but very keen. He's a chemist.' Jesse wrinkled his nose. 'With booze problems.' He looked up, violet eyes wide and dark. 'When he's drunk and thoroughly laid, he brags.'

Stone glanced sidelong at Jarrat. 'We're trying to establish a solid connection between Equinox and the Angel trade in this system. And maybe the supply of military weapons to the street. Any joy?' Then he held his breath.

'Oh, sure.' Jesse slipped the cockring into his wallet, drew out the image of Michael Rogan and Jack Spiteri, and studied it sadly. 'After Michael died, Jack was wrecked. I went to the funeral... took him home afterward and held him. He came to me after that, now and then. I didn't take money.' His eyes widened defensively. 'I told Jack everything I know. He said he'd get it to Grenshem. Then Grenshem was hit, and Jack vanished. I've been out of my mind.'

'You can stop worrying,' Jarrat told him. 'Can you carry another drink? You look a bit rough.'

But Jesse shook his head. 'I've had too much already. You want the Angel connection? Get Schaefer. He told me, he holds Equinox in the palm of his hand. Said he could have anything he wanted. One night he told me, Randy Dorne couldn't exist without him, he's the key to Dorne's success, his fortune.'

'A fortune build on Angel?' Jarrat asked very quietly.

The Companion smiled mockingly. 'You don't imagine he got control of Equinox and built Skycity on legal dealing?'

'We need names, dates, places,' Stone reminded him. 'Allegation is no good.'

'Names, dates.' Jesse knuckled his eyes. 'Four, five months ago, Kjell Wozniak put a bullet in an Elysium money man, three blocks from here, down in Rawhide. You know it?'

'We've heard of it,' Jarrat said. 'Rough place?'

'Depends. It's a great place to dance, so long as you stay out of the basements. It's a sex shop down below, and the crowd there like to hurt. I was drunk enough to go down once, had a whipping it took me days to forget. Why d'you think they call it Rawhide? Wozniak's there regularly. Tac must be blind. Don't they know it's where the money men deal this year?'

The leap of Jarrat's heart hit Stone in the chest. 'You sure, kiddo? Why haven't you told Tactical?'

Jesse gaped. 'There's easier ways to suicide! You mean NARC doesn't know the Angelpack uses Rawhide?'

'We just got here,' Jarrat said brusquely. 'We get these pearls of wisdom from people like you. Okay, so Tac's been hood-winked. If the brains behind Angel syndicates were made of putty they wouldn't be so dangerous. The Angel money men did business someplace else last year?'

'A restaurant in Sciaparelli.' Jesse waved in the general direction. 'I heard all this when Schaefer thought I was comatose. I was... extremely fucked and supposed to be asleep. He took a call from Wozniak. He'd been drinking, didn't even bother to hold the volume down. I heard it all. Wozniak shot a money man called Koop, the Angel was bailed, waiting for a mule. Schaefer was the one who gave Koop the job, Wozniak said Koop had been robbing them for months. He was furious with Schaefer, said he'd get him in trouble with Randy. What's that sound like?'

Both flat hands on the table, Jarrat looked levelly into Jesse's face. 'You weren't skulled that night?'

'I don't use dope,' Jesse said indifferently. 'Sweetheart, I can't afford to. If I was high as a kite, there's no telling what the customers might do to me. I can't afford to trust them. See?' He turned slightly to display a faint scar which curved about his left side. 'One terminal crazy wanted to pulverise me. You meet a few real psychos.' He opened his wallet and produced a bundle of tiny darts. 'I can take care of myself, so long as I'm wide awake.'

'Poisoned?' Stone glanced at the sneak-weapons.

'Drugged. Enough to drop the loon while I get the hell out.' Jesse put away his darts and sat back. He was calm now, and growing cynical. He threw the robe back over the chair as the humidity raised a sweat on his fair skin.

'So you were sober,' Jarrat said slowly, 'and you know exactly what you heard. Wozniak and Schaefer... and Schaefer bragged to you that he was the key to Dorne's fortune.'

'You got it.' Jesse helped himself to a draught of Jarrat's forgotten beer. The sound system boomed and the volume increased suddenly as a group of men took to the floor. Jesse watched them with absent admiration. 'This used to be a great place. I had friends everywhere, four, five years ago. Then it got full of Angel.' His face shuttered.

'And you lost a lot of mates,' Stone finished.

The blond head nodded. 'It's still a great place to prowl if you're looking for a night's lay. But it's not the same. Not after the Angel got in.' His teeth worried at his lip as he looked at the NARC men. 'You going to bust Equinox?'

'We have to find solid proof for everything you and Jack told us,' Jarrat said under the swell of the music as he turned off the voice recorder in his shirt pocket. 'But it'll be easier now. We know where to look. For what it's worth, sugar, I don't think they're onto you. You'd be dead by now if they were. If you want to be sure, we can take you somewhere safe. Even take you up to the carrier, if you don't mind bunking with the crew.'

Jesse considered the offer interestedly but declined with a smile. 'You're right, if Wozniak's goons knew I had anything to do with Jack or Mike or Grenshem, I'd be in a meat locker! If you don't mind —' he patted a yawn '— I'll go home. I'm usually asleep by now.'

'Can we give you a ride?' Stone stood, picked up the robe and held it for Jesse to put it on. He gave the Companion's body an appreciative look as Jesse got to his feet. Head to toe, he was beautiful, with lovely muscles and that gorgeous cock nested in golden curls. Stone patted the roundness of his buttocks as he sashed the robe.

'If you're going my way, I wouldn't refuse a ride,' Jesse agreed. 'I got a place in Rheims.'

Rheims, where Tactical HQ towered over the broadwalks, and Colonel Vic Duggan lived in a modest flat by Manitola Park, according to his personal file.

'As it happens,' Jarrat said easily as he picked up on Stone's train of thought, 'we're going that way. I'll see if I can scare us up a cab.'

At midmorning an aircab was easy to find. They stepped aboard at the kerb as a squadron of gyrobikes whisked by, and the vehicle rose straight up out of the deep, dusty shadows of the street into the sunlight at rooftop level. Above, Zeus loomed, green-faced, belted with blue and gold. Eos was a silvery crescent low in the west.

The sun was rising toward the bulk of the gas giant and would soon be eclipsed. Vast lighting towers lined every street and clearway, every roof was armed with lights. The instant the sun was gone Avalon would plunge into blue-green twilight, but billions of candlepower would flood the city. People who had been born here, like Jesse, would not even notice the augmentation of the daylight.

He was dozing on Jarrat's shoulder when the aircab dropped toward his building. He lived high in the apartment tower, in the expensive levels. Instead of parking on the kerb the cabbie set down on the roof. Jesse stretched, yawned and smiled sleepily as the gullwings lifted.

'I'll keep my ears open for more,' he promised. 'Where can I reach you, if I get something?'

'You can't,' Stone told him. 'Give us your number, and in a few days we'll buzz you.' From his wallet, Jesse produced a card with the number of his agency, and his own number on the reverse. Stone pocketed it with a smile. 'I'm Stoney, he's Kevin. If you need us, call —' he glanced at the deliberately inattentive cabbie – 'a guy called Vic. You know the one I mean?'

'Oh, I know.' Jesse smiled and held down the skirt of his robe as the repulsion lifted it about his slim hips. 'I'll be okay. But you watch yourselves. This city's getting rough.'

He was gone then, and Stone frowned after him. The gullwings dropped and locked, and the cabbie turned to his clients. 'Where to, chief?'

'Not far,' Jarrat told him. 'Do you know where we can rent a decent car?'

'Groundie, or flyer?'

As the cab lifted off Stone waved at Jesse, who stood at the block of service lifts. The kid was leaning on the wall, sunning himself, and waved back. 'A groundie will do,' Stone decided.

The vehicle's blunt nose rotated, and they could already see the immense Tactical HQ building in the distance. Radio masts and a groundstation dish crowned it. A cloud of air traffic buzzed like gnats about its head.

Minutes later, Stone stood leafing through a rack of pamphlets as Jarrat signed out a Chev sports roadster. He paid by card, and Stone watched discreetly, trusting to luck that the attendant would not try to check their travel papers through the Elysium Spaceport computers.

Perhaps the woman would have, but before she could slip Jarrat's ID into the machine the door opened once more, and an argument over the quality of vehicle maintenance erupted. Grasping the opportunity to leave, he swiped up his papers and keys.

An electric blue Chevrolette Mohawk swung out of the parking bay, and Jarrat threaded into the late-morning traffic. They were looking for an address on South Copenhagen, a quarter-hour's drive from Tac HQ.

Manitola Park was a swathe of trees and grass in the midst of the concrete jungle of the city. Duggan's building stood on the west perimeter. Jarrat slid the Chev in to park beside a rank of public vidphones, and sent up the canopy.

The residents' index was posted by the intercoms. Stone glanced down the listing and tapped one name. 'Duggan, V.H. He's not going to be home at this time of day. He may be hard to track down.'

'Try. We have twelve hours before Petrov and Cantrell panic.' Jarrat looked into the sky, as if he almost expected to see the carrier. 'Why don't you call the man?'

'Tac will be an open book to Equinox,' Stone retorted.

'They have to understand what they're hearing to make sense

of it.' Jarrat stood on the roadside, amber glasses perched on his nose. The warm wind stirred his hair. 'He was your instructor in rookie school? You must have used codes, and by now they're ten years old. Even if Equinox knows the Elysium Tactical codes, they'd never know ten-year-old codes from London.' He laid one hand on Stone's shoulder. 'In this whole city, I'd give you odds, there's two guys who'd know those. Vic Duggan's the other one.'

'You'd probably be right,' Stone agreed drily. 'Okay, I'll give it a shot.' He searched his pockets for a card and inserted it into the vidphone. The numbers for Elysium Tac, fire control and medevac were quoted on the transparent side of the booth. He punched digits and waited.

Jarrat's fingers drummed a tattoo on the booth until the screen cleared. A voice-only message appeared and the usual, androgynous synthetic voice said, 'Tactical.'

'I'd like to reach Colonel Vic Duggan,' Stone told the machine. 'It's a personal call. I'm an informant. If he can't talk right now, can I leave a message?'

'Go ahead, sir,' the machine invited.

'Message is as follows. Sundiver to the survivor from Moswell-Chow. I haven't forgotten Dominic, I know you never will. Got to see you. Get back to me soon as you can. Message ends. If he's in the office, I'll wait.'

'Colonel Duggan is in the building, sir,' the machine told him dispassionately. 'You are on hold.'

Music replaced the voice, and Jarrat nodded thoughtfully. 'Moswell-Chow was the college where Duggan was studying. Dominic was the guy he married, who died of Angel, which made Duggan switch from engineering studies to Tac like that.' He snapped his fingers. 'I don't get the reference to Sundiver. He'll know it's you?'

'I flew sailplanes when I was a kid,' Stone told him. 'There was this yellow glider with flame scallops on the nose, and the name *Sundiver* painted across the wings. I'd hire it when I had the money. One night I got into a game at the club, Duggan was there. I won the plane. Two days later a storm came in off the Atlantic, smashed her to bits. I got drunk, missed a class. Vic covered for me. He knew how much I wanted it, and then I had it, and it was wrecked. He nicknamed me Sundiver. Like a recognition code.'

'He'll remember.' Jarrat watched the traffic as they waited.

'You want to give him what Jesse told us?'

Stone's lips pursed as he considered the question. 'You can trust Vic. But I couldn't vouch for anybody else in that building. For all I know, Duggan might be the only decent man in Elysium Tac — which would account for how blind they are lately. The Angelpack is using Rawhide, and everybody knows but Tactical.' He took a breath to continue, but before he could speak the screen cleared and Duggan's face appeared. 'Morning, Vic,' Stone said levelly. 'Nice to see you.'

'And you,' Duggan said evenly. 'You want to meet?' His brows twitched in obvious warning: *be careful!*

'Manitola Park,' Stone said. 'Now?'

'Fifteen minutes,' Duggan said without expression, and the screen blanked.

'Done and done.' Stone withdrew his card and turned his back on the phone. Hands in pockets, he ambled back to the car a pace ahead of Jarrat. 'If there's a clipper outbound today, Curt Gable will be on it.'

'Great. Four days to Darwin's World, two days back on a Starfleet courier,' Jarrat said bitterly. 'And till then we don't dare run our computers or transmit telemetry, and meanwhile I'm going to have to sit on my duff up there and watch you jump headlong into a deep-cover assignment! That's a jump straight into hell. You want to talk about delayed stress syndrome?'

A storm of his emotion barrelled into Stone, making him wince. 'Kevin, it's not as bad as that. Jesse gave us what we needed. I'll at least know what I'm looking for.'

'The way I knew what I was looking for, in the bosom of Death's Head?' Jarrat glared across the park.

Stone said no more. He leaned on the car, watched the road in the direction of Tactical HQ and counted minutes which seemed like hours. A starlight black Marshall sports pulled up nose to tail with their hired Chev, and through the dimmed armourglass he saw Duggan's frowning face.

The frown deepened as the colonel joined them in the dappled shade beneath the trees. 'What the Christ is going on with NARC?' he demanded in lieu of a greeting. 'I've been trying to get a message to you since midnight! Scuttlebutt at Tac is, the bloody carrier's bugged out and gone!'

'We went dark, Colonel,' Jarrat told him in brittle tones. 'It's possible Equinox have hacked us, as well as you. After the circus at Caitlin-B, we're wondering if we're carrying a leech, or worse. We can't take risks. You'd hear the bang from here if they took the carrier.'

'Jesus.' Duggan swiped a film of sweat from his forehead with the back of his hand. 'It's worse than I thought. Okay, Stoney. NARC knows its own business. You got something for me? I'll trade you. I got something you want.'

'Such as?' Stone glanced sidelong at his partner.

'Kjell Wozniak was at Rawhide last night.' Duggan wore a faintly smug look. 'I had a squad there. Officer Rose Ryan took a beating for you. Enough to make it convincing when her backup bust in and slammed the manacles on Wozniak. She screamed rape, he howled blue murder, but we got him locked up. I can't keep him long. If you want to sweat him, do it soon.'

'Not bad, Vic,' Stone said appreciatively. 'Not bad at all. We'll do it now. We ought to have everything we need in the shuttle.'

'Some weird, classified shit out of a narco lab?' Duggan turned up his nose.

'Something like that.' Jarrat adjusted his amber lenses. 'We'll be with you in an hour. Get some mild sedatives into Wozniak to shut him up, move him to a holding cell in the most isolated corner you have, and meet us at Reception. We're carrying civvy ID, not NARC. We can't just walk in.'

Duggan's jaw slackened. 'You're going to screw Wozniak's head on backwards, inside Tac HQ, and you're not on official NARC ID?' His eyes squeezed shut. 'I'm going to be on the next clipper to Earth with my pension cancelled and a corkscrew up my ass.'

'You want to nail Equinox?' Jarrat asked in a disturbingly soft voice. 'We'll do it for you, Duggan, but we can't do it alone. Spiteri might not make it, but we connected with the source of his information. You know Jesse Lawrence?'

'Should I?' Duggan was agitated.

'No. He's an uptown Companion,' Stone told him. 'But he's the key to this. You know the Angel money men are doing business at Rawhide this year?'

'No kidding?' Duggan said acidly. 'Now prove it. Six times I put men in there, and I got nothing. It's a dance shop up above, a fuck parlour down below, and stay out if you don't want your buns roasted. That's all my squad ever found. Face it, Stoney, Tactical was hacked years ago. Equinox is always two jumps ahead of us. We might as well crack our heads on a wall.'

'We worked that out all on our own,' Jarrat said drily. 'You obviously know who you can trust on your team, or you wouldn't have grabbed Wozniak. Got another name for you. Find him, and hold him any way you can. Gary Schaefer, started at Equinox a couple of years ago. He's a chemist with a booze problem and expensive tastes, one of which is Jesse Lawrence.'

'And,' Stone added, 'he has a big mouth. In a post-coital haze he likes to brag that he has Equinox in his fist, and Dorne wouldn't exist without him.'

The colonel's brows arched. 'The hustler had all this?'

'It's what Grenshem died for.' Stone said darkly. 'Find Schaefer and you're at the heart of it.' He rubbed his hands together. 'Meanwhile, we have to be very careful with Wozniak. Vic, is there a clipper for Darwin's today?'

'Uh, yes. It would have left three, four hours ago,' Duggan said blankly. 'Why?'

'We had a man on it.' Jarrat watched the macaws in the trees overhead. 'Like you said, NARC knows its own business.' He stirred and dropped a hand on Stone's arm. 'Get Wozniak somewhere secure, and get us in. We'll be with you in an hour.' He brandished the keys to the Chev and strode toward the car without a backward glance.

One hand on Stone's shoulder held him back. He looked into Duggan's worried eyes. 'I hope you know what you're doing,' Duggan whispered. He nodded after Jarrat. 'Is he all right?'

'He's my partner.' Stone smiled faintly. 'My lover. I'd trust him with my neck. In fact, I frequently do.' The Chev's jets exploded into life and he gave the Tactical man a wink. 'False ID or no, this is on our ticket. Stop sweating.'

The Chev reversed into the road and Jarrat swung through a wide arc. The traffic had begun to thicken and they made slow time back into Alexandria. Stone's eye was on his chrono as they parked in the chill, windy basement under the Taipan.

A maglev lift raced up the outside of the building and they found the roof hangar busy, and the video surveillance on. Cabs, passengers and civvy pilots milled about, and Stone swore. In the discreet corner the shuttle was undisturbed, its shape indeterminate under the swathe of kevlex sheeting.

While Jarrat drew the attention of a lounging mechanic, Stone released the seals about the undergear and wormed inside. Working by touch, he felt along the belly of the plane until his fingers found the manual release to the external cargo compartment. Clamped to the inside was a hand light, and he flicked it on.

Survival gear, radio tracers, ammunition, a spare sidearm, power cells, medical kit... and a box of 'nasties'. Stone withdrew the latter and pried it open. The drugs were capsuled, pre-measured dosages which clicked into the hypo. Four types were provided, with six shots of each. Stone could not even pronounce their names, but one was a hypnotic, another smothered the will of the individual, rendering deception impossible; the third was a powerful sedative, the last a broad-spectrum blocker agent which neutralised the others.

Stone tucked the kit under his arm and sealed the compartment. He peered cautiously under the kevlex shroud, but Jarrat had manoeuvred the technician away. By the time the man looked back the plane was secure once more.

They were on the road in minutes, and late by a quarter of an hour when Jarrat parked in the visitors' bay. Duggan stood in a side court, chainsmoking as he waited. He ground out the cigarette as the NARC men approached, and urged them away from the main foyer.

'Tradesmen's entrance?' Jarrat asked glibly.

The remark earned him a glare. 'You're lucky, we're right on shift change. Use the private lifts and you probably won't be noticed.' Duggan's eyes flicked to Stone. 'Probably.'

The shift that had come on at 04:00 was just going off. How well Stone remembered the routine. Tired, strung-out officers, yearning for a drink, a shower, a meal, would be ploughing through reports before they were free to go. Efficiency was as low as the staffing level. Duggan was right, the timing was perfect.

The holding cells were underground. The service lift fell with sickening swiftness. Stone counted six sub-basement levels before it slowed, and they stepped out into a white walled corridor. Jarrat arched one brow at their host.

'You sure you couldn't get Wozniak any further away?'

'We put the drunks and dopeheads down here to keep them quiet. I can take anything but spaced-out screaming.' Duggan pointed at the corner cell. 'That's him. He had a hit of tranks with his breakfast, though he didn't know he was getting it. He should still be out.'

'Check,' Jarrat said quickly. 'We can't let him see Stoney's face. Looks like he'll be inside Equinox in a few days, and recognition would be blow us sky high.'

'Right.' Duggan cracked open the door, peered inside and grunted. 'He's comatose.'

Stone stepped into the cell, opened the medical case on the side of the tiny table, and clicked a capsule into the hypo gun. The room was a standard three-metre square with white walls, a cot, toilet and basin. Kjell Wozniak lay on his back, snoring lightly.

His file said he was forty but he looked older. Expensive clothes disguised a body which had begun to run to seed. The good life was taking its toll. Dark hair had begun to thin and silver; the skin was tough and lined, the mouth lax.

'What are you giving him?' Duggan stood back to observe.

'A cocktail,' Stone said as he checked the hypo. 'I'll skinpop it, it won't leave a mark by tomorrow, and in any case I'll put it in his back. A blocker to stop the tranks you gave him, a hypnotic that'll make him receptive to anything he's told, and a shot of what they call "honest john". Let's say, lying is the last thing he'll be able to do.'

'Legal shit?' Duggan leaned on the door as Jarrat helped Stone roll the man and lift his shirt.

'They are when NARC uses them,' Jarrat told him. 'You don't find them on the street. We developed them.'

The shot popped into Wozniak's shoulder and Stone stood back. In seconds the blocker stopped the tranquillisers and he was coming to. Eyelids fluttered and he groaned. At the same time the hypnotic would spin his senses, blur his vision, and Stone was unconcerned as he looked down into Wozniak's eyes. The pupils were vast, black, the irises just thin rims of blue. Jarrat thumbed the voice recorder and took a sound level.

'Kjell Wozniak?' Stone asked clearly.

'Yeah. What's happening?' Wozniak swallowed repeatedly.

'Who do you work for?' Jarrat spoke slowly.

'For... Equinox,' Wozniak slurred. He pawed his eyes and tried to sit up. 'Where am I?'

'At Rawhide,' Stone told him. 'You were doping and you passed out. Remember?'

Wozniak clenched both hands into his hair. 'There was a girl.

Screaming.'

'Tell me about Equinox,' Jarrat purred.

The black eyes peered at him. 'What about it?'

'Whose orders do you take?' Stone sat on the side of the cot. 'Where do you come from?'

'I answer to Randy,' Wozniak groaned. 'I come from... from Cygnus. Answer to Randy Dorne.'

'What work do you do?' Jarrat adjusted the voice recorder.

'Security, top level.' Wozniak scrubbed his eyes, leaving them bloodshot.

'Details,' Stone insisted. 'Tell me about your special assignments.'

'Special?' Wozniak peered at him. 'Like Angel jobs?'

'Yes.' Jarrat stepped closer. 'Tell me about the money man, Koop.'

Wozniak dragged in a breath. 'I killed him. Been stealing.'

'Who gave the orders?' Stone looked up into Jarrat's attentive face.

'Randy. Can't use thieves. Don't trust them. So I shot...'

'What work did Koop do for Dorne?' Jarrat's hand fell on Stone's shoulder and squeezed.

'Money man in Sciaparelli,' Wozniak slurred.

'What trade?' Stone insisted.

'Trade? Waddaya mean?' Wozniak shook his head as if he could fight off the mist. 'Angel. Only Angel.'

Duggan had shuffled steadily closer. He leaned down over Wozniak now. 'You use Rawhide for business?'

'Yeah.' Wozniak cleared his throat. 'Got to move soon. Seen Tac squads there.'

'Where will you go next?' Duggan growled.

'Dunno.' Wozniak sighed. 'Ask Randy.' His voice was more slurred by the moment.

'Vic...' Stone fended the colonel off. 'Wozniak. Tell me about the Angel. How does it get into Avalon? Wozniak!'

But the man was on the fringe of unconsciousness, and Jarrat stood back. 'Want to try another shot? I think he can take it, he's got a lot of body weight.'

Duggan's fingers clenched into Stone's arm. 'For Christ's sake don't kill him. I don't gave a fuck for his life, but if you leave a corpse here this narco shit of yours in his blood will show up in the autopsy and I got no explanation to give.'

'We'll be careful.' Stone clicked another capsule into the gun as Jarrat rolled the man over. The cocktail popped in and he jerked awake. 'Wozniak,' Stone said loudly. 'Wozniak!'

'Oh, Jesus,' Wozniak moaned. 'What happened to me? I got some bad dope?'

'Yes,' Jarrat said slowly, clearly. 'You're having a bad trip. Can't you see the rats?'

'Rats? Where?' Wozniak pulled his arms and legs in close.

'You're in an alley among the trashpacks,' Stone said into his ear. 'You're lying in the garbage. The rats are going to eat you alive.'

'Christ!' Wozniak curled tightly into a ball. 'Get me out of here!'

'We will,' Jarrat promised, 'as soon as you tell us the Angel route into Avalon.'

'Get me out!' Wozniak bellowed. 'They're eating me!' He kicked and flailed at rats only he could see.

Stone grabbed both his wrists. 'Tell me how the Angel gets into Avalon and I'll take you out.'

'Angel?' Tears streamed over Wozniak's face. 'Doesn't get it. Can't get it in.'

'You brought in a stockpile after the Black Unicorn bust on Cygnus?' Jarrat demanded.

'No. No way into the system, Tac got smart,' Wozniak panted. 'Get them off, get them off me!'

Jarrat pressed a finger to the pulse in the man's neck. 'He's on the edge.'

'Stoney!' Duggan hissed. 'Get him down before you kill him. Stoney!' The blocker agent fired into the back of Wozniak's neck, and Jarrat held him down for long seconds until the threshing began to ease. Wozniak relaxed slowly and lay panting. For a moment Stone regarded the hypo gun, but Jarrat made negative gestures, and Duggan had already withdrawn to the door.

They were outside before Wozniak came to. Stone leaned on the wall, arms folded, eyes closed. 'Jesse heard right. That bastard is a shooter, and Dorne is running an Angel syndicate from inside the bastion of Equinox Industries.'

'Okay.' Jarrat rubbed his neck and glanced at his chrono. 'But where the hell is the Angel coming from?' He frowned at Duggan. 'He said Tac got smart. You killed the Angel smuggling totally?'

'Years ago,' Duggan said emphatically. 'When I got here there was a scam among handlers on the Orion line. They'd just falsify the readouts of baggage coming in through the scanners and offload the crap by the tonne. It was as simple as programming a computer to show prerecorded data over and over, instead of displaying current scans. Took me half a year to work out how they were doing it, but I got them.'

His eyes gleamed with the unholy light of the zealot. Stone clasped his shoulder. 'You've had Dominic's revenge a hundred times, Vic. You've got nothing to prove.'

'No?' Duggan jerked one thumb at the cell. 'I've got trash like Wozniak peddling Angel at whim on these streets. I've got one kid in ten between fifteen and twenty-five snorting that garbage, screwing his way through fantasy-land till he cocks his toes and they sweep him out of an alley one morning. Nothing to prove?' He drew both hands through his hair and his eyes closed. 'D'you know, Stoney, I still wake up some nights in a sweat when I've dreamed about Dom.'

'Hey.' Stone gripped him by the arms. 'Every kid in that rookie class knew what you went through with him.'

'Did you?' Duggan looked haunted. 'Nobody knows, Stoney, unless you've held somebody you love while he putrefies, while Angel turns him into a rutting, craving, rancid animal in heat.' Colour drained from his face and he turned away.

Stone looked at Jarrat in mute conference. How much should he say? What would Duggan believe? Surely, he would never believe that a man could breathe Angel into his lungs and his brain, and leave it behind. Jarrat shook his head minutely: say nothing. Stone sighed deeply.

'Believe me, Vic, in our job we see it all, and we see it often,' he murmured. 'Like I said, I haven't forgotten your Dominic. NARC isn't just a job, it's a way of thinking.'

With an effort of will, Duggan seemed to drag himself back to the present. 'You know you can't use a word Wozniak gave you. There's no legal system, not even on Earth, that'll indict on a dope-testimony.'

'We know.' Jarrat toyed with his amber glasses. 'But with what we got here, and from Jesse Lawrence, we know where to start. We've got a hell of a lot more to go on than we started with when I went into Death's Head.'

'You went in?' Duggan's brows rose.

'And this time,' Stone added, it's me.'

'What's the plan?' Duggan shoved his hands into his pockets and strode back to the lift, eyes on the floor.

Jarrat and Stone shared a blaze of tension. 'We consult a clipper schedule,' Jarrat said levelly. 'When the next arrival stands off waiting for tugs, one of our gunships will rendezvous and put Stoney aboard. A set of improvised ID, travel vouchers, employment records, the lot. Good enough to get him into Equinox.'

'When I'm in, I grab whatever it takes to turn dope-testimony and allegation into proof,' Stone finished. 'Then I get out, the fastest way I can.'

They stepped into the lift and Duggan thumbed for ground level. 'You, uh, ever had a deep-cover assignment go bad?'

'Yes.' Jarrat looked away. 'It's happened, and I dare say it'll happen again.'

'But not this time,' Stone murmured. Jarrat's stormy feelings barrelled into him like a punch, no matter their attempts to block the assault. 'Lightning doesn't strike twice so fast, Kevin.'

It took a moment for Duggan to make the connection, and then he swore. 'The Death's Head job went sour?'

'The less you know right now, the better,' Stone told him. 'Hold Wozniak a few days if you can. When he comes to, tell him he got some bad dope at Rawhide, went buggo with a girl and passed out among the rest of the trash. He'll remember the rats, so he'll buy every word.'

The lift went up fast. 'He'll expect charges.' Duggan stepped out into the ground-level passageway and took a swift glance around. 'Go, while you got the chance.'

'We're gone.' Jarrat was heading for the door as he spoke. 'Tell Wozniak the girl was a dopehead. She vanished back under a rock, soon as she heard the word NARC. He'll buy that too.'

'Shit,' Duggan swore. 'I heard about you bloody NARCs, but I never had to work with you before. You know every answer?'

A pace into the side court, Stone smiled wryly at his old instructor. 'Half of them, Vic. We're working on the other half.' He cast a glance at the green velvet face of the gas giant. 'Home, Kevin? We have work to do.'

'Home,' Jarrat agreed bitterly, and tossed him the keys to the Chevrolette.

Chapter Twelve

The carrier was transmitting, but its radio traffic was a mix of audiolab re-recordings and irrelevant data. When Stone asked for a status report, Petrov handed him a sheet of paper. Budweisser had shanghaied two squads of Ravens. The synthetic aperture units had been dismounted from three gunships to augment those available from Engineering, and the systematic, exhaustive task of making a fresh holo blueprint of the electronics had begun. Bud's estimate was eight days for completion of the scans before analysis could really start.

The clipper *Sirius*, with Curt Gable aboard, was bound for Darwin's World. It would dock in orbit over Venice in four days; a Starfleet courier would deliver Gable and a cyber specialist to Avalon two days later. Meanwhile, the carrier was running literally silent.

'We left one reactor on line,' Petrov told them as they stood in an ops room which seemed eerie with every screen dead. 'The flight systems are dormant. We're piloted on manual, around the clock. There's a lot of overworked, angry Starfleet people up front.'

Stone grunted in agreement and turned the paper. On the back was the clipper schedule. The next inbound was the *Rigel*, in three days. Petrov's name was called and he ambled away. Alone in the inert ops room, Jarrat read the report over Stone's shoulder.

'Three days. Gives us time to get your cover into shape,' he mused. 'You'll need it all, right down to a name. This isn't like the Death's Head job. That was cityside. Mavvik didn't know we had a carrier over Chell until almost the end. This is sky high. Dorne's toadies know your name, if not your face. You won't hit trouble unless you run into someone who saw us on Skycity, and the chances of that —'

'Are nil,' Stone said drily. 'I'll in as a grunt, the lowest form of life. Career mercenary. Ex-Army, fought in the corporate bloodbath on Sheal. Kicked out of the military for...' he snorted with laughter, '...screwing my CO for a promotion.'

'Thanks a bunch,' Jarrat said philosophically. 'You'll never let me live that down.'

'I also know you paid for that promotion, and not in bed.' Stone stirred. 'I'll see what the library has available. It won't be easy with the computers down.'

The archive was an annex off the briefing room, and that too was dormant. The duty librarian was operating a personal terminal similar to Budweisser's, and Stone's request for access to materials elicited mild hysteria. The woman slapped down a case of datacubes, twisted the terminal toward him and offered him a chair. With a sigh, Stone sat and began to search for what he wanted.

First, a name: Strother, Jon D. Add personal statistics, birth and education records. Born in Lisbon, educated in London. Parental details: Jon Strother Snr. and Marguerite Netley. Education: Bremner Institute of Space Sciences. Graduation without honours. Army enlistment after two years unemployed. Distinguished service on Roth, Hellier and Sheal. Dishonourable discharge.

Now Stone began to improvise. He had fought with an officer over a civilian lover both wanted. The officer was almost killed. Strother was suddenly back in civvies at the age of 27, with no trade but soldiering. It would do.

Here the fabricated personality became harder. For hours he rummaged, and chose four mercenary units which operated at least six weeks' flight time from Zeus. Two had been broken by provincial forces, one had gone to ground following a defeat. Strother had fought with them all and come out alive.

He memorised names and faces belonging to military and mercenary squads, dates and events where he would swear he had been. A victory in the jungles of Calleron, a crushing rout in the glacial hell of Roth.

His head was throbbing, but he had compiled a believable identity when he smelt fresh coffee, and Jarrat appeared in the archive with a cup in either hand. The door closed behind him, and they were alone. Kevin sat on the edge of the desk and read swiftly through the printout.

'This is pretty good,' he said at last. 'Strother is a son of a bitch, Stoney. You happy with the role?'

'Strother is a patented bastard.' Stone took a welcome swig

of coffee. 'He'll need to be to survive, where I'm going. You think grunts at the boot end of Equinox live the way they do on Skycity?'

'Barracks, routine, discipline, uniform.' Jarrat touched his face. 'You're doing it rough. I was in a palace.'

'But it'll be quick,' Stone reasoned. He sat back, swivelled the chair and looked up at Jarrat. 'Two weeks. Maybe less.'

'Can you guarantee that?' Jarrat chewed his lip. 'You'll have to access databases. That means subterfuge, stealing access codes, old fashioned sneaking. If you get caught — '

'I'm too good.' Stone rested one hand on Jarrat's thigh. 'All I want is get in, get the goods and get out.'

'Fast,' Jarrat added. 'I'll stay with you, Stoney. I can monitor you better than machines anyway.'

'I'll be counting on it,' Stone said softly.

'Yes.' Jarrat's eyes were still closed. 'I'll stay tuned in to you, and I can pick you up in minutes if you make it to the roof or the street.'

Stone rubbed his temples. 'When it comes to the payoff I'll be sending either panic or euphoria. You'll know it's all come together... or gone bad. Either way, pull me out.'

'I will.' Jarrat moulded his palm about Stone's face. 'I'm going to miss you.'

'The feeling,' Stone said quietly, 'is mutual.' He turned his mouth to Jarrat's palm and then stood. 'I've got a lot of study to do. I've got to *be* this bastard, Strother. Let me get under his skin, and I'll be convincing.'

'Go for it.' Jarrat looked at the time. 'I'll organise your gunship rendezvous.'

'How's Bud doing?' Stone asked as he returned to work.

'He's started the analysis.' Jarrat lingered at the door. 'We're loaded with Equinox components, like most ships. Bill Dupre is going to have kittens.'

He was gone with that remark, leaving Stone to ponder the situation. Rear echelon cost-cutting had always been the blight of technicians in three services. It seemed a dismaying karma was about to catch them up, with a vengeance. Sobered, Stone's eyes went back to the screen.

***

199

His bags lay beside Jarrat's door, and Stone was content to lie against Kevin's body while they waited for the buzz which would call him to the gunship. Quiescent, resigned, Jarrat appeared relaxed but Stone knew the truth. Beneath a surface calm Kevin was disturbed. They had made love an hour before and thrills of pleasure lingered on. Stone clung to them, yet at the same moment rejected the soldier's old fear. Every assignment could be the last; every farewell could be the finale.

He propped himself on an elbow and looked into Jarrat's face. They were dressed and Stone was ready to leave, still yawning, an hour before he would normally wake. Kevin was in his customary denims; Stone wore paramilitary fatigues, dustgrey, noticeably lacking insignia. The personality of Jon D. Strother was at his fingertips, but for the moment the mercenary was filed away.

Gentle hands caught Stone's head, pulled him down to kiss, and he opened his mouth to Jarrat's tongue. An hour before it had been Jarrat laid open for Stone's hands, and his cock. Jarrat had been silent, almost sombre, and the act was slow, deliberate. Racked by climax, he had looked up into Stone's eyes and the flood of his emotions was overwhelming. Something for Stone take with him, to embrace when he became Strother, and he might have been a lightyear separated from Jarrat.

Shiptime was 05:00. NARC crews passively monitored Elysium while Budweisser commandeered every off-duty man to operate the synthetic aperture equipment. The carrier was not much more than an observation platform.

The buzz they had been waiting for intruded and Stone sat. 'Stop fretting, honey,' he told Jarrat fondly. 'You'll get grey hair.'

Jarrat pulled himself up against the pillows. 'You'll be in Elysium by noon.'

'And in Equinox by tonight.' Stone shouldered his bags and looked back at the bed. Jarrat was still solemn, tousled, very beautiful in the soft cabin lights. 'If I can get a shift off I'll call Duggan and Jesse, leave a verbal message, if there's news. They're the only ones I trust in Elysium.' He held out his hand. Jarrat clasped it tightly. 'I'm a big lad,' Stone said, mock-sternly. 'Trust me.'

'I do.' Jarrat watched his fingers slip through Stone's. 'I love you, Stoney.' The empathy spiralled to a peak and diminished once more. 'Be careful.'

The cabin was empty without him. Jarrat sat on the side of the bunk and glared at the chrono. The terminal on his desk was dark, leaving him disturbingly isolated. But he knew to the moment when the Blue Raven gunship launched. His empathic shields were down, and if he concentrated he could even feel Stone breathe.

Restless, he left the cabin and looked in on the flight deck. NARC personnel were rarely seen there, since the running of the carrier was Starfleet business. To his surprise the Master Pilot, Colonel Helen Archer, was on watch. The woman was fifteen years Jarrat's elder, lean, sinewy, with silverblond curls and probing green eyes. She wore plain clothes by preference, but the snug white coveralls and sport shoes could have been uniform. Archer had flown everything Starfleet had. She had transferred to NARC when her son became an Angel statistic.

If the boy had lived he would have been twenty, Jarrat calculated. He gave the pilot his hand as she turned toward him. She was not beautiful, but striking, with strong features that would age well.

The viewports were open, the armourglass undimmed, since the carrier was over Avalon's night side. Instruments filled the forward consoles but despite its kilometre length the ship was actually piloted by the same delicate, pressure-sensitive cyclic stick as the shuttle. Four seats, side by side, flanked the consoles; only two were occupied.

The Engineering and Communications officers were absent, leaving a duty pilot and copilot to stand this watch. Archer stood behind the two lieutenants, hands about a mug, watching without comment. She was an insomniac, Jarrat remembered.

'Help yourself to coffee, Cap,' she invited. 'It's the real thing, not synthetic robochef bilge.' She indicated a percolator on a hotplate behind the vacant programmer's console. 'A gunship just launched. Cap Stone on his way?'

'Yes.' Jarrat poured coffee and leaned on the back of an empty seat. He looked down on the dark face of Avalon, and up, into the blue, green and gold belts of Zeus' atmosphere. 'How much do you know about the QuantumData brains that make this ship tick?'

'Not enough.' Archer finished her coffee and poured another. 'I just fly them, I don't design 'em. Bud told me you sent for a specialist.'

'Three days ago.' Jarrat sampled the strong, black brew. 'You know the name of McKinnen?'

Archer's brows rose. 'I read about her work. She's the one who developed the brain implant that let us talk to monkeys.'

'Did she?' Jarrat smiled cynically. 'That doesn't surprise me. She wants to install biocyber implants in the brains of field agents.' He tapped his forehead with one finger. 'Well, not in this brainbox, lady!'

'Damned right.' Archer gestured at the lights of Elysium and surrounding cities. 'You saw the political vidcasts?'

'I haven't had time.' Jarrat gazed, half hypnotised, at the diamond glitter in the darkness.

'They're brawling for Tigh Grenshem's job,' Archer told him. 'Tactical's on alert. There's been more fighting.'

'I saw their telemetry on an Angel riot in Alexandria,' Jarrat said quietly. 'Nothing Tac couldn't handle.'

'No military weapons,' Archer mused.

'No Equinox involvement.' Jarrat drained his cup and toyed with it absently. 'Did you see what we got from Wozniak?'

Her face was bleak. Unlike most Starfleet personnel, who pulled a tour with NARC and then returned to their usual units, she had deliberately requested the permanent rank of carrier's Master Pilot, and took an active interest in NARC business. Jarrat gave a thought to her long dead son.

'I saw it,' Archer said sourly. 'It must have been tough, walking out of Tac HQ, knowing Wozniak would be free to go.'

'It was,' Jarrat admitted. 'But Stoney and I bent the rules close to snapping. We could have hung something on Wozniak, but it would have alerted Equinox to the fact we're getting close. His time will come. Soon.'

She cocked her head at him. 'The Angel isn't smuggled into Avalon?'

'So the man said,' Jarrat affirmed. 'And Duggan is adamant about that. This system is rough on smugglers. For a start, it's so full of rubble it takes a big ship, running flak deflectors, to get in without a major collision. Big ships get tracked, draw attention and get searched.'

'Then Duggan's not just bragging. He knows damned well he has the smuggling plugged.' Archer folded her arms. 'Then where's the shit coming from?'

'That,' Jarrat said softly, 'is the question. NARC has had these people under surveillance for six months, and we still don't have an answer.' He smiled faintly. 'My money's on Stoney. He'll be in by tonight.'

He left the flight deck as the chrono showed 06:00 and rode the lift down several levels. The Infirmary was quiet. Kip Reardon was yawning over breakfast in his office, and Jarrat pulled a chair up to the cluttered desk. The surgeon studied him overtly, but Jarrat was too preoccupied to care. In every nerve he felt Stone. He was anxious, deliberately trying to relax; eating something sweet and talking.

A scanner whirred over Jarrat's chest. Reardon made disapproving sounds which snapped the younger man back to reality. 'I'm fine, Kip,' he said shortly.

'You're stressed out,' Reardon corrected, though he sat back and returned to his breakfast.

'That would be normal when we're running an assignment,' Jarrat said sharply, 'and when we may be sitting on top of an enormous bomb — you want me to be happy?'

'Point.' Reardon thrust a plate at him. 'Eat. Do you know where I can reach Spiteri's next of kin?'

The question diverted Jarrat. 'That would be his brother, I guess. And no, I don't. He said he'd left them in some safe place, but he didn't say where. On Avalon, it'd be somewhere isolated, out of touch. Why?'

'I put him in cryogen.' Reardon gestured at the tanks which stood in the darkened hall beside his office. 'I did what I could, but the damage was extensive. He needs a lot of transplant surgery, and it's going to cost. A bundle. Any chance you can get NARC funding?'

'Maybe.' Jarrat chewed mechanically on a croissant. 'I can ask. He was the major link in this chain reaction, and we owe him. I'll see if Dupre's office will sanction it. Let me have a medreport.'

'Done.' Reardon handed him a folder. 'He needs liver, heart and lung transplants. I fixed what I could but the rest packed up. I tanked him before brain damage could accumulate. He'll make it if he can get the work, but I need authorisation to proceed.'

'Leave it with me.' Jarrat skimmed the top sheet in the folder. 'It'll be some time before I can send this. I'll give you a permit to hold him tanked as long as necessary. Damn. It's a shame. It took guts to do what he did.'

'There's idealists everywhere,' Reardon said soberly. 'They're

203

the ones who pay the biggest price.'

'While the crazies on the street snort anything they can get,' Jarrat added. He rubbed his eyes. 'Sometimes I think, let them do it. When they're dead and gone, that's the end of it.'

Reardon sighed. 'You don't believe that.'

'I... don't believe that,' Jarrat admitted. He thought of Michael Rogan; of Vic Duggan's Dominic, and Stoney. His heart squeezed painfully. 'Ignore me, Kip. I'm just talking drek because he's out there, and he's on his own.'

'Like I said,' Reardon repeated quietly, 'idealists are everywhere. You and Stoney are two of the worst I know. Or the best,' he added. 'Did you sleep last night?'

'You must be joking.' Jarrat licked crumbs from his fingers and stood. 'I'll sleep later, when he does. I'm too aware of him, every minute, now.'

The surgeon leaned back. 'Where is he, what's he doing?'

Eyes closed, Jarrat reached out. 'Sitting. Eating. He's talking. Strung up, heart beating hard.'

'On his toes,' Reardon observed. 'Stage fright, Kevin? Two old hands like you?'

Jarrat discovered a little genuine humour. 'Every time, Kip. Every damned time.'

***

Elysium Field lay under a thick overcast and the air was taut with the electric feeling of an incoming storm. After seven hours on the clipper and another two on the ground, queuing for visitor's registration, Stone was tired. Wide glass doors swished shut behind him and he stood on the cab rank in the shade of the terminal building. His bags were at his feet. In his pockets were the entry permits, ID and cards of a man called Jon Strother. And he was wasting time.

He snatched up the bags and whistled for the cabbie at the head of the rank. As the trunk in front of the ride capsule popped open he dumped his two cases in.

The cabbie stubbed out a cigarette and the jets fired with a howl. The car was an old, battered Rand. 'Where to, chief?' The man was just as old, with a face like worn leather.

'Equinox Towers,' Stone said without hesitation. No need to ask if the cabbie knew it.

Three buildings so tall, clouds seemed to gather about their crowns, set in a triangular pattern and connected by aero-bridges, monorails, maglev tracks. Stone caught sight of the incredible structure from kilometres out. It dwarfed the Chandler sector just as Equinox Industries eclipsed the entire Zeus system.

It was mid-afternoon and traffic was thick. The Rand stood in a blistering canyon street, trapped by ten lanes of ground traffic while skyvans and aircabs scudded overhead against the brooding face of Zeus. Stone glared at them through the transparent gullwing canopy. He could have been at Equinox half an hour sooner, but the flight would have been inconsistent with Strother's profile.

He was broke, so far down on his luck that he was seeking the worst kind of job he knew. Security goon with a corporate army. No professional soldier would take the work unless he was out of options. Strother was ripe for it. His last mercenary unit had been cut to bloody shreds on Tannis, he had a gambling habit and his lover had put paid to his chances, taking most of the credits Strother had saved, and leaving him.

The cab rocked to a halt on its unstable repulsion field and Stone handed over a few notes. The gullwing lifted and he stepped onto the kerb. The street was in shadow but the heat was oppressive. He twisted his neck to look up, and up, at the building towering above. The crest seemed lost in the sky, and beyond was Zeus, faintly seen through the gathering overcast.

Stone lifted his bags from the trunk and turned his back on the cab. Wide, mauve glass doors opened onto the street beneath the name of Equinox Industries. With a glare at the holographic logo he strode into the foyer. He saw midnight blue carpets, ice grey walls, silver trim on a tall reception desk before him. Screens flickered and the young man behind the desk looked down a long, disapproving nose.

'Are you sure you're in the right building?'

'Positive.' Stone dumped his bags beside the desk and dug out his ID. 'I'm looking for work.'

The receptionist glanced at the papers. 'Wait over there.' He pointed to a corner out of sight of the doors.

'Thanks.' Stone snatched back his documents, picked up his bags and lounged against the wall in a corner where upmarket visitors would not notice him. The young man made a call, and

Stone watched the lifts opposite with an unfamiliar flutter in his belly.

Sure enough, a man in uniform stepped out. Fifty years old, severe, with the ringed-planet Equinox crest on his left breast and colonel's insignia on his collar. He looked Stone up and down without crossing the foyer. Stone drew himself up to attention, lifted his chin and stared into the middle distance. He had never served with any Army, but had heard more than enough from Jarrat to go through the motions.

The behaviour was right. The officer approached, and when Stone offered his cards they were taken. The ID bar on the man's breast read Malone, A.L. The cards were handed back, and Stone maintained the rigid posture.

'Looking for work, Strother?' Malone examined him again. 'What makes you think there's a place for you here?'

'I'm good, sir,' Stone said stiffly. 'I need the job, and I heard you need good men, sir.'

'Where did you hear that?' Malone's accent was local, with broad vowels and clipped consonants.

'On Tannis, sir.' Stone did not look the man in the eyes. 'I heard Equinox might have some... business soon.'

'I see.' Malone seemed to consider both him and the statement, but at length relented. 'As it happens, you heard right. You have your service record?'

'Yes, sir.' Stone stooped toward his bag.

'Not here. Bring your gear, I'll take you to Induction.' Malone returned to the lift without a backward glance.

If Stone expected it to go up, he was disappointed. He counted eight sub-basements before the lift slowed, and Malone led him into a labyrinth of white walls and sign panels. Uniformed guards stood duty even here. Stone's eyes missed nothing as he tailed Malone to an office deep in the complex.

A man with lieutenant's insignia and cropped blond hair stood and gave Malone a smart salute. Malone did not return it. Stone scanned the name plate on his desk: Sorenson, B. 'Fresh meat, Lieutenant,' Malone said brusquely. 'Name of Strother. His papers seem to be in order. I'll leave him in your capable hands.'

'Sir.' Sorenson inclined his head, remained stiff-backed till Malone was gone, then returned to his more indolent norm. Stone was wary, taking nothing for granted. 'Papers.' Sorenson held out his hand.

Mute, Stone produced his ID, entry permits and service record, set them on the desk beside three vidphones and a terminal, and waited. Sorenson seated himself, read them in minute detail, punched keys, checked and double checked, and at length regarded him with a bored expression.

'It's a six-month hitch. You work eight-hour shifts, we stand three shifts around the clock. You work where you're told, do what you're told. Drink, dope and fuck on your time, not ours. Screw up, and your sergeant will take you to pieces. You'll be under the orders of Security Captain D.L. Greaves, but you're tagged for Warlock Company. Sergeant Neville's group is shorthanded since last week.'

'They fought an action?' Stone asked carefully. The only battle it could have been was the streetwar which NARC had finished, at Duggan's behest.

Sorenson did not seem to hear the question. 'You work seven days, get two free, a standard Avalon week. Miss a shift, you lose pay. Sass your officers, and they take it out of your hide. Discipline around here is the end of a lash. It usually takes one flogging to learn, so you probably got it due. It's called Company Punishment, and you'll find Neville has a heavy hand. Get your pay at the end of each seven days, bonus if you do good, fines if you bungle. Standard pay scale.' He thrust a paper across the desk. 'Put your mark on that and you're in for the hitch. No right of resignation. Surrender your ID and cards to Company possession. Cut and run, and you won't get far. When you get back here you pull fines, flogging and double duty till your time's up.'

Stone's skin prickled. He had heard it all before, it was a normal corporate army contract, much more stringent than the regular Army because the men must be controlled in the midst of a civilian environment. Fear was the best method of control ever devised; loyalty was born out of dread.

Only the most desperate ever worked for these corporate armies, but once a man survived the first hitch, got a couple of stripes on his shoulder, some respect within his unit, he could climb to astonishing heights. A year on the street, and Strother might get triple wages, lounging on Skycity. If the threat of discipline was the stick that frightened men into obedience, the promise of the palaces of the moguls at the top was the carrot that seduced them to re-enlist.

He signed the paper, threw down the pen and picked up his bags. 'Where do I go?'

Sorenson touched the vidphone. 'Sergeant Neville? Got a new boy at Induction. He just sold his soul. You want him, he's yours.'

With his bags over his shoulders, Stone stood against the wall as Sorenson vanished with his ID. He was literally a prisoner until his cards were returned. Footsteps announced Neville, and he swallowed as he turned to the sound.

Big and broad, a Company man to the marrow, was Neville. Thirty-eight or forty, crop-haired, clean shaven, tanned, with dark hair and brown eyes that might have been Latin. Races were so mixed, it was hard to tell. He wore green fatigues with the Equinox crest on the left breast, and dull-finish black boots.

The sergeant looked Stone and down. Stone straightened his back. 'Strother, Jon D.,' he said stiffly. 'The lieutenant took my papers, sir.'

'You know what you've got yourself into?' Neville stood aside and gestured down the long, white walled passage.

'Yes, sir. I need the work.' Stone let Neville walk ahead.

'Mercenary?' He stepped past a sign reading Medical.

'Since I left the Army.' Stone glanced cynically about at the little infirmary.

A medic in immaculate white coveralls was servicing the diagnostic machines. Only one of the beds was occupied. A young man lay on his belly, shuddering. His back was a mess of bloody weals. Stone's own skin crawled.

'This is Medic Sergeant Yip,' Neville said curtly. 'You'll get a standard exam, tests and broad spectrum shots. Where did you ship in from?'

'Tannis, sir.' Stone set his bags on a vacant bed. 'I don't think I'm carrying anything regional.'

'Make sure, Yip,' Neville said firmly. 'There is nothing more pathetic than a twelve-man combat unit out of action because it can't get its collective ass out of the latrine.' He stepped back to the door. 'Leave your rags and personal junk with the Medic. They'll be held till you leave. After your exam, get down to Stores, draw uniform and weapons. Then grab a bunk in the Warlock Company barracks. You pull your first duty shift, 06:00 tomorrow.'

'Sir.' Stone shrugged out of his jacket as Medic Yip produced a large plastic sack. He stripped to the skin, folded his clothes into the bag and kept back only his wrist chrono and razor. Yip sealed the sack and labelled it with the name of Strother, and his 'out date'.

The medic was Stone's age, impersonal and efficient, good looking and intelligent. Scanners whirred and probes intruded into every orifice of Stone's body, leaving him sore and annoyed, but the exam was entirely practical. Blood, urine and semen samples were taken before the promised shot fired into Stone's buttock, leaving a livid bruise.

'You'll live,' Yip told him cheerfully. 'You should see some of the guys we get. Got to decontaminate them before we can put them into Company greens.' He labelled the samples. 'For what it's worth, you're healthy. Your tests'll come back good. Go get your gear.'

'Thanks.' Stone picked up his chrono and razor, and nodded at the infirmary's only inmate. 'What was his crime?'

'Him?' Yip looked indifferently at the young man. 'Hutton's a fool. You sass Neville, you hurt.' He gave Stone a hard look. 'Company policy, Strother. Don't rock the boat.'

'I won't.' Stone stepped out and consulted the index by the lifts. He rubbed the shot bruise ruefully. It felt odd to him to be buff naked, but Jesse Lawrence would not have been perturbed. Stone felt the shifting air against his skin and decided to enjoy it. He was still sore in several places after an exam which had been nothing if not thorough.

Stores were a hundred metres westward. To left and right along the way he saw six barracks, an armoury, another infirmary, communal latrines and showers. No one paid him a moment's notice until he strode into the vast, half-lit cavern of the warehouse.

There, an older man, not far short of retirement, looked up over a magazine, saw his state of undress and clicked his tongue. 'Don't tell me they caught another one.'

'They didn't hold a gun to my head.' Stone leaned on the long counter, behind which were innumerable racks and shelves of clothes and footwear. 'Come on, pop, I'm getting cold.'

Company greens, boots, underwear; a flakjacket and helmet with a thermoscan visor; a Colt AR-12 9mm automatic rifle with laser target acquisition and spare clips; kit bag. Dressed, Stone stuffed the bag with the gear he was not wearing and left the old man to his lurid magazine.

He had passed Warlock Company's barracks on the way in. It was a long hall with ten beds down either side, a locker beneath each; a communal table doubled for mess service and briefing. Lighting panels in the ceiling cast multiple shadows. The walls were a pale, indeterminate shade, the floor simple dressed concrete. Eight men were present as Stone approached. The doors stood open and he coughed discreetly as he stepped in.

Shrewd eyes examined him and Stone looked back, evaluating everything he saw. They were a mixed bag of the hopeful and the hopeless. The youngest would be twenty, the eldest mid-forties, and they seemed to come in every shape, size and colour. Stone pinned on a noncommittal smile.

'Strother,' he said simply. 'They told me to bunk here. My first shift is 06:00 tomorrow.'

The big, broad shouldered kid turned toward him. 'You just got in?'

'Yeah. Which bunk do you want me to take?' Stone glanced at the boy's ID bar and offered his hand. 'Do I call you Purl, or have you got a name?'

'It's Frank.' A beefy hand extended. 'That's Decker, and O'Hara, and Brin. You already met the sergeant.'

'Saw one of your guys in Medical,' Stone added as he clasped a wrist here and there.

'That's Hutton.' The small, sharp-faced O'Hara grinned, showing tobacco-stained teeth. 'Some got to learn the hard way. What about you, Strother?'

'I'm a quick study,' Stone said darkly. 'How many guys in this unit?'

'Nine, including you,' Purl told him. 'Take the bunk in the corner, if you want it. We lost a lot of men in the last action. Them playing cards, aint got the manners to come and take your hand, that's Treveno and Fushida.'

The kit bag dumped heavily onto the vacant bed. Stone turned back to the group, hands on his hips. Eyes smouldered on him. Treveno was as big as Purl but not as amiable. His hair was white blond, tied at his nape; his left cheek bore old, orange-peel scars from a chemical fire long in the past. Fushida was Jarrat's height, over Stone's weight, solid muscle. He wore his raven black hair in a thick braid which reminded Stone of the

Blue Raven, Joe Ramos. There, the similarity ended. Fushida was as silent and unsmiling as Treveno. Dangerous.

Every intuition Stone had told him to disregard the rest but never take his eyes off these two. He smiled without a trace of humour and inclined his head in greeting. Treveno's pale blue eyes narrowed. Fushida looked away.

'Nice to know I'm welcome,' Stone said acidly.

'Well, fuck 'em,' Purl advised. 'We got to get some new blood or Warlock Company ain't going to exist no more.'

'You fought an action last week,' Stone said pointedly. 'Heavy casualties. Where was that?'

Purl blinked. 'You didn't hear about that? Right here in Elysium, man!'

'In Sciaparelli?' Stone's belly fluttered. 'I did hear about it. Didn't know it was you boys.'

'Damned right.' Purl grinned. 'Ain't going to get no respect for it, though. We went out in civvies, really stirred 'em up. Till NARC riot troops jumped in and screwed us right into the ground.'

'NARC?' Stone echoed. 'They wouldn't deploy unless it was an Angelwar. What the hell were you guys doing, pratting about in an Angel shindig?'

'Search me.' Purl sat on the bunk opposite and clasped his big hands between his knees. 'S'what got Hutton a good flog. He razzed Neville about that. Real dumb.'

'I see.' Stone smiled grimly. 'We work where we're told, do what we're told, and we don't ask questions.'

O'Hara plunked onto the bunk behind Purl. 'Got it in one, Strother. You making a career in Equinox, or are you in it for fast cash, and then out?'

Make a career in what Gil Cronin often scathingly referred to as 'shit-kicking private armies'? Stone could have shuddered. 'I just want some credits in my pocket,' he said with feigned blandness. 'Then I'm gone.'

'Pity.' O'Hara's pointed face creased in a frown and he glanced along at the two playing cards. 'Warlock used to be my kind of people. Can't keep the good blood these days.'

'Shut it, Vin,' Purl hissed. 'You want to be with Hutton? Christ! Them and Neville'd flay you.' He shook himself a l stood. 'You want to eat, Strother?'

'Maybe later.' Stone tucked the kit bag under the bunk and

lifted his legs up. 'Right now, I want to catch some sleep.'

But in fact he did not sleep. His ears remained open, storing and analysing speech and accent, words and mood. It was often easier to tell who was bluffing, who was scared and who was downright psychotic, by listening. When men thought the newcomer was asleep they were unguarded. Most of the squad were locals, but one spoke with the Cygnus accent; Brin had the Chell vowels, and two were from Earth, like Stone himself. He learned a good deal about his fellows. Purl was big enough and tough enough to be relaxed, while O'Hara was terminally wary. Decker had only been in a month, and was terrified, of what, Stone did not know. The rest were bored, irritable, longing for the end of their enlistment. But Treveno and Fushida were career men — he learned this from the inarticulate but talkative Purl. From the two men themselves he learned nothing, since they said nothing.

He turned over, punched the pillow and surreptitiously checked his chrono. It was 20:25, and hunger had begun to make its presence felt. The rattle of a trolley announced the arrival of a meal and Stone sat. He kept well back, let the others have their pick of the utensils and food.

Neville dined with his squad and used the meal as an opportunity to brief them for their upcoming duties. Stone's ears pricked and he waited to be addressed directly. Sixty levels above, in the offices where men like Jack Spiteri and Michael Rogan had worked, were classified projects, meetings and archives. Much of the work performed by Warlock and the other Equinox squads was a matter of Company security. Stone was not surprised by his assignment.

'You're in Special Technics,' Neville told him after the others had drawn similar assignments and the debris of dinner had been dumped into the disposal.

Protocol was to stand, hands clasped at the back, when one was addressed by an officer. Stone stood smartly and wondered how much of this drivel went on in the regular Army. Not much, if Jarrat was anything to go by. Private armies were worlds apart. 'Sir,' he responded. He had said 'sir' more in one day than in the last ten years. 'Who do I guard, what can I expect, sir?'

'It's a classified Technics lab. Report to Dr Oscar Dunlop. Your priority is the integrity of Dunlop's material. Second and last, Dunlop's neck.'

'Have you had trouble recently, sir?' Stone asked. 'Can I expect violence?'

Neville sat back. 'Jesus Christ, Jon D. Strother, you ask a lot of questions for a new boy. Just get your dumb ass up to Floor 39, Special Technics, and do as you're goddamned told!'

The sergeant slammed down his spent cup and stalked out without a backward glance. His fist hit the door release as he exited. It closed behind him and the lights automatically dimmed. By Stone's chrono it was almost 22:00. Lights-out.

He pushed away from the table, resigned to a ridiculously narrow and horribly empty bunk. He had gone four paces when hands grasped his arms, spun him and slammed him into the wall. Without surprise, he saw Treveno's lint white hair and pale blue eyes before him. Fushida stood at his back, and it was the lackeys, Decker and Brin, too terrified to whisper a word of argument, who held Stone.

He looked for Purl and O'Hara, but they had withdrawn to the end of the hall. Purl's face was like a mask. O'Hara's shifty eyes were on a battered magazine. Stone was on his own. And he could not say he hadn't expected it. He took a breath and looked into Treveno's face.

'What do you want?' He spoke between clenched teeth.

'You're not a Warlock.' Treveno had not said more than three words in five hours. His accent was odd, Stone struggled to place it. The voice was husky, as if he had suffered damage to the larynx in the chemical fire which left his face scarred.

'I signed the paper,' Stone said grimly. 'Even you can't get rid of me for six months.'

'You want to be a Warlock?' Treveno's pale eyes widened.

Stone hissed an obscenity. 'You're the king of this rat pack, I can see that. Okay, I'm buying. We'll play it your way. Yes, *sir*, I want to be a Warlock, *sir*, what do I have to do, *sir*?' The mockery was barbed.

'Leave him,' Treveno snapped.

The hands holding Stone against the wall released. He tugged his sleeves down and glared at the men as they grouped before him. One by one they opened their shirts. On the left breast of each was a tattoo, a five-point star, like the ancient pentacle symbol. Stone swallowed.

'You!' Treveno barked at Purl and O'Hara.

Reluctantly, they joined the group and displayed the laser-branded tattoo. Treveno's brows arched at Stone.

'You want to be a Warlock?'

'Do I have a choice?' Stone's palms were sweating as he opened his shirt. 'What is it, a mark of squad honour? Trial by ordeal?'

'Initiation.' The blond man stood aside and Fushida took his place. In his hands was a small laser torch, a common workshop tool.

Stone threw his shirt into Treveno's hands and pressed his shoulders against the wall. 'Get on with it.'

Treveno traced the lines of his own brand with one index finger. 'Warlock's initiation, Strother. One squeal, and I got ways to put you with Hutton before you can blink.'

The torch ignited and Stone watched Fushida deftly tune the beam. He had done this countless times, which meant he was good. He could make it easy, or very, very hard. Stone clenched his teeth and closed his eyes as the mute, unfathomable Fushida stepped closer. The first caress of the torch tore the breath from his lungs but his throat was silent.

***

The cup fell from Jarrat's hand and smashed at his feet. He sagged against the littered briefing table, both palms pressed to his chest, and heard dimly as Cantrell's voice shouted, 'Dr Reardon to the ops room, fast!'

Hands caught him and he struggled to shield himself as he fell into a chair, but the more he tried to shut it out the less he was able to. He choked in a breath and felt acid tears on his face.

Reardon must have run. A hand scanner chattered over Jarrat's torso as he blinked up into the surgeon's worried face. 'What is it, Kevin? You're going to have to tell me. I've never scanned anything like this.'

'It's nothing,' Jarrat gasped. 'It's not me.'

'He's been green to the gills for hours,' Cantrell said doubtfully. 'In the middle of the briefing he'd twitch and yelp.'

'I'm monitoring Stoney, damn it!' Jarrat dragged a breath to the bottom of his lungs and fought the empathic shields up until he could think clearly. 'I sweated through a whole medical with him.'

Cantrell puffed out his cheeks. 'I should have known.'

'And what's this?' Reardon showed him the readings. 'What the hell is going on down there?'

'Initiation.' Jarrat pulled both hands over his sweating face. 'They do it in a lot of units. I expected it. So did Stoney. It's all right, Kip, it just surprised me.'

'Same as it surprised him, no doubt,' Reardon said caustically. 'You're in pain, Kevin.'

'No. But Stoney is.' Jarrat rubbed his chest. 'They're putting their mark on him. He'll want it removed as soon as he gets out. Feels like a laser brand. It's common in merc units. I've seen it before.'

The scanner turned off. Reardon's hand fell on Jarrat's shoulder. 'You ought to get some sleep.'

'I'll sleep when he does.' Jarrat knuckled his eyes. 'And I'll wake when he does.' He looked up at Reardon, Cantrell and Petrov, who hovered dubiously. 'Empathy may not be much, but's all we have to work with. He could be in there for weeks.'

'Then at least get some food inside you and have a drink,' Reardon advised. 'You want me to make that an order? Get out of here, Jarrat. You're off duty, as of now.'

He stood, still rubbing his chest. 'I was finished anyway. There's not much we can do till our cyber specialist arrives, except monitor the situation in Elysium.'

'It's simmering,' Reardon followed him from the ops room. 'I've been watching political vidcasts. The fight for Senator Grenshem's job is like a war. Colonel Duggan was interviewed.'

'I saw him. He's tipping real violence.' Jarrat sighed as he thumbed for the lift. 'And he's on his own, Kip. NARC can't get involved in politics.'

'Politics?' Reardon exploded. 'You told me, Randolph Dorne is running an Angel syndicate from inside Equinox!'

'And until we can prove it, we're hamstrung.' Jarrat stepped into the lift. 'The instant we have proof, we'll bounce the rubble, I promise you.' He rubbed his chest and licked his lips. 'Jesus, that hurts. They're finished now. He's... lying down. Seems it's over.'

The scanner chattered again and Reardon swore. 'I can't give you a painkiller. I don't think it would work.'

'Besides, I need to concentrate.' Jarrat smiled tiredly. 'It's Stoney who needs the pill, not me.'

'Would you take a shot of malt whisky?' Reardon offered.

'Park your rump in my office, watch some video dross from Elysium. You're not going to sleep tonight, and I want to keep you under observation.'

'I'm not sick,' Jarrat protested. 'But I'm obliged, Kip. Did you grab a copy of the political broadcasts?'

The lift diverted to the Infirmary level and minutes later Jarrat was in Reardon's leather recliner, mellow with one whisky in him and another in his hand. On the screen, the candidates went for each other, beak and claws, while Reardon returned to the bio work he had been finishing before he was summoned to the ops room.

The broadcast would be a diluted version of the truth. Only Duggan would know the whole story, and Jarrat hesitated to call him. The telemetry NARC was getting from Tactical since the Wozniak incident was routine and inspecific, which in itself warned Jarrat of the state of affairs: Duggan was deliberately trying to keep their eavesdroppers undisturbed. Jarrat approved.

Championing the people was Lenore Maddigan, a professional politician, smart enough to know she was literally fighting for her life. Her file said she was Grenshem's protégé. She lived in a three-way marriage, with two spouses, one male, one female, and she cut the perfect, spotless image of a senator.

In the other corner was Bryce Ansell, the Equinox man, an engineer, young and brilliant. Jarrat disliked him on sight and listened with scepticism. Avalon's survival depended on Equinox, he said. Without the industrial giant the system would be no more than debris and deprivation. Poverty must lead to escalating Angel addiction.

Perhaps he was right. Jarrat was tired and bitter enough to have lost what grip he ever had on idealism. He could see the possibilities of Ansell's case. He sipped the second whisky as Maddigan's face returned to the screen and the argument raged on.

If Equinox was to survive here they must have mining rights to Zeus. The key to future liquidity was fluorine. But the process of stripping the atmosphere of the giant would fill the sky with a veil of trash, plunging Avalon and Eos into perpetual twilight. Local agriculture would fail as plants perished, every bite of food must be imported.

Jarrat reached for the pad on the corner of Reardon's desk and made a note. Who owned or controlled the major freight lines between Avalon and the nearest agriculturally rich colonies, the Cygnus homeworlds? Cygnus... Buchanan, Wozniak, Schaefer...Randolph Dorne.

The screen blanked as Reardon turned it off. Jarrat jerked awake without realising he had fallen asleep. Reardon took the empty glass from him. 'Is Stoney sleeping?'

'Yes.' Jarrat rubbed his chest. 'He's very angry and very sore, but they got whatever they wanted. They're satisfied.'

'They marked him, that was all?' Reardon was serious. 'I've heard of military units where it goes much further.'

'So have I.' Jarrat got stiffly to his feet. 'But Stoney's no kid. The treatment you're talking about, they save for pretty boys with more balls than brains. Stoney's a man, and they're treating him like one. Thank God.'

'Amen to that.' Reardon stood aside. 'If he's asleep, why don't you crash? Use that bed, where I can keep an eye on you. I don't know what to make of this.'

'The empathy?' Jarrat stretched out gratefully, hand still pressed to his chest, which was almost as sore as if he had taken the brand himself. 'It's something we live with. We don't have much choice.'

'But you have a choice about *how* you live.' Reardon dimmed the lights. 'If you were bumming around on some beach in civvy land, you wouldn't be in this shit.'

He was right, and Jarrat sighed. 'But NARC isn't a job, it's a way of thinking. Stoney believes that, which is why he's down there.'

'And you believe it, or we wouldn't have seen you for dust after the Death's Head job.' Reardon set a camera to monitor his patient and glanced at the time. 'Sleep while you can.'

'He's on military service so he'll be called early,' Jarrat added. 'How well I know those bloody duty schedules.' He turned onto his side, away from the camera.

'Shall I leave a message for someone to wake you?' Reardon was on his way out.

But Jarrat grunted a negative. 'I'm wide open. If he even thinks too loudly he'll wake me.' His voice was already slurred. As Reardon left him he tuned into Stone more closely. He was dreaming, and Jarrat's breath began to pant. He curled into a ball and forced himself to relax. It was the Angel nightmare. And this time Stone would have to master it alone.

Chapter Thirteen

'You have a man in deep cover, and you're running silent?' Yvette McKinnen was stunned. Her Paris accent thickened as she looked from Jarrat to Cantrell and back. 'This is highly irregular.'

'That's putting it mildly,' Cantrell agreed. 'Then again, this entire assignment is irregular. Were you briefed?'

They were waiting for the robotrolley with McKinnen's baggage. The Starfleet courier had just undocked and Jarrat wore a thunderous face. Curt Gable leaned against the bulkhead by the shuttle docking port, listening warily. Jarrat left McKinnen to Cantrell's diplomatic tactics and beckoned Gable a few paces away, out of earshot.

'You gave Dupre the file?'

'I did.' Gable's handsome face was grim. 'He's routing us a couple of tenders, one Starfleet, one Army, but they can't get here inside of a week at earliest.'

'Damn.' Jarrat rubbed his face.

'I had my doubts about whether you'd still be here, Cap,' Gable confessed. 'I mean, we could be sitting on a hundred megaton fusion bomb, and there's a man down there with his finger on a button.'

'Tell me about it.' Jarrat cast a glance at McKinnen. 'How much does she know?'

'Everything Budweisser gave me, I gave her.' Gable's teeth worried his lip. 'Cap Stone went into Equinox?'

'Four days ago.' Jarrat's brows arched.

'And he can't even get a call out of that building.' Gable swore. 'You're, uh, monitoring him?'

Jarrat was watching McKinnen. 'The empathy is better than R/T. Stop worrying. He's safe so far. Bored, annoyed, anxious, but safe. Now, what the hell is she doing?'

The woman was gesturing agitatedly as Cantrell tried to smooth ruffled plumage, and as Jarrat strode back toward them she swung on him. 'Captain, you have probably jeopardised this entire assignment!'

'By doing what?' Jarrat looked at Cantrell. 'We had no more time to waste, waiting for a specialist to bail us out. We had two options, Doctor. Pull the carrier right out of Randolph Dorne's space and let him do as he likes, or put a man into Equinox, get what we need and finish it.' He lifted his chin. 'Right at the start, before we were sent to your lab, Colonel Dupre told us a ballbreaker job was coming. This is it, he knows what we're up against.' Jarrat turned away. 'I suggest you do what you were sent here for.'

She bristled. 'The only means you have of monitoring your deep-cover operative is this — this empathy? It's ludicrous!'

'Is it?' Cantrell tilted his head at Jarrat. 'Where is Stone, what's he doing?'

Eyes closed, Jarrat concentrated. 'He's on his feet. Calm and even. Feeling well. The weight over his left shoulder has to be a weapon. Somebody made him laugh twenty minutes ago, and gave him a coffee. He's bored, frustrated. But I know he's onto something. I feel... optimism. He's on his toes.'

'Impressed, Doctor?' Cantrell asked affably. 'You should be. No machine would give you all that.'

'You're wrong, Captain Cantrell.' McKinnen snatched up her lighter luggage as a robotrolley trundled to a halt beside her. Gable stooped for the heavier cases.

Three of them held assorted personal terminals, never slaved to a ship's computer, containing no Equinox components. McKinnen drummed her fingers on the largest. 'I developed a biocyber brain implant that would relay every specific Captain Jarrat has just given us, plus medical telemetry, right down to pulse, respiration and blood analysis.' She clicked the infra-beam trolley control. 'Show me to my quarters and give me everything Engineer Budweisser has gathered. How long since you reasoned that you may be carrying Equinox parasites?'

'Seven days.' Jarrat folded his arms. 'Bud's just about got the synthetic aperture work done, but we don't have facilities to go much further.'

Her eyes were like chips of ice. 'Fortunately, I have.'

A pace behind her, Cantrell winced visibly and pinned on a smile. 'I'll take you to your quarters, Doctor. The engineers are at your disposal.'

They had stepped into the service lift when Curt Gable threw up his hands in exasperation. 'What the fuck is it with that woman? I've been trying to get two civil words out of her since we left Darwin's!'

'She's got a whole carcass to pick with NARC,' Jarrat said cuttingly. 'First, Central puts her project on hold, then she's told to research Stoney and me. Then, in their wisdom they put her on a courier, tell her to rush into a hotzone, dig the parasites out of a ship this size, our ship, potentially one of the biggest bombs ever launched, and smile while she does it.'

'Shit.' Gable raked his fingers through his dark hair. 'She's not pleasant company, Cap.' He stirred. 'You mind if I grab a shower, get a meal and catch up on your data? What goes on in Elysium?'

'Power politics.' Jarrat made a face. 'If Grenshem's faction wins, Equinox is out. Wars have started over less.'

Gable's brows rose into his unruly fringe. 'Lovely. You got anybody on standby?'

But Jarrat shook his head. 'We're not even twitching, Curt. We watch, we listen and we wait for Stoney.' He paused. 'It's been a long four days.'

'You look rough,' Gable said quietly.

'Yeah.' Jarrat clasped Gable's shoulder. 'I'm getting feelings from Stoney. He's sniffed something out.' He fended off Gable's concern with a guarded smile. 'Go and clean up. I'd better try and make peace with McKinnen.'

'Just take care,' Gable said drily as he stepped into the lift, 'that she doesn't turn you into a pillar of salt.'

The remark made Jarrat chuckle for the first time in a week. He leaned both palms on the wall by the docking port and closed his eyes. Stone was in no better spirits, but he was unhurt, in no immediate peril, neither cold, nor hungry. Jarrat was thankful for small mercies.

He pushed away from the wall and thumbed for the lift to take him to the quarters set aside for McKinnen. 'Come on, Stoney,' he murmured. 'Make it quick, for sweet Christ's sake.'

***

The same thought teased Stone's mind as he walked the length of the Special Technics division for the sixth time that shift. For eight hours of unremitting tedium, he patrolled from the labs to the library to the guarded exit, and back. Floor 39 was his patch, and in four days he had learned most of the people working there, if not the work they did.

The eight-hour shift was a relief in disguise. For that time he was out of the barracks, away from Warlock Company and the men he had come to despise. Treveno and Fushida had swiftly assumed the aspect of his nemesis.

When he was in the barracks they would push, goad, trying to manoeuvre him into a 'disciplinary situation'. The fact that Stone would not be goaded seemed to infuriate them. They longed to see him draw Company Punishment, as if it was the keenest amusement they knew.

If he was in the barracks by 20:25, just before a meal hit the mess table, he broke no regs. Lights-out was 22:00, and the squad rose at 04:45, when the graveyard shift came off duty. Army routine was stultifying and Stone had grown weary of saying 'sir'.

But Special Technics was close to where he wanted to be, and in four days of silent, stiff-backed efficiency, he had earned the freedom to begin. Treveno scorned him, but Treveno scorned everyone. According to Purl, he set out to goad every new man into Company Punishment. Most were seduced.

Not Jon Strother. Purl had taken to laughing when Treveno failed yet again. The barracks foreman assigned the new man the chores no one wanted. Strother worked without complaint. Cheated at cards, he called the misfortune his own fault for gambling. Called all kinds of degenerate, he was deaf. The striking of a senior was all Treveno needed to consign Strother to the ruthless justice of the private army.

The trick was to be out of the barracks before Treveno and Fushida got back from their own work. With his shift over, Stone ditched his weapon and left. He returned minutes before Neville arrived, and kept his mouth shut.

His one genuine concern was that after lights-out the real fun and games would begin. Treveno and Fushida were the kind who rode roughshod over subservients, it was routine in mercenary units. To Stone's gratitude, surveillance cameras watched the barracks. He wondered what events had prompted their installation, who monitored the antics taking place after the lights doused, and where those officers drew the line. The ritual of initiation was clearly part of local lore.

After four days the brand was no longer sore. Stone seldom thought of it. In a way it did make him part of the squad, contributed to the character of Strother.

Amid all of it he had one solace. With the slightest effort he could reach out and almost touch Jarrat. If he closed his eyes Kevin seemed so close. At night the illusion was painfully real. It was the first time since becoming lovers that they had been separated, and it was a learning experience. He had felt the shivers of Jarrat's arousal, the strokes of his right hand as he took care of his own needs. Stone savoured every sensation, waited until Kevin finished and then began himself, knowing Jarrat would feel it all with him. In the early hours of the barracks' morning, solitary panting and heaving was not unusual. All it took was a little discretion.

Preoccupied by memory, he stood at the long windows, looked into the street and marked the time. He would be free in an hour. Two floors above Special Technics was the Archive, and Data Processing.

Out of duty hours, he was welcome to use the library, walk or ride a maglev car up to the landing bays on the roof. So long as he remained in the building he was within regulations. Stone claimed boredom, and explored. To his pleasure he discovered at once, the uniform and Warlock insignia took him anywhere. A crisp salute pacified any officer he ran into. A brisk march and a folder in one hand gave them the impression he was running an errand. Deception was cheap.

Special Technics encompassed Engineering, Construction, Imaging, Chemical, any project involving unusual technology. New fuels, opticals, generators, and much more were developed in seven laboratory complexes.

The floor was inaccessible to the public. Entry was by authorised permit and the staff lived in. Their apartments were a hundred metres from the lifts, past the labs. Exit was as difficult as entry, and if they left their floor they did so escorted.

Ruby Chan was a chemist. Fluorine fuel processing was her field. Her lab was airlock-sealed. Stone had seen her twice, fleetingly, in four shifts. Marc Estevez was on powerpacks that made argon laser cannon man-portable. Russ Isaacson worked with gravity repulsion. Stone knew them all by sight and had culled what he could from Archives. They were on contract, literally imprisoned, immersed in their work. Most were oblivi-

222

ous to the powderkeg situation in Elysium.

Their supervisor was a young man with more brains than Stone would have believed could fit into one skull. Oscar Dunlop was Stone's own age, small, slight, mouse-brown, not unattractive but as physically ordinary as Kevin Jarrat was remarkable. Stone liked him, and respected his enormous intellect. Dunlop had not become head of Special Technics before he was thirty by chance. As an academic he was without peer; as a human being he was wreckage, and as a man he was so insecure, Stone wondered how he had made it through puberty.

But Dunlop had his finger on the pulse of this section. On shift, Stone took his instructions, and of the entire captive staff, Dunlop alone had clearance to leave the department, access classified records, delve into the business of other sections. Stone had targeted him for intensive surveillance on his first shift.

The data he wanted was in the system somewhere, but it would be highly classified. Weapons. Mercenaries. Shipping schedules either for the drug or the raw materials from which Angel was made. Smuggling was impossible, so the cargoes of poison must come in on legit freighters. They would be heavily disguised, but analysis would ultimately find them. Equinox was a facade disguising a vast, flourishing syndicate.

It was brilliant. Tactical could only ever nibble at the edges and speculate. Duggan had always known he had no chance of getting at the truth when Dorne's criminal trade was woven so deftly into the legitimate business of Equinox Industries. The way in was through Archives and Data Processing, but without access codes Stone would never breach the system. Dunlop had those codes, which made him the pivot point of Stone's plans.

Keeping tabs on him was easy. Dunlop was a creature of routine. He drank tea, smoked too much, shuffled his feet when he was nervous, which was most of the time, and he had been watching Jon Strother unblinkingly for two days.

Whenever Dunlop could take a break from work he deliberately looked for the Warlock Company guard. It made surveillance that much easier. Stone glance at his chrono. Dunlop's routine was his single firm characteristic. Stone need only wait.

Soft footsteps, nearly soundless on the deep blue carpets, caught his ears. He turned, unslung the Colt, but relaxed as he saw the man. The scientist wore baggy slacks, a garish red shirt and sport shoes, dress which reminded Stone of Harry Del. He had been born on Sheckley, Jarrat's own birthplace. His voice still had the telltale inflections, and drew Stone like a magnet.

'Just the man I wanted,' Dunlop called. 'You can help me, Jon.'

'Me?' Stone was surprised. 'I'm no scientist.'

'But you do have muscles.' Dunlop regarded him with overt interest.

'Muscles,' Stone echoed. 'That means you want something pushed, pulled or lifted.'

'Lifted.' Dunlop frowned at him. 'What's wrong? You look blue.'

'Purple,' Stone corrected as he followed Dunlop into an engineering lab which reminded him too much of McKinnen's for him to like it. 'I'm bored and I have three days left before I can get out of this antheap.' He glanced about the grey-walled room with its white benches and ivory-cased machines, and set the Colt on a chair. 'Okay, Doc, what do you want done?'

'Call me Oscar,' Dunlop invited. 'I need the inferometer moved out of the storeroom onto that bench. I'm supposed to have a lab tech, but the damned man called in sick. You know... you don't have to be bored and deprived.'

Stone checked in mid stride. 'Come again?'

'You know what I mean.' Dunlop blushed. 'And as for coming again, I'd settle for the first time.'

The inferometer was a big piece of machinery. Stone cast about for a grav adjuster, but none was handy. Hence, Dunlop's sudden requirement for muscle. He cradled the big, surgical steel case in his arms and took the weight.

'Put it here.' Dunlop patted the bench. 'I'll set it up later. I'm having tea, if you'd like...' He flinched under Stone's blue-eyed scrutiny.

'If I didn't know better,' Stone said drily, 'I'd say you were trying to proposition me. And I'd say you were trying to do it since yesterday.'

The blush deepened. 'Well, why not? Oh, God. You're not a total het, are you?'

'I like guys,' Stone said warily as he dusted his palms and slung the Colt over his shoulder. 'You're going to get me into trouble, Doc.'

'Me?' Oscar recoiled. 'There's no rule about who you spend your off hours with. Didn't they tell you that?'

And Stone admitted, Sorenson had. 'Drink, dope and fuck on my time, not theirs,' he recited glibly.

'Right.' Oscar shoved his hands into his back pockets and fidgeted engagingly. 'Don't worry, you can talk in here. The lab's monitored but I hotwired the cameras. The morons don't even know I did it. So, you and me. How about it?'

Stone chuckled aloud. 'That's one hell of a line.'

The hopeful expression wilted. 'You're going to reject me,' Oscar groaned. 'It's because I work for Equinox? So do you, man. You're wading just as deep in the same shit.' He turned his back on Stone and hunched on a stool by the bench.

'What sort of shit are we both wading in?' Stone asked patiently.

'You kidding?' Dunlop toyed with the inferometer. 'You saw the political circus last night?'

'I don't see much,' Stone admitted. He put the Colt on the bench and stepped closer. 'Lenore Maddigan and Bryce Ansell?'

'The contenders.' Dunlop feinted a few punches into the air. 'If it was pistols at ten paces, you'd make a million on tickets.' He looked up anxiously. 'Equinox is going down the latrine. That why you won't frat with the likes of me?'

'You've got me dizzy,' Stone told him drily. 'You're cute, Doc, but I'm a basement-barrack grunt. I don't know what you're talking about.' But he thought he did, and his pulse quickened. After watching every scientist and technician on his patch for days, Oscar Dunlop most of all, he knew when these people needed to sneeze.

Dunlop sighed. 'You want tea?' He gestured at the robochef in the corner. 'Get me one. Lemon.'

'You're the boss.' Stone keyed the machine but never took his eyes off Dunlop. 'Equinox is flushed?'

'When Maddigan's elected.' Oscar swivelled the stool. 'Do you know what I design here?'

'Not my business.' Stone handed him a cup, took one for himself and leaned against the bench.

'I design the junk that'll tear Zeus apart.' Oscar patted the inferometer as if it were a dog. 'Except it won't get the chance.' He looked hauntedly at Stone. 'They're going to be in here, and I don't give a fuck for our chances.'

'Who?' Stone pulled up a stool.

Brown eyes gaped at him. 'Jesus, you can't be that naive! Or are you one of those gorgeous dumbells, all muscle, not enough brains to give yourself a headache?' He took a gulp from his cup. 'You think Equinox will take it lying down? They'll fight, goddamn it! It'll make the last fracas look like a party.'

He was scared, and Stone backed off though he could see exactly what Dunlop meant. Feigned naivety had its merits. 'You mean, the crowd'll be in here? The people?'

'Grenshem's mob. Maddigan's mob now.' Dunlop swallowed. 'They gave you buggers a run for your money in Sciaparelli, and they're not even armed. Yet,' he added darkly. 'They have Tactical on their side. And NARC.'

Stone's skin prickled and his pulse picked up. Jarrat would feel the sudden kick. 'Warlock Company went up against NARC. They say NARC destroyed them.'

'Trashed them,' Dunlop muttered. 'You can't fight that. Riot armour and gunships.' He looked nervously at Stone. 'You're gorgeous. But you're not dumb, you're crazy.'

'Thanks.' Stone made a face.

'I mean, you enlisted in this rat circus at this time,' Dunlop elaborated. 'You trying to suicide? They'll throw you in at the deep end when the mob comes to burn this place! You going to defend me? With that?' He stabbed a finger at the absurdly inadequate rifle.

'So run, before it starts,' Stone said cautiously.

The scientist's eyes narrowed. 'I was right, wasn't I? You're not like the rest. I saw it as soon as you walked in here. You're different.'

Alarms tripped in Stone's head now. 'I signed a contract. Like you said, I'm mad. Why don't you get out while you can?' Intuition coiled in his belly. 'Or are you on a contract too?'

'Equinox,' Dunlop said bitterly, 'doesn't buy paperclips without a contract. They own us all, Jon, body and soul.' He held out his hand. 'You're not with them, are you?'

Stone took the offered hand. 'I don't know what you mean.'

'Bullshit.' Dunlop bit his lip. 'You're not dumb, and you're not nuts. You're playing dense with me, and I wish I knew why. You're highly intelligent, and I can't name another basement-barrack grunt who is. Did they tattoo you? That means you had the guts to play Treveno's game. You're not like him. You've been here four days and you haven't had discipline, which means you're two moves ahead of the creeps. Who the hell are you? What are you?' Dunlop shook his head slowly. 'I spend my life analysing data. And you don't add up, Jon. Not as a security goon.'

The assessment was dismayingly accurate. Stone looked away. He had seen Dunlop watching him and had put the interest down to animal magnetism, old-fashioned lechery. He should never have underestimated Dunlop's intellect. It was a mistake, and he could be in serious trouble.

He cleared his throat and picked up his cup. 'Okay, Doc. What do you think I am?'

'I don't know,' Dunlop admitted. 'But I know what you're not. You're no grunt. You're no fool. You're too smart to sign into this godforsaken outfit on the brink of a battle that'll get you cut to scrap. You've got looks and brains, skills. You move like an athlete, not like Neville's clodhoppers. I saw you in the library last night.'

Stone's mouth dried. 'You followed me?' Damn. He had been so intent on his work, so convinced of Dunlop's ineptitude, he had not bothered to look over his shoulder. Mistake.

Dunlop nodded. 'I've been trying to proposition you. I saw you five floors up, followed you to the library. I saw the way you handled the terminal, Jon. I saw what you were reading.'

A pulse hammered in Stone's temple. 'I'm researching the Company. That's normal. I just started here.'

'Yes.' Dunlop's voice dropped. 'You handle a terminal like a pro, you ran the data four, five times faster than Neville's louts can read.' He paused. 'I'm an analyst. I see these things. It's part of my job.'

The extent of his mistake was becoming apparent to Stone. He stood, turned his back on Dunlop and looked for options. He saw few, and every one meant terminating the assignment. He rebuked himself viciously. He had outmanoeuvred the illiterate barracks savages with ease, but in four shifts Oscar Dunlop had cracked his cover wide. His eyes strayed to his chrono. He was off duty in half an hour. If went up to the roof he could steal a skimmer, make it out to Tac HQ, call Jarrat —

'I won't tell,' Dunlop said quietly.

'What?' Stone spun.

'I said, I won't tell,' Dunlop repeated. He rubbed his face.

227

'You work for Lenore Maddigan, don't you? She took over Grenshem's whole merry band of whistleblowers. He had scores!' The brown eyes gleamed. 'Most are dead now, and those that aren't won't last long. How long can you live, with your nose stuffed with Angel?' Dunlop took a breath. 'I won't betray you. But you damned well make me a promise.'

Relief rushed through Stone like a cascade of cold water. 'What promise?'

'When you go, you take me with you.' Dunlop caught his arm with fingers like talons. 'You're here to get the data Maddigan needs to shoot Ansell down in flames, aren't you?'

'Maybe,' Stone allowed. It was not so far from the truth. 'Did you know Jack Spiteri and Michael Rogan?'

Dunlop's face twisted. 'Jack was a project director six months ago. Two floors down, in Engineering. Christ, you know about Mike? Then you must be with Maddigan!' He caught Stone's hands tightly. 'How will you get out?

'Slow down!' Stone took him by the upper arms. 'I'll worry about that when the time comes. First I need something to get out *with*.'

'Data?' Dunlop steadied with an effort.

'You said it yourself,' Stone said quietly. 'Maddigan has NARC and Tactical behind her. You know why?'

'I've thought about it.' Oscar licked his lips. 'The only reason NARC would get involved in the brawl in Sciaparelli would be if Jack was right. Was it Angel money that put Dorne on Skycity?'

A bolt of electricity raced through Stone's nerves. Jarrat would feel it like a kick. 'NARC and Tac are trying to prove that,' he said evasively.

'And Maddigan sent you here?' Dunlop's eyes widened. 'You've got a way out!'

'Maybe.' Stone released his arms. 'You haven't told me where you stand yet. Which camp are you in?'

The scientist's hands clasped on the bench. 'Mine. I'm on an Equinox contract, I can't escape any more than you can. I don't want to see Avalon wrecked by some crank scheme to mine Zeus. For all I know, Grenshem's specialists are right and it'll kill us all. But I've seen Company data too. Do you know where we'll be if we lose the Equinox revenue?'

'I'm not a politician,' Stone said guardedly.

'But you're a survivor.' Dunlop's eyes flayed him. 'So am I. I told Randolph, the last thing we want is a fast decision. Moratorium. Research. Equinox can afford to delay one year or *ten* till we have the findings.'

'You know Dorne personally?' Stone was surprised.

'Professionally.' Dunlop leaned closer. 'I'll make you a deal.' Stone's ears pricked. 'I'm listening.'

'Get me out, when the time comes,' Dunlop whispered. 'I'll help you get what Maddigan needs. Deal?' He offered his hand.

'Deal.' Stone took it and shook. 'You know what I need?'

'I can work it out.' Dunlop seemed to steady. 'It'll be two days before we can try to get it. There's only one terminal in Data Processing that has the access. And you can't do it yourself. You need entry codes. How were you planning to get them?'

'From you.' Stone shrugged eloquently. 'One way or another.

The blush on Dunlop's cheeks was furious. 'You bugger. You'd have doped me, got me drunk or fucked me, got the codes and then dumped me!'

'Not necessarily.' Stone smiled faintly. 'What's special about the timing, two days from now?'

'That's when I have the terminal booked.' Dunlop rummaged for a cigarette. 'You don't just walk in and use it, and you don't use it without an armed escort.' He looked Stone up and down. 'By outrageous good fortune, that's you.' He flicked a silver lighter, dragged smoke to the bottom of his lungs and offered Stone the packet.

'Thanks.' Stone took a cigarette and the lighter. 'You can get the data?'

'On the first attempt?' Dunlop took another drag. 'Maybe. I have a regular booking for that terminal, so we'll get a second shot. I have a better chance than you ever had. I know the way the system works. It's littered with mantraps.' His eyes widened. 'If you'd doped me for the codes, you'd have tripped one, and one's enough.'

Stone's blood cooled by degrees. 'I never expected it'd be easy. I know my way around these systems.'

'Not this one. This one's a deathtrap unless you know it like your own backyard.' Dunlop sagged against the bench. 'It's lucky you have me, soldier.' He's eyes closed on the smoke. 'I'll work out a probable way in on paper, lick it into shape before we get there. You owe me one after this.'

'I owe you a bunch.' Stone took a last drag and ground out the cigarette. 'I'd better be visible.' He touched the tip of Dunlop's nose with one finger. 'I'm trusting you.'

'Same as I'm trusting you,' Dunlop added. 'You could get me crammed with Angel and dumped in a city bottom fuckhouse. I'm scared to death, Jon.'

'Don't be.' Stone dealt the man's cheek a small caress. 'You do good work, and leave the rest to me.'

With that he slung the Colt over his shoulder and stepped out of the lab. Nothing moved between the service lifts and the private apartments. He checked the time and settled into a last routine patrol, but his belly churned with apprehension, and he knew Jarrat would fret with him. Taking a deep breath, he cultivated a sensation of optimism. 'Read that, honey,' he said to Jarrat, and wished to God he had the capacity to send thoughts or words.

Chapter Fourteen

A ream of printout lay strewn across the briefing table under the ops room's overhead lights. Yvette McKinnen pored over it, line by line, and once in an hour she would make a note. To Jarrat it was so much gibberish, but he knew what she was doing. Colonel Helen Archer could make better sense of it, and had offered to test McKinnen's theories with a portable terminal. McKinnen accepted the aid of a Starfleet officer more readily than she could tolerate NARC participation.

Jarrat appreciated her annoyance and did not interfere, but he was often aware of McKinnen's professional scrutiny, and this he resented. She was waiting for him, or Stone, to foul the assignment so badly it fell apart. Jarrat's mouth compressed in anger though he said nothing.

Groundside, Stone was filled with a continual inundation of feelings which were near to overwhelming Jarrat. From one moment to the next, he might be elated, angry, scared. He was riding an old, familiar rollercoaster. Being in the middle of it, knowing the cause of the emotions, made them easier to endure. Being three hundred kilometres away, otherwise in the dark, made them acutely distressing. Jarrat longed to put up his shields and block the empathy, yet knew he could not.

Five days after Stone entered Equinox, he felt a deep throb of expectation, quick pulse, racing heart, a faint sweat, almost sexual sensations. Stone was excited, on his toes. Something was simmering. Jarrat had kept a private log since the beginning, and noted his feelings by the hour.

He's onto something. Found the answer to some problem. He thinks he sees the way out. He feels sure. If he's right this could be over sooner than expected. I hope it is... it's taking a heavier toll of me than anticipated. Not sleeping. Can't eat. Getting tired. Reardon gives me pills, stimulants, I guess. It's been a tough week.

The log was handwritten, he was taking no chances. The sheets were passed to Cantrell, who collated the data for Intelligence. McKinnen would have liked to read the file, but

Cantrell whisked it out of her reach.

Shiptime, it was evening. Jarrat pacing restlessly about the ops room. A session in the gym had left him exhausted, but his mind continued to race. Cantrell and Petrov were reviewing the carrier's records, which would normally have been transmitted as telemetry. Archer's fingers flew over the keys as she ran another test sequence.

McKinnen's soft French oath took them all by surprise. Jarrat stilled and frowned at her as she straightened from the scatter of paper. One shell-pink fingernail tapped an obscure subsection in the mechanical printout of the labyrinthine Quantum-Data programme.

'There it is.' McKinnen pressed both palms into the curve of her spine as she straightened. 'I'd gamble a year's salary, Captain.' She stood back as Archer moved in to see. 'Run an analysis, Colonel, everything from here... to here.' Red ink labelled the obscure material. 'This whole section has nothing to do with guidance or navigation. It's nested in a part of the prog where it has no business being.'

A textscanner passed over the hard copies and the computer began to run. McKinnen shouldered in beside Archer and moments later allowed herself a small crow of victory.

'That's it, Cap.' Archer tapped the screen. 'That's the leech. My guess is, Tactical's computers carry the same one. Question is, Dr McKinnen, is it passive or active?'

'I would said, *re*active.' McKinnen toyed with a pen. 'You have something here that lies dormant till a command is received.'

Cantrell cleared his throat. 'Can you tell from that if we have parasite devices among our Equinox hardware components?'

'Indications are, you do,' McKinnen mused. 'It will take some time to decipher this. It's complex, clever.'

'Some time?' Jarrat echoed. 'You mean, an hour or a week?'

She glared at him. 'Hours at least. I can get lucky and stumble over the answer, or I can fight for it.'

'The quicker the better, Yvette,' Cantrell said smoothly. 'I'm sure we'd all like to see this done. Kevin —'

'Message incoming. Uncoded on the civvy band, voice only,' Petrov interrupted. He was monitoring the carrier's sporadic, bogus radio traffic, and looked across the cluttered table at Jarrat with surprise. 'It's for you, Cap.'

'Duggan?'

'No.' Petrov listened for a second. 'Lenore Maddigan.'

Astonished, Kevin pulled up a chair. 'Jarrat.'

The voice in his ear belonged to a girl. 'Captain Jarrat, I have Madame Lenore Maddigan for you, if it's convenient.'

'Put her on.' Jarrat gestured toward the comm console, and Petrov turned on the voice-stress analysis. 'Good evening, madame,' he said evenly.

He recognised Maddigan's voice from innumerable vidcasts. 'Captain Jarrat, good evening. I won't dissemble. I imagine your time is as precious as mine. Colonel Duggan advised me to call.'

Jarrat's brows rose. 'About what, ma'am?'

'I can't discuss it on open channel,' she said flatly. 'I wish to meet you personally.'

'I ought to advise you,' Jarrat said slowly, 'Narcotics And Riot Control cannot enter any political arena.'

'I understand.' Maddigan paused. 'Still, I must speak with you, Captain, privately.'

A note in the woman's voice alerted Jarrat. He glanced up at Cantrell, and the older man nodded. Gene had heard it too. 'All right, ma'am. How urgent is this?'

'Extremely.' Maddigan took an audible breath. 'If you'd meet me at once, I'd be grateful. Do you know my home?'

Who did not, after endless political biographies? 'Flinders Park, north of Elysium,' Jarrat told her. 'You'll be there tonight?'

'All evening.' Lenore Maddigan hesitated. 'And take care, Captain. Goodbye.'

The recorders shut off as Jarrat stood. 'I'll go now. She could have something for us.'

'Alone?' Cantrell asked quietly.

'I want at least one command rank officer aboard,' Jarrat said shortly. 'That's you, Gene.' He gestured at the printout and Archer's personal terminal. 'It may not look like it, but the crucial work is going on right here.'

He left the ops room in Cantrell's care, and strode to his cabin with a sense of agitation. Stone's unease, or his own? It was difficult to tell. A pace inside the cabin he stopped, eyes closed, and reached for Stone.

There he was: his hands were raw with some heavy work, Company duty. But his belly was full and though he was annoyed he was not worried, and above all that Jarrat read excitement, optimism. Something was on the boil, and it was close to completion.

He changed quickly and was in the shuttle in minutes. Tight brown slacks, cream lace shirt with green trim, tan leather jacket, black boots. Elysium chic. Beneath the jacket was an old, familiar ally, the Colt AP-60. Rarely did he leave the carrier without it.

The hangar bay cleared and he consulted the navigation deck as the hatch opened to space. He was passing over the terminator into the night side, and below him the lights of the towns and cities were like jewels on black velvet.

The wings glowed cherry red in the darkness as he bucked through re-entry. Elysium Field picked him up and he identified as NARC Airborne, but declined the offer of landing assistance as he dropped in over the sprawling city on a heading for Maddigan's residence.

The house stood in floodlit private grounds, not as regal as the mock-Roman palace on Skycity, but lavish enough to impress. Five thousand metres downrange, instruments warned Jarrat he was being tracked, and not by spaceport radars. He rode straight down the beam and kicked in his floods and spinners as he shut back to hover, two hundred metres over Flinders Park.

Below was a fleet of vehicles, an army of security men. He saw Tactical uniforms, heavy weapons, and swore softly. 'NARC Airborne. Where do you want me?'

Unsurprisingly, Vic Duggan's voice answered. 'East wing of the house, inside the cordon, Captain. It's the safest place.'

Trees thrashed in the downwash and the jets screamed back off the mansion's grey stone walls as the shuttle settled on the lawn. The repulsion would scorch the grass, but Duggan must have known that. Jarrat lifted off his helmet as the canopy rose, and took a breath of the warm, windy night air.

Stone was not ten kilometres away. He was on his back, comfortable, tired but too restless to sleep. Jarrat felt a stir of erotic sensation and gritted his teeth. *Not now, Stoney! Save it!* Did the protest carry through the empathic bond? Did Stone tune in on him and feel with Kevin's nerves as he climbed from the cockpit and hit the ground? Perhaps he felt the weight of the machine pistol against Jarrat's ribs, and the wind in his hair.

Arousal faded and Jarrat took a breath as he felt Stone's tangible presence. Stoney knew he was groundside, and now was monitoring *him*.

'This way, Jarrat.' Duggan's face appeared about the corner of the house.

'This had better be good,' Jarrat said tersely. 'I've told you people time and again, NARC is not political.'

'This has shit-all to do with politics,' Duggan said darkly. 'Where the hell is Stoney?'

'Inside Equinox.' Jarrat strode past him and entered the dim, quiet house by a side door. He smelt fresh flowers, beeswax and wine, and gave the scores of framed photographs of a bygone age which mosaiced the walls a curious look before he turned back to Duggan. 'You've got half an army here.'

'Talk to Lenore. Second on your right.' Duggan let him go ahead.

The door was open, she was waiting for him. Jarrat inclined his head as he entered. Lenore Maddigan was seated behind a wide desk. She was the consummate politician: not a hair out of place, in conservative, pastel-blue slacks and blouse, discreet jewellery, perfumed with the faint reek of money. She extended a hand across the desk, and Jarrat took it before he seated himself in a stuffed leather armchair. The antique hearth and bookcases gave the study an old-world flavour which reminded him of Grenshem's home in Belreve. Maddigan was Grenshem's protégé, groomed to take his place.

'It was good of you to come, Captain.' She steepled her fingers on the desk. 'Colonel Duggan said you might not, but quite frankly, I don't know whom else to petition.'

'For what, ma'am?' Jarrat flicked a glance at Duggan.

'Help.' She sat back. 'If you've followed the broadcasts, you know the election is in two days. And you know there will be violence.'

'War,' Duggan added.

Jarrat frowned at the burgundy drapes behind the desk. 'I don't see what I can do.'

'You can deploy the riot troops who are sitting on their backsides on your ship,' Maddigan said in caustic tones.

He shook his head slowly. 'Not to fight your war for you. You want a warship, not a NARC carrier.'

'The nearest is the *Ambush*, ten days away,' Maddigan said

brusquely. 'We sent signals. I don't think they got through.'

'Jammed at source?' Jarrat looked at Duggan, who was leaning on the closed door.

His brows arched. 'If you were Randolph Dorne, would you let your rival send for a warship to depose you?'

'Right.' Jarrat turned back to Maddigan. 'But I can't give you NARC deployment till I have concrete evidence of what we all know damned well is going on. We have a man in Equinox even now. He's close to the truth.'

Her dark eyes widened. 'How long before you have what you need?'

'Impossible to be sure,' Jarrat said carefully. 'A day, a week. Believe me, I'm as impatient as you are.'

She regarded Duggan soberly. 'You know Equinox maintains a vast private army which makes the token defence force of this colony look like a set of toy soldiers. When the votes are counted two days from now and I formally assume Grenshem's office, Equinox Industries will unleash that army on the people of Elysium, crush them, and continue with their lunatic project to mine Zeus.'

The assessment of the situation was painfully astute. Not for a moment did Jarrat try to argue. 'I can't take NARC into a corporate war. It's not just my job I'd be putting on the line, I'd be compromising the integrity of the whole department. You want me to deploy like a mercenary force.' He stood. 'You know damned well, I can't.'

'Not even to save lives?' Maddigan followed him to his feet. Her voice rose sharply. 'You know what Dorne is doing as well as we do! For years he's used Equinox to cover the biggest Angel syndicate between the rimworlds and the deep sky! He has this system in the palm of his hand.'

The remark took Jarrat back to Jesse Lawrence's tale of the chemist who swore he had that same grip on Equinox. He frowned at Duggan. 'You found Gary Schaefer?'

But Duggan made negative noises. 'He's disappeared.'

'What do you mean, disappeared?' Jarrat demanded tautly.

'Gone, vanished, not on Avalon or Eos, no record of him leaving the system, no body in the morgue that fits his stats, nobody using his stolen ID,' Duggan snapped. 'We turned up totally blank. It's like he never existed at all.'

'Jesus.' Jarrat draw a hand through his hair. 'They sent him after Spiteri and the other whistleblowers.'

'That,' Duggan said sourly, 'is their style. I'm telling you, Jarrat, it'll be war. And there's sweet fuck all I can do to stop it or slow it down.'

Jarrat took a breath, exhaled slowly. NARC could stop it. Four gunships, one hundred riot troops, two heavily armed spaceplanes. It would be an act of total war, with no concrete connection to the Angel trade. Jarrat's belly knotted. 'All we need is a lousy handful of data,' he said quietly.

'If you had it, you'd deploy?' Maddigan was tight lipped, desperate.

'Yes.' Jarrat thrust his hands into the pockets of the brown slacks. 'It's a matter of time. I know Stoney's onto something.'

'He got a message out of there?' Duggan guessed.

'Oh, yeah.' Jarrat pressed a hand to his chest. At that moment Stone was so finely attuned to him, shared tension snapped between them as if they were in the same room. He stirred fretfully. 'You're going to have to wait. I'll deploy when I can. Till then, you're asking me to compromise the entire foundation NARC is built on, and I can't do it.'

'Won't,' Maddigan corrected acidly.

'Have it your way, ma'am.' Jarrat nodded goodnight to her and paced from the study. Duggan was behind him, all the way to the shuttle. Jarrat waited for him to speak, but the Tactical man was silent.

On the point of climbing into the cockpit, Jarrat turned back. 'Give me a groundcar.' He thumbed the infrabeam to lock the canopy.

'You going into Elysium?' Duggan was dubious. 'It's not safe. Like you said, I've got half an army trying to protect Lenore. Their shooters have tried two long hits, they bombed her car, torched her office in town this morning. You think Dorne doesn't know exactly where you are, Jarrat?'

'He knows.' Jarrat frowned at the dim, green velvet face of Zeus. 'We found the parasites in our flight systems, just before Maddigan called.'

'Christ.' Duggan looked away. 'If you're going into Elysium, don't go alone. Where are you headed?'

'The less you know —'

'The better.' Duggan drew a Stery pistol from the holster beneath his left arm. 'Sod that, Jarrat. I know Elysium better than you ever will. Where are we going?'

Jarrat permitted himself a faint, grim smile. 'Get us on the road first. Something bulletproof but fast.'

'I've got a Marshall Thunderbird.' Duggan produced the keys. 'Good enough?'

The car was a long, low aeroshell with triple jets in the tail, each rated at three hundred horses. The apple green and gold paint job concealed kevlex armour, and the gullwings were manufactured of the same material as the shuttle's canopy. It was parked in the lee of the Tac mobile command post. Jarrat took the keys as Duggan informed his squad he was leaving.

The jets exploded into life and the Thunderbird rocked on the tractors which held her in position. Duggan settled in the passenger's seat, and as Jarrat dropped the gullwings he was already arcing about the house, toward the gateway. Tactical guards stepped out before him, but Duggan spoke tersely to the R/T and they cleared the way.

The gates opened onto Southbound 9. Jarrat turned right, turned on the autonav and requested a fast route into Rheims. Duggan's eyes raked every vehicle they saw, but they were still unchallenged when Jarrat parked, just short of the Rheims exit, in a bay beside a rank of vidphone booths.

'Watch yourself,' Duggan warned. 'They won't be far away.'

'You watch me.' Jarrat lifted himself out of the bucket seat. He felt a flashfire of stress and gasped as he walked toward the booths. 'It's okay, Stoney,' he muttered. 'Do your own job, let me do mine!'

From his pocket came a personal card, which he slid into the phone as he took a backward glance at the road. Ten lanes of moving traffic confused the darkness with dazzling halogen. He blinked his eyes clear as the screen lit. Jesse Lawrence's face appeared, but he was not looking at his own screen.

'I'm not working tonight. Call my agency.'

'It's Kevin,' Jarrat said quietly. 'Your friendly NARC.'

The boy gave a start. 'My God, are you psychic?'

'What do you mean?' Jarrat's pulse picked up.

'I've been trying to get a message to Vic Duggan,' Jesse told him. 'Every time I call Tac, they say they'll pass it on, but he's busy. He never calls back.'

'Surprising.' Jarrat glanced at Duggan, who was out of the car, leaning on the nose, away from the blistering heat of the jets. 'You in trouble, kid?'

'I think so,' Jesse said bitterly. 'I told you I'd keep my ears open for more... and I found it. I've been talking to people, asking questions. I must have said the wrong thing to the wrong person somewhere. You've got to help me.'

'I'm groundside in Elysium right now,' Jarrat told him. 'Where do you want to meet? And I have to warn you, it may not be safe. You didn't reach Duggan because he's covering Lenore Maddigan, and now he's with me. If Equinox shooters are behind us, and they probably are, I'll lead them straight to you.'

'Wouldn't matter.' Jesse raked back his hair. 'I'm scared spitless, Kevin. I know I was followed home. I mean, am I paranoid? They're watching this building, waiting for me to leave. It's a safe building, we've got guards, but they're waiting for me!'

'Which means your phone's bugged, they're getting every word of this.' Jarrat took a breath. 'Get out, fast, kid. Your doormen won't hold them off for long. Where will I meet you?'

'Oh, Jesus.' Colour drained from Jesse's face. 'Do you know Palomino, in Alexandria?'

'I'll find it. Go! I'll be there before you.'

Jesse did not need telling again. The screen blanked, and Jarrat turned back to the car with a grim look for Duggan. 'What the hell is Palomino?'

'A sex shop in Alexandria.' Duggan was in the car as he spoke. 'You desperate for a quick blow?'

The jets screamed up and Jarrat jumped the Marshall back onto the clearway. The Alexandria exit lay ten kilometres away and he flattened the accelerator as soon as he had nudged into the fast lane. Duggan swore as the digital speedo spun over.

'What the fuck are you doing, Jarrat?'

'Trying to get to a sex shop in Alexandria before some bastard Equinox shooter gets there,' Jarrat snarled. 'We're not being followed.'

'They'd have a tough time keeping up,' Duggan muttered.

The jets howled as the speedo touched 400k. Jarrat scanned ahead for the exit and swung the Thunderbird wide through two vacant lanes to take it fast. Duggan clung to his straps as Jarrat met slower traffic and hit the brakes. Now he wove, lane to lane, leaving a trail of cursing civilians.

'Make a right, and for godsakes slow down,' Duggan shouted.

'The place is a mess of gyrobikes.'

He was not exaggerating. Jarrat braked hard as he swung into a broad thoroughfare lined on either side by glaring neon. He had already picked out the holosign over the wide neon foyer of Palomino, and cruised down at the kerb opposite.

His view along the street was good, and he checked the time. Jesse could not have made it here in six minutes. If he was going to make it at all. Jarrat's belly knotted. The kid could already be dead. Fury blazed through him like a live fire. He knew he would be panicking Stone with the intensity of the anger, and deliberately reined it back.

If Jesse did not make it, he would be another statistic in a war which had been going on for months, perhaps years, albeit underground. Maddigan and Duggan were right, it should be NARC business. Shackled by regulations, Jarrat felt a pang of unaccustomed impotence. A man could learn to loathe the feeling in seconds.

Duggan leaned forward on squeaking bronze leather. 'We got company. Shit, Jarrat, you know how to get me into trouble.'

'I see them.' Jarrat had picked out the figures in the alley across the road in the moment Duggan spoke. 'Jesse was well bugged. Damn.'

Three shooters — dressed in dark garb, heavily armed, common contract executioners — approached from the shadows, hoping for one clear shot. The Colt AP-60 slid out of the holster and Jarrat thumbed the safety off.

He had the armoured body of the Thunderbird between him and the shooters, and set a hand on Duggan's arm as the colonel drew his own weapon. 'Stay put!'

He cracked the gullwing up just enough to slither out into the gutter, and hugged the side of the car, around the nose. His view into the alley was poor, but he saw them with seconds to spare before they picked him up. One was shouting into an R/T, and Jarrat took the Colt in both hands.

On full auto, he held the trigger down for under two seconds. A welter of scarlet, a peppering of returning rounds which smacked into the side of the Thunderbird, a scream from the alley, and it was over. Jarrat stood, the Colt still in both hands, and scanned the street and alleys. Civilians screamed and ran, but panic was to his advantage. Someone was sure to call Tactical, but he was carrying NARC ID.

'They R/T'd base,' he told Duggan. 'We're not safe, but it's the car they'll be looking for. Get it out of here.'

'And go where?' Duggan was hurrying around the nose.

'Hide it.' Jarrat's grip relaxed on the Colt. 'You said you know this town! Mark the time, give me fifteen and then *be here*. If you don't see me, ditch the car and run.'

'I'm gone.' Duggan had slid in under the wheel and the gullwing locked before he had finished speaking.

Jarrat backed up against the wall as the jets blew scorching air over him. He reholstered the Colt and watched sightseers gather under Palomino's holosign to peer at the bodies. The steelrock from the sex shop had not even paused.

He almost did not hear the soft-soled footsteps and panted breaths, and spun at the last moment to see Jesse, winded and flushed, bolting up from the downtown arcades. He was in brief cutoff denims, a short black robe which he clutched about himself as he ran, and rope sandals, all he had managed to grab before he fled. He fell into Jarrat's grasp with a cry.

'They behind you?' Jarrat caught him. 'Jesse!'

'I lost them.' Jesse whooped for air. 'I had to double back — I thought you'd go without me.'

'Not a chance.' Jarrat tucked him under his arm and glanced at the time. 'Ten minutes, and we're out of here.'

'Ten? Then, come on!' Still panting, Jesse grabbed him by the arm and pulled him into the street toward Palomino.

With an animal wariness, Jarrat followed. As far as he could see, they were unobserved, and if Equinox shooters came out to finish the job, it was a hundred to one against them guessing their quarry had entered the sex shop. The smart move would be to run, fast and far.

Steelrock blazed out of the transducers. Hustlers of both genders lounged along the counters, naked, painted, alluring, in all sizes and dispositions, but all blond and long legged. Palominos? Jesse ignored them, and Jarrat allowed himself to be urged to the back of the dim, candy-sweet shop. Dreamsmoke buzzed the ears and steelrock reverberated through the brain.

Stairs led down into a basement warren. Cubicles opened on either wall; the glory holes were busy; the pool was full and thrashing. The dreamsmoke made Jarrat's head swim. He longed for a draught of clean air as Jesse began to look at faces

241

and pry bodies apart. Couples protested, but customers and hustlers alike were too groggy to do more than shout. The place reeked of sweat and sex.

Just as Jarrat began to watch the time and prepare to pull the boy out, Jesse found what he was looking for in a dark booth far from the stairs. A big man, naked and bodypainted, reeled drunkenly out of the cubicle, leaving a boy face down and spreadeagled over the cot. Jesse turned him over and swore.

'Kevin! Help me,' he called back into the dim corridor. 'I can't move him!'

Jarrat choked back a curse and shouldered into the booth. 'One of your friends? Looks like an Angelhead.' He stooped, slung the barely conscious body over his shoulder and turned carefully. 'You think we're just going to walk out of here with him?'

'This way, I know the place,' Jesse panted as he dove back into the shadows.

Sweating under the man's weight, swearing passionately, Jarrat followed. He was blind in the near darkness and the dreamsmoke was starting to fuddle his brain. He focused on Jesse's long, bare legs and kept moving.

Concrete steps led upward. He shifted his grip on his burden and climbed carefully. A door whined open and a gust of cool air hit him in the face. He dragged in a deep breath and his senses began to clear.

They were in the alley behind Palomino, and Jesse stopped only to set the door's electronic lock. Jarrat twisted his head to see his chrono. 'We're out of time, kid.' He spun, gripped the dead weight of the unconscious hustler, and ran.

To his credit, Duggan was right on time, cruising the kerb at walking speed with the left hand gullwing up. He was a scant dozen metres from Palomino when Jarrat hit the street, and the driving lights flashed in recognition.

With a breathless groan of relief, Jarrat stumbled into the road. The gullwing lifted, and as Jesse folded down the front seat he dumped the body onto the rear bench. The hustler was out cold. Jarrat dumped Jesse on top of him and lifted the seat into place.

'What the Christ are you doing?' Duggan shouted as the canopy slammed and locked.

'Ask him.' Jarrat jerked a thumb over his shoulder and

buckled his harness. 'Move!'

'I got us some topcover.' Duggan spun the wheel over and took the Thunderbird back the way he had come. 'Two Tac squads are waiting on Northbound 7. You want the good news?'

'Equinox shooters picked you up,' Jarrat guessed. The Colt slid out of its holster and he twisted to look back. 'Where?'

'The white Rand,' Duggan told him. 'They won't try it before we hit the clearway.' His teeth bared, not a smile. 'This one's on me, Jarrat.'

The Colt lay heavily across Jarrat's knees as Duggan wove at speed through the midnight traffic. The white Rand was never more than a hundred metres behind, but Duggan had read his men accurately. Until the Thunderbird exited onto the clearway they were unmolested. Then they were in trouble.

A hail of bullets pelted the side and tail, and Jesse yelped hoarsely. 'Go faster!'

Duggan crammed his foot to the floor as Jarrat slid open the hand-hatch in the bulletproof canopy. The muzzle of the Colt nudged into the windstream. He squeezed the trigger as the Rand shot up alongside, but it was as armoured as the Thunderbird. The Colt could punch through it, but Jarrat must target the same area with three or four rounds before he would breach it.

The ammo counter dropped to fifty and he let go the trigger. 'Not going to take them that way.'

'I told you. This one's mine.' A scanner flickered in the darkness, and Duggan redlined the jets. They screamed into overboost and the Thunderbird bolted ahead of the Rand, slamming Jarrat back into the seat.

Proximity alarms clamoured though the road ahead was empty, and some sixth sense made Jarrat look up. Through the armourglass he glimpsed the red running lights of two skimmers in the instant before a burst of laser-bright tracer momentarily blinded him.

The eruption in the road behind flung cartwheeling shrapnel into the Thunderbird, and Jesse yelled in fright. Jarrat covered his eyes as burning gases shrouded the car before Duggan outran the fierce explosion.

Breathless, Jarrat twisted to look back. The Rand was gone. Duggan snatched up the R/T. 'Wildcard to Airborne. Bloody nice shooting. Stay with us.'

'With you all the way,' the pilot sang. 'Thanks for the invitation, Colonel. We ought to do it more often.'

Jarrat righted in his seat and thrust the Colt away. The barrel shroud was hot against his ribs. Stone would feel it and know he had missed a firefight. But he would also feel Jarrat's swift elation. In the back, Jesse whimpered softly, and though Jarrat longed to demand to know what the hell this was all about, he swallowed the words. The kid was too shocky to make sense yet.

The grounds of Flinders Park blazed with light. Tactical would get Maddigan through the election alive one way or another, but Jarrat wondered what would become of her, and Elysium, afterward.

The scarred, paint-blistered Thunderbird pulled in under the wing of the spaceplane. Duggan leaned into the back to move the doped body.

'This kid,' he said tartly, 'stinks. Where'd you dig him up?'

'He's a cheap sex-shop bumboy,' Jarrat said mildly. His brows arched at Jesse.

The Companion had regained his wits and composure. He shook his head in bitter anger. 'He's a programmer. Or, he was. He worked for Equinox, with Jack and Mike. He isn't a hustler. He was a brilliant, beautiful man.' Jesse's eyes brimmed. 'Look what they did to him, Kevin. Oh, look.'

Jarrat was looking. He was thin, halfway to emaciation. His muscle tone was gone, his skin blotched. His cock was at half mast even now as the Angel rampaged through his system. 'Put him in a rug,' he said to Duggan. 'What's his name?'

'Tim.' Jesse scrubbed his eyes. 'Tim Kwei. He's the same age as me.'

Looking down into Tim's haggard face, Jarrat would have guessed the boy was years older. Sighing, he slipped an arm about Jesse. 'Come on, sugar. Hold it together. You're coming with me.'

A Tac medic rolled the unconscious Kwei in rugs, strapped a repulsion unit on him and manhandled him into the rear acceleration couch. Built to accommodate the bulk of a hardsuit, it easily held two slender young bodies. Jesse squeezed in beside his friend and the harness ran up about them both.

With a helmet on, already tuned into the carrier, Jarrat looked gravely at Duggan. 'Thanks, Vic. That was good of you.'

'Any friend of Stoney's.' Duggan paused. 'Maddigan gave

you the truth. There's only NARC left between us and Randolph Dorne. The thought scares shit out of me, Jarrat.'

'I know.' Jarrat looked up at the brooding visage of Zeus. 'What I can do for you, I'll do. You have my word on that.'

'Then, make it fast.' Duggan extended his hand, and Jarrat took it.

He was in the shuttle moments later, and Tac squads ducked as the twin ramjets ignited. Repulsion hammered and the spaceplane fell upward into the night sky. Jarrat called Elysium Field to log his exit, swept the wings and threw the aircraft fast toward the carrier's parking orbit.

Fifty kilometres out, with the ship on his CRT, he called Petrov. 'Got a casualty. Buzz the Infirmary.'

Petrov's voice was harsh. 'Christ, not Stoney?'

'No! Just an Angelhead.' Jarrat shut back speed as he saw the glowing sterntubes. 'Another victim.'

In the back, Jesse was silent, overwhelmed by the thrill of flight or consumed by grief, Jarrat did not know.

He left the boy to his thoughts until a gurney team had rolled Tim Kwei into the Infirmary. Then he sat Jesse on the side of a bed in the observation ward and at last demanded answers. A voice recorder picked up every word.

'I found Tim yesterday.' Jesse's eyes strayed to the treatment room where Reardon was cleaning the patient before he could begin to work with him. 'I'd been trying to call him since I met you and Stoney. It was his brother who told me where he was. Tim was down yesterday. He'd start to crave this morning.'

'I know.' Jarrat hopped up onto the bed opposite, 'He was lucid, you got some sense out of him?'

The violet eyes were sombre. 'He's not alone. This is how Equinox puts the frighteners on its people. Maybe you stumble over Dorne's business, but you keep your mouth shut, or your lover, your kid, gets 'accidentally' addicted. Or sometimes they vanish, like Tim. They turn up in bordellos in other cities, or on Eos, fucking for their next snort.' He shuddered. 'People at Equinox are too scared to tell what they see. If they knew it all, they'd never tell. You want your lover or your kid turned into that?' He was watching Reardon.

The surgeon had Tim clean outside and was working on the battered inside now. Jarrat looked away. 'Tell me about him.'

'He was a clever programmer. He booked me a few times, we

got to be friends, started seeing each other outside of business. He was good to me, never treated me rough.' Jesse swallowed hard. 'He went to Equinox to design simulators to train pilots. They asked him to do battlefield simulations instead, for top money.' Jesse smiled bitterly. 'He thought he was writing games. He was working late, and saw one of his progs running when it shouldn't have been. He peeked into the files support- ing it.' Jesse took a breath. 'He saw the size of the Equinox army.'

Jarrat's mouth was dry. 'He wrote the battle simulations Equinox has been running to plan a real, live war?'

'He thinks so.' Jesse slumped onto the bed and curled up. 'He said, they have city sectors designated as first-strike targets. I didn't know what half of it meant. Tim would know, he's good with this crap. So he went to his boss, spoke out.'

'And this was his reward.' Jarrat stood.

'There's hundreds like him.' Jesse looked up hauntedly. 'Thousands. Kevin, I can't go back to Elysium.'

'Don't fret.' Jarrat tousled his hair. 'I have to leave you here, sugar. That's Dr Reardon. Anything you want, you tell him. We'll find you somewhere to bunk. Right now, I have work to do.' On impulse, he kissed the young man's forehead. 'Try to rest. You need it.'

Shiptime, it was long past midnight and Jarrat was tired. The ops room was still working. Petrov had gone but Cantrell, McKinnen and Archer were sweating through some task. Jarrat's appearance brought Cantrell to his feet but the women were too busy to even glance at him. Gene offered him a coffee and Jarrat was pleased to accept.

The personal terminal was still running and McKinnen had to be on uppers. She was working fast, juggling calculations which to Jarrat meant nothing at all. He watched for a time and then looked at Cantrell for answers.

'She's designing a tapeworm,' Cantrell told him. 'We can probably install it tomorrow. It starts in QuantumData and burrows through everything we have, to find every parasite.'

'And neutralise them?' Jarrat asked wearily.

'That's not so easy.' Cantrell rubbed the back of his neck. 'To lop the brains of this thing, maybe ten thousand little buggers hidden in the works have to be snipped in a few nanoseconds, or we're history.' He watched McKinnen bemusedly. 'I hope to

God she knows what she's doing.'

'She's the best.' Jarrat swivelled a chair toward him and sat. 'I don't like the woman, but she's the best.'

Cantrell leaned on the back of the next chair. 'What the hell happened down there? You look bushed.'

The report was verbal, terse, but he promised a sheet for the Intelligence file, and at last fell into a moody silence. Cantrell had taken notes for his own observer's log, and as Jarrat finished he said levelly,

'I'd pull Stone out now. One wrong move, and he's dead.'

'Aren't we all?' Jarrat's thoughts were with Jesse, Tim Kwei, Mike Rogan and countless others like them. 'Stoney's okay. It feels like he's on top of it. Give him a chance.'

'Two days,' Cantrell advised. 'Any longer and he's pushing his luck.'

'The way I pushed mine with Death's Head?' Jarrat murmured.

'I didn't say that.'

'You didn't have to.' Jarrat stood. 'I pushed till it broke. Stoney's got more sense.' He paused as the comm called his name.

'Cap Jarrat to the Infirmary.'

'Sounds like Kip might have got that poor kid back among the living.' Jarrat frowned at McKinnen. 'Keep me posted. I don't know what McKinnen's doing, but keep her busy.'

The Infirmary was quiet in the early hours, between shifts. Jesse was dressed in a soft white Starfleet jumpsuit which hugged his body beautifully. He stood in the annex, looking into Jack Spiteri's cryotank. Reardon was in the biolab. As Jarrat entered the ward he saw Tim Kwei. He was clean, awake, groggy, miserable in the aftermath of the trip. Addicts woke to the truth. Death was one step closer. As Jarrat appeared, Reardon beckoned him into the lab and closed the door for privacy. Jarrat folded his arms and gave the surgeon his attention.

'He's dying,' Reardon said simply.

'They're all dying, from the first fix.' Jarrat was tired and irritable.

'I mean he's got a month left, maybe less.' Reardon picked up a framed holosnap of his wife and three daughters. 'Makes you feel your mortality, Kevin.' He frowned at the image. 'I've done all I can for him.'

'You changed his blood, like you did for Stoney?' Jarrat looked out through the glass, into the ward. Jesse was sitting with his friend now, holding his hands.

'No.' Reardon set down the frame. 'I learned a lot when I was treating Stoney. A lot more, I got from Harry Del. We've been trading data since that incident. He sent a case of the latest batch of his experimental drug with Curt Gable. Thank Christ he had the intuition to do that. I just gave Tim a shot, and he's coming down gently. It might buy him an extra few weeks. For what that's worth.'

'The devil's claw fungus extract?' Jarrat's brows rose. 'It was the only thing that did Stoney any good.'

'It's cushioning Tim,' Reardon added, 'without me having to pump more synthetics into him. Not that the devil's claw isn't a drug! It is. But not as damaging.' He coughed. 'What are you going to do with him? You're collecting strays.'

Jarrat smiled faintly. 'I know what I'd like to do with him. Put him on a courier and send him to Darwin's. Harry's still there, finishing up his project. He could mend this kid the way he mended both Stoney and me.'

'Then do it.' Reardon returned a box of glass tubes to the freezer. 'That's the best suggestion I've heard. Send Spiteri as well. Jiggle the paperwork till it fits. You have a Starfleet courier due in the morning.' He blinked at his chrono. 'In about six hours, in fact.'

'Loaded to the cargo hatches with odds and sods, spare parts, Yamazake original components,' Jarrat finished. 'McKinnen ordered them before she came over.'

The surgeon grasped Jarrat's arm tightly. 'Do it. There's nothing I can do for either of them. If it was Stoney in that tank, or in that bed, you'd move heaven and earth. In fact, I recall you did.'

'I'm convinced.' Jarrat stretched his shoulders. 'Is Tim well enough to talk?'

'So long as you go slowly, speak clearly. The devil's claw is bringing him down.' Reardon released the lab's door. 'Any word from Stone?'

A familiar fist grasped Jarrat's insides. 'Not yet. Give him time. He's working on something, I feel it.'

'Queer,' Reardon breathed. 'I don't envy you.'

The boy was gaunt, his skin was blue-veined, transparent, with charcoal smudges beneath the eyes. His sinuses were so congested with the Angel, he was mouth breathing as if he had a cold, and his hands shook as they held a glass of sugar-rich fruit juice. He looked up and flushed as Jarrat appeared. The sheet was tucked about his chest, disguising a mottling of bruises. Jesse had combed his hair, he smelt of soap, shampoo and cologne, but Tim was weak and very ill. The mattress dipped as Jarrat sat on the bedside and offered his hand. 'Do you know where you are?'

'Jesse said... a NARC carrier.' He blinked owlishly.

'I'm Kevin Jarrat. I'll do what I can for both of you.' He glanced into the annex holding the cryotanks. 'And for Jack.'

'You're an officer?' Tim asked thickly.

'Doctor Reardon told me.' Jesse blushed rosily. 'You're a damned Captain. I didn't realise.'

Jarrat smiled at him. 'Don't let it trouble you. You'll be guests of Starfleet in a few hours. I'm sending you both and Spiteri to Darwin's World. Do you know it?'

'Only as a dot on a map,' Jesse confessed. 'I've never been out of Elysium.'

'There's a healer on Darwin's.' Jarrat took Tim's hand. 'He's working on an experimental cure. Are you willing?'

'Cure for Angel?' Jesse's voice rose. 'It's impossible!'

'No. Just extremely difficult.' Jarrat looked into Tim's dark, dopy eyes. 'It's experimental, but it has to be worth a try. You can be there in two days, if you're game.'

The young man's eyes flooded. 'Why are you helping me?'

'I'm... involved.' Jarrat tousled Jesse's dark blond hair. 'And because I need you. Can you tell me about Equinox? Your work, your bosses, the mistakes you made.'

The story was told haltingly, wearily, and it distressed Tim until grief assailed him. Jesse held him while he wept useless tears, and Jarrat waited patiently. It was the same tale Jesse had told, enriched with details, names, dates. In Jarrat's pocket, the voice recorder captured everything without Tim being aware of it.

'So I went to my boss, the Special Programming supervisor. He said, go back to work, he'd make inquiries.' Tim struggled with his congested sinuses. His cheeks were bright, his eyes feverish. 'The next night I thought I'd go out for dinner. They caught me in the basement under my building, where I park. I... woke a whole day later. I was in a sex shop. Not Palomino. I went there later, traded off when Gemini got into debt. They doped me, Captain, over and over, till I didn't know what day it way. Didn't remember my own name. I'd wake sometimes, filthy and...' He clung tight to Jesse.

Jesse was weeping soundlessly. He looked over Tim's head at Jarrat. 'Took me days to find him. From some of the things he's said, he's been traded a few times. I think he was on Eos for a while, serving the industrial crews. Equinox runs the sex shops there. His brother found him at Palomino a month ago, but he was so disgusted, he left him there. He thought Tim took the shit for fun, got himself addicted.'

'I see.' Jarrat's blood was running cold. 'Can you talk some more, Tim?'

'Yes.' Tim settled against Jesse and would not lift his head. 'What d'you want to know, Captain?'

'You saw facts and figures, the manpower and dispersal of Dorne's corporate army,' Jarrat prompted. 'What do you remember? Don't guess, tell me only what you recall for sure.'

'I ran the support files that were feeding the simulation I wrote for the bastards.' Tim dragged his hands across his face. 'Two thousand men, armed, stashed all over Avalon. Most are mercenaries from Cygnus, they've been coming in for the last two years. They're camouflaged as construction workers, crane chasers, freight pilots.'

'Weapons?' Jarrat added. 'You looked that far?'

'They're well armed,' Tim said bitterly. 'Not like NARC, but far in front of Tac. I think I know what they're doing.'

The truth was clear. 'Equinox Industries hasn't controlled government in over half a century,' Jarrat said softly. 'They want the reins back. Corporate coup. Smash the civil defence force and Tactical, grab government. This is sovereign territory. Not even the government of Earth has jurisdiction to invade without an engraved invitation. And after the coup, Equinox *is* the government.'

'Jesus,' Jesse breathed. 'Can't we get a warship?'

'The nearest is too far out.' Jarrat stood, slipped his hands into his hip pockets and tipped back his head. 'You're on your own... and NARC can't budge until we have an Angel connection, or we're no better than tame mercs.'

250

'But you know what Equinox is doing!' Jesse protested.

'I know.' Jarrat leaned over and kissed his cheek. 'But without proof, it's just allegation.' He touched Jesse's lips with one fingertip. 'Get some sleep. You'll be on a Starfleet courier before you can blink, and your only responsibility is getting Tim, and Jack's tank, to a man called Harry Del.'

Tim sucked in a breath. 'An experimental cure?'

'It's worked before.' Jarrat hesitated. 'You remember Stoney, my partner?'

'Tall, dark and gorgeous?' Jesse wrinkled his nose. 'Course I remember!'

'He was a user,' Jarrat said softly. 'Forced addiction, on a job. Harry brought him back.'

The two boys were stunned. Without another word, Jarrat left them in each other's arms and headed for his cabin. Scalding water eased the tension from his spine, but as he sprawled on the bunk he saw the time and groaned. Stoney would be roused in an hour, and Jarrat's job was to be awake and alert.

He turned over and dimmed the lights. An hour's rest, a meal, a drink and a hit of Reardon's patented pickup juice. One way or another this assignment was almost over. Maddigan's supporters would send her into office, and at the same stroke consign Avalon to the kind of corporate war which had made many worlds into bloodbaths. When it began, if 'Jon Strother' was still groundside in an Equinox security squad he would be deployed with his fellows.

He would be out before the first shot was fired, Jarrat vowed. Memories of Sheal haunted him as he tried to rest. He turned over, punched the pillow and whispered into the darkened cabin. 'Come on, Stoney. Make it quick, for godsakes. We're out of time.'

251

Chapter Fifteen

Oscar Dunlop was a trembling, chainsmoking bundle of anxiety. Stone cornered him in the lab, out of view of the surveillance lenses, probably the only safe place to speak in the whole building.

'What's wrong with you?' He peered into Dunlop's eyes. 'What are you taking?'

'I'm not using anything.' Dunlop glared at him. 'If I was, I'd have a blast right now — I'm shit scared, and not too proud to admit it!'

'Calm down.' Stone set both hands on the man's shoulders, which quivered inside a loud blue and yellow shirt. 'You know how you'll access the classified files?'

'I worked it out, researched it.' Dunlop fidgeted. 'Jon, it's dangerous. Are you sure —'

'I'm sure.' Stone cupped the scientist's face in both hands. 'I saw the political vidcasts last night. So did you.'

'Equinox's man, Bryce Ansell, denying that his ratpack had anything to do with the attempts on your boss. Duggan made a statement. Maddigan nearly bought it, four times. Tac have her under guard.' He flung himself against Stone. 'Avalon votes tomorrow.'

With an exasperated sigh, Stone held him. 'We'll be out today, with the data. If you can pull yourself together long enough to get it!'

'I —' Dunlop shook himself, peeled himself away from Stone's broad chest. 'I'm sorry. I never committed espionage before. Obviously you have.' He drew away.

'I'm counting on you.' Stone picked up the weapon he had deposited on the nearest workbench, and waited for Dunlop to fetch his briefcase.

'You owe me after this,' Dunlop warned shakily.

'I'll put you somewhere safe, and we'll call it even.' Stone pointed him at the door. 'You can't afford to be late.'

Procedure was for the supervisor to summon an armed

escort, take the service lift to Data Processing and use the time he had booked on the restricted access machines. All ID would be checked and double-checked. Stone found the circus faintly ridiculous, but was properly silent as he shadowed Dunlop into the lift.

They rode up two floors and stepped out into a world he had seen in library images, never in reality. Academics and professional soldiers rubbed shoulders; the loudest sound was the hush of soft shoes on carpet, a hum of thinking machines, whisper of airconditioning. Vast windows overlooked Elysium; potted plants throve in profusion. The Archive smelt of hot electronics and carpet cleaner.

Guards stopped Dunlop twice between the lift and the cloisters which held the security terminals. He showed his ID, placed his palm on a scanner and looked at Stone with wide, anxious eyes. Stone hung back, showed Strother's Warlock Company authority and smiled at the men from Viking Company. They had come upstairs from boot-end squads like Warlock, in the basement barracks. Strother was a new boy making a good start. In his second hitch he could be up here. In his third, he might work the 'top end' of Equinox Towers, even Skycity, with double pay, easy duty and his pick of the Companions.

Each terminal stood in a recess, screened from the main facility for total privacy. The escort stood at the operator's back. Stone took his place, unslung the Colt rifle, and his eyes swept the vast Archive as Dunlop sat to begin.

His voice was almost inaudible. 'How long?'

'As long as it takes,' Dunlop hissed. 'I booked two hours. It could take all of that. Shut up and let me work.'

So Stone shut up, watched the Archive and covertly monitored Dunlop's progress. Before him was an engineer's design pad. One leaf was covered with a confusion of command lines, codes and what Dunlop called 'get-outs'. If he tripped a booby trap he knew override codes to assure the machine he had made a keying error.

Twice, he did just that, and Stone's heart leapt into his throat. Dunlop was hyperventilating as he entered the get-out, but each time the machine accepted. 'I told you,' he muttered. 'If you'd tried this, you'd have been in a meat locker by now!'

'Get on with it,' Stone said quietly while his blood iced, and

253

he admitted the probability of Dunlop's words. Getting the entry codes by deceit and using them himself had been his plan. He doubted if he would have succeeded. His best option would have been fight, flight, and a fast pickup. Kevin was with him, every second, waiting, poised to spring.

Jarrat had fought last night. When Warlock Company was dead asleep, Stone's body prickled with cold sweat as he felt Kevin's racing heart and taxed muscles, anger, alarm, even grief. He had felt the shudder of an airframe, the impact as Jarrat hit the ground beside the spaceplane. He had been in Elysium, he had fought, but beyond that, Stone knew nothing.

He watched the morning vidcast as he forced down a little food. Three men were shot in an alley beside a sex shop; two vehicles raced out of the city and a Tactical squad destroyed a car on the road. Was this Jarrat at work? Stone had no way of knowing. But Kevin was unhurt, merely tired and stressed, safely back on the carrier.

At a grunt from Dunlop Stone turned toward the screen. Columns of data had replaced the endless requests for coded ident, and Dunlop was rubbing his palms together. 'You're in?' Stone whispered.

'I'm a genius, remember.' Keys pattered and Dunlop dropped in a datacube. 'This is what you want. I had to dig so deep, I don't think I'm interrogating a computer in this building anymore. I may be talking to a machine on Skycity.'

'That would make sense,' Stone murmured as his eyes skimmed the data. 'Dorne would hide his private business behind the best lock-outs he could devise. You copying?'

'Of course. I'll only get one chance.' Dunlop looked up anxiously. 'I dug into Equinox security, supply, requisition and freight. I've hit some strange shit. These are manifests. Weapons, soldiers, aircraft. Am I reading what I think I'm reading?'

'You're the genius,' Stone said drily. 'They're ready to fight. Look at this.'

'Two thousand mercenaries... came in via Cygnus.' Dunlop tapped keys. 'That's all we'll get on military issues. What else do you want? Fast, before the system picks us up! There's random surveys of what files are being accessed.'

'Now he tells me.' Stone's own palms sweated on the rifle. 'Angel. Supply, freight, any connection to Cygnus, raw materials, lab staff, ships to move it, money men, incoming cash, anything. Three names. Buchanan. Wozniak. Schaefer. And it'll be well hidden. Can do?'

'Can *try*,' Dunlop panted. 'Oh, Christ, what am I doing? I need my head examined!' But his fingers flew over the keys, trying reference after reference, cross-matching and collating at high speed until he had a coincidence of data. He zeroed in from there, and grunted as the picture began to go together. 'Damn, I've found it. Copying everything.'

The data raced through the screen so fast, even Stone, who was trained in rapid ingestion of information, could get only snatches. Buchanan was a rimrunner. He hit every port in two weeks' flight time from Zeus, and the cargoes he ran for Equinox were contraband dressed as legit freight. Wozniak was a king shooter without a scruple, notorious on many worlds, including Earth. Contracted to the Black Unicorn syndicate on Cygnus, until a matter of months before the arrival of a NARC carrier. Schaefer was a chemist with no employment record, yet he was rich beyond credibility. In two years he had become the hub around which Dorne's operation revolved.

'There's more,' Dunlop muttered. 'Shipping schedule. Looks like freight. Chemicals.'

Stone's pulse quickened. 'To and from this building?'

'No. See? Orbital data, and it's not Avalon, and they've never referred to this building by code before. Look.' He touched the screen. 'What the hell is Hera?'

A place, a person, a ship? Stone had no idea. 'Cargoes of chemicals. Get a match between them and money movements.'

'You want miracles,' Dunlop groaned. 'Wait... ah. Jackpot. You're a clever boy. It ebbs in waves and patterns.' He looked up grimly. 'It's Angel, isn't it?'

'How long have you known?' Stone asked tartly.

'Suspected,' Dunlop corrected. 'How dumb do you think I am? Spiteri and Rogan got what they asked for. See nothing, hear nothing, say nothing, that's the rule here.' He paused. 'I think you've got all you're going to get.'

The datacube popped out and Stone's hand closed about the small, white metal case. 'Can you exit the system safely?'

'I'd better.' Dunlop pulled his sleeve across his face. 'It'll take a while. Most of your data came out of a machine God knows how far away. I have to back out step by step and leave no footprints.'

The cube was folded in Stone's palm as he returned to a position of vigilance. Elation fired his blood. It had taken almost a week, a time which had seemed nearer months. Without Dunlop success would have taken much longer, or might not have been possible at all. He owed the man a flock of favours, which Dunlop was eager to call in.

The exit sequence was as important as the entry, but Dunlop's research was painstaking. Ten minutes before his two hours expired, he stood, crammed his papers into his case and stepped out of the cubicle. He was exhausted and Stone smelt the tang of his body. Fear made a man sweat.

'You did good,' he told Dunlop honestly. 'I stand my last shift tomorrow. When I go off, I'll head for the library. Meet me there. I'll use my ID to get you onto the roof for a breath of air, then I'll hit somebody and grab something that flies. That's all there is to it.'

'That's all?' Dunlop demanded fatuously. 'They'll be voting by the time we get out. It'll be over by evening.'

'You mean, they election will be over,' Stone corrected as they approached the lifts. 'The storm will be about to break. They're only going through the motions, Doc. If they rig the ballot to give Grenshem's job to Bryce Ansell, Maddigan's camp will explode.' He paused as the Viking Company trooper looked out of the guardroom, then thumbed for the lift. 'A coup is Dorne's only chance to snatch total power, and he knows it. But with this data, he's up against NARC. And that, my son, he didn't reckon with.'

Dunlop had begun to calm. 'Do you —'

The lift opened with a quiet rumble, and the words died on his lips. Stone's heart stood still and then raced as he saw the muzzles of four big machine pistols, and four men in plain clothes behind them. Not security troops. These were contract shooters. One was Kjell Wozniak.

From far off he heard Dunlop scream, but his legs propelled him in an instinctive, headlong dive. He came up against the wall in the cover of a bank of data towers and the big ceramic pots of the ferns which throve here. The Colt rifle unslung, he pulled it into his shoulder and leaned out around the edge of the grey metal towers.

Shots *whanged* past him. He returned them and heard a cry as a man went down. Wozniak's shooters were aiming far too wide, they had no hope of hitting him, as Stone would have expected. If they put a bullet into the data towers they might short out the whole facility. Dorne would feed them balls-first into a grinder.

But Stone was completely pinned down. The lifts were the only exit, and the route was cut off. He cast about feverishly, looking for anything he could turn to his advantage, but all he saw were the fire-escape capsules.

In buildings this size the risk of fire was minimal but still very real. Dousing the blaze involved flooding a whole, sealed section with a pressurised fire-retardant gas. With the oxygen forced to floor level and extracted by reversed aircycling fans, an inferno would stop. But no one on the sealed floor would survive. With the lifts inactive, the only exit was by escape capsule.

Multiple pods were installed along outside walls: a seat with straps, a tough aeroshell, a pyro charge which blew it out and up, a chute to feather the capsule to street level with its occupants more or less intact.

But the outside wall was beyond the lift bays, twenty metres past the shooters, and Wozniak was already shouting into an R/T. Stone's heart beat at his ribs as he leaned out once more and sprayed a dozen rounds toward the group. They were in the cover of the doorway, and he knew he hit nothing. Dunlop was on the floor, face down and still. Stone choked back a pang of regret.

The ammo counter read 24, and now he held his fire. He adjusted to single-shot and pressed into the corner between the data towers and the wall. He would take them, one by one, as they stepped into his field of fire, and make every round count. Sometime, somehow, one of them would make a mistake. All he needed was a chance.

Jarrat would be feeling it all. Fear, anger, the kindling of despair. Stone gripped the datacube in his left hand. How futile it would all have been if he died here. As futile as the Death's Head assignment had seemed, when he lost track of Jarrat in an alley in Chell.

The faint vibration of an approaching lift resonated through the floor. Reinforcements? Dorne's men were alerted to the breach of their boss's private records, and those reinforcements would be king shooters coming down from the 'top end', not basement grunts on their way up.

Angry voices called from the lift and Stone got to his feet. Braced against the wall, he shouldered the rifle and waited. Twenty-four rounds, properly used, were better than a hundred wasted.

Something popped only metres away with a sharp, plastic *crack*, and he smelt a bittersweet odour which at first he did not recognise. His head had begun to swim when he placed it, and knew he was breathing Triacid vapour. It would knock him off his feet in seconds.

Instinct, training, some nerve which would not permit him to yield hope, steered his hands as he fell to his knees. The datacube slipped into the back of the ceramic pot, where the tree fern concealed it and not even Dunlop knew where to look for it.

Then the rich blue carpet smacked Stone in the face, and his thoughts dissolved.

***

'He's in trouble.' Jarrat's hands clenched into the back of the engineer's seat.

Before him the viewports were unshielded. Avalon was a cloud-swept panorama. Yvette McKinnen sat at the programmer's console, hands splayed over the keyboard. Her work had been input moments before, and now they could only wait. Cantrell, Petrov, Budweisser and Archer stood at the rear of the flight deck, acutely aware that they were mere observers.

If McKinnen's hunter programme worked, it worked. If it did not, they could only pray that it did not trigger a reprisal in the system. In the event of a failure, the best they could hope for was a clean abort. McKinnen would redesign it and try again. The alternative was a cataclysm.

The gunships and shuttles had launched and gone to safe-distance minutes before, overloaded with both the NARC and Starfleet crew. Only officers remained aboard, and most were on the flight deck as McKinnen input her programme.

Which was the moment Stone's fear and futile rage barrelled into Jarrat like a punch. His hands clenched into the seat as his belly knotted. Cantrell stepped closer, put a hand on his arm, but Jarrat shook his head.

'There's nothing either of us can do from here. Get Gable back. I'm going down.'

'Where is Stone?' Cantrell asked quietly.

'In the building.' Jarrat took a breath.

'You can't get in there,' Petrov said doubtfully. 'You're up against the whole security force.'

'You'd do better to monitor him from here,' Cantrell advised. 'If he can get out —'

'If he can't, he's dead.' Jarrat gasped as his senses reeled. 'Jesus, what was that? He's out, but I felt no pain.'

'Gas?' Cantrell guessed.

Jarrat straightened as his balance returned. 'I think so.' He dragged a deep breath, as if his own lungs had taken the gas. 'They'll kill him, Gene. Get Gable back!'

'Kevin.' Cantrell caught his arm. 'There's no way you can get into Equinox!'

'But maybe Tactical can. A ruse, bomb alert, anything.' Jarrat was already moving. 'Tell Curt to hangar that shuttle!'

Then he ran. The ship was empty; machines operated everything, the crew was gone. Jarrat had never seen or heard a ship so silent, so dead. His feverish mind likened it to an open coffin, and the simile sickened him.

He was at the observation port, looking into the hangar as Gable returned. Airlock and repressurisation were on manual, under Gable's control, and all Jarrat could do was watch the status board and listen to the beat of the pulse in his ears till the inner hatch released.

The canopy was going up as he sprinted toward the plane. Gable was out, frowning in confusion. 'What's wrong? You going groundside?' He tossed his own helmet to Jarrat for the sake of speed.

'They've got Stoney,' Jarrat panted as he tugged it on and cut into the loop. 'It's going bad, Curt, and I've got no chance up here. They're on the flight deck if you want to watch McKinnen's act. Move — I'm leaving!'

As Gable ran, Jarrat climbed in and strapped down. His eyes skimmed the instruments instinctively as the hangar depressurised fast. The hatch rumbled open when he read quarter pressure, and the last air gushed into space as he fired the twin engines.

Descent was a bucking, heaving rollercoaster ride. The Spaceport radars picked him up but he shucked every rule, and ignored their mechanical request for identification. 'Raven Leader to Tac 101. Come on, Duggan!'

Elysium expanded before him as he raced in from the west. Seconds dragged before Duggan was on the air: 'Tac 101. What the hell's going on, Jarrat?' He knew what the shift in callsign meant as soon as he heard the words 'Raven Leader'. An action had begun.

'I'm over Elysium. Where are you?' Jarrat cut speed as the altimeter showed five thousand. Elysium filled the plane below.

'Same place,' Duggan said shortly.

Jarrat put the stick over, scanned the air ahead for civvy traffic and sent the spaceplane twisting between several slow, underpowered skybuses. 'Give me touchdown space and an acquisition beam, Duggan. I don't have time to wait for you!'

'You're in an ass-burning hurry,' Duggan observed. 'There's your beam. What the fuck is your problem?'

A light winked on the CRT and Jarrat teased the nose about a few points. 'I'm coming in. Be there, Duggan!'

***

The aftermath of Triacid gas was a metallic taste in the mouth, nausea and a throbbing head. Stone had not smelt that vapour in years. Tactical sometimes used it to control an Angel packriot and avoid a brawl, given calm air. If NARC was unavailable, they used what they had.

He was in an armchair. Light seeped through his closed eyelids as he took a breath and swallowed the hot nausea. Memory hit him hard. Archive, Dunlop, datacube —

'Ah, you're with us. I'd say it was nice to see you again, Captain Stone, but in fact you're the last man on Avalon I desired to see.'

Randolph Dorne's voice was silken. Stone cracked open his eyes and squinted against the light. He tried his hands, expecting to be secured to the chair, but he was loose. Then he saw the three pistols levelled on him. Tying him would have been pointless. Dorne sat in the opposite, matching chair, one long leg crossed over the other, an HK pistol on his knee. Kjell Wozniak stood behind him, to his left, a Steyr .44 in both big hands. Flanking Dorne's right, similarly armed, was the secretary, Enrique.

'It seems,' Dorne said affably, 'you infiltrated my security force. Your ID papers are exceptionally good, they duped everyone. You've been here almost a week. For what purpose, Captain?'

The gas thickened Stone's throat. 'Fun.'

'Of course.' Dorne nodded. One hand smoothed his russet brown jacket. 'Naturally, you need Wozniak to beat you a little before you speak the truth... a matter of ego.' He gestured to Wozniak. 'Oblige him, Kjell.'

'All right!' Stone's head was clearing. 'You know damned well why I'm here. We can't move on you without solid fact behind us. Dope testimony and allegation won't hold water with your legal-eagle mates.'

'That's better.' Dorne smiled. 'You solicited the help of Oscar Dunlop. Luck, Captain, or astute work?'

'Both.' Stone rubbed his smarting eyes. 'I guess Dunlop tripped a booby trap even he didn't know about, somewhere in the system.' He coughed harshly. 'Did he make it?'

'No. He tried to run and Kjell did what comes naturally.' Dorne leaned back and stretched out his legs. 'Kjell wants to kill you now, but I see a certain value in having you alive.'

Wozniak took a stride forward. 'He's trouble. So long as you got him, you got NARC right behind you.'

'And if we hand them his body,' Dorne added, 'someone somewhere will be thirsty for vengeance.'

'Cute problem,' Stone said acidly.

'But not without solution,' Dorne told him. 'You see, it's possible, though I admit, unlikely, that I may joust with NARC in the future. The more I know about them, their strengths and weaknesses, codes, every little secret, the less I have to be concerned about them. You'll tell me every detail you know.' He smiled, snakelike. 'And as a Captain, you know them all.'

Dry mouthed, Stone looked about the room. It was an elegantly appointed office so high above the street that beyond the wide windows he saw nothing but windswept clouds and Zeus. He felt a rumble, a tremor, echoing down through the building. From the roof landing bays? Then they were *very* high up. The only door was behind him, the windows before.

'You won't get out,' Dorne told him as he saw the movement

of Stone's eyes. 'It's a hundred floors to street level, and every one of them guarded. Kjell is eager to begin, and unless I get co-operation, I have no choice but to let him. He tells me he can extract everything you know at the end of a whip, and I... tend to believe him.'

Stone's heart thudded hard but his face was blank. 'You don't know much about NARC, do you? Pain is something you learn to disconnect.' It was sheer bravado, but convincing. 'I've been through psyche simulations that'd make your little friend puke. NARC weapons testing do drugs, virtual reality programming of the mind, that make you think you're being boiled alive.' He settled in the chair. 'I've been there, done that. Save yourself the bother.'

'Randy —' Wozniak exploded.

'Shut up,' Dorne snapped. 'Look at the man. You won't frighten the data out of him, and he's strong. Your crude methods would kill him before we got enough. Very well, Captain. There are other methods.'

'Drugs?' Stone closed his eyes. 'NARC's forgotten more about drugs than you'll ever know. Fill me with any crap you like. They expect it to happen if we blunder into a scene like this. My subconscious was programmed before I was cleared for street work. Dope me, and you'll get nursery rhymes.' This was the truth. He did not open his eyes, but listened intently.

For a moment Dorne was silent. 'I can believe that, too, Captain, since my labs are developing similar psyche methods. I imagine you'd overdose before I got close to what I want. And you're too valuable a resource to waste.' He paused. 'That wasn't what I had in mind.'

Now Stone opened his eyes. Wozniak looked angry, Enrique merely wary. Dorne wore a thoughtful frown. 'I'm listening,' Stone told him.

'A trade,' Dorne offered. 'You tell me what I want to know, and I won't kill you.'

'I'm supposed to believe that?' Stone almost laughed.

'Perhaps not.' Dorne set down his pistol and stood, hands in his jacket pockets. Slightly built, immaculate, elegant, he was not the archetype of the Angel baron. Then, who was? 'You see, Captain, the only weapon you leave me is fear,' he said reasonably. 'And I'll find your phobia. Not heights, not close spaces, nor even death. Insects, perhaps? Rodents?'

'I told you,' Stone said indifferently while his innards ravelled into a blazing knot. 'I've done every psyche simulation you can think of, and a lot you can't.'

Dorne tilted his head at the younger man. 'Still, those are simulations. Now, imagine the ruin of your *real* life. Oh, not blindness or quadriplegia. These are easily repaired. But picture yourself a ten-credit fuck in a labourers' sex shop on Eos. I've sent men there, traded them like pieces of meat, brothel to brothel. You want to be like them? Your colleagues would never find you, and you'd never rescue yourself. Where would be the point?' From his pocket he took a plastic capsule. 'Recognise it?'

It was filled with golden dust, and Stone choked audibly. He gripped the arms of the chair and looked up into Dorne's eyes. 'I know Angel when I see it. If that's the way it's going to be, you bastard, get on with it.'

'Ah.' Dorne toyed with the capsule. 'There are ways and ways to die, Captain. You're aware of this. I'm going to send you to a bordello in Orlando for a few weeks. When you come back, you'll be glad to talk in exchange for comfort, clean sheets, medical care to extend your life and a humane death in the end. Or, you'll surely deal with me after a tour of duty on Eos.' He picked up the pistol, levelled it on Stone's belly and beckoned Wozniak. 'Do it.'

The shooter swore lividly. 'For Christ's sake, will you just put a bullet in his brain?'

'When I have his data, you can put a whole magazine in his skull,' Dorne said agreeably. 'For now, fear is the only effective weapon I have, but fortunately I'm very adept with it. Do it!'

Sharp gestures betrayed Wozniak's anger as he twisted the capsule to crack it. Stone's eyes slitted as he watched the big hands coming closer. Instinct was to fight, to run. A hundred nightmares coalesced, flowed together into the same terrible reality. If he ran they would cut him down.

If he breathed in the golden dust —

Reason controlled terror with an iron grip. Stone closed his eyes as Wozniak took him by the hair and crammed the broken capsule under his nose. The muzzle of a gun pressed his ear, pinned him to the chair. He held his breath until his lungs burned but Wozniak waited until he must breathe or faint.

His lungs spasmed deeply. He took the Angel by nose and mouth, coughed, retched, and toppled to the floor.

***

Tac 101 had spoiled the grounds of Flinders Park, but Lenore Maddigan was alive, running her campaign from her home office, since her building in Chandler sector was a charcoal ruin. Duggan's command truck stood at the head of the rank of heavy vehicles. Radars turned on the roof, a ground-station dish tracked across the sky. The air was busy with radio traffic.

Duggan wore a bleak face as Jarrat outlined the situation. The rear of the truck stood open. The colonel had a beer in one hand, a bottle of bourbon in the other, and sat on the corner of his littered plotting table as Jarrat spoke. Offered the bottle, Jarrat refused. He needed his wits.

'I can't get in,' Duggan said flatly. 'There's no ruse, legit or not, that would get me into Equinox Towers. You're on your own, kid. And I don't say that lightly.' He looked away. 'It's Stoney in there.' He took a swig of beer. 'How the hell did he get a message out?'

'Doesn't matter how.' Jarrat leaned on the table and closed his eyes, the better to focus on Stone. 'He fought, I think they used knockout gas. He's alive, unhurt.'

'He's carrying an implant?' Duggan slammed down his beer. 'You buggers put a device in his skull. They probably picked up your frequency!'

'It's not an implant.' Jarrat gasped. 'He's waking.'

Disbelief replaced anger, and Duggan studied him shrewdly. 'Shit, you're reading him like a machine.'

'I'm not a machine,' Jarrat said windedly as he felt the hot nausea, the throb of Stone's head. 'But I know where he is. If I could get into that heap I could go straight to him.'

'Put on a hardsuit and blow a hole in the wall,' Duggan said sourly. 'That's the only way in I know.'

Jarrat steadied his breathing with an effort. 'Don't think the thought hasn't occurred to me.' Dry mouthed, he swiped up Duggan's beer and drained it.

'Stoney was always resourceful,' Duggan offered. 'If there's a way, he'll find it.'

'If,' Jarrat echoed bitterly, and stepped down out of the vehicle into the hot wash of the repulsion.

264

Floods of sudden panic shafted through him, dumped him into the side of the truck, and he fought for orientation. Stone's heart was pounding but he was not in pain. He was sitting, not even restrained. Jarrat stifled a cry as the dread peaked. He felt a rush of sheer terror, the sharp echo of an impact as Stone fell heavily and then, inexplicably, wanted to sneeze.

'You okay, Jarrat?' Duggan leaned out of the truck. 'You look like hell.'

'I don't know.' Sweat prickled Jarrat's spine. 'He inhaled something.'

'A drug?' Duggan's fingers caught his shoulder. 'If you can read him, tell me!'

'I don't know.' Jarrat searched the echoes of Stone's sensations, feeling for something, anything, but all he could get was an insane melange: fear, which was healthy, and hysterical amusement, which was not. 'I just don't know, Duggan,' he whispered. 'And it scares hell out of me.'

***

His sinuses burned with the desire to sneeze and sneeze, but Stone choked the reflex. He hit the floor and stayed down, eyes closed, ears alert. Wozniak bitched for minutes; Dorne walked out with one parting shot.

'I've heard enough, Kjell. Put him in the conference room until you arrange transport to Orlando. I have better things to do than stand watching a NARC captain try to fuck a carpet. He'll give us what we want, and then you can have him, I don't even want to know about it.'

Cursing, furious, Wozniak and Enrique laboured under Stone's considerable mass. He lolled, every muscle lax, and when they dumped him again, did not even twitch. A man's first headful of Angel would keep him out for six or eight hours, depending on his body weight. Wozniak saw no reason to lock the door.

Alone, Stone listened for long seconds before he sat and rubbed his nose. His mind was clear, his sinuses were no more congested than if he had inhaled common house dust, though he tasted the acidity of the drug at every breath. He felt a wave of ridiculous humour and smothered it fast. The time for hysteria would come later.

He cracked open the door and peered out. He saw no one, but every passage was covered by cameras. He was still in Company greens, but if his face showed on a monitor, alarms would erupt. And he was unarmed.

A weapon was his first priority. Orientation was his second. Of two things was he certain: he was very high in the building, and he would meet less opposition by heading up than down. Service lifts opened along the passage from the conference room, and on the elite levels they were unguarded. This was Dorne's domain, inaccessible to anyone not on his staff. Where was the need for guards? Stone slipped out, kept his back to the surveillance lenses and summoned the lift with a sharp jab.

He was in a second later, and swore as he saw the indicator. He was already on Overlevel 3. Three floors above the top level available to anyone save Dorne's crew. The roof landing facilities were right above. He hit the switch and stood back from the door.

A smoked-glass vestibule opened onto the windy landing bays. On the far side were hangars, closer at hand a broad field of jet-stained concrete. Through the armoured glass he saw two skyhoppers and four limousines, several mechanics working with their heads in an engine cowl, two armed guards. Every instinct was to take one of the cars and get out. Every grain of his NARC training overrode that.

Glass doors swished open as he approached and he slipped sidelong into the shadows. One of the guards was by the parapet, smoking as he enjoyed a view bettered only by Skycity. The second patrolled the landing bay. Over his shoulder was a Steyr AR-24, and Stone's eyes lit as he saw it.

The guard was complacent and careless. His neck snapped cleanly, death came in a merciful split second and Stone caught his weapon before it fell. The ammo counter read 90, the barrel reeked of oil and cordite, a guarantee that it was well maintained.

The doors opened again and Stone dragged the body inside, out of sight. No human had observed him, but he had no idea how surveillance was arranged up here. He left the body propped in the corner, between a potted palm and an obsidian casting of Eros. It could be minutes or an hour before he was found. Stone was down to luck.

He stepped into the lift, took a breath as the doors closed, concealing him, and traced down the index. He gritted his teeth as he pressed the key marked Archive. The thought crossed his mind that what he was doing was insane. But an old NARC instructor once claimed, the more insane the scheme, the more likely it was to work, for reasons of logic. 'If you can't blind 'em with science,' Stone muttered, echoing a teacher he had not recalled in years, 'baffle 'em with bull.'

The lift dropped fast, and since it rode Dorne's private shaft, did not stop along the way. Stone took a breath, knocked off the safety and primed the Steyr.

It was then that he felt Jarrat so clearly, Kevin might have been beside him. 'Christ, you're near,' he whispered. 'You're groundside!' Hope flickered like a naked flame. 'Do you feel me, Kevin?' He knew Jarrat did.

He shouldered the weapon and stepped into the passage where he had escorted Dunlop only hours before. Viking Company guards looked impassively at him, and Stone accorded them a crisp salute. He knew the duty roster by now.

They were on the next shift, they would know there had been a fracas, a man killed, and they would also know the situation had been resolved. The insurgent had been seized, it was over.

Stone marched briskly into the Archive and saluted again as he reached the guard room. A red-haired sergeant looked out, bored and uninterested. 'Sorry to intrude, sir,' Stone said stiffly. 'A datacube from Programming was left up here. I know where it'll be, sir.'

Brown eyes flickered, and the sergeant waved him by. 'Make it quick. Jeez, these scientists are supposed to have brains, you think they'd collect their trash before they leave. One old jerk left his lunch up here last week.'

With a polite chuckle Stone marched into the enormous hall. A quick glance back, and he saw the sergeant shuffling papers. Deft, swift, he ducked behind the machines and slid his fingers into the ornamental ceramic pot. His heart beat like a drum as he scrabbled for it. There is was, against the enamel. He folded it in his palm, straightened and marched back toward the exit.

The klaxon cut across the silent facility like a knife. Boots pounded in the passages, doors slammed and sealed. Stone spun, and saw the sergeant before a vidphone. The game was up. His luck had just expired, and the only chance he had left was speed.

Five rounds spun the sergeant about, flung him over the vidphone, and Stone fled. Through the Archive's doors he saw a lift open, saw four Company shooters barrel out, and he held down the trigger. The Steyr cycled ten 9mm rounds per second, but over distance it was badly inaccurate. He sent Dorne's men diving left and right, but heard only one scream.

Before they were up again, Stone spun and sprinted. Shocked faces appeared down the length of the Archive; shots ripped into the wall behind him as a scientist's armed escort tried to target him. Stone sent a peppering of rounds into the general area, and someone screamed as people lunged away. If he had taken the guard, he could not guess.

The fire escape capsules were nested in closed alcoves along the outside wall. Stone turned back, hosed short bursts toward the doorway to hold Dorne's men and buy himself the seconds he needed. He whisked aside the instruction panel and hit the switch with the side of his fist.

The mechanism was designed for the use of panicked civvies with a fire raging behind them. A hatch slammed back, revealing a moulded seat, and Stone flung himself in. He did not pause to strap down, but punched the illuminated red bar marked *Eject*.

As the interior hatch slammed and the seat rotated in its cradle, he glimpsed the oncoming contract men. Gunbarrels swung toward him, shots pelted into the hatch, but the seat assembly revolved too fast. As it locked he saw the aeroshell a hand's span from his knees.

It was all automatic. Stone was still clawing for the harness when the pyros detonated under him and the capsule fired out of the building. Acceleration crushed him for long seconds as it went up in a ballistic arc. The aeroshell was transparent, he saw the facia and roof of the building opposite rush toward him and held his breath, waiting for the upward jerk as the chute opened.

The straps grabbed as the chute plucked up the capsule like a toy, and Stone cast about for his bearings. Equinox Towers lay behind him. Below was Stuyvesant Boulevard, ten lanes of congested traffic. Faces peered up, cars rocked on their repulsion. Stone released the straps and his hand hovered over the switch which would blow off the aeroshell.

'Kevin,' he muttered. 'You're close. Where the Christ are

you? Kevin!'

And then he saw the glare of sunlight on outswept wings as the spaceplane dropped into the street. There was no place to land on Stuyvesant at ground level. Stone searched his memory. He had two options: run for the fountain garden at the junction of Stuyvesant and Takahashi, or make for the nearest building and ride the lift to the roof.

The capsule swung like a pendulum as the wind caught the chute, but it hit the ground softly in the space between two lanes of stalled traffic. The aeroshell tore off as miniature pyros burst like gunshots, and Stone was out.

With the datacube in his left hand and the Stery primed in his right, Stone bolted into the road.

***

'Not the park, Stoney,' Jarrat muttered as he dropped in between the buildings, 'get off the street. Yes!' Stone had vaulted the hood of a Rand sports and dived into the crowd on the broadwalk. He was in the DeSilver building seconds later, and Jarrat bobbed up on repulsion. Equinox Towers was three times higher. If Dorne's shooters were going to try their luck, they would do it from the roof.

The shuttle bounced up into the sunlight and he saw them: five men by the parapet, setting up a heavy, bipod-mounted piece with a long lens and laser acquisition. From there, they could pick Stone out of the crowd, knock him off the roof. Jarrat's triggers had been armed since he left Tac 101. A delicate pressure tripped the twin rotary cannons in the nose, and he watched the macabre dance as the shooters ripped apart.

He felt a shudder in his legs, knew Stone was going up and pulled the plane around to scan the Equinox roof. Vestibule and hangars invited a brace of Hawk missiles, and received them. Flame and smoke enveloped the whole landing bay, and Jarrat took the spaceplane down and eastward.

The roof of the DeSilver building was not stressed to take the weight of the shuttle. Landing was a trick of balancing the repulsion until he touched down with a negligible weight. He had five metres' space off each wingtip, nose and tail, and instead of making a visual descent he nudged down on instruments.

The pall from Equinox veiled the DeSilver building as the wind picked it up. The canopy rose and Jarrat coughed on the chemical smoke. Now he was a sitting duck, begging to be hit, and he concentrated on Stone: his legs pumped as he climbed. The public lift did not go all the way, but he was almost there. Almost. Jarrat sucked in a breath as Stone's chest began to burn.

There! The maintenance hatch slammed open and Stone stumbled out. Jarrat ignited the main lifters and kept them just above idling. He held the shuttle on the concrete by balancing the repulsion as Stone sprinted, scrambled up the hardpoints and tumbled into the rear cockpit.

The canopy whined down and locked, and as Jarrat cut repulsion the plane went up fast. Red lights winked, warning that a laser target acquisition beam had picked him up, and he swore lividly. 'Strap in, Stoney, they've seen us!'

Just above DeSilver's towering transmission aerials, he threw open the throttles, folded wings and canards and stood the plane on its tail. In the back, Stone grunted under the shock of acceleration as he crammed on a helmet and cut into the comm loop.

'Missiles!' he bawled. 'They've locked on. Heat seekers.'

'Hold on!' Jarrat flung the shuttle onto its back, pointed the nose into the glare of the sun for three calculated seconds, then dropped a wingtip, rolled fast and watched his CRT.

'They're ballistic,' Stone crowed. 'Chasing the sun. For Christ's sake, get us out of here!'

'Grab something,' Jarrat panted as he turned the plane's nose toward space and lit the afterburners.

Chapter Sixteen

Still weak with relief, Stone dropped onto the hangar bay deck and gratefully accepted Jarrat's quick embrace. Flight crews glanced curiously at them but did not intrude. Stone withdrew with a self-mocking grin and held the datacube between thumb and forefinger.

'Have that analysed. A man died for it.'

Jarrat took it from him. 'Get yourself a drink, get out of that bloody awful uniform. Right now, you look good enough to shoot.' He gave Stone a push and beckoned Gil Cronin and Curt Gable, who were loitering by the Blue Raven gunship's massive hydraulic pylons. 'And Stoney.'

'Yeah?' Stone turned back tiredly.

'Welcome home.' Jarrat's grey eyes were warm and dark. 'What I've got to say to you, you'll want to hear in private.'

A deep chuckle rumbled in Stone's chest, and Jarrat watched him amble across the hangar. Cronin passed a hand over his shaven skull and leaned one elbow on Gable's shoulder. Gable was intent on the datacube.

'Is that it?'

'Stoney thinks so.' Jarrat palmed it. 'Lets take a look.' He was still following Stone as they strode up to the ops room. He felt the spreading warmth of a double whisky, the rustle of fabric, hot water. Stone was as weary as Jarrat. What they needed was six hours' sleep; what they were likely to get was a shot of uppers.

The ops room busy, Cantrell wore a brilliant smile and Yvette McKinnen looked smug. She sat at an unused console, cradling a mug, and gave Jarrat a triumphal look as he, Gable and Cronin appeared.

'Obviously, your programme ran,' Jarrat observed.

She took a bow. 'You are free to manoeuvre and transmit. I found the lot, snipped it out. You also succeeded, Captain. You got him out. I'd like to examine your flight recorder.'

'If you want to.' Jarrat flourished the cube. 'But before you put Stoney and me on trial, read that.'

Her eyes widened. 'Damn. He got it.' She took it from him, dropped it into the nearest terminal and studied Jarrat with a frown. 'You knew where and when to effect the pickup.'

'To the last metre and second, Doc.' Jarrat was too tired to spar with her. 'You know better than anyone what we're capable of. If we'd been made empathic before the Death's Head job, Stoney would have whisked me out of Chell, no trouble. I might have taken the beating, but I'd have been back aboard so fast, Kip could have got to me before...'

'Before the brain damage became technically irreversible,' McKinnen finished for him. 'You're a medical singularity, Captain. Papers are being written about you.'

'Should I be flattered?' Jarrat turned his attention to the screen as Stone's enormous cache of data finished loading and began to display. Cantrell, Petrov, Gable and Cronin gathered in a knot behind him. 'Now, what have we here?'

Manifests, schedules, orbital data, requisitions, logged movements of freight, men, money. Gable whistled through his teeth. 'How the hell did Stoney get this?'

'I'm afraid to ask,' Jarrat said drily. He shivered as he felt Stone in every nerve. He was naked, drying off in the warm cabin air with a third whisky in him and some highly spiced food scorching the roof off his mouth. Stone liked all things hot, food, sun and sex alike.

'It's going to take hours to make sense of this,' Cantrell estimated. 'Reardon wants you and Stoney in the Infirmary.'

Jarrat groaned. 'Not now, Gene.'

'Kip said he won't brook arguments. Unquote,' Cantrell informed him. 'You've both been on the edge too long.'

'That's true.' Jarrat looked into McKinnen's face. 'We never said the empathy was a walk in the park, Doc. There's a price to be paid when we work, and we pay it.' He gestured at the data which raced through the screen. 'Let me have a preliminary compilation, soon as you can.'

The aftermath of a run was almost like the comedown from a narco trip, without the benefit of a blocker agent. Jarrat wished he could sink down and sleep as he stepped into the cabin; then he saw Stone, and the weariness dispelled.

He was still naked, still eating, sitting on the bedside with a handful of pastry. And on his left breast was a laser-branded pentacle.

'So that's how they marked you.' Jarrat rubbed his own chest. 'It hurt like hell.'

'You went through it with me?' Stone dusted off his palms and held out both hands. 'Come here, for godsake.'

They tangled, ate each other alive for long minutes, but a torrent of mutual relief eclipsed passion. At last Jarrat pinned him to the bed and explored the tattoo with fingers and tongue. Stone's hands cupped his head and massaged his sensitive scalp. He lifted his knees to hug Kevin's hips.

'I'll get it removed, soon as this shindig's over,' he promised. 'I don't like looking at it. It reminds me.'

Jarrat's eyes were sombre. 'It was rough.'

Stone kissed him deeply. 'Let's say, I'm glad it's over. You ran the data?'

'They're starting analysis.' Jarrat sat and straightened his clothes. 'Reardon wants us.'

'Damn.' Stone knuckled his eyes.

'I'd be happy if he did check you over,' Kevin said thoughtfully. 'They crammed you full of Angel. Didn't they?'

Rueful, Stone rolled to his feet. 'You felt that?'

'I didn't feel anything much,' Jarrat admitted. 'A little congestion, but no buzz. Take it as read, sunshine, you're immune.'

The debris of Stone's quick meal fell into the disposal, and his brows rose as he pulled on fresh slacks and shirt. 'You were groundside last night.'

'Read the report Gene filed.' Jarrat opened his arms. 'I brought Jesse out, and his friend. An Angelhead I took out of a sex shop. I sent them to Darwin's six hours ago. I thought maybe Harry could fix the kid. And Jack Spiteri.'

'That was a nice thought.' Stone held him tightly, took his mouth again, hungrily. 'I missed you.'

'Understatement.' Jarrat was husky with affection.

An exam room was prepared, waiting for them. Reardon palmed a scanner and took Stone first, while Jarrat watched with heavy eyes. Stone stood, sat, turned this way and that, and ended flat on his back while Reardon inspected the tattoo. 'I'll erase this for you,' the surgeon promised.

'I'd be obliged.' Stone pillowed his head on one forearm. 'All I need is some sound sleep.'

'Grab it while you can,' Reardon advised. 'Avalon votes

tomorrow, and according to their vidcast, the street'll go up like a flashfire. Okay, you'll live.' He beckoned Jarrat.

Jarrat hopped onto the bench and pulled his shirt over his head. His eyes followed Stone as Reardon took readings but finished off with his hands, as if he distrusted machines. Stone looked grim, and as Jarrat eased down the empathic shields he felt his partner's solemn mood.

'What's wrong, Stoney?'

'Two thousand Cygnus mercenaries,' Stone said quietly. 'They'll butcher Tactical and Avalon's token defence force. I hate to say this, Kev, but the only thing between Dorne and the coup he's been planning for years —'

'Is us,' Jarrat finished. He turned to give Reardon access to his back. 'Your data looks good, at first glance. If we can follow it to source, we're home free.'

'Source,' Stone mused, 'seems to be something called Hera. I couldn't find out what that was.'

'Analysis will find it.' Jarrat turned again, flat on the bench. 'Kip, are you finished?'

The surgeon grunted. 'And so are you. You're at the end of your rope, *Captain*, and you've been on uppers too long.' Jarrat yawned in his face. 'I'll give you a blocker shot,' Reardon said as he charged a hypo. 'Then, if you don't hit the hay I'll personally tie you to a bed.'

'I'll be good.' Jarrat's teeth bared as the shot fired in, but it was Stone who yelped.

The hypo clattered back into its case. 'Get out of here,' Reardon said fondly. 'You've got about five lives left — between you two tomcats!'

The lure of a soft mattress and Stone's hard body were more than Jarrat could resist. The cabin lights dimmed and he stood still in the semidarkness, luxuriating in the sense of touch as Stone stripped him with breathtaking sensuality. He was swaying as Stone knelt at his feet. His face pressed to the flat of Jarrat's belly, arms circling his hips. A kiss for his reluctant cock, and Stoney tumbled him onto the bed.

'The doctor said, sleep,' he reminded as he pulled the sheet over their heads.

'Don't seem to have much option,' Jarrat said mournfully. He caught Stone's hand, tucked it between his thighs and breathed a sigh. 'The spirit may be willing, but the flesh has gone to hell.'

Stone laughed softly. He dealt the soft, captive genitals a companionable squeeze and wriggled a hand under to knead Jarrat's buttock. 'Later. I'll show this little fanny a deep, sweet fuck it won't forget.'

'Threat or promise?' Jarrat turned over and went limp.

'Go to sleep, beautiful.' Stone set his face against Kevin's tousled hair and followed.

It could have been an hour or a year before the comm buzzed, and they both started awake. Jarrat's arm snaked out, selected voice-only, and his eyes were still closed as he slurred, 'Yeah, Jarrat, what?'

'Ops room, Cap.' Petrov. 'You wanted a preliminary.'

Fighting out of the torpor, he peered at his chrono and was astonished. He had been out for eight hours. 'Christ, is that the time?' He dug a sharp finger into Stone's ribs.

'I'm awake,' Stone mumbled. 'I wish I wasn't.'

'I, uh, interrupted something?' Petrov snickered.

'You woke us,' Jarrat told him tartly. 'Give us an hour, and call a briefing. We want the latest from Elysium too. Call Duggan, tell him this ship is officially un-hacked. If Dorne is eavesdropping — great.'

'Will do,' Petrov responded.

Jarrat stretched and looked down into Stone's stubbled face with a smile. 'You look disreputable, dissolute, and bloody edible,' he growled as his hands splayed over Stone's chest, ruffled the hair and tweaked both nipples teasingly. Pleasure rushed through Stone. Jarrat murmured as he was caught by stronger hands than his own, pulled close and dumped down between long, muscular legs. 'You soldiers don't know your own strength,' he accused fondly.

'Oh, yes we do,' Stone growled. His hips lifted in a slow, seductive rhythm.

'Thought you were going to fuck me.' Jarrat was already breathless as the empathy rang like a bell.

'We need time to do it right.' Stone devoured his ear. 'It's no quickie you're getting, my lad. You're due the de luxe job.'

A groan escaped Jarrat's throat at Stone's words, the grip of his thighs, the tang of his musk. In minutes the empathy overloaded him, seemed to squeeze his balls, and finished him like an over-eager adolescent. He went down on Stone's chest, panting, cursing and sticky. Still moving under him, Stone arched into the bed, dug in his heels and came with a cry. Dark, sleepy blue eyes looked into Jarrat's face, and Kevin subsided.

'You did that to me deliberately.'

'Certainly,' Stone agreed. 'And you didn't need much prompting.'

'We've got a week's worth under pressure,' Jarrat allowed as he sat and stretched. He wriggled as Stone kissed his back. 'Shower, shave, breakfast, briefing, in that order.'

'Yes, sir, Captain, sir.' Stone swung his legs off the bed. 'Remind me to stop saying "sir". I said it so often in the last week, it's a habit.' He angled a glance at Jarrat as Kevin hit the taps. 'You were Army. Please, God, say it wasn't like the mob of crazies Dorne recruits.'

'Nothing like.' Jarrat stepped under the water and sluiced away the milky blend of their semen. 'We were trained to a peak, taught to think for ourselves. If you said "sir" too often, they assumed you were taking the piss! They recruited smart kids for the officer corps.'

'Like you?' Stone joined him and soaped his chest.

'Like me.' Jarrat ducked his head under the water. 'It was rough, but they break you in gently. A hundred simulations before the real thing, then they put one rookie between two veterans. The mortality rate is low. You bunk on the ship. Six men to a cabin, and your officers are pleased if you buddy up. Sex-starved soldiers get careless, and dead. You'll always get barracks tyrants, but good surveillance keeps kids from being mistreated.' He leaned over to kiss. 'Good food, good friends. There's danger, but the vets look out for you while you learn. Then one day you're a veteran yourself.' He paused, hands on Stone's strong hips. 'You realise it in the middle of a fight, when you're pulling some boy out by the seat of his pants, bawling orders that save a guy's hide. Overhead is an airborne observer. Your officers watch the videos later and your first promotion just happens.'

Stone's arms draped over Jarrat's shoulders. 'You were good, even then.'

'I still am.' Jarrat lay heavily against him as the hot water eased his muscles.

Five minutes early, they strode into the briefing room and Stone ordered a meal as Jarrat began to page through a folder of printout. The senior Ravens and the ops room staff gathered, and Stone was not surprised to see Yvette McKinnen. She wore a pensive look, studied them overtly, and he waited for her to speak. Judge, jury and executioner.

But McKinnen offered her hand, and Stone took it. 'I reviewed Jarrat's flight data,' she said quietly. 'Understand me, Stone. My biocyber implant is the equal of your empathy.'

'But you haven't scan-shielded it,' Stone added.

'Yet.' She withdrew her hand. 'Gene showed me Jarrat's log covering the whole assignment. It's remarkable, but to me, much more remarkable is your sanity.'

'Our what?' Stone recoiled.

Across the table, intent on the printout, Jarrat did not look up. 'She said, our sanity. We ought to be cuckoo by now. We're empathic, remember?'

McKinnen made some small noise of disdain. 'You are also committed lovers,' she added. 'I think, in your case this makes the difference.'

'As Harry Del told you,' Stone added sharply.

'Yes.' McKinnen smiled faintly. 'Everyone is permitted one mistake, Captain. Perhaps I have made mine.'

Surprise echoed between Jarrat and Stone. Jarrat gave the woman a curious look. 'Is this a peace pact?'

'We were never enemies,' McKinnen said mildly as she pulled a chair up between Cantrell and Petrov. 'Now, I have been studying that dossier. You're in trouble, Jarrat.'

'What?' Stone hardly believed his ears. 'Everything we need is on that cube, lady!'

'Captain Cantrell?' McKinnen sat back.

But Jarrat had already skimmed to the bottom line, and cautioned Stone with a minute gesture. 'She may be right. What you've got here is a brilliant picture of one of the richest Angel syndicates I've ever known. And not one scrap of hard evidence you could lay your hands on if we blew our way into that building with a gunship.'

Stone sagged into a chair. 'What about the shipments of raw chemicals? They've got labs galore in there. You telling me the Angel isn't coming out of Equinox Towers?'

'Got it in one.' Jarrat turned the folder toward him. 'Here's a breakdown of prohibited scientific projects in there, and yes, they have a chemical facility as fine as our own. But it doesn't make Angel.' His voice was hushed. Stone felt him shiver and waited. 'It's nerve gas, Stoney. It reads as a neurotoxin that paralyses the central nervous system, kills in three, four seconds. If they use it they could kill millions.'

The words punched. 'If they're pushed hard enough, they'll use it,' Stone whispered. 'We could be the ones who provide that final shove. It's midnight in Elysium. They vote tomorrow.'

'I know.' Jarrat sat and rubbed his face. 'There's more. Records of abduction, blackmail, bribery, assassination.'

'Angel?' Stone rasped.

'Oh, yeah, lots of that.' Jarrat's fingers drummed on the open folder. 'With one thing missing.'

'The actual Angel itself,' Petrov finished. 'No lab, no stockpile, no smuggling. The shit just seems to appear on the street by magic. Face it, Cap, all we've got there is a bunch of allegation. We could have written that file ourselves.'

'And that,' Cantrell added, 'is the ammunition any syndicate lawyer would use to shoot us down in flames.'

Stone's teeth closed on his lip till he tasted blood. 'Wait. There was a codename. Hera. I saw orbital data, flight schedules. I couldn't make sense of it. What do we have on that?'

Paper rustled as Jarrat paged back. 'Not a lot. It's your Angel link, but we know what's it's *not*, rather than what it is.' He counted off on his fingers. 'It's not in the building, it's not on Avalon or Eos, the orbital data is all wrong. It could be a ship in space, even a disused smelter, but none of these shipping schedules correlate with space-tracking data from Elysium.'

'Which means it could be hidden,' Stone speculated. 'A ship parked on or even in a smelter?'

'Or behind one of the dead moons, or on an asteroid.' Cantrell puffed out his cheeks. 'We're not totally in the dark. There's a project report in there. Kevin?'

'Uh... here.' Jarrat turned pages. 'I see what you're driving at. Christ, it's lucky this was grabbed right out of Dorne's own computers. This data would be transmitted in the same codes we busted our buns on!' He skimmed the pages and Stone felt his pulse quicken. 'Damn, it's a chemical analysis.'

'Let me see.' Stone turned the dossier and read quickly. 'It's a lab report, a batch test, and a request for resupply of basic chemistry.'

'Take a look at the chemistry, Stoney.' Jarrat's voice was taut. 'Those are the building blocks of Angel.'

Stone took a deep breath. 'Then, the Angel is coming out of Hera, whatever and wherever Hera is.' He looked from Jarrat to Cantrell and back. 'Find it, and we find our connection. Have you talked to Duggan about this, Gene?'

'He's being monitored,' Cantrell began.

'Bugger that! Dorne knows we're so close, we can smell him!' Jarrat leaned toward Petrov. 'Get me Duggan. And find out what happened to the food — I'm wilting.'

Their meal arrived moments after Duggan responded to Petrov's insistent calls. Jarrat deferred to Stone, who knew the man much better, and was pleased to see unaffected delight in Duggan's face on the screen as he saw Stone safe.

'It's good to be out,' Stone told him honestly.

'All hell erupted at Equinox, ten minutes after Jarrat grabbed his helmet and bolted out of Tac 101,' Duggan said smugly. 'That was you on the loose? Outstanding. What can I do for you, Stoney?'

'You got anything on the codename Hera?' Stone asked.

But Duggan shook his head. 'Never heard of it. That's an Equinox code?'

'*The* Equinox code,' Stone corrected. 'Okay, you're blank. A warning, Vic. There's a chemical lab in that building, and they're not making Angel. We read it as a neurotoxin. Nerve gas. Kit your boys up with environment suits... they may use it.'

'Jesus Christ.' Duggan paled. 'Deadly?'

Stone glanced at Jarrat. 'Lethal.'

'Then fuck your NARC directives!' Duggan shouted. 'You can't sit it out up there and let Dorne pull a coup at the cost of millions of people!'

'Vic,' Stone said quietly. 'Take a pill, lie down. They may not use the nerve gas unless they get a fight they stand to lose. You follow?'

'You mean, NARC involvement may make them use it?' Duggan backed up and reconsidered.

'Possibly.' Stone's fingers drummed on the table. 'If we deploy, it has to be so fast, so hard, they haven't time to spit. Or it's your city that'll pay the price.'

The colonel cleared his throat. 'This codename, Hera. That's your Angel connection? Where is it? What is it?'

'We don't know,' Stone admitted. 'But we will. Stay in touch, Duggan. We found our leeches, dug the bugs out of this old bucket. We're back in business.'

'Yeah.' Duggan's eyes were frightened. 'Don't go away, will you, Stoney?'

'Count on it.' Stone closed down and glared at Petrov. 'Okay, we have orbital data and shipping schedules. We're down to analysis. Can we locate Hera? If not, why not?'

The Russian's face was bleak. 'We got one shitty half of a kiddy puzzle, Cap. The computers have been running for three hours already. This is a big, dirty system with more places to hide a ship than you'd believe.' He hesitated. 'In the end, we could be down to smart-ass guesswork.'

'Well,' Cantrell said slowly, 'NARC makes a policy of recruiting the smartest asses we can find.' He regarded Jarrat and Stone levelly. 'Yvette isn't saying much, but her reading of the data is that it's a question of time and painstaking attention to detail. We'll find it.'

'The question is,' Jarrat said bitterly, 'will we find it in time? If we had the absolute, irrefutable sanction of hard evidence, we could break Equinox before they knew the blow was coming. But if we deploy before we have it, and then for whatever reason, we don't find it, we could break NARC, and ourselves. Syndicate lawyers from here to Earth would queue up to flay the department alive.' He toyed with his food. The thought of eating made him faintly nauseous. 'What's the situation in Elysium?'

Many hours of video coverage had been recorded, augmenting Tactical telemetry, and a sixty-minute edit had been compiled. Lenore Maddigan's speeches were inspired. Given the vote of the people, she would deny Equinox the celestial mining treaty. She would expedite their departure from the system, and then the people would begin to clean up the toxic wilderness left by the company.

Bryce Ansell painted a different picture. Where Maddigan spoke from the podium, Ansell recorded his interviews in an office, addressing a camera with a dry skeleton of statistics. Avalon's survival pivoted on Equinox's prosperity. Drive Equinox out, and impoverishment would lead to want, disease and a wholesale plague of Angel use.

Next, a physicist spoke, backed by animated illustrations of the consequences of Equinox's plan to mine Zeus of its fluorine. In a decade, as the veil of debris output from the refinery accumulated, the sun would cease to shine on Avalon. Plant life must perish, almost a billion people would depend for every bite of food on rimrunners, immense freighters plying between Zeus and the Cygnus colonies.

There, Jarrat halted the video. 'Mischa, did you find out who controls the major freight lines?'

'You guessed dead right, Cap,' Petrov told him sourly. 'Dorne owns huge shares in Cygnus industry and freight. He's invested in mariculture. Oh, he'd feed Avalon, at a profit. We accessed his tax audits, back twenty years. He made his first big killings in shipping. Used some kind of a scam, just this side of the law, to get control of the biggest rimrunners in this elbow of space. Not much moves between here and Cygnus that he doesn't control. These poor buggers are in a no-win situation, unless they get rid of Equinox.'

'Or get rid of Randolph Dorne,' Stone added. 'Do we know where those mercenaries are?'

'Here.' Petrov punched keys, and a grid map replaced Maddigan's face on the screen. 'All inside an hour's flight time of Elysium. That's your battlefield. The city.'

'If we're going to take them,' Jarrat mused, 'with four gunships, we'll have to wait till they're in one relatively small area. We can't afford to chase them all over the planet. Stoney?'

'Right. When the party begins they'll pour into Elysium. The people will fight. It's going to be bloody. Duggan doesn't have a chance.' He felt Jarrat's chill and knew Kevin was haunted by memories of another corporate war. Sheal had been bloody, a long, agonised conflict in which the Army was trapped in the crossfire between mighty industrialists. Jarrat had survived; many had not.

'Still,' Cantrell added, 'Equinox will take losses. And every man and machine they lose is one less for us to contend with.'

Jarrat felt the sting of Stone's quick revulsion. He could have been down there himself, if he had stayed with Tactical, even stuck with Duggan. 'All right,' Jarrat said quietly, 'we go with the data analysis, but we put everything we have on standby, Lieutenant. Monitor anything that twitches in Elysium.'

'It might be intelligent to move out of orbit,' Stone said thoughtfully. 'They have some nasty hardware, Kevin. It's possible they could take a shot at the carrier, either from the ground or from a mobile firebase out here.'

'Do it,' Jarrat agreed. 'Inform Colonel Archer, safe-distancing procedures.'

'And arm the gunships with the lot,' Stone added. 'When the time comes to move, the one thing we won't have is time.'

Cronin made noises of agreement. 'Will do, Cap. Give me a target strike sequence, I'll programme the onboard decks.'

'Target strike designation,' Jarrat echoed. 'That's going to be interesting. One, Equinox Towers. Two, any assembly of their military.'

'Three, their armouries. Four, landing facilities.' Stone tapped the folder of printout. 'It should all be in there.'

'It is.' Jarrat stood, hands laced at the back of his neck. 'Christ, if we can find Hera. If we can't...' His eyes closed. 'Dorne pulls his coup, declares Equinox the legit government of Avalon, formally withdraws any allegiance to the government of Earth —'

'And tells NARC to screw itself,' Petrov finished, 'because our jurisdiction just got fritzed.'

The words were as leaden as the silence which followed. At last Stone stood. 'I think that's all. Petrov, work out the target strike sequence, get it to Gil, soon as you can. Let's pull this ship out of orbit, we make a big, fat target. Doc McKinnen, I hope we can entrust the hunt for Hera to you.'

'You can.' She toyed with a pencil. 'It is a matter of time, and exhaustive evaluation of scanty data.'

'That touches all bases,' Jarrat said brusquely. 'We want updates on the hour. Questions? No? Then get busy, people.'

***

It was afternoon over Elysium when the sporadic violence began. Since morning the election had dominated every vidcast, and by noon the early counts were in. Maddigan commanded over ninety percent; only hard line Company people supported Bryce Ansell. Ansell himself seemed to have vanished.

Duggan called at 14:00, Elysium time. Jarrat and Stone were reviewing Petrov's target priority estimations, and groundscan had located several task forces of machines, traced by the emissions of hotcore generators. The ops room was fully manned, and the week's delayed telemetry had already been boosted to Central. Jarrat looked over the illuminated plotboard, into Duggan's worried face as he appeared on the screen.

'It's started, Jarrat. I've got riots in three sectors. Two of my squads were just shot down by Maverick missiles out of a highrise vehicle park. That's military.'

'And it's political,' Jarrat added. 'Where's Maddigan?'

'Safe. I moved her to a nuke shelter, a bunker by the spaceport. They won't be able to hit her there.' Duggan hesitated. 'You making progress?'

'Maybe.' Jarrat met McKinnen's eyes, but the woman made negative gestures. 'No joy yet, but we're close. You're running surveillance on Dorne?'

'He's on Skycity,' Duggan said promptly. 'Wozniak is in the Towers. No sign of your man Gary Schaefer — you sure he ever existed at all? Coded signals are up two hundred percent. They're on the move, I swear it.'

'I believe you.' Jarrat straightened from his work as Stone and Gil Cronin entered the ops room. 'Look, Vic, if they shoot at you, drop them. Tactical can handle the current situation. Keep us informed of Dorne's movements.'

The man's face was bleak. 'You can expect ECM jamming, two seconds after it starts. The Tac-NARC band won't be worth shit. Run your own surveillance on Dorne, it's got to beat anything I can do for you.'

'Roger that,' Jarrat responded. 'Watch yourself, Colonel. We've located some heavy equipment.'

'Tell me about it,' Duggan said sourly, and shut down.

Petrov leaned over the plot table. 'We're monitoring Skycity with everything we got. Nothing's moving, in or out, but their radio's running hot. If an executive aircraft bugs out, it's a safe bet, that's Dorne.'

'Stay with it.' Jarrat leaned his hip on the table, and regarded Stone and Cronin soberly. 'It's started to rumble, Stoney. It won't take much to touch off the real circus.'

'I heard.' Stone studied the latest groundscans. 'They've still got their men and machines barracked. What's Dorne waiting for?'

'Night?' Cronin guessed. 'His grunts'll be using thermo, vision intensification, every scan system they can get their hands on. Gives 'em an advantage if the civvies are blind.'

'Makes sense.' Stone glanced at the chrono. 'Sunset over

Avalon is in six hours. That gives us a chance.'

At the programmer's console, McKinnen was working at a steady pace. Jarrat stood behind her, watching her piece together a coherent picture from orbital vectors and the acceleration parameters of ships moving through a cluttered system. When two calculations agreed, she locked in a coordinate and moved on.

She frowned deeply at the NARC men. 'The field is at least narrower. It's in the inner system, which means we can discount nine thousand abandoned smelters and refineries in the asteroid belts. You see, these trajectories may indicate a spiral course, calculated to confuse with a flyby around a stationary, parked object, which I took to be Elysium's deep space tracking platform. It's a cheap way of getting from point to point without your destination being obvious. I guessed Hera would be in the outer system. I was wrong, or I'd have found it by now. The same trajectories might indicate flightpaths around a deep gravity well.'

'Which means,' Stone mused, 'either the star —'

'Or Zeus,' Jarrat finished. 'Which, Doc?'

'Uncertain. I assume it's the star, since, if Hera was an object in proximity to Zeus, I'd expect to see it on instruments sooner or later, if only serendipitously. And neither NARC nor Elysium Control ever registered it. That does not mean it isn't there, just that Equinox is resourceful. I suggest,' McKinnen advised, 'you launch a gunship, swing it around Zeus and look at the whole system with long-range probes.'

Cronin winced. 'Sixteen moons, four close-in smelters, nine refineries, three radiation belts, two asteroid fields. Jesus Christ, Cap, you're asking me to find a fucking needle in a haystack, without a magnet!'

'Then the sooner you get started,' Stone said drily, 'the better your chances. How long? Best guess.'

'Ten, maybe twelve hours.' Cronin closed his eyes. 'You damned well give me a Starfleet crew. If my Blue Ravens are going to jump into hell come nightfall in that godforsaken city, they do it fresh, not worn to a nub with this bloody paper chase!'

Stone gave Petrov a nod and the Russian quietly called the standby crew. Cronin marched away, every stride betraying his aggravation. Stone turned back to McKinnen. 'You're probably right, it's more likely deep in the sun's gravity well.'

But McKinnen's lips pursed doubtfully. 'If it was, these trajectories would be right. But the flight-time estimates to Avalon are so short, they only add up if Hera is near Zeus, or if Dorne's ships exit a close solar orbit at near optic velocity... in space so full of rubble, a pebble takes on the characteristics of a missile.'

'Flak deflectors?' Jarrat speculated, and slammed up the shields protecting his empathy as Stone's annoyance began to get under his skin like glass powder.

'Maybe.' McKinnen tapped a line on the screen. 'Everything says Hera is somewhere around Zeus. But it *can't* be unless Dorne has discovered how to make it invisible.' The Paris accent thickened as she concentrated. 'None of it makes sense.'

'But you're winning.' Stone consulted his chrono. 'We're still in with a chance.' He looked over the scatter of papers on the plot table. 'Did you finalise a strike priority, Kevin?'

'Getting there.' Jarrat pulled a paper toward him. 'The Towers. Skycity. Major troop congregations, including in-hangar vehicles. Ground installations, including stockpiles. I figure, allocate one gunship to each ground target, and one shuttle to suppress Skycity while the other flies topcover and observation.' He looked doubtfully at Stone. 'Everything we have will be in the air in five directions. There'll be no way to call for backup, since they'll jam our comm... and no backup to send, even if a signal punched through.'

As he spoke Cantrell stepped into the room. His face was grave as he heard Jarrat's evaluation. Stone rubbed his face. 'Words of wisdom, Gene?'

'You mean, I've thirty years on you, I'm supposed to know the answers?' Cantrell could have been their father. He shook his head. 'It's an old superstition, that long experience makes better commanders. Oh, seasoning is precious. But captains are given a crew with an aggregate of *centuries'* experience. The truth? Young men request advice and value it. Old men *know* they've seen it all, give orders and often blunder. That's the lesson of history.' He smiled at Jarrat and Stone. 'It's why we recruit young blood, two by two, train you to bounce ideas, evaluate advice... use the vigour of a fresh approach to get answers.' He cocked his head at them. 'How old was Alexander when he conquered his world?'

They shared a wry look. 'Thanks a bunch,' Jarrat breathed.

'That's a flattering way of telling us we're on our own.'

'Maybe.' Cantrell sobered. 'I'm just an observer. But... if Dorne pulls an iron-clad coup and proclaims his independence, we're out of jurisdiction. It'll take an invasion force to get in, and for Avalon, the next stop is hell, one-way ticket. Against that, you've got the survival of NARC. If Hera is already dismantled, demolished, and we get a fistful of air instead of irrefutable proof, this offensive,' he gestured at the table, 'is the act of a mercenary army. And a hundred syndicate lawyers will rip NARC to bloody tatters.' He paused. 'The decision is yours, gentlemen. I don't envy you.'

Stone took a breath and exhaled slowly. 'We prepare, we watch, and we play a hunch.'

'A hunch?' Cantrell smiled once more. Young blood was about to prove NARC recruitment policy.

'Hera,' Jarrat said flatly, 'must be worth billions of credits. They wouldn't destroy it, they'd hide it. And we'll find it.' He looked at Petrov. 'Has that gunship launched?'

'They're launching now, Cap.' Petrov was listening to the loop via a headset. 'Telemetry coming in from Tac. They're fighting in Alexandria. Riot turning into a battle.' He routed the data to a monitor and stood back to watch.

A mix of videos and text filled the screen. Jarrat and Stone watched images from a Tactical skyhopper. They saw the characteristic black uniforms and Tac men, and the blue and green garb of the planet's token defence force.

Missiles erupted from the roof of a building; phosphor grenades exploded in the middle of the Tactical ranks. A medevac skytruck stood off on the perimeter, unable to get in. The air crackled and spattered with interference but Tactical overrode it with signal power.

A flak curtain burst across an eight-lane clearway and a Tac ground transport shattered into spinning, blazing debris. Stone turned away from the screen. 'Doctor McKinnen.'

She was also watching the nightmare images, and shook herself away. 'I'm doing the best I can, Captain Stone. If I abandon my analysis, I can only start to guess. I don't advise it.'

'Stoney.' Jarrat set a hand on his partner's arm as Stone's feelings of furious impotence cut him to the bone. 'I think it's time we checked our gear. You want an inspired hunch?'

'I'd be grateful.' Stone calmed with an effort of will.

'Hera was built after Duggan arrived and took a grip on this system so tight, Dorne's smuggling days were over. His Cygnus connection was neutralised. It's probably a platform, manufacturing Angel in-system. Nobody's insane enough to fly at near light speed through a fog of gravel, so it's somewhere around Zeus. It cost Dorne an arm and a leg, so he won't destroy it, he'll hide it.'

'Then, you want to risk deployment?' Stone's brows rose.

'I say, go in the last minute,' Jarrat said carefully. 'Search until we're out of time... then deploy, and find it later. It's there, Stoney. We both know that.'

'Yeah.' Stone looked at Cantrell. 'I'm buying. Take over here, Petrov. We're going to go over our gear.'

In a ritual was as old as combat, warriors assembled and checked their own weapons. The riot armour was taken from the lockers, each section and system inspected for integrity. Rotary cannon, stun projector and snapper were tested while the armourers plied between the magazine and the hangar deck, equipping both shuttles with every missile and round they would carry.

Jarrat clicked his chrono over to Elysium time as they walked back to their cabins. It was 16:40. As Stone took the personalised Ingram-Kalashnikov from its case, Kevin turned on the monitor.

Scenes of havoc dominated every channel coming out of Elysium. Lenore Maddigan was in the throes of a desperate speech, begging for order. She offered to deal with Equinox, reach some viable alternative to the mining treaty. Then her face was replaced by a sight which made Jarrat's heart squeeze.

'Christ, Kevin, what is it?' Stone felt his shock and was with him at once.

'That's Tac HQ. Or, it was.' Jarrat watched the inferno which gushed up out of the city like an active volcano.

'Oh, my God.' Stone touched the comm. 'Petrov, are you still getting telemetry from Tactical?'

'Two sources, Cap,' Petrov reported as the open comm loop chattered in the background. 'Tac 101 is set up out of the city on Mount Valeris, and we're getting telemetry from Duggan's own squad, airborne, by the Spaceport. Civvy air traffic is grounded, space to surface is prohibited. The Spaceport radars have been rocketed. Senator Maddigan is transmitting from a nuke bunker. Duggan's providing airborne target vectoring for whatever's still intact, which isn't much. It's a cock-up. The defence force scattered half an hour ago.'

'Then who's fighting?' Jarrat asked hoarsely.

'The people,' Petrov told him. 'Duggan's two thousand over Elysium, on open transmission, telling every civvy shooter with an R/T what to shoot at for best effect. It's the best he can do. Tactical's stretched thinner than a G-string on a belly dancer.'

'Has Equinox deployed the main mercenary force?' Stone asked as he watched a brace of missiles launch from a high roof.

'Nope. You're looking at Company security goons, straight out of the Towers,' Petrov reported. 'Safe guess is, they'll throw them in to bust Tactical, deploy the mercs to clean up.'

'Give me Dr McKinnen,' Jarrat whispered into the loop.

'I'm listening, Captain,' the woman said at once.

'Tell me you've found that thing,' Jarrat entreated.

'I'm close,' she said cautiously. 'An hour, and I might have it. It's near Zeus, I'm sure of it.'

As they watched the city erupt, Stone's arm snaked about Jarrat's waist and held on. 'Can you quote me the time of the last logged flight data to or from Hera?'

Jarrat twisted to look at him. 'Meaning?'

'We may be chasing the location it was *moved* from three days ago,' Stone said bitterly. 'Or if they destroyed it —'

'The log-time of the last data was less than an hour before you left Equinox Towers,' McKinnen told him. 'If they'd moved it since then, we'd have seen it.'

Stone took a breath. 'Thank you, Doctor. Petrov, where's the Blue Raven gunship?'

'Swinging around Zeus, fast orbit, coming up on — shit!'

The expletive tore from Petrov's throat in the same instant the screen before Jarrat and Stone blanked. 'Petrov, what happened?' Jarrat barked.

'We just lost every telemetry feed, radio is out, the lot. We're down to our own groundscan data,' Petrov shouted. 'I'm reading ten tenths ECM over Elysium, and you can bet your ass that's full frequency jamming. They just moved.'

Jarrat's hand tightened on Stone's shoulder. 'Stoney?'

Stone's insides shook once and then settled. He felt a rush of sudden resolve — his own or Jarrat's, in that moment he could not tell. 'Yes,' he said quietly, then, into the loop, 'Lieutenant, get the gunship back here, best speed. Intensive groundscan, track anything that moves. You'll see their merc units coming in. Pinpoint them.'

'Standby all crews,' Jarrat continued. 'Flight deck, drop us into a low insertion orbit and track for missiles. All Raven units, standby your gunships. Gable?'

'Yo!' Curt Gable shouted across the loop.

'Take out the standby shuttle, and for chrissakes stay down-range of them,' Jarrat told him. 'You on observation.'

'And you?' Gable was breathless, already on the run.

'We'll take Skycity,' Stone said tersely. 'Petrov, where's that gunship, and can you see the mercenary units?'

Petrov: 'Blue Raven gunship will rendezvous in twenty minutes... and we see their mercs, airborne, coming into Elysium on six headings. They'll be in strike range in thirty minutes. Wait.' A pause, then, 'I've got something outbound, heading for space so fast its tail feathers are alight.'

'Missile?' Jarrat barked.

'No, an aircraft,' Cantrell called. 'Looks like a civvy bus. They'll outrun the jamming in a few minutes.'

Gable: 'Coming this way?'

Cantrell: 'On this general heading.'

'Launch, Curt,' Jarrat said sharply. 'Move it along if it's civvy... if it looks like an Equinox aircraft, waste it.'

The loop was an angry chaos of chatter. Stone watched seconds tick over as the Blue Raven gunship piled on every erg of power Tanya Reynolds could get. Red, Green and Gold Ravens were already aboard as Gable launched, and Petrov cut in.

'Blue Raven gunship is fifteen minutes out. Civvy Outbound should be clearing atmosphere and jamming about now.'

'Hail them,' Stone growled.

'Trying, Cap,' Petrov said acidly. Minutes dragged before he quit in disgust. 'They don't answer.'

'Boost your signal, you're getting slop-over jamming from groundside,' Jarrat guessed.

And there it was. Vic Duggan's voice was knife-edged with panic. 'NARC carrier from Tac Wildcard!'

'Vic!' Stone shouted. 'There's a shuttle coming your way. Just tail it in. What the hell are you doing?

'I've got Senator Maddigan aboard,' Duggan panted. 'You

getting anything from Elysium?'

'Nothing but our own groundscan,' Stone said tersely.

A blast of white noise cut across Duggan. 'The Senator wants to talk —'

'No!' Jarrat snapped. 'Not one word, Duggan, till the show's over. This is a NARC assignment, don't cloud the issue with politics. Captain Cantrell will give her visitors' quarters. Right now, we don't have time to chat.' He spun, snatched up the Colt AP-60 which he had dropped on his bunk and dragged on a headset.

Petrov: 'Gunship is ten minutes out. Reading six bogeys inbound to Elysium, twenty minutes from strike range. It's going to be tight.'

'We're on our way,' Stone told him as he pulled on his own headset and followed Jarrat from the cabin. 'Hold all units till the gunship docks, then launch everything, as fast as you know how. Cronin!'

'Blue Raven 6,' Cronin called. 'All targeting computers are preloaded with the priority sequence.'

'Make it fast,' Jarrat panted as he jogged toward the lift to the suiting room and hangars. 'Give them a chance to gas that city, and they'll do it.' His eyes flicked to his chrono.

It was afternoon in Elysium, warm, humid under a tropical overcast which masked the face of Zeus. He wondered fleetingly how many men would not live to see morning, but grimly ousted the thought. Stone's caustic emotions scalded him raw, and he toughened the bulwark of his shields against the painful empathy as he stepped into the suiting room.

Chapter Seventeen

The communications jamming was absolute. As the shuttle dropped through normal re-entry signal blackout, Stone heard only white noise on any channel. Below, Elysium lay shrouded in smoke, as if half the city was ablaze. Jarrat was flying. Though Stone was skilled, when it came to low-level work Jarrat was the best he had seen in NARC. In the rear cockpit, three CRTs were alive with data, and Stone's own hands were full.

He cut out the impenetrable static of the loop, leaving only cable audio between them. 'I'm tracking the gunships,' he reported. 'I see Gable... and the incoming bogeys. Blue Raven are targeting the Towers. Contact in two minutes. Dorne's aircraft look industrial. Heavy lifters. They'll be armed, with geocannon if nothing else.'

Ahead, Skycity was a single track on Jarrat's screen. The throttles were wide open but the spaceplane handled like a pig under the full ordnance load. 'Seven klicks out. Christ, they've seen us. What are you reading?'

'Three warheads leaving Skycity. Safe bet they're Avengers,' Stone said calmly. 'Here's your intercept bearing.'

'Got it.' Jarrat punched keys. 'Arming Mavericks. Three thousands metres. Two. Mavericks away. One thousand... we're clear.'

Three Maverick missiles ambushed the heat-seeking Avengers launched from the platform in a nimbus of blazing gases and cartwheeling shrapnel. The scorching blast envelope seared the shuttle's nose, instruments went wild for half a second before target acquisition came back on line.

'The bloody jamming's coming from Skycity too,' Stone said quietly. 'I'm on long-range visual. See the big aerials on the belly? Get them, and the air should clear.'

'What about the missile launchers?' Jarrat added. 'I'm picking up the three tubes that just fired on us. Hold on.'

Four Phoenix IIIs left diverging exhaust trails as his thumb hit the triggers, and Stone watched the CRT. A blossom of blue-white vapour wreathed the belly of Dorne's platform, shook the structure, tangled the mighty aerials, and before the explosion had cleared Stone was crowing.

'They won't launch anything else out of this side.'

'Chances are their shooters are galloping for the nearest escape pod,' Jarrat said drily. 'I'll duck around and put a few stingers up the tubes on the other side.'

He threw the shuttle up and over on her back, dipped a wing and righted on gravity resist. Skycity's defensive blindspot was right above. He caught a glimpse on the CRT of tumbled masonry under the vast transparent dome. The mock-Roman mansion seemed to have suffered an earthquake.

As he dropped in on the opposite side of the platform he fired almost intuitively. Again, Skycity shuddered, and this time Stone murmured in apprehension. 'Damn, their repulsion's on the fritz. The whole thing's losing altitude.'

'Going down at ten metres per second,' Jarrat read off his instruments. 'They'll be trying to get power back on. Christ, there's hundreds of people on that monster!' He pulled up, let the massive platform drop away beneath and watched for the inevitable fusillade of escape pods.

'Bug-out capsules,' Stone sang. 'There they go. Damn. If Dorne's in one of those we'll lose him.'

'You're kidding,' Jarrat said acidly. 'Dorne, jump out in a pod, land in the street? You know the man better.' He glanced back at his instruments. 'Rate of descent is slowing. Five metres per second... three. Looks like they've got their grav compensators back. Try the loop. The aerial arrays are shot to hell, that should have killed the ECM.'

Stone plugged back into the loop and was rewarded by a confusion of callsigns, warnings, invective. 'We're back on the air. I'm getting signals from Blue Raven. They're taking fire from Equinox Towers. Listen.'

He plugged Jarrat into the chaotic loop as Kevin took the plane about, away from the crippled platform, and turned the nose for an overview of Elysium. Even from altitude, the triple towers at the heart of Equinox Industries reared over the surrounding city. Missile flaretails chased upward like fireflies. The gunship answered with intercept warheads and the air was filled with a thickening shroud of chemical smog.

'They're in strike range in five seconds,' Stone murmured.

'Two... one. Picking up their acquisition. Here we go!'

Thirty missiles, in ten groups of three, fired out of the gunship and impacted with the Towers, spaced evenly between street level and the massive radio masts. Like a house of cards, the three monstrous buildings collapsed together, inward and downward, in a mushroom cloud of dust, smoke and flame. Jarrat caught his breath.

'They'd have been empty,' Stone said softly as he picked up Kevin's horror at the immensity of the blast. 'Everybody in that building knew it was coming. The only people in there would have been a handful of Company goons in the basements, handing ammunition to the shooters, and good riddance.'

He was right. Jarrat cleared his throat. 'Blue Raven 6.'

'Right here,' Cronin called. 'You want we should jump?'

'Sample the air,' Jarrat corrected sharply. 'That place was lousy with chemicals. Sniff for that bloody nerve gas.'

'We were too quick,' Cronin snorted. 'It'd take them half an hour to break that shit out of storage. They didn't get enough warning.'

'Test the air anyway,' Stone repeated.

'I'm doing it!' Cronin paused to work.

On the CRT, Jarrat watched as the gunship circled the blazing mountain of rubble. A hundred chemical sniffers would taste the wind and provide a complex analysis of the harmless and lethal alike. Cronin knew what he was looking for.

'Negative on the gas, Cap,' he reported a full minute later. 'There's a lot of serious crap in that smoke, but nothing that reads like a neurotoxin. We're ready to jump.'

'Hold where you are,' Jarrat told him. 'I read six bandits, inbound, they look like industrial heavy lifters. You got them?'

'On my screens,' Tanya Reynolds, the gunship's pilot, called. 'They'll be in strike range in under a minute, Cap.'

Stone was watching the same tracking data. 'Knock them down,' he said tersely. 'Fast as you can, any way you can.'

'Stoney!' Jarrat's voice barked over the loop. 'Christ, that has to be Dorne! Scan the platform!'

Even as he spoke, Stone had seen the blip on the tracking CRT. The shuttle spun on one wingtip and Jarrat opened the throttles, cramming Stone into the acceleration padding with the shock of soaring G-forces. Skycity's rate of descent had almost halted. The platform was stable, five thousand metres over Elysium, when a hatch in the belly, aft of the jumble of warped antennae, released a fugitive

'It's a skyhopper,' Stone said breathlessly. 'And bloody damned fast. Too fast to be civvy'

'I've got it on visual. Well, well. This is going to be interesting. That's a Yamazake Lightning.' Jarrat's hand settled about the cyclic stick with a faint prickle of sweat in the palm. 'He's suborbital, but in atmosphere he's as fast as we are. Jesus — he's armed!'

The spaceplane flung into a backbreaker as Jarrat dodged a brace of Hawks, launched from the tail of the Lightning. Proximity alarms clamoured but the missiles self-detonated in roaring airbursts a thousand metres behind.

'Where the hell is he going?' Stone puzzled over the CRT. 'You sure he's suborbital? He's heading for space, southbound, in a polar orbit.'

'No Lightning I ever saw was orbital,' Jarrat said, preoccupied as he registered another brace of missiles. These, he intercepted swiftly with three Mavericks, and the shuttle bolted through the storm of billowing, incandescent gases.

'This one might be modified,' Stone guessed. 'Can you knock him down?'

'I can try.' Jarrat read his remaining ordnance load. 'We haven't got a hell of a lot left.' He thumbed the trigger, launched a precious Phoenix III and watched the CRT.

'Intercept warheads away,' Stone called. 'He's not stupid. Woah! Pull up!'

Jarrat threw the spaceplane onto her back. The surface of Avalon filled the canopy and their apparent mass soared over five G's as he dodged the immense explosion as the Phoenix was intercepted. Stone grunted with reaction and Jarrat shared the cold sweat of his shock.

'That was close,' Stone muttered.

'I'll let him run ahead,' Jarrat panted. 'Get us some manoeuvring room.' The sky was indigo, he saw the stars. Seventy kilometres high, they were on the edge of space. When Jarrat read his instruments again he swore. 'He's levelled off. He's not going to make it into orbit.'

'Then what's he doing up here?' Stone demanded.

'Heading for a rendezvous,' Jarrat guessed. 'Raven Leader to *Athena*.'

Petrov: 'Carrier.'

'You tracking a blue-ass fly, buzzing south in one hell of a hurry?' Jarrat opened the throttles to keep the Yamazake in sight and missile range. 'Is he trying for an in-flight rendez-vous?'

'Negative,' Petrov said at once. 'There's nothing in your airspace, Cap. You're on a heading for the low continent. Maybe he's got a groundside destination.'

With a flash of intuition, Jarrat guessed. 'Best place to hide half an army. Caitlin-B, the extinct gas field, Stoney.'

'Where you picked up Spiteri.' Stone hissed through his teeth. 'That's half the world from Elysium. The carrier won't hold a track on us, we'll be on our own. If he's got heavy backup down there, we're running into a hornets' nest.'

Jarrat gasped as he felt the surge of Stone's foreboding. 'Blue Raven gunship. Status report.'

A burst of white noise sheeted the loop before Reynolds was on the air. 'We got one of the troop lifters, Cap. They went down hard. We took a big rocketing, got some damage.'

'You're disabled?' Stone shouted into the radio clutter.

'No, but we lost a couple of antennae,' Reynolds returned. 'We're holding, two thousand over Elysium.'

'Groundside looks secure?' Jarrat asked as he nudged the throttled forward.

'The street's a riot, shooters everywhere. They're fighting hand to hand. Boost your signal, Raven Leader,' Reynolds called. 'We're starting to lose you. Where are you?'

'Southbound, in a hurry, edge of space.' Stone poured power into his transmission. 'Blue Ravens, insert. Red Raven gunship, fly topcover for Blue boys. Then pull that gunship out and get after us, Reynolds. We have a nasty feeling we'll need you.'

Reynolds: 'Got you on tracking. Five minutes, Cap, and we'll be climbing your back. Blue Ravens away!'

Eyes on his instruments, Jarrat launched the last Phoenix III. 'Move it, Reynolds! This bugger's giving away altitude.'

The Yamazake skyhopper had entered a descending hyper-bolic curve. Stone punched his readings into the computer and read the result with displeasure. 'You guessed right, Kevin. The son of a bitch is making for Caitlin-B.'

The final Phoenix erupted in a gush of chemical fire, and Jarrat held his breath, hoping, praying. But as he shot through the firestorm of blazing vapours he picked up the track once more. 'We're out of missiles, Stoney.'

'I know.' Stone was reviewing their ordnance situation. 'He can't have much left either. A civvy sportplane just can't carry much. Switch to cannons.'

'Oh, lovely.' Jarrat armed the rotaries in the nose and test-fired the laser. The energy weapon was formidable, with one drawback: it guzzled both power and lasing gas. Ten shots with the kick of twenty kilovolts, and it was dead.

The skyhopper's sternflares were close now. Jarrat sighted on the superhot exhausts and triggered an argon laser bolt. Instruments reported a near miss, a neat hole burned in a tail fairing. Dorne's pilot took instant evasive action.

Now, the Yamazake tore up the sky, not merely with speed but with gymnastics which would not have disgraced a Starfleet pilot. Jarrat throttled back a notch and swore. 'He's not going to let me take a shot, Stoney.'

'I'm reading Caitlin-B,' Stone was hoarse with the punch of Jarrat's anger. 'Eight hundred k's downrange, and... oh. That's not nice. Reynolds!'

The gunship's pilot came through loudly. 'Riding your tail. Be with you in one minute.'

'Make it fast,' Jarrat said bluntly. 'We've got company. Jesus, what is that thing?'

'An ore tug,' Stone guessed as he watched long-range visuals. 'Wallowing like a pig in mud. Coming up fast. Don't let it get between us and the Lightning!'

'You want to tell me how to stop it?' Jarrat crammed the throttles forward, targeted on the mammoth shape of the industrial lifter and triggered five shots from the laser. Every hit drilled into the side armour, but the tug did not even stagger. 'Useless,' Jarrat said bitterly.

'Can you hit the skyhopper from this range?' Stone asked doubtfully.

'Only if he stands still and lets me target on his exhausts.' Jarrat locked the triggers, conserving the remaining power and gas. 'The best option we have left is cannons.' He glared at the CRT, where the squat, ugly tug was framed on visual. 'And I'm not game to take on that with a couple of 30mm gatlings.'

'Give it one shot.' Stone switched to visual. 'Depleted uranium rounds, target the cockpit blister.'

'You can hope,' Jarrat said cynically. 'Hold on.'

The rounds punched in accurately, the tug was shrouded in radiant vapours, but the damage was minimal. Stone's eyes had not left his CRT.

'They're running flak deflectors. We don't — *pull up!*'

Jarrat's reactions were just as quick. As the Lightning dove into cover behind the tug he saw the gunport in the chin of the big ship gape open. The barrel of a geocannon extruded, already rotating for a shot. Afterburners alight, streaming flame from both tailpipes, the spaceplane hurled upward. Alarms lit across the board. A demolition shell skipped so close under the port wing, Jarrat thought he felt it go by.

'Reynolds!' Stone bawled. 'Where the Christ are you?'

'Right here, Cap. Shift your asses, gimme some space. I might be able to take him.'

'Might —?' Jarrat panted as he levelled out, high above the abandoned gas field. 'Watch your own ass, lady!'

'Kevin!' Stone called. 'You can get a shot at the skyhopper from here. We've got the altitude, and that tug's going to be busy.'

Five hundred metres below, the Yamazake Lightning was trying to stay in the cover of the tug, but as Reynolds loosed a brace of Phoenixes the tug's pilot had more urgent things on his mind than providing protection. The missiles impacted shockingly, the tug staggered in the air, and the skyhopper bobbed out to a safe distance as the big lifter's flightpath became erratic.

'Got you, you son of a bitch,' Jarrat whispered as he held down the triggers. The rotary cannons moaned as a thousand 30mm rounds burned off.

A jet flamed, the Lightning whirled crazily, and as Stone watched it went 'divergent', spinning in all axes. 'She's gone,' he shouted. 'He hasn't time or height to pull her up. He'll punch out.'

'There!' Jarrat confirmed. He throttled back and spared a glance for the screen monitoring the gunship.

Pyros blew the ejection capsule out of the skyhopper, and a yellow chute deployed. Scant moments later the Lightning belly-flopped in an incandescent blue-white firestorm.

Below was a wasteland of derelict buildings and machinery, and Jarrat tailed the capsule as it drifted into the oxidising ruins. 'It's coming down on that roof,' he murmured. 'Looks like a control building. You reckon it'd take our weight, Stoney?'

'Try it,' Stone suggested tersely. 'I can hold her on repulsion.

Like a feather, the spaceplane skimmed the tangle of a toppled crane and Jarrat nosed down into the landing bay atop the abandoned building. The chute billowed like a kite as the capsule touched down and lodged against a parapet, fifty yards from the aircraft.

The gear unfolded and the repulsion increased a fraction at a time under Stone's sensitive hands. 'We're down,' he reported. 'Holding at six hundred kilos. The roof'll take us. Christ, Kevin, look at your screens.'

Jarrat watched as the canopy rose. Heavy weapons filled the air with thunderous concussions, chemical smoke and fire as the gunship broadsided the ore tug. Both were damaged. The industrial lifter was streaming coolant, venting black fluid from its hydraulics. One of its three engines had shut down. The gunship limped about, sideslipping as Reynolds tried to tuck in behind. She was trying for a shot into the sterntubes.

'The capsule just cracked,' Stone said sharply.

'I'm going.' Jarrat released the harness, snatched the Colt AP-60 from its bracket by his left knee, keyed the apparent mass of the riot armour to fifty kilos and vaulted lightly over the side.

Shots pelted out of the ovoid ejection module but the gesture was futile. Jarrat stepped into the stream of 9mm rounds and took them on the mirror black kevlex-titanium breastplate. He strode toward the capsule and made out two figures he knew. One was Randolph Dorne, the other, doing the shooting, was Kjell Wozniak.

Six rounds from the Colt picked Wozniak up bodily, spun him like a marionette and dashed him against the side of the capsule. His blood spattered Dorne's legs as he fell, before Jarrat swung the Colt to cover his real quarry, and switched in the audio.

His voice echoed off the concrete. 'Get out and stand still. I want you alive, Dorne. Run, and I'd love to put a bullet in you somewhere trivial but painful.'

Even now Dorne was cool. The fight, flight and ejection were enough to shake even an experienced professional, but he had pulled himself together. He climbed out, cast a contemptuous look at Wozniak's body, brushed down his dark blue coveralls and faced Jarrat calmly.

'My compliments, Captain. You made it interesting.'

Stone was listening. 'Good Christ, the man's incredible.'

'Blue Raven gunship,' Jarrat called. 'Reynolds! Stoney, do you see them?'

'On instruments. They've drifted five k's downrange. The tug's shot to hell. Reynolds'll get a rocket up its tail soon. The gunship looks damaged, one engine's down. She won't make orbit, but she's still flying.'

'Raven Leader to *Athena*,' Jarrat called as Dorne turned and leaned both hands on the parapet.

'Carrier,' Petrov responded. 'We're getting telemetry from the gunship. She's crippled, Cap.'

'I know. Can you route something to extract a prisoner? We've got Dorne, alive.'

'You win the cigar,' the Russian said drily. 'The engineer's tractor's on launch procedures in any case, to standby the gunship. They'll take the man off your hands.'

As he spoke a thunderclap rolled over the rooftop, and Jarrat's eyes flicked into the south-west. A distant plume of grey-black smoke rose skyward, and he would have worried if Reynolds' voice had not crowed over the loop in the same instant.

'Got the fuckers! Major reactor spill, Petrov. Buzz the local Tac, get a clean-up crew. I'll dump a marker, label this area as a hotzone.'

'Do that,' Stone called. 'Then put that bucket of yours on the ground! They've launched a tractor. Abandon the gunship, get your crew off.'

'Will do. They cut us up for scrap.' Reynolds sounded bitter and furious.

Watching the smoke as he stood by the parapet was Randolph Dorne. His face was the same impartial mask Jarrat and Stone had seen, the night they met him on Skycity. Only his eyes moved. He gave the wind-drifted pall marking the position of the ore tug one glance, and turned back into the east. Those slitted eyes raked the sky as if he was intent on Zeus, which loomed forbiddingly over Avalon.

Some nerve in Jarrat's spine crawled though he said nothing. Stone felt the creeping disquiet as clearly as in his own flesh, but before he could speak Petrov was on the air with uncharacteristic, boisterous enthusiasm.

'We got it! You wanted some shithouse called Hera?'

Disquiet was eclipsed by overwhelming relief. Jarrat took a quick breath as his partner's exhilaration hit him in every nerve. 'Where, Mischa? Where the hell did they hide it? And how did she find it?'

McKinnen's French voice replaced the Russian. 'I told you, Captain. Painstaking attention to detail. We'd never have seen it in a decade of searching around Zeus. Give Dorne his due, it's brilliant. Hera is probably a platform, parked on gravity resist — in an clear-air pocket, inside the upper atmosphere of Zeus. Radiation belts shield it from any scanning method we possess. I haven't seen it, Captain, but I can pinpoint it to an accuracy of under a thousand kilometres.'

'Thank you,' Stone breathed with feeling. 'I needed that. I've aged ten years since this morning. Where's that tractor?'

'It launched two minutes ago,' Petrov told him. 'What's your hurry? You've got Dorne.'

But Jarrat's animal foreboding slithered through Stone's belly, and on impulse he extended the range of the shuttle's airsearch envelope. Nothing. He cleared his throat. 'Kevin, what is it?'

'I don't know,' Jarrat admitted. 'It's this son of a bitch, Stoney. Look at him. He's... waiting. Watching. You scanning anything east of us?'

'Nothing in sensor range,' Stone said slowly.

And then Reynolds intruded: 'You will. Holy shit. Raven Leader, get out. Move, while you can!'

Jarrat spun to look at Stone's armoured figure in the cockpit. 'What does she see?'

'I don't...' Stone took a breath and Jarrat felt the icy fingers playing down his spine. 'One track on the extreme edge of sensor range. Coming in fast. It's big. Reynolds!'

'Looks like another ore tug, Cap,' she shouted. 'I'm down, three klicks from you, two engines totally fucked, and I'm out of missiles. You're on your own. *Go!* It's coming in hotter than hell!'

Desperate fury bared Jarrat's teeth behind the featureless visor. He could see the tug now, a black wedge-shape rushing out of the overcast. Behind him, the shuttle's main lifters ignited as Stone primed the systems.

'Kevin! Get him up here!' Stone bawled.

Jarrat wound an arm about Dorne's neck and manhandled him as if he were a child. He threshed, but the struggles were fruitless. Jarrat threw the Colt into Stone's waiting hands and lifted Dorne's flailing body.

Where the shot came from, he would never know, but the targeting was close enough, the calibre heavy enough, to throw Jarrat clean off his feet. He sprawled under the shuttle, rolled onto his back, and as his grip slackened Dorne scrambled away. Jetwash buffeted Jarrat as he fought to his knees. Heavy rounds slammed into the concrete a metre from his shoulder armour.

The only reason the gunners were not launching demolition shells was that Randolph Dorne was still alive, still on the roof. His inelegant, headlong scramble took him behind the skyhopper's tough escape module, where Stone could not get a clear shot at him with the Colt.

The shuttle's cannons had a narrow, forward-raking field of fire. Stone had nothing that gave him the option of a shot, while the incoming tug had begun to pepper the rooftop with heavy rounds that would have maimed the NARC aircraft if the targeting had been accurate.

Panting, cursing, Jarrat dove and rolled out of harm's way. He was on his knees for the second time, still under the spaceplane, when the roasting downwash of the repulsion knocked him flat. It bobbed up fast, and his breath caught in his throat as he watched it lift.

'Stoney!'

'Jump!' Stone shouted. 'Get off the building, put it between you and that thing! If I don't get her off they'll junk us. Jump for it!'

Every nerve in Jarrat's body echoed Stone's cold dread. He keyed his weight to twenty kilos, bounded to his feet like a deer and dove over the parapet. The ground was forty metres below, the shuttle was already on the carbonised concrete which rushed up fast.

At ten kilos he touched down in the scorching wake of the jets, rolled, absorbed the shock and bounced up again. The thunder of engines reverberated through the derelict building as he ducked the outswept wing, jumped and caught the edge of the cockpit.

She was off before the canopy slammed, and the harness clinched about Jarrat's armour. The sweat of fear stung his eyes and palms as he grasped the cyclic stick and opened the throttles. Was it Stone's heart pounding, or Jarrat's own? Did it matter? Adrenalin coursed through them as the shuttle climbed fast, out of range of the tug's punishing geocannon.

'Raven Leader!' Petrov shouted. 'Carrier to Raven Leader!'

'We're still in the air,' Stone gasped as the spaceplane levelled out and Jarrat shut back speed. 'Petrov, are you getting telemetry from Reynolds?'

'Not a chance,' Petrov told him. 'The gunship's sitting there like a dead duck. Systems are malfunctioning, everything's shot. The crew bugged out. But I'm getting feedback from the tractor — forty k's downrange of you. Budweisser's aboard. He'll lift out Reynolds' crew.'

'Great,' Jarrat said breathlessly. 'The tug snatched Dorne. We'll stay with it. Can you route us anything out of the battle?'

A pause, a blast of white noise, and Cantrell's voice: 'You can have the Gold Raven gunship. Elysium is pure turmoil. Every Raven is groundside, but it's hand to hand now. They're fighting it out on the street, NARC, civvies, Tac, giving Dorne's shooters a run. I'll have the Red Raven gunship fly double duty for Gold. A few Tac squads are coming in from Orleans and Albany to back us up.'

Jarrat's pulse had begun to slow. 'Fine. You getting our telemetry?'

'Monitoring your visuals,' Cantrell assured him. 'Looks like the tug's pulling out now they have Dorne.'

'Yeah.' Jarrat took a breath. 'Here we go again, Stoney.'

The flare of Stone's grim emotions hit him hard. 'Yeah, well, you give the buggers plenty of space, Kevin, because we're down to 30mm, and we might as well spit at that thing.'

Jarrat's throat made some dry, humourless sound. 'I wasn't thinking of picking a fight. But I'm damned if we're going to lose him now.'

The ore tug lifted on repulsion and turned its blunt nose skyward. The sterntubes were incandescent as the pilot opened up. Jarrat threw the throttles wide, tailing the bigger craft in a westward ascent. With the added kick of Avalon's rotation they were off fast; the sky dimmed from blue to mauve to black.

At sixty kilometres altitude the tug's acceleration rate slowed, but Stone's hopes of an intercept were doused. The lift engines shut down but the sterntubes darkened for only moments before main drive ignition lit them blindingly. The tug lunged away.

'Jesus,' Stone murmured. 'That's not your garden variety drive. Look at the acceleration he's making.'

'I am. Petrov, where's the gunship?' Jarrat's throttles were ten percent over maximum, and still the tug raced away before them.

'Coming up,' Petrov reported. 'Rendezvous in five minutes.'

'We're losing him,' Stone warned. 'Gene, are you tracking that thing?'

'Got him,' Cantrell said grimly. 'It may look like an ore tug, but his powerplant would move this carrier. You're not going to run him down in the shuttle.'

'The gunship could take you aboard,' Petrov suggested.

Cantrell made doubtful sounds. 'You won't catch him in a gunship, either. He's still accelerating, the main drive is rammed to maximum and holding.'

Eyes skimming the boards, Jarrat saw the first warning indicators as engine overheat began. 'That's as far as we go,' he said bitterly as he closed the throttles. 'Ah, Christ, tell me he's not on a heading for McKinnen's Hera co-ordinates.'

His acid fury scalded Stone's belly. 'You know he is, and you know he'll destroy it.'

'And then he'll destroy NARC with a ratpack of syndicate lawyers.' Jarrat hesitated. 'What do you say, Stoney, all or nothing? You thinking what I'm thinking?'

'Why not?' Stone's fingers drummed on the canopy. 'Send the gunship back. Tell Gable and Cronin to mop up as and where they see fit. Colonel Archer?'

'Captain.' The Master Pilot had monitored every word of the action from the flight deck.

'Plot a course for Hera,' Stone said grimly. 'Pull the carrier out of orbit, pick us up en route, and get after that bugger. Give me a time to intercept.'

Helen Archer was not even mildly surprised, though the action was highly irregular. 'He's still accelerating, but we'll overhaul him in sixty minutes, just short of the radiation belt hiding Hera.'

'Standby a guncrew,' Jarrat advised. 'Waste him before we lose him in the sensor deadzone.'

'If we can,' Petrov said darkly. 'If we take the carrier into that radiation belt, we'll be blind and deaf to our people in Elysium. We can't do that.' The statement was unequivocal.

'We won't,' Jarrat agreed quickly. 'Stoney and I'll stay in the shuttle, take on fresh ordnance. If he makes it into the deadzone, we'll be right behind him. He'll have to decelerate when he enters Zeus' atmosphere. Twenty assorted missiles up the sterntubes have got to blow back through his reactors.'

Stone was tracking the carrier. 'She's swinging out of orbit, coming up fast.'

Jarrat overran the engines to match velocity as the big ship loomed behind. The hangar was open and an acquisition beam invited them aboard. Sweat prickled his ribs as he nudged up and in at synchronised speed. It was the most dangerous docking manoeuvre in the manual, a scant plane's length from collision.

Furnace temperature air exploded into the bay and tech crews raced to restore the spent ordnance. Jarrat lifted off his helmet but remained in the cockpit. Eyes closed, he listened to the loop from Elysium and the commentary from the flight deck. Helmet and gauntlets off, Stone climbed down and paced restlessly.

Sixty minutes seemed nearer six hours. Stone was fretted, Jarrat furious. Their shields were up, blocking the empathy, lest they exhaust each other.

As Archer reported the tug dead ahead, Stone climbed up and sat on the edge of Jarrat's cockpit to watch the gunners' data on his CRT. Two guncrews had been in the forward cannon pods for minutes. Their weapons were armed and tested. The long-range visuals were awesome. The tug showed as a bright bar of superhot stern against the dusky face of the giant world.

The carrier's own massive defence cannons drew power from triple fusion reactors. Arcs of pure energy lanced against the blue-green and gold cloudscape of Zeus, which had swelled to fill the heavens. Multiple volleys carved into the dead of space, but the tug was still running.

'Flak deflectors,' Stone murmured. He looked into Jarrat's bleak face. 'We're going to lose him. Petrov, how far to the radiation belt?'

'Not far enough,' Petrov said sourly. 'Tracking will start to break up any second.'

Stone touched Jarrat's face with his bare fingertips. The

tenderness seemed at odds with the situation. 'It could be a one-way ticket.'

Jarrat shared the raw apprehension, and the wellspring of affection. He summoned a faint smile. 'Let's get it done.'

The harness was still running up about Stone's armour as the canopy locked. Spinners and sirens sent the hangar crew running and at thirty percent pressure, as tracking data began to distort, Jarrat ordered the bay open.

Instruments were wild as the carrier turned back. The shuttle plunged into Zeus' hotzone and Stone ignored the multiple radiation alarms. 'Keep a visual on him,' he advised quietly. 'We can't trust any readings.'

'I can see his engine flare.' Jarrat brought the nose about a fraction. 'He'll brake soon. We'll drop through the hotzone in ninety seconds.'

'I've lost the carrier on instruments,' Stone added.

'Raven Leader to *Athena*,' Jarrat called.

Interference was major, but Cantrell responded at once. 'We can barely keep a fix on your voice track. Boost your signal.'

'Better?' Stone shunted power to the transmitters.

'Better, but we're not tracking you,' Petrov warned.

'We have Dorne visually,' Jarrat shouted. 'Tracking is starting to come good. We're almost through the sensor blind.'

All at once, like flying out of a cloudbank into clear air, the instruments stabilised. Stone ran a quick systems check, recalibrated, and Jarrat felt his tingle of impatience. 'I'm reading something big, Kevin. It's in an oxygen-nitrogen pocket. Come right 088°.'

'Got it.' Jarrat shut back speed as the shuttle began to buck. 'Riding the upper atmosphere. I'm going to lose the visual fix on the tug, but he's on instruments now. Jesus, this is going to be rough. Carrier!'

'With you,' Petrov shouted, but his voice was distant and badly broken up.

The wings glowed dull red as the shuttle dove into the upper tendrils of Zeus' stormy atmosphere. The tug had raced on ahead as the lighter, much more fragile aircraft butted through the turbulence of re-entry. Jarrat gave away speed, increased repulsion and the ride smoothed out.

It seemed Zeus was gone, and the shuttle bolted through golden, sulphurous clouds. Chemical analysis indicated chlorine, ammonia, sulphur, methane, cyanide.

'It's toxic outside,' Stone observed. 'Air temp is eighty below. You've got an oxygen-nitrogen layer ahead. Tracking the tug... I read two marks converging. The second track can only be Hera... ah, now reading one mark.'

'They docked,' Jarrat said tightly. 'Range?'

'Two hundred kilometres. Slow down!'

'Slow down, and we turn into prime targets,' Jarrat panted. 'Christ, we're targets anyway. I think a laser designator just picked us up.'

Stone's eyes skimmed the CRTs. As the shuttle leapt out of the yellow mist into a nitrogen blue sky bisected by white liquid oxygen crystal clouds, he augmented tracking with long-range visual. 'One hundred kilometres. Fifty. There it is. It's a platform like Skycity. The tug's docked over the stern. Missiles!'

A thousand metres below, the platform rode serenely in the blue vault of the sky. Sulphur and ammonia clouds reared like mountain ranges to the west, and far below was a layer of dense, billowing chlorine cumulus.

'Intercept bearings,' Stone whispered as he tracked the missiles, and Jarrat primed everything he had. Then Stone's mouth dried. 'They've launched again. 'Tracking sixteen warheads. That's too many. Get us out of here!'

The shuttle pulled up in a backbreaking arc, tipped a wing and dove, but not even Jarrat's reflexes were fast enough. The airframe shuddered, red lights peppered the boards as an electrical fire raced through a dozen systems. Power cut automatically, leaving half the instruments dead. Other missiles proximity-detonated in shocking airbursts that pelted the shuttle with whirling fragments.

Terror and adrenalin overload were so mutual, Stone did not need to tell his feelings from Jarrat's. His CRT was alive with data. 'Hit in the starboard engine, repulsion's out. We're going down.'

Jarrat sucked in a gasp. 'Raven Leader to carrier, we're hit!' The stick was dead in his hands, the plane handled like a brick. His own CRT displayed one word. *Eject.* Eject into what? Nothing lay below but endless toxic clouds, growing hotter, denser, toward a distant core of liquid metallic hydrogen. 'Raven Leader!' He fought the dying aircraft for critical seconds as the grey-skinned platform, codenamed Hera, rushed closer.

In his ears was only a crackle of static.

'Kevin!' Stone bawled. 'She's breaking up!'

The windstream ripped at the wings as Jarrat hit the canopy release.

Nothing.

He hit the release again, but he knew the whole pyro system had shorted. Horror stole his breath. Stone was shouting but he did not hear the words. Instinct sent his hands to the Colt, in its bracket by his knee.

Ten hollow-nosed, teflon-coated rounds per second ripped out of the magazine, and at close range tore out the canopy with an explosive roar. Flight harnesses quick-released, suit repulsion went to maximum, and as the aircraft began to disintegrate they were out.

Below, the platform drifted gently, a hundred metres long and fifty wide, grey hulled, with the bulk of engines in eight pods on the periphery. The dorsal surface was smooth but for the protrusions of radio masts and missile tubes.

In midair, Jarrat twisted slowly. The empathy flared luminously. 'Stoney?'

'I hear you.' Twenty metres away, ten below, Stone's helmeted head rose. 'The second the air clears of debris, they'll see us. I'm going down.'

As Jarrat watched, he adjusted his grav resist and fell toward the grey metal hull. Fragments of wreckage from the shuttle and the many missiles whirled about Hera, confusing scanners as efficiently as deliberate ECM. Jarrat keyed his repulsion and followed.

It seemed they touched down on a smooth, geometric plane which sprouted radio pylons like trees. The tug had docked at one end, though neither end could rightly be called bow or stern.

Landing lightly, Jarrat jogged toward Stone and dropped to one knee as he reloaded the Colt. In Stone's own hands was the Ingram-Kalashnikov pistol. The rest of their weapons had gone with the shuttle. By habit, Jarrat carried plenty of reloads among the armour's basic equipment.

'If I was Dorne,' he said bitterly, 'I'd be covering my tracks. I'd get rid of this platform, fast, and swear NARC wrote the evidence.'

'Rig the reactor? Makes sense,' Stone panted. 'If we can get in we might stop him.'

'I'm glad you said *might*.' Jarrat stood and cast about. 'Air-lock, service hatch, anything.'

'Like that?' Stone gestured at the fascia panel labels, columns of instructions printed on a vertical surface just below the radio masts. 'That's got to be a maintenance hatch.'

'Not bad,' Jarrat said approvingly. 'Make it fast, Stoney. We won't have much time.'

How long could it take to programme a reactor detonation sequence? Stone examined the service manhole, lifted a control plate and simply touched the key marked *Entry*. The hatch slid aside, revealing an airlock large enough to accommodate two hardsuits with a squeeze. He sidestepped into it and levelled the Ingram on the inner hatch as Jarrat slid in beside him.

Closed to the toxic sky, the airlock purged and reflooded with breathable atmosphere. A green indicator lit, and Stone hit the hatch release. He poised his finger on the Ingram's feather trigger and stepped out.

The interior passages were white walled, quiet. Offices and labs opened to left and right, and on thermoscan Jarrat picked up the heat signatures of working machines, but no people.

'Where are they?' he murmured as he and Stone passed from door to door.

'I imagine they all rushed to the docking port. If Dorne's going to rig the reactor, I wouldn't want to stay aboard.' Stone looked into a fourth lab, and Jarrat felt his sudden surge of delight. 'That's pretty.'

The narco lab was filled with busy machines, but otherwise deserted. On one long bench was a stack of plastic cylinders, batch-labelled.

'Place your bets.' Jarrat stepped in, took a cylinder and smashed it between steel fingers. Golden dust showered from within. 'Pure and uncut. There's enough here to keep Elysium delirious for weeks.' He picked up two, tossed two more to Stone. They went neatly into the forearm weapons mountings.

'And take that.' Stone pointed out the case of datacubes beside a processing machine.

Jarrat swiped it up, thrust it between the cylinders and turned his back on the lab. 'Thermoscan, Stoney. We find Dorne, or we go up with the platform.'

The visor display adjusted at the touch of a key beneath the chin of the helmet. Stone's head turned slowly. 'The reactor deck is dead centre, in the keel. Engines... people.'

'A control facility,' Jarrat speculated. 'I count five figures. Forty metres forward, three metres below.'

Stone was already moving. A service lift opened thirty metres nearer the knot of figures. Jarrat sent the lift down, and they returned to normal visual. As they stepped into the corridor they heard voices, sharp with anger, or panic. Four men and a woman stood on a wide flight deck amid a stunning array of technology. The viewports were sealed, the lighting was dim. The group was so intent on in-fighting, the NARC men were unnoticed until they were a pace inside.

The tall, ebony-skinned Natasha was in a curve-hugging silvermesh bodyskin. Dorne and his pilot were in white metal industrial armour, helmets under their arms. A third man was a contract shooter in street clothes, jittery and fidgeting. The fifth figure was in slacks, tee-shirt and sandals, as if he had just left his work in the laboratory where this system's Angel was produced.

It took little intuition to connect a name with the man's passable looks and physique: was this Gary Schaefer, who held Equinox, and Dorne, in his palm, and who had vanished out of Elysium as if he had never existed?

Natasha had the instincts of a black panther as well as the looks. She spun as she glimpsed the NARC armour, and shrieked Dorne's name. Dorne twisted clumsily in the bulky armour, saw them and crammed his helmet on, all in one awkward but efficient movement. An HK assault rifle lay on the console at his side. As he snatched it up Jarrat and Stone dove into the cover of the machines.

Not that they afforded any protection. Projectiles punched through and into the deck a hand's span from Stone's legs. He swore, pulled up the Ingram and held the trigger down. The magazine burned off fast, he heard a chorus of shouting and screams. Someone was down but it would not be Dorne. The armour he and his pilot were wearing was not the equal of a NARC hardsuit, but it was tough enough.

A figure dove by Stone, and out. Jarrat sent a volley after him, but the man was gone. 'The pilot,' Jarrat panted. 'I'll go after him.'

'Let him go!' Stone slammed a fresh magazine into the

Ingram. 'Can you see Dorne?'

'I —' Jarrat began, and dove again as another round of wild shooting ripped into the deck. He rolled fast and came up against the bulkhead below the sealed viewports. Stone knew he was unhurt, but shock and anger made his heart pound. Jarrat emptied the Colt into Dorne's white metal armour as the man stooped to reload the HK.

Ricochets tore into sundry machines and a barrage of alarms signalled electrical fires. Jarrat rolled again, scrabbled for reloads and ejected the spent magazine. Schaefer was cowering behind a bank of terminals, coughing violently in the smoke and magnesium-bright spatters. Natasha lay sprawled at Dorne's armoured feet, her silvermesh bodyskin stained scarlet. The company shooter was screaming soundlessly and clutching at his belly.

As Jarrat realigned the Colt, Dorne whirled and triggered with desperate speed. Stone caught his breath as the first round detonated against the deck. 'Christ, Kevin, move! He's loaded with depleted uranium!'

The warning was less than a second too late. A dozen rounds hammered the bulkhead where Jarrat lay, smashed through, and Stone saw the brilliance of the sky beyond.

The interior pressure was considerable, compared with the toxic atmosphere so high in Zeus' upper clouds. As the rupture opened, the explosive decompression swept Stone across the deck. He punched his mass to two hundred kilos to hold himself down, but before he could even call Jarrat's name, Kevin was gone.

'Kevin! Kevin!' He gave the transmission every erg he had.

Jarrat was breathless, furious and sweating with animal fear. 'I'm out, Stoney, three hundred metres below you. I've got plenty of repulsion power, stop worrying. Get yourself out!'

The whole platform would relentlessly decompress through that aperture, and the storm of racing air continued unabated. Stone keyed his mass to two-fifty and got to his knees. Natasha's dead body was wedged in the rent, slowly buckling. Another second and it followed Jarrat. The contract man was already gone. Dorne's armoured hands clung to a console, fingers embedded in the plastic.

'Help! Help me!' Schaefer's voice was shrill with terror as he lost his grip on the legs of a chair and began to slide. His eyes were huge, dilated with horror, as if every nightmare were coming true.

Stone lunged toward him but the tremendous mass that held him steady in the windstream made him slow. Schaefer clawed for his hand, but their fingers never touched. For a terrible second he braced himself in the gash, struggling against the overpowering decompression storm. The last Stone saw of him, his mouth was open to scream as he blew back and out, and was lost.

'Kevin, talk!' he shouted.

'I'm okay,' Jarrat told him. 'Drifting. Going into clouds, sensors read chlorine and ammonia. Losing sight of the platform.'

The windstream eased little by little, and Stone cut his mass back to two hundred. Dorne was moving. He was down on his side, one hand stretching after the rifle he had dropped, and Stone's heart squeezed.

Far away, Jarrat mirrored the dread. 'Stoney!'

But Stone had no time to respond. He was looking into the broad muzzle, and every movement seemed stretched in a surreal slow motion.

He pulled the Ingram into line and squeezed the feather trigger hard. Armour-piercing rounds battered Dorne's gauntleted hands and tore the HK from them, before Stone brought the pistol up and emptied the rest of the magazine into the armoured visor.

It was tough, but not tough enough. The concentrated battering split it wide. As scarlet spattered from within Stone looked away. Catharsis roared through him like a purifying fire and left him trembling.

'Stoney!' Jarrat shouted for the fourth time.

This time Stone heard. 'I'm okay. Dorne's dead. I'll take a look at the computers, but there's not much working.'

Two terminals were alive, by luck alone. What he needed was a status report on the whole platform; what he got, without having to touch a key, was a barrage of warnings of fire, atmospheric toxicity, low pressure, hull breach. And a bottom line that rendered the rest insignificant.

He swallowed as he read the indifferent machine display. '05:22 to reactor detonation. Sweet Jesus Christ.' Sweat stung his eyes. 'Kevin! Key up your repulsion and *drop*! Get some distance between you and this junkheap! I'll know where you are.'

'He rigged it?' Jarrat's voice was harsh.

'I'm sitting on a bloody hydrogen bomb,' Stone breathed as he cast about for a functioning link to the transmitters. His eyes darted back to the screen. 04:41 to reactor detonation. With shaking fingers he set the chrono in his helmet to pick up the countdown.

Power was on but the keyboard was carbonised. He could not tell if it was working, and wished he believed in something to pray to as he cut into the NARC band.

'Raven 7.1 to *Athena*. I don't know if you're getting this, and I can't receive. Key on my transmission, I'll set it on auto, then, God help me, I'm going to jump. The reactor's set to blow. I've got four minutes, I can drop like a brick to safe distance. Kevin's already out. We'll drift on repulsion. For chrissake, pull us out when you can!'

The auto repeater would send the message over and over. Stone locked it in, and dove through the ruptured hull at two hundred kilos, dead mass.

He rolled onto his back and watched Hera shrink with distance. The tug was moving, lumbering through a tight turn to clear the docking port. The drive was alight too soon — the pilot was panicked. The blunt nose clipped the side of the platform, crushed a whole section, and the radio masts fouled the docking mechanism.

'He won't make it,' Stone whispered as he plummeted away and counted dwindling seconds.

The lift engines wrenched the tug about, and for a moment Stone thought the pilot was free, before a firestorm out of nowhere enveloped the whole craft. His visor dimmed, he flung an arm over his face and read his helmet chrono. 01:45.

'Cap Stone! Stoney, kill your descent!' Petrov's voice bellowed. 'Kill your descent, we'll grab you in tractors!'

Stone's heart battered his ribs as he searched the nitrogen blue vault above him. He fumbled with the repulsion, zeroed his mass and spread arms and legs wide to airbrake. 'Where are you? It's going to blow! You've got ninety seconds!'

But even as he spoke he felt the snatch of the tractors, saw the cloudscape begin to race by as he was hauled into a mountain of ammonia cumulus. He tumbled, breathless with fear and exhilaration, and watched his chrono and proximity sensors.

Fifteen kilometres downrange, he burst through a mist of sulphur and chlorine and saw the belly of the carrier. Massive as a blue whale, it filled the sky before him. One hangar bay was open; an armoured flight crew had tethered to the deck, arms outstretched.

As he plunged toward them he looked back at the chrono and caught his breath. 'Kevin! Black your visor!'

Jarrat might have answered, but the electromagnetic storm sheeted the air with impenetrable interference. Stone tumbled into the hangar, the hatch slammed before he saw the flash, and his radiation counters still read normal as he felt the carrier ride the shockwave.

He sat, panting and sweat-damp. The helmet wrenched off and he resettled his earpiece. Eyes closed, he concentrated every nerve on Jarrat.

There we was: blind, buffeted, intent on his instruments. Radiation counters had gone wild; skin temperature soared as the pressure wave flooded over him and he was plucked up in the convection on the extreme edge of the blast. The armour would take it. His heart was like a drum, but he was unhurt. Fear was healthy. It kept a man alive. Stone counted seconds, let the EMP diminish, and touched the headset.

'Kevin? Come on, honey, you can hear me. Kevin!'

He was breathless and hoarse: 'I'm all right. The hardsuit's sound, but I'm hot as hell. Anybody tracking me?'

Petrov, from the ops room: 'Keep talking, we'll align on your audio.'

'Okay. Standby a decontamination crew,' Jarrat panted. 'That was a rough ride. You found me yet?'

'Got you,' Cantrell assured him. 'Taking you in tractors. We'll put you in Decon 4. You know the procedure.'

Shakily, Stone clambered to his feet and walked out of the hangar. Jarrat's adrenalin overload sang through him as he tussled with the sections of the armour, thrust them into the locker and found himself sweat-soaked.

He leaned both hands on the locker, for long minutes intent on Kevin, sharing the relief, the sudden weariness. He was decontaminating now, and Stone walked aft to the restricted area to watch.

The whole airlock jetted high-pressure boron steam, and in

the midst of it Jarrat stood with arms and legs spread, waiting for the radiation counters to read normal levels. At last the compartment flooded with common water, purged and re-flooded with scorching air.

Jarrat was tired, annoyed, shaky about the knees, longing for a drink, rest, peace. The empathy was so clear, his feelings could have been Stone's own. He took off his helmet as he stepped from the airlock. Technicians hurried to help him desuit, but Stone would have done it for him.

Silent, hearing only the empathy, Stone closed his eyes. They were not touching, yet seemed to touch everywhere, all at once, like the most consuming lovemaking. As Jarrat made some quiet sound of humour Stone opened his eyes. The techs were trundling the armour away on a trolley, leaving Jarrat plucking at his sweat-dark shirt. He swept off the headset and ran both hands through his hair.

'That was too close.' Stone offered his hand.

'Understatement.' Jarrat laced their fingers, tipped back his head to savour the rush of Stone's affection and bounced it back, twofold. 'Who the hell is taking responsibility for bringing the carrier down here?'

Gene Cantrell's voice surprised them both. 'As a matter of fact, Colonel Archer was following my orders,' he said drily as he appeared from the nearby lift. It... seemed a good idea at the time. You're going to argue?"

'Me? Not a chance.' Jarrat's grey eyes sparkled with rueful humour. 'Just so long as it's not my butt in a sling.'

'Shouldn't be anybody's butt,' Stone argued. 'We were only sensor-blind to Avalon for minutes.'

'And the fighting there's almost over,' Cantrell added. 'You got everything we need. Your telemetry, and this.' He weighed a hefty drum of Angel in his hands. 'We enter orbit over Elysium in ten, and we've monitored their radio, every second. They didn't miss us.'

'It's nice to feel wanted,' Stone quipped. He slid an arm about Jarrat's waist and propelled him toward the lift.

'Duggan and Maddigan want to talk to you,' Cantrell called after them.

'Later.' Jarrat did not look back. 'Tell 'em they can talk themselves hoarse, but I want to clean up first.'

The lift closed and Stone sagged against the wall. 'You okay,

Kev?'

'I'm alive,' Jarrat said wryly. 'There's a lot to be said for it.'

Stone gave him a tired smile. Moments later he followed Jarrat from the lift, and in the sanctuary of their cabin caught him in both arms. Oh, Kevin was alive. He was flushed, hot, every muscle tense, sinews roped. Pungent with fresh sweat, he was so masculine, Stone was entranced for the hundredth time. Jarrat lifted his mouth and hunted blindly for a kiss which celebrated survival. Stone was pleased to respond.

Chapter Eighteen

The midmorning sun of Darwin's World, shafting under the half-drawn blind, found the summer blond in Jarrat's hair and spun it into gold. Stone buried his face in his lover's tousled mane, inhaled the rich scents of him as he stopped to rest and catch his breath.

Beneath him on the bed, Jarrat was taut, spread wide, hands clenched into the linen. He pressed his cheek into the pillow but his lashes fluttered. Beautiful, Stone thought, and kissed his ear as he began to move again.

The Colonial Hotel stood at the edge of Lake Theresa. Their room was at ground level, with a private access to the shore. The city of Venice lay just over the northern horizon, the NARC weapons-testing range beyond that.

The long, easy rhythm stopped again, and Jarrat took a breath as Stone rested on his back. They had not spoken in minutes; words were unnecessary. Empathy was clear and pure. Stone kissed the wide, brown shoulders, and felt the deep possession of Jarrat's body as if it were his own. Kevin wriggled, closed his eyes and smiled.

'Hedonist,' Stone accused fondly.

'Is that what you call it?' Jarrat stretched his arms out, across the bed. He tilted his hips the little he was able, and the lance of Stone's cock shifted inside him.

'Sensualist,' Stone elaborated, and rocked into him once more in the slow, gentle cadence of loving.

After two days' R&R, the fireworks were spent. Stone moved back, slid his arm under Jarrat's narrow hips and lifted him to his knees. Kevin pillowed his head on his forearm and gave a bass groan. Stone shared the silvery tingle of humour and laughed quietly.

'You're incredible, you know that?' he said honestly.

'Me, or my ass?' Jarrat was luxurious with comfort, well-being. He looked up and back and Stone.

Stone's right hand slid into the nest of his groin, caressing as cleverly as his cock pleasured the inner man. 'I mean, all of you, honey,' he murmured. 'I love you. If I forget to tell you, remind me.'

'You'd do anything for me?' Jarrat affected a naive tone, but his humour tickled Stone's belly.

'Anything.' Stone's fingertips traced down his spine to the place of their joining, his hands spanned the strong, slender pelvis.

'Then get on with it!' Jarrat humped back into him, teasing and demanding at once.

Mutual desire flared like a torch, rebounding through the empathic link. Their shields were down, every sensation shared. Jarrat bucked like a colt, and Stone took a firmer grip on him. 'Your word is my command,' he intoned breathlessly, and obeyed to the letter, with relish. Free time and the absence of duty and responsibility could be more precious than a cache of diamonds.

Two weeks' uninterrupted R&R stretched out before them, followed by a week with Starfleet, retraining with the new aircraft NARC had just acquired. The Athena was still over Elysium, but the situation there was defused. Most of the city was a ruin, but Equinox Industries was gone, and what became of Avalon now the affair of its people.

In a month, unless Angel trouble recurred, the carrier would be reassigned. Jarrat and Stone did not know where, but soon enough they would be briefed on the new location.

Colonel Vic Duggan and Senator Lenore Maddigan were confident they would make order out of anarchy, and Stone hoped they could. It was no longer NARC business. The political aspect of the job never had been...

With a shout, Jarrat stilled, not even breathing, and surged into climax. His milk filled Stone's hand, the spasms of powerful internal muscles seemed to pull climax out of Stone as the torrent of his pleasure overwhelmed them both. Stone's teeth bared, his head flung back as he lunged once more into the body he loved, and surrendered.

Exhaustion swiftly followed rapture. With his last erg of energy, Stone gently withdrew and sprawled on his back. One hand searched the floor by the bed for the washcloth and towel he had left there a century before. Jarrat was inert, on his belly, panting lightly into the pillow.

'I could get used to this,' Stone admitted as he regained breath and wits. 'Idleness, pleasure and excess. Sheer debauchery.' He leaned over and dealt Jarrat's buttock a pat. 'A life of beauty and... consummation.' He pronounced the word with rich, round vowels.

Jarrat gave a ribald snort as he enlivened at last. He rolled to his feet with a trace of stiffness and one hand pressed to his back. 'We'd be soft as pasta and bored to tears inside two months.' He stretched luxuriously. 'Enjoy it while it lasts. The reason it's so great is because it *doesn't* last.' He regarded the tub and wrinkled his nose. 'I'm going to swim. Coming?'

'I just did.' Stone smiled smugly and settled back.

'Sometimes,' Kevin said thoughtfully, 'I worry about you.'

But his infectious good humour strummed Stone's nerves. The room opened onto the lake front. Morning sun flooded the room as Jarrat stepped out, and Stone stretched with a pleasured groan.

Kevin had swum like a fish since he was a boy. While Stone ambled leisurely after him he was already sculling out into midwater. Stone shared the water's chill, the working of muscles in arms and shoulders as he paddled on his back, and shivered. It was easier to dive after him and share the reality.

The fleeting post-trauma, delayed stress syndrome which had shadowed Jarrat was purged. During debriefing after the Equinox assignment, Colonel Dupre's psyche evaluators explored Kevin's deep subconscious, with as little to show for their efforts as Yvette McKinnen had produced after the Death's Head job. Jarrat wore a faintly self-satisfied expression as he walked out of the lab for the last time. Stone was prideful. They were 'back on the horse', as Harry Del put it.

Still, memories of Equinox would haunt them both, Stone most of all. Kip Reardon had erased the Warlock Company tattoo, his chest was neither marked nor sore. But he would never forget his first night in the barracks. Neither would Jarrat.

NARC Central had had its own unwelcome excitement. McKinnen's hunter-killer programme was methodically running through every thinking machine in three services. Equinox parasites turned up randomly in Starfleet and Army ships, and even civilian vessels. Stone's blood chilled as he pondered the terrible implications of Randolph Dorne's ambition. And how close he had come to succeeding.

They were lying in the dappled shade on the shore, warm and almost dry, when voices laughed on the path leading to the hotel foyer. Stone sat, eyes narrowed against the glitter of the lake. Jarrat's eyes were closed, but he knew the voices.

'Sounds like Jesse.'

'And Tim, and Jack,' Stone added. 'They come as a three-some, remember... and I do mean *come.*'

'You're fixated on the word,' Jarrat accused as he sat and dusted grass from his chest.

'An entirely natural compulsion,' Stone argued as the younger men approached.

Tim Kwei was reborn. He was still frail, thin, but Jesse Lawrence had sworn he would put flesh on those bones. Jack Spiteri still mourned for Michael Rogan, and always would, but his grief had found perspective. With the destruction of Equinox, Michael was avenged. For the first time in months, Jack was at peace.

The three were inseparable. They had rented a penthouse in an expensive Venice block and had rarely been apart since Tim and Jack were released from medical care. The hallmark of Harry Del was on them all. Jack's dusky brown skin carried no surgical scar, his body contained no transplant organs. Harry had not cut him. Whatever the healer's magic was, Stone did not know, but Harry was a master in the art, and he operated on NARC funding now.

'Hello!' Jesse stooped, kissed Jarrat's mouth and then Stone's. He was bare, save for brief, frayed cutoffs, flimsy sandals and his jewellery. 'We tried to call you at the NARC building, but they said you were here.'

The other two were clad in gaudy track pants and running shoes, barechested. Kwei's skin was golden, perhaps a legacy of his genes. Spiteri brandished an eightpack of beer, and cracked a can as he sat on the grass. 'We just had the news from Avalon! I mean, you came back by Starfleet courier, but news takes a week to get here.'

'Wonderful news.' Tim blushed rosily as he looked at Jarrat. He would never forget what Kevin had seen one night, in a city bottom sex shop.

'You'll be going back?' Stone sampled the beer. It was the local brew, bittersweet and insipid.

But Jesse's blond head shook. 'We took a vote, and decided

to stay here. We like Venice.'

'Elysium's hardly worth returning to,' Jack added. 'Christ, what a mess they made.'

'And it's got a lot of bitter memories,' Tim added, 'for us all. Jesse's dancing now, he got a booking at an uptown club, did you know? I won't let him hire out his ass anymore.'

Jarrat chuckled. '*You* won't?'

'We sort of made a commitment,' Jesse told him. 'The three of us. So I dance. The money's good and the work suits me.'

'He means, he's an exhibitionist,' Spiteri added teasingly. 'Tim's writing virtual reality games, and I wanted to tell you, I was offered a contract to design for NARC. That's what I did for Equinox — project design.'

Stone's arms draped about Jarrat's body and he rested his chin on Kevin's shoulder. 'I'm pleased for you.'

'Thanks.' Jesse finished his beer. 'Where do you go, after your R&R?'

'We'll know when they tell us.' Jarrat leaned back against Stone. 'Some other place where Angel's become a plague.'

'Can't you find an easier way to earn a living?' Jesse wrinkled his nose. 'You two won't make old bones.'

Tim tugged his hair in admonition. 'It's a vocation.'

'I suppose it is,' Jesse mused. 'You don't have to be mad to apply for the job, but it helps.' He bounced to his feet and dropped the cutoffs. 'Who's going to swim?'

Minutes later, as the three young survivors splashed in the shallows, Stone considered Jesse's words with a wry smile. Jarrat was drowsing in the dappled sun, brown, bare and beguiling. Stone leaned over and kissed his throat. 'You don't have to be mad to do this job, the kid said —'

'But it helps.' Jarrat caught him by the shoulders and pulled him down. 'That's enough shop talk, Stoney. 'If these lips are on overtime pay, think of something creative to do with them!'

'Was than an order, Captain?' Stone demanded drily.

'Why not?' Jarrat's sultry tone invited, seduced.

For the second time in an hour, Stone followed orders to the letter, and with pleasure.